MEADOWLANDS

MEADOWLANDS

A CHRONICLE OF THE SCOVIL FAMILY

VIRGINIA BLISS BJERKELUND

FOREWORD BY
MARION BEYEA

CHAPEL STREET EDITIONS

Published by
Chapel Street Editions
150 Chapel St.
Woodstock, NB E7M 1H4
www.chapelstreeteditions.com

ISBN: 978-1-988299-32-7

Library and Archives Canada Cataloguing in Publication
Title: Meadowlands : a chronicle of the Scovil family / Virginia Bliss Bjerkelund.
Names: Bjerkelund, Virginia Bliss, 1930- author.
Identifiers: Canadiana 20200332473 | ISBN 9781988299327 (softcover)
Subjects: LCSH: Scovil, Elisabeth Robinson, 1849-1934—Family—Fiction.
Classification: LCC PS8603.J47 M43 2020 | DDC C813/.6—dc23

Cover painting by Morris A. Scovil, *Meadowlands from the Gagetown Side of the St. John River*. (See page 410)

Book design by Brendan Helmuth

Chapel Street Editions, Ltd. gratefully acknowledges the financial support of the Department of Tourism, Heritage, and Culture, Province of New Brunswick.

In the end, we'll all become stories.
Margaret Atwood

Table of Contents

Foreword

Often in my archival career I have come across a document (or a collection of papers) that I was excited to share for its humour, or poignancy, or the light it shed on a little-known aspect of history. However, to be appreciated and enjoyed by an audience larger than the archivists who might discuss its potential for researchers, the record needed a context and detail. It needed a story. In *Meadowlands*, author Virginia Bjerkelund provides this kind of story. Drawing on letters and diaries preserved by various Scovil descendants, memories and information from family members, and creative nonfiction techniques, she faithfully recreates the events and mores of the time in her telling of the Scovil family story.

Meadowlands is a non-fiction novel set between 1903 and 1934 along the St. John River opposite Gagetown, a historical area of New Brunswick settled by pre-loyalists and loyalists who counted the Scovils among their numbers. It recounts the rhythms of daily life on their prosperous farm through the seasons, planting and harvesting and raising horses. It makes us part of family meals and their preparation, of friendships, interactions with hired help, and the entertainments the young people enjoyed—skating, boating, swimming, hiking, and various games, including tennis played on a grass court they built on orchard ground near the house.

The story of the family plays out through such world events as The Great War with the experience of having a son captured and held as a prisoner and the beginning of The Great Depression with its repercussions on the fortunes of the family. Many subjects are touched on as they are the stuff of conversation, events, and contemplations of the family members—education, medical care, the arrival of the automobile, trips by riverboat to Saint John, women's suffrage, courtship, and marriage.

Central to the novel are the lives of Scovil women, foremost Elizabeth Robinson Scovil, whose illustrious nursing and writing career we are promised by Virginia Bjerkelund will be chronicled in a separate biography. Elizabeth Scovil's professional achievements are part of the *Meadowlands* story, but its foundation is her raising of her nephews and nieces, her philosophical insights on child rearing, her thoughtful reflections on her career, and her satisfaction with her single state, a situation that permits her to assist financially many of the members of her family.

The stories of the nieces she helped care for, including two educated at Edgehill who went on to further education and careers, and their youngest sister, perhaps the brightest of them all, who foregoes education away from home after a horrible experience at private school, continue the theme. While things were changing for women in the period, higher education, travel, and careers were not the norm for rural women.

Meadowlands comprises tales that are sad as well as jubilant. It recounts events that from the vantage point of the present day are frustrating and sometimes shocking. These stories reinforce the history we have learned and bring it to life. They help us remember that history and recount it in a memorable way. They lead us to have a clearer understanding of its events or give consideration to something we have not thought of previously. Importantly, they take us beyond facts and statistics; they give us a palpable connection to history and to the lives of those who came before us in the not too distant past.

Marion Beyea
Provincial Archivist of New Brunswick
1978-2013

Preface

My original plan was to write a biography of my Great Aunt Bessie, Elizabeth Robinson Scovil—she was such an unusual and interesting figure for her time. However, I knew so much about the Scovils that grew up on the Meadowlands farm—much of it through my mother—I decided to write about their lives from the time Aunt Bessie "rescued" the family in 1903 until her death in 1934. I have hinted at some of her accomplishments beyond the family, partly through flashbacks. Her actual biography is well on the way to completion.

Meadowlands is in the form of creative non-fiction, in other words it is based on fact, but when facts cannot be known the "creative" aspect takes hold as with dialogue and details of some actual events. For this reason, long time residents of Gagetown, New Brunswick may have heard other versions of some events from their grandparents. Most names are historically correct but a few are in the "creative" category.

My aim in writing *Meadowlands* was to tell the story of the Scovil family and the place on the St. John River where its members grew up during the early decades of the twentieth century. The context of the story is, of course, an era of momentous cultural change, so in telling the family story, the larger story inevitably comes into view. Although Meadowlands was a farm, the Scovil family was in many ways on the forefront of the changes taking place. *Meadowlands* chronicles the last years of one era, and the coming of another—a journey the Scovils made in a way that has always seemed to me to have the scope, drama, and, above all, the characters of a great family story.

Virginia Bliss Bjerkelund
Fredericton, New Brunswick

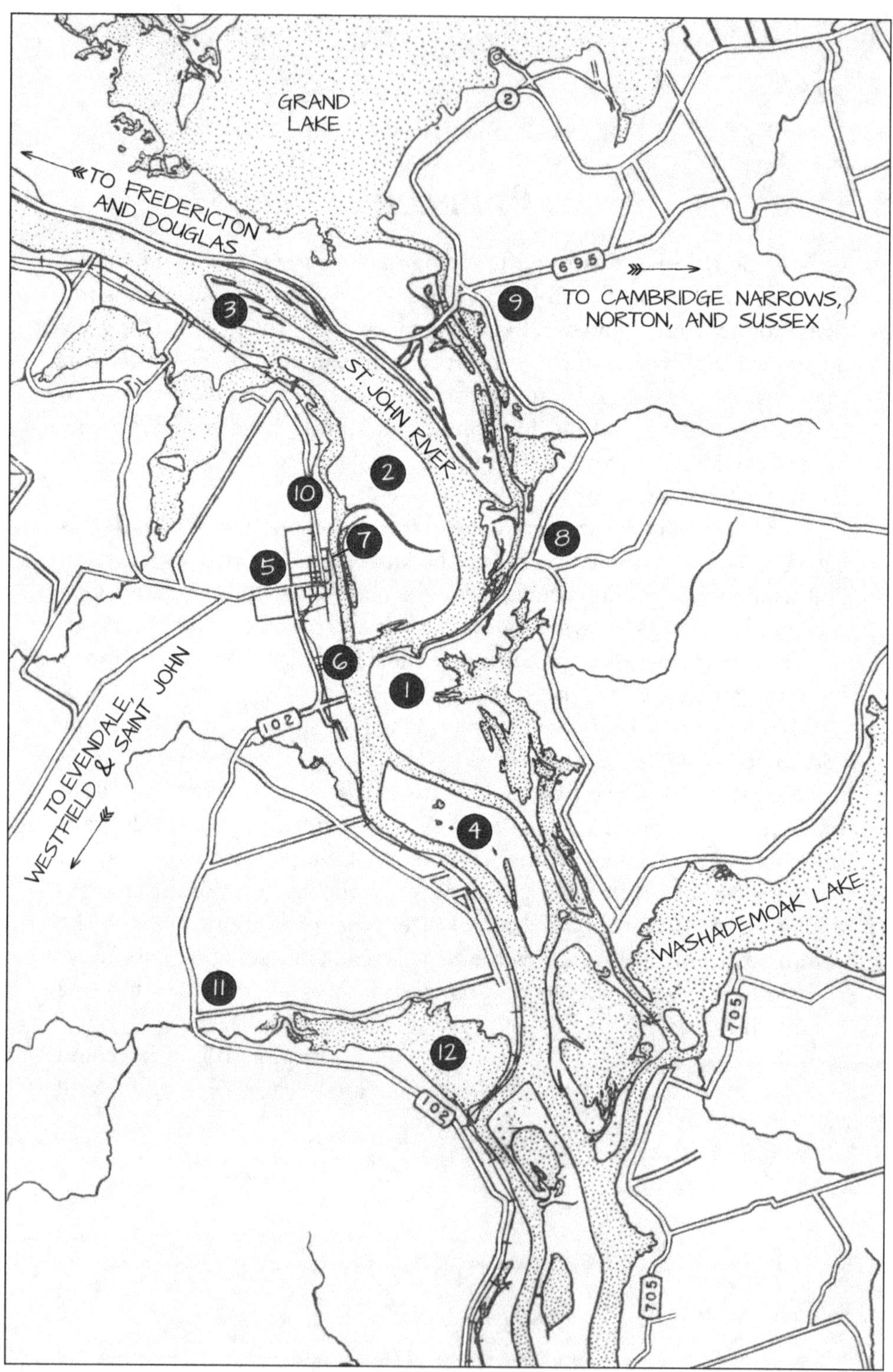

GRAND
LAKE
TO FREDERICTON
AND DOUGLAS
2
695
TO CAMBRIDGE NARROWS,
NORTON, AND SUSSEX
9
3
ST. JOHN RIVER
2
10
7
8
5
6
1
102
TO EVENDALE,
WESTFIELD & SAINT JOHN
4
WASHADEMOAK LAKE
11
705
12
102
705

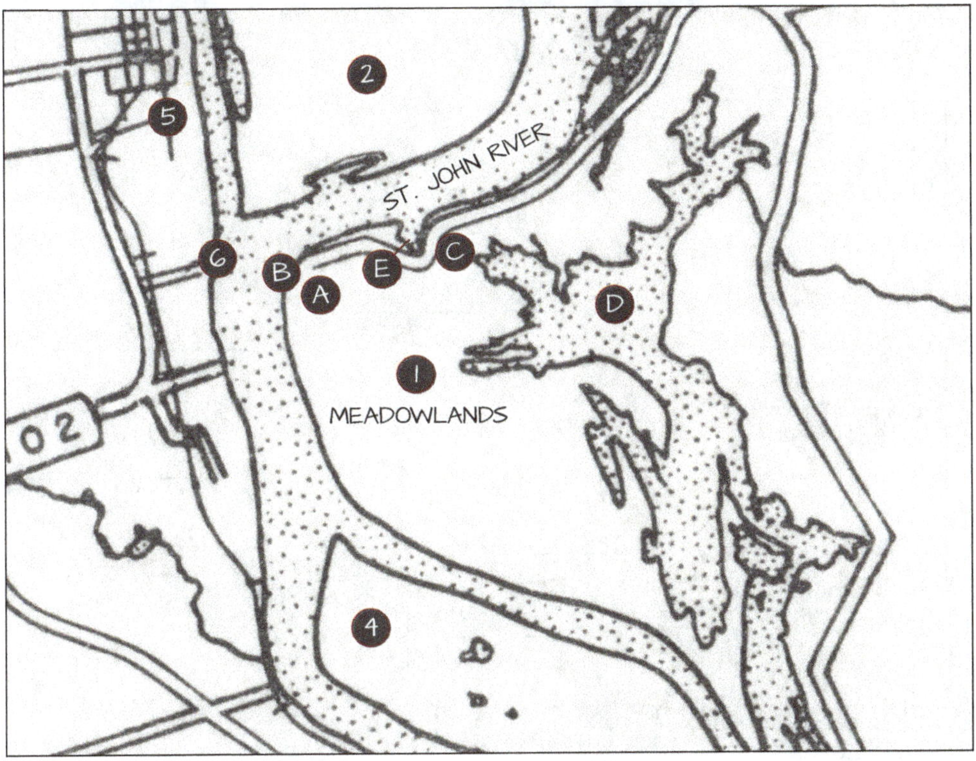

Map on facing page

1. Meadowlands
2. Gagetown Island
3. Grimross Island
4. Upper Musquash Island
5. Gagetown
6. Gagetown Lighthouse & Landing
7. Gagetown Wharf
8. Lower Jemseg
9. Jemseg
10. The Mount
11. Otnabog (now called Elm Hill)
12. Otnabog Lake

Map above

1. Meadowlands
   A. House and barns
   B. Scovil Point & Scovil Wharf
   C. Nelson's Mound
   D. Foshay Lake
   E. The Cut

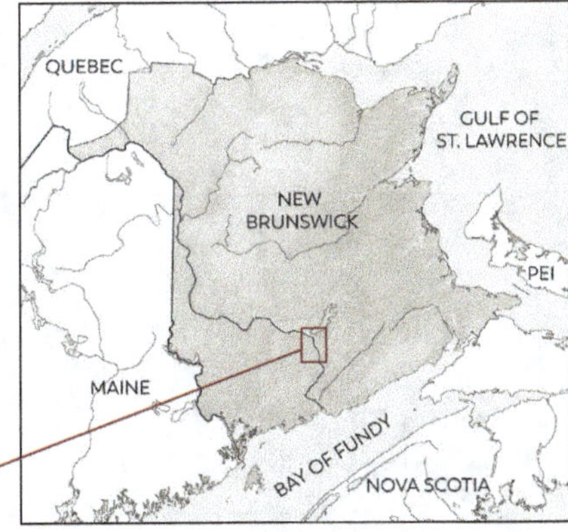

Detail enlarged on facing page

FAMILY TREE

(Rev) Elias Scovil
1771 - 1841
Elizabeth (Eliza) Scovill
1783 - 1869
Samuel James Scovil
1816 - 1883
Mary Eliza Robinson
1824 - 1894
Elizabeth
Robinson Scovil
1849 - 1934
Barclay
Allaire Scovil
1867 - 1947
Samuel John
(Jack) Scovil
1856 - 1917
Eliza Adeline
Barker
1859 - 1928
John Delancy Scovil
1884 - 1935
Charles Barker Scovil
1886 - 1983
Elizabeth (Bess)
Adeline Scovil
1889 - 1982
Morris (Mod) Scovil
1860 - 1935
Harriet Lavina DuVernet
1866 - 1903
Morris (Morrie)
Allaire Scovil
1889 - 1968(Nov.11)
Mary
Madelaine Bliss
1896 - 1978
Gertrude (Trudy)
Jervis Scovil
1891 - 1959
Elizabeth
Courtenay Scovil
1922 - 1995
Anne
Delancey Scovil
1927 - 1941
Richard Scovil
1928 - 1947
Elizabeth (Wowsie)
Robinson Scovil
1890 - 1966
Charles
Haydn Villers
1891 - 1952
Mary
DuVernet Scovil
1896 - 1990
Denison Bliss
1894 - 1970
Roger (Rog)
Peniston Scovil
1897 - 1983
Sophie Rose
Herbert
1893 - 1976
George Haydn Villers
1923 - 1944(Burma)
John Hyde Villers
1925 - 1981
Barbara Elizabeth Villers
1934 - 2003
Diana Elizabeth Bliss
1925 - 1997
Virginia Scovil Bliss
1929 -
Roger Morris Scovil
1929 - 2020

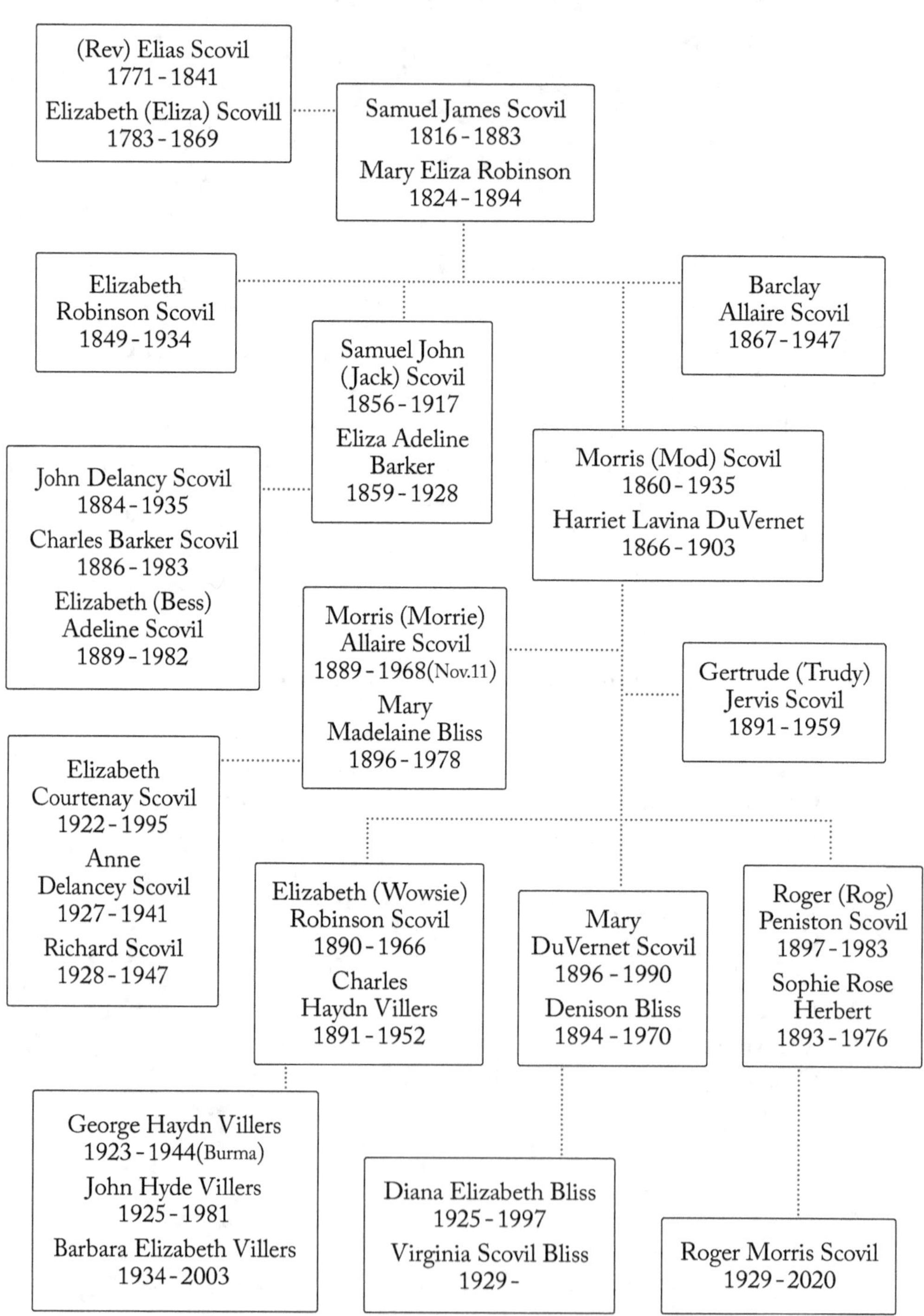

Scovil family, 1902 or early 1903, Studio photo.
Front row, L. to R.: Morris, Morris A. (Morrie), Elizabeth, Hattie
Back row, L. to R. Mary, Gertrude, Roger

Elizabeth Robinson Scovil wearing her treasured
Honiton Lace collar and cuffs. Shortly before 1903.

Mary and Roger in front of Meadowlands' house before verandah was built.
Note window under peak behind which was Bessie's "writing corner."

Early WWI. Patriotic Canadian flag in the background.
Front Row, L. to R.: Elizabeth and Morris A. (Morrie) holding hands
Back Row, L. to R.: Bessie, Mary, Morris, Molly Otty,
brother Alan Otty (killed in WWI).

Mary, studio portrait, Boston, 1917

Dorrie Lee, St. John friend and relative, on left, & Mary, wearing their popular "Middy" blouses on the river with "Mr. Evinrude."

Loading the boat at Scovil's wharf to catch the riverboat at Gagetown. L to R.: unknown, Morris, Elizabeth standing, Bessie, possibly Bess, Mary (looking cross), probably Constance Carr (cousin), DeLancey (Jack's son, also a cousin) wearing a clerical collar.

Meadowlands' tennis court with family and visitors playing.
Note long skirts. Before 1920.

Back Row, L. to R.: Roger, Gertrude, Morris, Elizabeth, Morris A. (Morrie)
Sitting, L. to R.: Delancey, Mary & friend (unknown), Bessie, Constance Carr.

Morris, early 1930s, on the verandah of Morris A.'s (Morrie) house in England.

Bessie, on Roger's verandah in Greenville, South Carolina, early
1930's, wearing the cameo broach she willed to her niece, Elizabeth.

1946 Reunion of four siblings and cousins, Weymouth, Nova Scotia
at the home of Ayleene (Starr) and Glidden Campbell.
L. to R. Roger M. Scovil (son of Roger P.) age 17, Campbell son, Ayleene
(Starr) Campbell, Frances (Caswell) Jones, Gertrude, Glidden Campbell, Mary.
Kneeling, L. to R.: Virginia Bliss (author) age 17. Morris A. (Morrie).

1946. Four siblings on the lawn of cousin Frank DuVernet, Doctor's Hill,
Gagetown. L. to R.: Roger, Gertrude, Mary, Morris A. (Morrie)

Prologue:

A Beginning and an Ending
1934

The little girl had not seen her mother cry before this moment. But there she was, kneeling on the parlour floor over a spread-out newspaper, big tears falling, sinking into the paper, spreading into larger dark spots. The mother removed her round, gold-rimmed glasses, something she did rarely because of astigmatism, took a handkerchief out of her apron pocket and caught the next flow.

If the little girl, Virginia, had been asked her age that day, November 28, 1934, she would have said she was five and a quarter. Her mother had told her she was "five and a quarter." Five and a quarter sounded more important and older than just plain "five" and she dearly wanted to catch up to her big sister, Diana, who was already nine, big enough to wait at the end of the lane by herself every morning for Roy and Guy's grandfather to stop for her and drive them all to their school, nearly five miles away. At five and a quarter, Virginia was aware crying meant pain, disappointment, hurting, something you wish would go away. Perhaps something dreadful was happening to Mummy. A hot feeling came into her own eyes, as though her mother had too many tears and needed to give some away. But Virginia decided not to cry. She walked nearer Mummy.

"What's the matter?"

"Aunt Bessie died; oh...oh.... I grew to love her so."

Virginia put her arm over Mary's back and looked down at the newspaper, at the photograph of an old woman with a middle parting of grey hair tightly pulled back. She wore a large important looking lace collar at her neck. It was the same person, but not such a clear picture, as the one in the birds-eye-maple frame, upstairs on the dressing table, where her head seemed glued to her shoulders by a black velvet band around her neck.

Both pictures reminded Virginia of their visitor of the summer before last, partly because there are photos of them together — Aunt Bessie, Grandfather and her — under the white painted arch meant for climbing roses, which had yet to appear. But more than that, she remembered sitting on the floor with her back to the brick fireplace watching Aunt Bessie's foot wearing a black shoe fastened with a strap and a shiny button. Round and round, very slowly, went the shoe and the shiny button. Then, it changed direction, round and round the other way.

At the other end of Aunt Bessie, her head looked like the one in the square frame, firmly connected with the rest of her by a black velvet ribbon. There was one difference; Aunt Bessie had smiled down at Virginia, an approving smile, as she had not at the person who took her picture.

Virginia sat on the carpet as Mary read the article out loud, partly in order to calm her emotions and partly to show her little girl the importance of the person it was about.

ELIZABETH R. SCOVIL NURSE AND AUTHOR DIES IN ENGLAND

Oldest graduate nurse on the North American Continent and friend of Florence Nightingale, who revolutionized nursing during the Crimea War, Elizabeth Robinson Scovil, died in England on November 24th at the age of 85 years, according to word reaching the City today. A native of Saint John, she obtained nursing qualifications after a two-year course at the training school of the Massachusetts General Hospital in Boston in 1880. She was, for a number of years, in charge of the Infirmary of St. Paul's School, Concord, New Hampshire and eventually became superintendent of the Newport Hospital in Rhode Island. Co-operating with Lady Aberdeen, wife of the Governor General, she was one of the founders and a member of the Victorian Order of Nurses, also a founding member of the National Council of Women and the International Council of Women and an honorary member of many women's organizations. In addition to her nursing interests and those promoting women, Miss Scovil was a capable writer. For thirteen years from 1890, she was an Assistant Editor of The Ladies' Home Journal *and for twenty years from its inception in 1901, an Assistant Editor of* The American Journal of Nursing *and a department editor of the* Canadian Nurse. *Apart from her works on nursing, she was the author of over 20 books, including one of her poems, adult reflections on religious themes and children's books. One of her groundbreaking books was* Preparation for Motherhood *in 1894. This book, and* The Care of Children *so changed women's* lives that when she travelled by train to British Columbia to attend a meeting of the National Council of Women, groups of women gathered on station platforms, calling her name so they could thank her for her gift of knowledge. Of pre-Loyalist and Loyalist New Brunswick stock, Miss Scovil was the descendant of an old Virginia family. At the time of her death, she was visiting, along with her brother Mr. Morris Scovil, his son Mr. Morris A. Scovil and Mrs. Scovil, the former Miss Madeline Bliss of Amherst, N.S.

I

A Request and a Response:
Aunt Bessie Comes to Meadowlands
1903

As Bessie was taking her morning break from her infirmary duties in late April, she relaxed in her rocking chair looking out at the early signs of spring in the countryside around Concord, New Hampshire. She was under no pressure as there were only three boys in her care, and they would be discharged in a few days, though there would be the usual steady trickle of sports injuries and stubborn infections. She sipped her tea and nibbled ginger snaps as she absorbed the warmth of the mid-morning sun pushing nature in the direction of spring. Small leaves were already showing, though scarcely larger than a mouse's ear. In a reverie encouraged by the warming tea and the optimistic sun, she found herself thinking about the farm and how the ground might still have a few patches of snow, with not a sprouting leaf in sight. Her musings were interrupted by the morning mail. There were two personal letters for her. One was in her brother's hand and one in her sister-in-law's, both postmarked, "Gagetown, N.B."

Bessie thought that was strange. Normally, when more than one letter came from home in the same mail they were always in one envelope. Though the time she allotted for her mid-morning refreshment was nearly used up, this departure from normal was unusual enough for immediate attention. She took up her silver letter opener with the mother-of-pearl handle and slipped it under the flap of her brother's letter. She soon realized she should have opened Hattie's first as much of Mod's letter referred to his wife's request.

When Dr. Caswell diagnosed pregnancy onset diabetes some time ago, Bessie knew that Hattie's nine months would be more of a burden than her other pregnancies had been. She also knew that Hattie's type of the disease might vanish after the baby's birth in July. With five live births behind her, Hattie was no novice to the restrictions and discomforts of a normal pregnancy. Until now, her letters had been generally cheerful and optimistic about the coming happy event and her ability to manage the home and the children. Bessie had assured Hattie she would be there before the end of June for her confinement and would stay until school began in mid September. By then the new mother would have regained much of her strength. However, this letter changed the picture.

Meadowlands, April 26, 1903

Dearest Bessie,

I have debated, these last few days, whether I should write this letter, but today, with all its complications, confirmed that I should. I have a very big favour to ask of you, dear sister. Is it possible you could see your way clear to taking your summer break earlier than usual this year? I am increasingly exhausted and unable to fulfill all my duties, not least, caring for the children properly. The doctor has told me I must rest more but if I do, I will certainly be neglecting the little ones. I must protect my health and that of my unborn baby, but I do not want to do it at the expense of those already needing me. Let me know what you think.

With best love ever, dearest Bessie,

Your loving sister, Hattie

Bessie then reread Mod's letter more carefully.

Meadowlands, April 26, 1903

Dearest Bess,

I am sending this separately as I do not want Hattie to be upset by my remarks. I confide in you that I am very worried about her as her state of tiredness is much worse than when she was carrying the other children. We really appreciate her sister visiting often, but Mira is also adding to her family and has many responsibilities at home, as you know. The ice will be breaking up soon which means no Mira for two or three weeks. I am thinking of asking Amelia to live in so she can be of help in the evenings. I hate to ask you to dislocate your life in order to help, but you have always been a steady rock for me since childhood. Please consider the earliest date that is possible for you to depart which will forever put me in your debt.

Your loving brother, Mod

Bessie summoned her assistant and asked her to be in charge for the next half hour. She sat down at her little desk and took the first steps — a note to Dr. Coit toward a leave of absence beginning in mid-May. Bessie was glad she had responded positively to Dr. Coit's plea for her to return to St. Paul's School as matron of the infirmary after her previous seven happy years there. It was her first job after graduating from the Massachusetts General Hospital in Boston over twenty years ago.

She and Dr. Coit, the headmaster, or, as he was usually called, the rector, had developed a warmer relationship than most employers and employees. There was a mutual appreciation of the other's interest in good literature and music and their general approach to life. Bessie felt like a treasured cousin, especially as Mrs. Coit often invited her to family celebrations. Bessie might have continued at St. Paul's well past the initial seven years but even Dr. Coit urged her to accept an invitation to apply for a plum position as head of nursing at the Newport General Hospital in Rhode Island. They both knew her professional and organizing abilities were far from stretched at St. Paul's.

The Newport General turned out to be a satisfying challenge. She was not only the Matron of Nursing but in charge of the nursing school in its infancy. She was able to lay down an early basis of excellence of which she was proud, as were those who graduated from the school. The position was, indeed, much more demanding than St. Paul's, not least because of no long summer holidays.

After six extremely busy but satisfying years at Newport, Bessie decided advancing middle age should carry fewer responsibilities so found work in private nursing, always taking time for herself between positions. When Bessie was fifty-one, she could not resist replying positively to Dr. Coit's request for her to return to her old position to see him through to his retirement in five years. Partly because of their special relationship and because she was finding the physical and emotional seesaw of her middle years somewhat trying, she accepted and had not been sorry. As well as the advantages of not having to look for new positions after each patient recovered or died and being welcomed back by familiar faces and circumstances at St. Paul's, she was again able to spend her long summer vacation back at Meadowlands. This was the year when that flexibility was more needed than ever before.

The mere promise of Bessie's presence relaxed Hattie and allowed her to put off certain chores "until Bessie arrives." Mid-May, as it turned out, was good timing. The St. John River in front of Meadowlands ran completely clear of ice floes and debris so a row boat was safe to collect Bessie from the Gagetown wharf after the river boat from Fredericton had deposited her there. The train from Boston ran through Bangor, Maine, made a convenient connection with Fredericton Junction, and then on to the capital city, Fredericton, allowing an overnight stay at Pine Grove in Douglas with the Robinson cousins as a gentle re-introduction to New Brunswick rural life.

After a day to recover from her travelling, and with Hattie's approval and gratitude, Bessie embraced the domestic scene completely, including meal planning, supervising Amelia and keeping an eye on the children when Hattie was resting. Bessie was struck by how this pregnancy was taking its toll on her pretty and still youthful looking sister-in-law. With Hattie in mind, Bessie had brought several books, which she thought would be suitable for reading aloud when Hattie was putting her feet up between chores. The books would also give the two women casual time together with an opportunity to discuss female problems and, in particular, for Bessie to learn of any symptoms which otherwise might not reach the doctor's ears.

In a few days the household took on a comfortable rhythm. The children, who were entirely used to having their aunt there for the summer, accepted her authority as they could see their mother looked so much more rested and less harried. Aware of her multi-faceted role, including that of self-appointed health expert, Bessie was quick to spot the symptoms of scarlet fever shortly after her arrival. Young Morris was first, then Elizabeth and Gertrude before a week had passed, and then Roger. They went through all the stages of sore throat, swollen glands, high fever and a bright red rash and the need to be confined to bed in a somewhat darkened room. Bessie had immunity, she knew, and mercifully so must Hattie and Mod as neither produced symptoms. It looked as though little Mary would be spared, too.

Bessie was feeling exhausted after many nights of broken sleep. By the time the affected young were up and convalescing, an invitation to visit Robinson cousins for a few days in Saint John was irresistible, especially as Hattie was feeling quite strong and was very much in favour of Bessie taking a break for a few days.

The day after Bessie took the morning riverboat to Saint John for her short visit, Mary complained of a sore throat and headache. Her mother sent her to bed. Hattie did not want to interrupt Bessie's few days of relaxation so she did not inform her sister-in-law of the latest invalid. As Roger already had suffered through his dose he was allowed to spend time with Mary, playing with paper farm animals on her counterpane when she felt like it. The two little ones amused one another, which meant Hattie, had fewer trips up the stairs to check on the patient. She knew Roger, though only five, would be a willing go-between.

Elizabeth's godmother had recently given her a Brownie box camera for her twelfth birthday, along with three rolls of film. She now desperately wanted to take a few photographs of her whole family, especially as her Aunt Bessie had confided in her that her mother was very seriously ill and her paleness and lethargy was not just because she was going to have a baby. The problem for the would-be photographer was that Mary was in bed with the blinds drawn. Her rash had not appeared, so her fever was still high.

Elizabeth asked her mother whether they could dress Mary in her favourite ruffled dress and have her join the others. Hattie agreed, thinking a short time on the verandah in the fresh air might even do Mary some good. The sun had just come out much to Elizabeth's delight, but it was a shock to Mary, coming from a darkened room. She did her best to hover in the background under the overhang of the verandah roof and to twist her head in such a way as to avoid the direct sunlight.

They were quite a group, so arranging everyone to the camera owner's satisfaction took some time. In addition to the immediate family, Hattie's young stepbrother, Frank and his grandmother, Mrs. Buzza, from just across the river, were visiting for the afternoon. It seemed to take an age before Elizabeth was satisfied that she and the box Brownie had done their work and Mary was allowed, at last, to return to her sunless room.

The day Bessie returned, Mary was at the height of her red rash and complaining of sore eyes. Bessie gently reprimanded Hattie for not writing to her about Mary. But Hattie was already conscious she could do little and Bessie knew there was no need to make an issue of the fact; she had, uncharacteristically, just blurted out her disappointment. Bessie's annoyance was really directed at herself, as she could not possibly blame Hattie, already with two burdens, pregnancy and diabetes, and less knowledge of disease.

There was no point in scolding Elizabeth as she had only the purest of intentions, and at twelve was completely self absorbed in her recently acquired knowledge of photography. Bessie was aware that most diseases were carried by personal contact or infected water or food. Years of nursing gave Bessie far more knowledge about ailments in children than most mothers or mother substitutes. After all, she had written several books on children's diseases and the care of children generally. She was still contributing a monthly page to *The Ladies Home Journal* called "Mothers' Corner." She had been providing that for over a dozen years. Giving advice by putting pen to paper in an unemotional setting was one thing, but Bessie knew well that putting that advice into practice in a distracting and busy environment was another. All she could do was her best, as she told her nursing students, but pressure often eclipsed her softer side, which she was in the habit of masking in her professional life.

It was hard to suddenly abandon years of habit—learned in training—of not becoming emotionally involved with her charges. She knew that a professional approach sometimes alienated the children temporarily, especially Mary, who was a naturally precocious child and whose feelings were never far from the surface. Bessie knew she did not always deal as well with the small children as she should, but felt more confident with the three older ones. Except for short periods long ago with her young relatives on the Kingston Peninsula and more recently with occasional patients, her charges were usually at least twelve and often subdued by illness.

Now that it was known in the communities of Gagetown and Jemseg that she had returned to help look after the five Scovil children while Hattie was preparing for another birth, Bessie felt the eyes of all upon her, expecting her to be a highly positive influence on the household, especially in matters of health and behaviour. She was relieved when all the children appeared to recover from the scarlet fever attack without leaving any particular weakness, with the possible exception of little Mary, who had been complaining about her eyes ever since, especially on bright days. When Mary was outdoors, a white, cotton sun hat was now always on her head to protect her eyes from direct exposure to sunlight. It had the added advantage of keeping her long, fine hair slightly tidier as well.

All the quarantined children had returned to school by mid-June, except Roger, who was too young for school. By then the teachers were organizing school closing. Miss Trenholm, well known for her musical ability announced that she had composed a musical play about the life of one of the Fathers of Confederation, Sir Leonard Tilley, who, as all knew, was born in Gagetown in a house close to the school.

Children who showed ability in singing were asked to try out for the main parts. Others were included for lesser parts, including non-speaking villagers. By now, nearly all required schoolwork had been completed. The children generally welcomed this departure though a few rowdies needed to have it pointed out the alternative to taking part in a play was doing more arithmetic.

Young Morris had always shown a sense of creative humour, often turning around a spat with his sisters by his ability to make them laugh. He was just beginning to put on his growth spurt as well as being nearly over the most embarrassing aspect of acquiring a deeper voice and was generally able to order his feet to be where he wished. The big delight for Miss Trenholm was that Morris could sing. With those useful qualities, his teacher gave him the lead role—Sir Leonard. Elizabeth and Gertrude, who could also sing quite well, were also given important roles—wife and sister to the great man. Miss Trenholm briefly tussled with assigning the three most important roles to the children of one family, but gave it up when she knew they had the most musical voices.

There were other factors that set the Scovil family apart in a community where all lead fairly predictable lives. Not only should they be rewarded for being a reliable resource for augmenting meagre school supplies, but Miss Scovil once had tea with Queen Victoria as well as being friends with Florence Nightingale, which elevated her well above everyone else and should not be forgotten. Bessie, when told of the three "star" parts, quietly thought it was a pity little Mary was not old enough yet to attend the grammar school. Two years ago, when she was five and attending a kindergarten in New York while living with her Aunt Addie and Uncle Jack, she was selected to sing as one of the "Three Little Maids from School." The Gilbert and Sullivan operetta was performed at the Waldorf Astoria, a great feather in her cap forever afterward. Those who were knowledgeable about such things said Mary had perfect pitch.

While Bessie felt confident singing hymns in church, she knew she tended to sing a little flat and could recognize that shortcoming in herself and in others. With that in mind she decided not to interfere with home rehearsals for the play, but would try to make encouraging remarks. Partly to divert Hattie from her expected confinement in three or four weeks and partly to encourage the children to perform as well as they could, Bessie organized practices after supper in Hattie's bedroom where she was resting on a wicker chair with a substantial foot stool. They started with printed scripts, but after a week they were word perfect and their singing, mostly to well known tunes, improved to a more than acceptable standard. They all enjoyed the smile on their mother's face and the clapping of the three adults, as their father was usually part of the audience. Mary, who often sang along as she quickly learned the words, sat on the floor next to Roger who was completely entertained. Bessie regretted there was no piano at Meadowlands as she could have accompanied them, having learned to play as a girl in Saint John.

Not wanting to tire Hattie too much, Bessie insisted that the rehearsal in their mother's bedroom not last more than a half hour at a time and if more were needed it could happen elsewhere, even outdoors, underneath a large elm tree near the house. Amelia volunteered to augment the audience, if she had finished her chores, while Bessie sat with Hattie or retreated to her desk in the upper hall to work on her next month's magazine articles.

When the last day of school arrived, the closing concert took place in the afternoon at two o'clock. Hattie was past the stage when a pregnant lady could appear in public so made do with a final song rehearsal the previous evening. Mod agreed to take time off from supervising the men on the farm and, with Bessie and Roger, took the rowboat across the river to Gagetown and picked up Mary at her little Porter School. She had been granted permission to leave early after her aunt had written a note requesting a short day.

Though it was still early summer, the June day had come on warm and humid. The Grammar School hall smelled of a mixture of soap, sweat, and excitement with a suggestion of sweet baking nearby. The Scovil family was shown to the front row as they had three children performing and because they were the largest landowners in the community. The usual formalities began. Small book prizes were handed out to those who had distinguished themselves during the year. Then came what the entire audience was waiting for after the makeshift curtains could be persuaded to fully open. Sir Leonard Tilley came to life in Morris's mostly adult voice, his wife and sister in those of Elizabeth and Gertrude, the maid in that of a Kelly girl with orange red curls appropriately corralled in a mob cap, and in several others with small parts, nearly perfectly remembered. The words were so familiar Bessie had difficulty not mouthing them. Mary's feet, not yet touching the floor, waved back and forth to the piano's beat. She needed Bessie's gentle finger on her arm and a small frown to discourage her from singing out loud.

The half hour of enthusiastic presentation was well received. Bows and curtsies, somewhat less than perfectly synchronized were accomplished during prolonged clapping, not least by those in the first row. At the back of the hall, jugs of lemonade and plates of cookies awaited audience and performers alike. Most held back until the red faced performers, flushed with success and the 90 degrees of heat, had been served. Several mothers came up to Bessie to congratulate her on having such a talented nephew and nieces and hoped Mrs. Scovil was feeling well and looking forward to the new arrival soon. Bessie thanked them and said she was, on both counts, the former being not exactly truthful, but socially acceptable. This was not the place to elaborate on Hattie's frailties, especially to people with whom she was not closely associated. There were not many men, except a few grandfathers, as most men were still working in mid-afternoon. Mod gravitated toward them, accepting their compliments on his children's performances, while they drank their refreshing lemonade faster than intended, wishing it were something stronger.

The boat ride across the river, in spite of the still intense heat, carried an air of light-hearted gusto overflowing from the concert, helped by energy from the sugar cookies. A repeat performance of the songs, with everyone joining in, drifted over the smooth water to Amelia's ears, as she was standing at Scovil's wharf. Hattie had asked her to see whether the family was on the way home as she was so curious about the outcome of the school year's closing ceremony. Mrs. Scovil was relaxing on the front verandah but large elm trees obscured her view of the river toward Gagetown, so she needed a spotter. Amelia rushed back to report that it must have gone well as they were all singing.

As the children crowded around their mother, Bessie asked Amelia to open the last bottle of last year's raspberry cordial and to serve them all on the verandah. Bessie was somewhat alarmed to see how pale and tired Hattie looked. The dark half circles under her eyes were more noticeable, more sunken than she remembered them being recently. She assumed Hattie was not able to have her usual sleep because of the afternoon excitement. Bessie was familiar with the euphoria that comes to children once holidays begin. Like a boat on choppy waters whose anchor has been pulled, a certain recklessness infected them all for a few days.

*　*　*　*　*

Early July's sunny days helped ripen the strawberry crop, producing enough for bowls of berries topped with thick cream on Morris's fourteenth birthday on the fourth. In order to keep the noise level somewhat controlled so Hattie could benefit from frequent rests, Bessie suggested a picnic four times during that first week after the end of school. The children helped to put them together with Amelia's eye on choices to make sure the pantry was not depleted of supper's ingredients. Morris was put in charge, otherwise he might have preferred hanging about in the barn with the hired help, grooming the horses and hearing the conversation he wished he understood better. With this assigned responsibility, Morris carried the heaviest basket; Elizabeth and Gertrude shared carrying the lighter one.

Their favourite picnic place was always under an ancient tree, out of sight of the house, on the road to Jemseg. When the dusty feet of the picnickers reached an indentation from the river called The Cut, which was said to be where long ago an Indian had landed his canoe, they knew there would be a big bend in the road and then their destination, The Mound. The Mound was where Nelson, their dear old patient horse had been buried. By the time they reached The Cut, the anticipation of savouring the baskets' contents overcame their heaviness and pushed them faster to their chosen spot. The house was now completely hidden from view, which added an air of independence and excitement, especially for little Mary and Roger.

Hattie could go into labour any time so Bessie did not entertain the idea of accompanying the children, though she still dearly loved picnics. Instead, she busied herself making sure she had everything in readiness for the birth. It was all in her popular book of a dozen years ago, *Preparation for Motherhood.* As far as she was aware it was the first of its kind. She knew it brought confidence to inexperienced mothers-in-waiting based on dozens of letters in its praise from readers. She had not delivered a baby for a long time so thought she had better review the requirements. She had no problem finding them as they were all listed in her book that she kept on her carefully arranged bookshelf at the side of her desk. There were the columns of necessities. She checked her stacks of soft towels, pins, bands, aprons, basins, and diapers. She should have a large pile of small cotton linings to be thrown away when soiled and at least two dozen full sized diapers, but she was six short. Her recommended solution to this was to raid the linen closet of a well-worn, white linen tablecloth. After unfolding several she found one that fitted her book's description. It sported several darns and was beginning to fray again at one edge. It would be sacrificed for a good cause. She hoped it was soft enough for the little mite's tender skin.

Dr. Caswell's hired man rowed him across the St. John River from Gagetown every week to check on Hattie. The sugar in Hattie's urine continued to be high, a fact he shared with Bessie out of Hattie's hearing. Though he knew Bessie was perfectly capable of delivering a baby, he urged her to send a message for him to come immediately when Hattie showed signs of labour. Dr. Caswell prided himself on his good record of saving both the mothers and the babies, even against the odds. And Hattie was his sister-in-law. He did not go in for sentiment but he had grown fond of his wife's pretty and gentle sister. This could be a quick birth after so many already and the baby might need special attention with so much sugar in the mother's urine, in spite of the special foods that had been imported from London for her.

Hattie found it almost impossible to sit or lie in a comfortable position. The heat of early July did not help. Bessie cooled her with a large fan woven from dried palm leaves, which was very light and did not tire her wrist. Even when Hattie was sitting on the verandah, the palm fan provided relief on a still day and gave Bessie an opportunity to listen to her sister-in-law's worries, some of which she could genuinely dispel, some she could not.

2

A Family in Loss

After the children had left for their fourth picnic on that first week in July, Bessie and Hattie took advantage of a small breeze on the verandah, sipping lemonade, Hattie's favourite cooling drink.

"I feel like a prize winning pumpkin," Hattie said and began to laugh.

Bessie joined in. The two women welcomed the shared humour. Then, without warning, Hattie realized her waters had broken and labour was not far off. Bessie sent Amelia to tell Mr. Scovil, who was attending to a sick horse, that he needed to fetch the doctor immediately. As Bessie was helping Hattie up the stairs and into her room, she put her nurse's brain into action, thinking first about preparing the bed with a waterproof sheet under a clean one with a draw sheet on top.

Hattie quietly began to undress, pulling on a fresh nightdress, with a little help. She knew the routine, but being two weeks early she was not quite mentally prepared. Bessie listened with one ear for an indication that Mod was on his way to fetch the doctor. Finally, she heard his hurried steps as he came in the house and up the stairs to check on his wife so he could inform the doctor of her progress. After a quick conversation and a kiss on Hattie's cheek, the expectant father raced to the boat.

Bessie washed her hands, put on a clean apron, and brought a basin of warm water to freshen Hattie's face and hands and to clean up her lower extremities. Partly in order to give them both some meaningful activity, besides waiting, but also because it was part of the pre-labour routine, Bessie unpinned Hattie's upswept, light brown hair and plaited it in two long braids which she arranged on either side of her head so they would not be uncomfortable. The braids, together with flushed checks and her curled bangs, which had been encouraged with tongs heated over a kerosene lamp, made Hattie looked like a young girl.

Though the contractions were still at least ten minutes apart, Bessie knew events could speed up without warning. She told Amelia to put kettles on the back of the stove so warm water would be available for the first bath and then bring the little tub used for such rituals up the back stairs. Bessie believed in being prepared as much in advance as possible.

An early delivery would spare dear Hattie the last, difficult-to-navigate, full-term days. As she was stroking Hattie's forehead, Bessie remembered the children would probably be away until late afternoon, when their more than ample picnic was only a happy memory and their appetites would have bounced back.

Mira Caswell, their aunt, had agreed to take them for the expected day and even keep them overnight while her sister was in the throes of childbirth, but this was not to be. The original arrangement had been to load the children into the rowboat when their father went to fetch their doctor uncle and to reverse the procedure after the delivery. Bessie told Amelia to inform her if she saw the children coming along the road so they could be encouraged to play outside, if Hattie were not finished her inevitable groaning.

While Bessie was musing about the might-have-been, she realized Hattie's contractions were coming more frequently. She timed them. They were now every six minutes. She laid out a small table with a white cloth and put supplies on it she knew the doctor might want to augment those he would have in his Gladstone bag. Hattie napped between her waves of pains, much to Bessie's satisfaction, as she knew her energy must be conserved for later use.

An hour and a half passed without much progress. Bessie suddenly remembered she had consumed no food since breakfast. She walked halfway down the back stairs. She called to Amelia and, in spite of the heat, asked for a tray of tea for two, one small bowl of broth from the soup still simmering the last benefit from Sunday's joint, and a proper bowl full for herself, plus a slice of bread and butter. The experienced nurse knew she might not have an opportunity to eat again for many hours and needed to keep her own energy at a useful level. Hattie managed to sit up between groans and consume nearly all the bowl of broth and a half-cup of tea.

The contractions were now coming every three minutes. There was still a way to go, but Bessie decided it was likely this birth would be between Hattie and herself. Suddenly, through the open window, she heard the two men talking, as their boats were made secure on the wharf rings. Then came the reassuring tread of their feet on the stairs. Mod pressed his wife's hand and kissed it just as another spasm overtook her. He grimaced in sympathy but knew this was no place for a husband, and said, "I'll be downstairs."

A brief exchange of relevant information between doctor and nurse was all that there was time for before another spasm, not more than a minute after the last. The doctor examined the patient and announced the head was crowning. After several minutes of Hattie's most valiant efforts, out came a seemingly perfect little boy who took one breath but could not be persuaded to take any more in spite of his uncle's and his aunt's using every trick known to the medical and nursing professions, including a warm bath, which cleaned him for his parents' eyes but had no additional effect. Bessie wrapped the tiny bluing baby in two of the diapers on top of her pile, placed him in the cradle and set to work to clean up Hattie.

"A boy or girl?" Hattie half smiled.

"A boy" said the doctor.

"Where is he?"

Bessie tried to collect the right words. "I have to tell you something, Hattie. Your little boy did not live for more than one breath."

"I think the diabetes was too much for him," said the doctor.

Hattie looked as though someone strong had slapped her pretty face. Tears poured from her eyes.

"I want to see him."

Bessie lifted the tiny figure out of the cradle and put him in Hattie's arms. Except for a deepening blueness he looked like a healthy newborn, sleeping soundly.

"I'll wash up and tell Mod," the doctor said as he slipped out of the grieving room.

Mod hit his forehead with his fist in sadness and frustration as though inflicting pain on himself might lessen it for his wife and his family. The doctor pulled a bottle of brandy out of his bag, which he kept for such occasions and poured them each a small glass.

"I was afraid of this. Babies sometimes don't do well when the mother has diabetes," confided the doctor. "I'll wait here while you see Hattie and have a look at the baby, before I go back. I have another birth to see to."

Bessie stepped out of the bedroom so Hattie and Mod could comfort one another and joined the doctor downstairs.

"Thanks, Bess, for your help. Too bad the local nurses aren't up to your standard. I'll be back tomorrow to check on her sugar. Mira will be upset. What have you done with the children?"

There was no need to answer that question. The Scovil children could now be heard and seen coming along the Jemseg road laughing and swinging the empty picnic baskets. The doctor was not one to put off difficult encounters, the sooner the better was his approach.

"They need to be told before they come into the house. I'll do it unless you want to."

Bessie told him to go ahead and that she would talk with them when he left. She could see the children's expressions change from happy smiles to sober attention to eye rubbing. Mod came out of the house and put his hands, like soothing poultices, on their shoulders but found he was no stronger than his children. Seeing the sad family comforting one another through their tears at the end of a day that held such promise only a few hours earlier, pierced Bessie's professional armour.

She dabbed at her wet eyes as she walked toward her family, hugging her brother before he joined the doctor at the wharf and then each of the children in turn.

Bessie checked on Hattie who was sleeping lightly.

"The children have been told. May I bring them in briefly?"

"Please", said Hattie weakly.

Bessie told them to wash their hands and tidy their hair and then they could see their mother.

"I'd like to see him", squeaked Elizabeth in a voice she didn't recognize.

Hattie raised an eyebrow in Bessie's direction.

"It's your decision, Hattie".

Stunned into silence, they all peered at the lifeless little form wrapped in white linen. Elizabeth held Gertrude's hand. Morris took Mary's in one of his and Roger's in the other as they stood around the cradle.

Elizabeth offered a tiny, "How sad," that loosened their tears again, joined by Hattie's.

Bessie stayed near the door, not wanting to intrude. When Mod returned from seeing the doctor off at the wharf, Bessie took her brother out of the children's hearing range and pressed an urgent requirement. As the weather was so warm, the baby ought to be buried soon. He had not been baptized so there was no need to place him in consecrated ground. Bessie suggested to Mod he might wish to make a little box in the carpentry shed for the baby, and bury him before nightfall, perhaps at the edge of the far pasture. She thought it better if the younger children did not know where it was, but perhaps Morris could accompany his father, for support. Mod agreed, almost pleased to have a role.

The little pine box was quickly assembled. He took it to Hattie for her approval, after Bessie lined it with another of the linen diapers. Mother and father said "good-bye" to their little tragedy before Mod set off for the pasture with only a small spade and his grief for companions, not wanting Morris to see him break down. Bessie settled the children around the table for supper that Amelia had prepared. No one was especially hungry in spite of the energetic day full of laughter, eclipsed so suddenly. For want of something else to do, they quietly cleaned their plates as a way of behaving well at a time when even the grown ups were falling apart.

Bessie was waiting outside Hattie's door the next morning when the doctor came out with a glass vial in his hand. He held it up to the light. "Loaded" he said to nurse Bessie. She knew what that meant. Hattie's urine was thick with undigested sugar. Her dear sister-in-law had not shaken her diabetes and would gradually decline. Bessie was aware there was still a small chance of a recovery, which, if possible, would show in a few days. Had the baby been able to nurse, perhaps it would be greater. The doctor told Bessie to send for him, if there was a need, but if not he would be back in two days to test again. He spoke with Mod briefly, telling him of the disappointing news, along with a small dose of hope as the two men walked toward the wharf and the doctor's boat. When Bessie entered Hattie's room after the doctor left, she found her patient silently crying.

"You have every reason to cry, Dear, so don't feel badly that you can't control your tears."

Bessie empathized, sitting on a bedside chair and gently holding Hattie's pale hand, noticing her unusually long fingers. Bessie remembered her own mother's similar losses and for a moment was unable to say anything, overcome by sadness. Hattie managed a tiny smile in appreciation of her sister-in-law's tenderness.

"Do you think my diabetes will go away now?" Hattie asked, looking vaguely in the direction of the window and then directly into Bessie's eyes.

"It sometimes does, providing the symptoms weren't there before the baby began. We'll just have to wait and see."

"How long?"

"There's no set time. The doctor will check on your urine often and will be able to tell from that. You will have an idea too, especially if your usual thirst and your other symptoms lessen. Speaking of thirst, would you like to share a pot of tea with me?"

As Bessie left the bedroom to produce a tea tray, Hattie tried to remember her state of health last autumn. It had been an unusually warm September and mild October. She recalled making lemonade more often than usual to please the children, as they all liked the specialness of it. But perhaps it was to quench her thirst. And then by December her thirstiness lost its importance in the general confusion of morning sickness and digestive upsets. The doctor diagnosed diabetes sometime after Christmas, Hattie recollected. As Bessie opened her door with a tea tray crowned by a little vase holding a bunch of gold and orange nasturtiums, Hattie decided she would not burden Bessie with her musing.

Repeated visits from the doctor showed no change. Bessie recognized a well-known symptom of diabetes — hair thinning. Hattie's beautiful hair lost its fullness. Her thirst was still present. Her cheekbones became more prominent. She continued to relish the special foods for diabetics that came from a distant relative in England, mostly conserves made without sugar. Bessie now directed Amelia to make Hattie dishes without starch or sugar, difficult but possible with plentiful vegetables and meats.

*   *   *   *   *

A month after Hattie's confinement, a letter came from her favourite cousin in Saint John, Frank Starr, saying he would like to visit her a week from next Saturday. Frank was a wealthy Saint John businessman with the largest coal importing company in the city. He had recently moved into a spectacularly large, architect designed house at 127 Carleton Street. The house had seven bathrooms, more than enough space for his wife and four children, plus a suitable number of servants. Hattie did not know Bessie had written to Frank suggesting he might like to visit his cousin as she was showing no signs of shaking off the diabetes and it was probable she would not survive more than a few weeks.

On the appointed Saturday, cousin Frank was collected off the riverboat at the Gagetown wharf by Mod and young Morris. While that was happening, Bessie helped the girls into clean pinafores and checked that they were generally tidy. Hattie thought this was a perfect occasion for Roger to wear the splendid white sailor suit which a New York Robinson relative had sent earlier in the year along with some other beautiful clothes her own son had outgrown. They were all a little large for Roger at the time, but she thought the sailor suit should be tried. It fit him quite well; in fact Hattie thought he looked like a little Saint John fashion plate.

Frank would have had a meal on the boat, so Bessie placed the basics of a tea tray, plus cucumber sandwiches, a caraway seed cake, and some little chocolate cakes that were favourites with the children. She covered them with upturned bowls to prevent them from drying out and to keep the flies away. In spite of the sticky amber coloured flypapers dangling from the ceiling, there were always a few flies about. All the children were ready earlier than they needed to be. Mary and Roger were fidgeting in the heat of August. Hattie said they could go and play but to stay clean. She suggested they be official spotters and as soon as the boat could be seen, to let her know.

After a few minutes of staring at the empty river, except for two scows with cows going to an island pasture, Mary's perpetual need for dramatic action as a relief from boredom and unexpressed emotion took over. She was feeling left out. There was no new dress for her with pretty puffs and frills. Though she dearly loved her brother, jealous thoughts raced through her little head. They increased as she compared the perfectly white sailor suit with the navy braid next to her much washed pale blue pinafore. Mary enticed Roger out to the barn, hand in hand, skipping through the dusty summer day.

Whether the brilliant idea hit her as they approached the pot of black tar or whether she had it in mind before they left the riverbank, she was not sure, when she thought about it later. They paused before this shimmering pot with its own convenient stirring stick. Mary grabbed the stick and began to stir. The tar became more co-operative as the movement mixed with the heat of the day. She stopped, stood back and waited. Roger didn't take the bait. Mary stirred again with more gusto, making the tar almost as appealing as molasses taffy. She stood back again. It was too much fun for Roger not to take a turn. His little hands were not as well controlled as his older sister's. In the middle of a vigorous stir his hands slipped on the stick. Out flew several globs of tar landing on his white sailor suit trousers. He wanted to do a better job of stirring, like his big sister, so he tried several times more, bending over the pot. When his suit became thoroughly decorated, Mary was satisfied. Brother and sister then drifted off for other amusement until they were called to greet cousin Frank.

Though Hattie spent much of her time resting in her bedroom, she decided to join the family in the parlour when her cousin arrived. All the others were there, listening to Frank's amusing adventures on the riverboat, when Mary and Roger joined them. Had Bessie been given to fainting, this would have been an appropriate time. She recognized that triumphant look of Mary's, so she knew it was her idea, and decided to have a firm talk with her later. This was not the time. Hattie's face registered disappointment until she saw Frank laughing uncontrollably. His reaction to the disaster was infectious. Soon everyone was laughing, which set the tone for the rest of the afternoon.

After tea, Hattie announced she needed to rest. Frank asked if he could accompany her to her room. Even though they both knew this might be the last time they would see one another, the gaiety over the tar disaster still floated around them. They talked of their partially shared childhood in Saint John, when Hattie visited her aunt and uncle and played adventurous games with her cousins.

"I don't remember any black tar, though," laughed Frank.

*　*　*　*　*

21

Bessie did everything she could to make Hattie's recuperation tranquil, trying to orchestrate the day to have as little noise in the house as possible, especially in the mornings. She looked for a way to keep the girls and little Roger quietly occupied on the few rainy days. Elizabeth and Gertrude were trying to master the art of needlework and were now doing smocking. Mary was encouraged with simpler embroidery using hoops to hold her work in position. Since her bout of scarlet fever earlier in the summer, her eyes tired easily so she made little progress. Reading seemed too much like school, but she did like cooking, especially when there were sweet edibles to follow all that hard work of beating and stirring.

The occasional wet morning found all four children in the kitchen, with Bessie supervising. At least they are learning the rudiments of baking, thought Bessie, justifying the mess. Most days they were all outdoors. Mod devoted as much time as he could to being with his adored wife, sometimes just holding her hand as she rested or slept. By mid-afternoon, when Hattie often experienced a spurt of energy, she came downstairs, and if the day were pleasant—as it usually was in August—would sit on the verandah. The children joined her, hoping to see her smile, to hear her laugh, the older girls bringing their needle work, asking her to untangle their messes. Roger wanted to be on his mother's lap. Mary always tried to sit next to her, touching her shoulder or her arm, curiously drawn by the unusual smell of her breath, like old apples at the bottom of the barrel when winter was past.

Morris liked to stretch on the first step just below the verandah, conscious of taking in the scene, storing it in his memory box. He sometimes helped the hired men with haying in the mornings but came to the verandah in the afternoons when his mother was there. Bessie made sure there was always a jug of water and a glass by Hattie, who had a perpetual thirst.

*　*　*　*　*

One morning in mid August, when Elizabeth and Gertrude were in Gagetown playing with their Caswell cousins, Mary decided to explore the orchard with Roger. She told her aunt where they'd be, who approved. The orchard was a relatively safe place; it was away from the river and from farm machinery and far enough from the house that their play was not likely to disturb Hattie. As Mary, with doting Roger close behind, was scouting about looking for apples ripe enough to nibble on, she began to pick up green apple windfalls to give the pigs a treat. As she stashed the apples in her pinafore pockets, she found a length of string in one pocket left over from a previous adventure. With that discovery, Mary hatched a new plan; she picked more green apples directly from the tree and added them to the collection.

When they reached the pig house at one end of the pig pen, Mary moved a little ladder from a nearby shed, suggesting to Roger they climb up on the low, almost flat roof of the pig house. When they were perched on the front edge of the low roof, Mary tied one end of the string to the stem of a green apple and lowered it slowly toward an unsuspecting porker. She waited for him to take a bite and then attempt to swallow the rest. At this stage her mischievous creativity took over! She deftly pulled on the string. Much to the pig's surprise, he was not allowed to swallow the treat but was keen to try again. Mary obliged. The pig was again disappointed but not disheartened. Mary repeated the trick, letting the apple descend further down the pig's throat before pulling on the string. Roger wanted a turn, which added to the glee. After a half hour of hilarity, Mary's pockets were empty and piggy-porky had been allowed to eat all the green apples. She turned her twisted tail toward the miscreants and, feeling distinctly queasy, staggered off to her favourite wallow.

At the supper table, after Father whipped through "For what we are about to receive ..." young Morris announced that one of the pigs seemed to be oddly lazy; she wouldn't come at feeding time but had stayed stretched out in the dirt. His father said he'd check on her later. Mary noticed Roger looked as though he was about to say something, so she started talking about the apples still looking very green, and shouldn't some be ripe soon? This produced a mini-lecture by Mod on when the different varieties of apples ripened. The conversation took a turn away from pigs and apples, but still on orchards when Bessie asked her brother when he expected to hear more from the government about experimenting with different types of plum trees to see whether they would grow in that area.

This left Mary feeling fairly secure their adventure would not be discovered, though she kept her eye on Roger, in case he blurted out something that she would have to deal with. She wasn't too worried as he followed Amelia's every move while she carried in the dessert, a wobbling blancmange cooled in a mould, which, when turned out, looked like a castle. The glistening concoction was accompanied by this year's strawberry jam to spoon on top, lifting the milky blandness to more than acceptable heights.

*　*　*　*　*

As August came to an end, Hattie could no longer collect enough energy to walk downstairs in the afternoons. She remained in her room, but welcomed the children, trying to re-create the intimacy of those verandah hours. By September first she slipped into a coma. Bessie and Mod took turns sitting with her. On September third, at 5 a.m., while Bessie stroked her forehead, Hattie stopped breathing.

In her declining days, Hattie asked Bessie to make sure she was buried in the St. John's churchyard in Gagetown. She had always preferred attending the church there, it being familiar since childhood, as the DuVernets lived on the Gagetown side of the river, near the lighthouse, just opposite the Scovils. She found the architecture and decoration of the humble little St. James church in Jemseg less inspiring. After she married, she fell in with the Scovil family routine — St. John's for matins and St. James for evensong, especially in the summer. In the winter, the weather sometimes prevented them from attending either.

Harriet Lavinia DuVernet Scovil had her wish. The St. John's church overflowed, with all niches for standing completely filled. Three of her five surviving siblings swelled the family pews: Ned, who practiced medicine in Digby, Nova Scotia, her unmarried sister, Lizzy who resided with him and his family, and Mira, Dr. Caswell's wife. One brother, Will, had died of a fever in Florida and another, Rob, living in South Carolina sent his regrets as his wife was about to produce another baby and insisted he stay near her. Gagetown citizens flocked to the funeral.

Hattie's father, Harry DuVernet, nicknamed "The Squire," died seven years previously, but his second wife, Pricilla Buzza, younger by twenty-five years, sat with two of their six offspring two pews behind Bessie with Mod and his five very sad children. There was some discussion between Bessie and her brother about whether Mary and Roger should stay at home with Amelia but in the end they decided it would be better for their memory of their mother if they could be part of the service. There was no reason for Amelia to stay at home. She asked Miss Scovil whether she might attend. Amelia was very fond of Mrs. Scovil.

A granite stone was erected over Hattie's grave a few weeks later, with a simple inscription, "Harriet Lavinia wife of Morris Scovil Esq. Died Sept 3rd 1903 Age 37 years" topped by a cross made of the same stone. Eighty-five years later, on a visit to the churchyard, Mary noticed there was still unoccupied space around her mother's resting place, as though no one wanted to intrude on her specialness.

3

The Search for a Housekeeper

Bessie now had to make a formidable decision. She was not expected back at St. Paul's until late in the month and had asked for an extension of a week or two, in case she needed it. With no children of her own, her brother's held a very dear place in her heart. She had become even closer to them in the last four months, but felt she must return to her profession, not least because she did not want to let Dr. Coit down by retiring before he did. With that in mind, a few days after Hattie's burial she set about finding a suitable housekeeper for her brother as he was in no state to make decisions. She knew word of mouth was the quickest and most effective way to advertise one's need in the rural community. She asked the doctor, the owners of the two grocery stores in Gagetown, the rectors on both sides of the river, and relatives and friends to pass the word around that she would like to interview possible live-in housekeepers who were capable of child care.

By the time a week had passed she had been told of three women who were interested and made appointments for them to come to Meadowlands to be interviewed, and of course to meet the children and their potential employer. Her brother was still very emotional, so she decided to do the initial interviewing and just ask Mod in when they were having cups of tea. While waiting for the first applicant, Bessie made a list of the basic requirements all must have to be seriously considered. They should be Anglican, as another religion would confuse the children; literate and numerate, capable of keeping basic accounts; reasonably well spoken; clean and neat and well groomed; practiced in good, plain cooking; not easily flustered, strong enough for housework with satisfactory references and of course experienced in the care of young and older children.

As she sat waiting to see the first applicant, a disturbing memory surfaced in Bessie's mind. She recalled a story that made the rounds several years ago of a Fredericton gentleman who employed a housekeeper to help care for his motherless children and look after the running of the house. She was an attractive and vigorous woman, though a little rough. But she was well recommended so the desperate father employed her.

It was not long before the lonely widower sought solace in the housekeeper's generous arms, and then she had difficulty buttoning her coat. Marriage was the only gentlemanly solution, which produced social isolation and endless problems.

Bessie was shaken from her reverie by a knock at the door. The first applicant had arrived. She allowed herself to be agreeably impressed by this neatly dressed woman of about thirty-five and was able to mentally tick off many qualifications on her requirement list. Unfortunately, however, when Bessie asked Ethel about her previous involvement with young children, she received a disappointing reply.

"I've never had nothing to do with small children. I was the last of seven and them all boys who took off as soon they could. Since I was fourteen, I done housekeeping for old people. Mrs. Fitch was the last and she just died, so that's why I'm lookin'."

Ethel would not do. Better grammar and some knowledge of children were both necessary, though the former could be overlooked if the latter were acceptable. As Ethel would be walking back to Jemseg, Bessie thought it only civil to offer her tea and biscuits. She excused herself, put the kettle on and told Mod—snoozing in the parlour—there would be no need to meet the applicant and would he tell the children, who were near the barns playing under the watchful eyes of Elizabeth and young Morris, they could continue with their games.

Neither of the other two applicant passed scrutiny for various reasons. One was unnecessarily pretty with a tendency to roll her eyes and would be too much of a threat to her brother's morals. The other was only sixteen and frail looking. Although a day woman would be coming twice a week to do the laundry and other heavy work, like carpet beating twice a year, this applicant was too near the children's ages to expect any discipline.

Bessie was not easily defeated. She again made the rounds of the local clergy, friends, and relatives she had previously contacted to say the position was still open. After a week a woman wrote with a very good hand and equally acceptable grammar. Bessie was hopeful but when she saw the corpulent woman waddling to the door, with a slight limp she knew this was her fourth failure.

The following evening, with Mary and Roger in bed and the three older ones doing their homework at the dining table, Bessie decided to share a pot of tea with Mod and discuss what they should do to find a housekeeper so she could return to work. As she entered the sitting room with a tray of tea, she was surprised to see the top of her brother's balding head first and his face in his hands. When he looked up at his sister's approach, she could see his eyes were red from weeping and his face blotched. Being over a decade older, Bessie was used to comforting her brother, so neither was embarrassed by this unmanly behaviour. After putting down the tray, Bessie placed a hand gently on Mod's shoulder.

"It is still early days, dear. Hattie was a fine woman. We will always mourn her in our hearts."

As she sat down to pour the tea, an image of her sister-in-law, as she died early on September 3rd, surfaced in her mind and she found herself swallowing hard to keep her eyes from watering unduly. She concentrated on putting just the right amount of milk and sugar in the cup and passed it to Mod. He cleared his throat, trying to get a grip on his emotions. After they each took a few sips, Bessie knew it was time to bring up the difficult subject. Since she had been unsuccessful at finding a suitable housekeeper, she had been thinking of alternatives. The children were all still dazed by their mother's death. This was no time to send them off individually to relatives. So that fleeting idea, often grasped by families of children needing mothering, was quickly abandoned. They needed to remain together and with their father for mutual support. She hoped that Mod would eventually find a suitable lady to marry and mother his children, though taking on five would be embraced only by an unusually kind or a recklessly foolish one. Bessie was aware of what was sitting at the bottom of her barrel of solutions. She was staring at it, now that all others had evaporated.

She hesitated to go back on her word to Dr. Coit, but she knew he would understand if she put off returning to her position in charge of the infirmary. Yes, she decided. Mod's face in his hands was the tipping point. During her year's absence from St. Paul's she would have ample time to find a perfect fit for the job. She refilled Mod's cup and told him of her decision. His face brightened with relief at his sister's generous offer.

"I've been hoping you'd come to that conclusion," he replied. "You've been so good to be here all summer, but I can't possibly manage with just Amelia and run the farm. I hate to take you away from your work, but you know I've always relied on you."

After living in urban parts of the United States over most of the last twenty-five years, Bessie was aware just how isolated life was at Meadowlands. She dearly loved the place and was already falling in with the natural rhythms, dominated by the changing seasons and the preparation required to be comfortable with them. Her brother Morris, whom she always called Mod, had lived here since 1880 and the children since their births. They were all in tune with their surroundings, though Bessie was beginning to think a more stimulating environment was needed to fit the young for the modern world, especially the three girls. Young Morris was doing well at school and might be expected to take over the farm from his father. Mod had established a thriving farm based on his success in breeding and selling thoroughbred horses plus the lush hay crop produced annually on 500 acres of interval land that was well nourished by the flooding of the spring freshet. The farm included an additional 400 acres of woodland. With such a large base, young Morris, and perhaps Roger, could well make a living at Meadowlands, as well. Bessie promised herself she would have to give more thought to the girls. For now, she had to keep the children occupied during their period of intense grieving—that lost feeling, which spreads to everyone when a mother has left the family.

Bessie was especially conscious how very bereft her brother felt and tried to cheer him in little ways. She knew from the days when he was a little boy that Mod had a sweet tooth. Though she also knew that too much sweet food was not good for anyone, she decided always to try to have a little ritual with him, after the children were in bed—cake and tea in the parlour. It was something to look forward to when they could read the papers sent from New York by their brothers, Jack and Barclay. It was also a good opportunity to talk over any happenings of the day that needed attention.

*　*　*　*　*

Bessie kept the cake tin on the top shelf in the larder and did not share it with the children, except occasionally when Amelia's latest entry into creative cooking provided an inedible lump for supper's dessert. Little Mary's watchful eyes were aware of the grown up cake ritual. She had inherited her father's sweet tooth and was hoping for at least some frosting lickings as she watched her aunt getting ready to adorn a round white pound cake cooling in the pantry. She stood as quietly as a tree, controlling her constant need to talk and wiggle. She knew her aunt wanted to enjoy a degree of tranquility during this creative activity. As Mary watched every move, she noticed Bessie plunge her scoop into the large jar of baking soda, instead of a similar one of frosting sugar, standing next to it, sifted it and in the usual way mixed in the melted butter, vanilla, and chopped walnuts.

Mary tried repeatedly to interject her discovery, especially as she was expecting to scrape the frosting bowl clean. She even jumped up and down, a mark of complete frustration. She was told to "Shush," to go and play and allow her aunt some peace and quite. All right, thought the child, I'll wait and see. Mary decided her revenge would be to peek-witness the expressions on the faces of the two cake eaters when the frosting made with baking soda instead of sugar hit their taste buds.

It seemed a year before evening came and her aunt tucked her into bed. Mary made herself stay awake until she could hear the grown ups talking in the hall before they walked into the sitting room. She then tiptoed down the stairs and hid in such a way that she could peek through the space provided by the door hinges. What Mary saw was worth the wait. The expression on the faces of the cake eaters biting into the baking soda frosting remained with little Mary for the rest of her life! After that fiasco, Bessie was very careful and even put new, large labels on the jars to replace those so smeared with various ingredients they were no longer legible, or at least that is how she explained the disaster to Mod. She was determined there would never be a repeat of this lapse of concentration.

There was, however, another spot of drama involving the same three characters — Bessie, little Mary and a cake. Not many days later, Mary observed a cake with its generous mound of butter frosting cooling in the pantry. She decided her ever-present sweet tooth must be satisfied. She had just come in from playing outside with Roger, who had now gone off somewhere with Morris. An urge for action grabbed her. She was still wearing her white, cotton sun hat with its large turned down brim, now always on her head to keep the sun from hurting her eyes. She nipped into the pantry, deftly cleaned the frosting from the cake with her speedy little hand, depositing it in her sunhat. She then placed the hat on her head and made a dignified escape to the Jerusalem artichoke bed, a safe distance from the house. There she sat, completely protected by the tall, leafy, dark green fronds. Mary tipped her hat into her lap, which made a perfect bowl from which she then scooped and savoured mouthful after mouthful of butter frosting. By the time nothing was left in her hat but a few buttery spots, the little thief was feeling decidedly sick. This coincided with Aunt Bessie's discovery of the missing frosting and her missing niece.

Bessie first searched the house while Amelia was sent outside.

"Miss Mary, Miss Mary," Amelia called, looking in the most likely places.

Little Mary was as still as an artichoke stalk, well hidden in the leafy cover. She knew her crime would be punished by being sent to bed without supper and without the company of brother Roger. She knew she would have earned the disapproval of her father, which was especially hard to bear. She decided she would not move until dark and Aunt Bessie would think she had drowned in the river, just a few skips and hops away. Then she'd be sorry she kept the frosted cakes for the grownups. Mary's tummy was still complaining about a surfeit of sugar and to add to that she was getting thirsty. The calling became much farther away; she could hardly hear it, then it gradually came nearer again. They're hunting all over everywhere, she thought.

Aunt Bessie's voice called, surprisingly loud, "Mary, come back. You won't be punished."

Mary couldn't believe her ears. All this fun and no punishment! Aunt Bessie must be getting scared I'm really lost or run away, she said to herself. Father would miss her. Secretly she knew that she was his favourite among the five children and that he really wanted to take her part, but she also knew he could not openly side with her against his sister who was in command of domestic affairs, including children. If her father called for her, she would run into his arms, but she knew he would be sitting in his usual chair, smoking his pipe, trying to read, but worrying instead.

The thought of not wanting to hurt her father, the promise of no punishment, chilly darkness not far off, and a thirst she could no longer ignore pushed little Mary out of hiding. No one saw her emerge from the artichoke bed wearing her nearly white, cotton sun hat, sticky with frosting smears. She walked slowly around to the front lawn and nonchalantly looked at a scow being towed up river.

"There you are, you naughty child," Bessie spat out against her intention, but nonetheless relieved when she spied her.

"You said I wouldn't be punished," piped up the culprit.

"Don't be impertinent," answered Aunt Bessie. "Go and wash your face and hands and your knees are filthy."

Bessie wanted to open her arms to the willful and adventurous child, tell her how happy she was that she was all right and to ask her whether she enjoyed the frosting. But she could not. Such complete forgiveness would encourage more bad behaviour leading to goodness knows what in the future. She had her reputation to think of. What if Mary became a real tear-away, known in the community for her unacceptable antics? Fingers would now point at Bessie; everyone would think, "not enough discipline at an early age."

As Mary was drinking a large glass of water, and washing some of the mud off her knees, Bessie remembered an advice to a mothers' column she had written in *The Ladies' Home Journal*. She collected herself, quickly wiping a tear from her eye, feeling relief Mary was not discovered face down in the river. A mother had written to ask her views on how to deal with a naughty child. She had suggested the mother try to discover why the child was being naughty—boredom, jealousy, loneliness, heightened creativity, enjoying the attention, unhappiness because of certain events etc.

Bessie smiled slightly, realizing this good advice now applied to her and her little charge. She vowed she would try to be more understanding. She would talk it over with Mod this evening as they ate their cake, devoid of frosting. Due to the drama of the day, Bessie was preoccupied by how to improve her relationship with the children, especially with little Mary, and had no problem launching the subject over their tea and cake, now hastily sprinkled with a sifting of icing sugar.

Her brother thought for a minute, putting himself back in his childhood years and remembering how he had liked Bessie to soothe him after an upset or before bed.

"You have a gift for reciting poetry, Bess. Try that." Mod offered.

"I should save my eyes for working on my articles, so reciting is a good suggestion. You and Jack always seemed to like it. I'll unearth my copy of *The Sunday Book of Poetry* by a woman writer I've admired since the early 1860s, a Mrs. Alexander. I think I still remember "The Burial of Moses".

Bessie began,

By Nebo's lonely mountain

On this side of Jordan's wave,

In a vale in the land of Moab there lies a lonely grave.

And no man knows that sepulcher, and no man saw it e'er,

For the angels of God upturned the sod, and laid the dead man there.

After the first two lines, sister and brother were reciting together, slowly and deliberately with the same inflection. Half way through Bessie caught herself thinking this was not a good choice, considering Hattie had been buried so recently, but Mod's recalling his childhood pleasure seemed to override his sadness.

Bessie decided she would try something lighter for her first bedtime versifying with little Mary. The following night, when the seven year old was tucked in bed, her aunt asked the still wiggling child whether she would like a goodnight verse. Always ready to put off the removal of the kerosene lamp to the top of a chest of drawers in the hall, Mary said she would. A few years ago, for a Christmas gift, Dr. Coit had given Bessie a copy of Jean Ingelo's *Poetical Works*, recently published in 1898. She was so enthralled by the prolific English poet's long narratives that before the holidays were over she had memorized several.

She decided to try "Supper at the Mill" on Mary, which she recited to Roger not long ago when she was baking.

She began:

> *My neighbour White—we met today—*
> *He always had a cheerful way, as if he breathed at ease.*
> *My neighbour White lives down the glade, and I live higher, in the shade*
> *Of my old walnut trees. I see his thatch when I look out, his branching roses*
> *Creep about, and vines half cover it.*
> *And there his eldest daughter stands with downcast eyes and skillful hands*
> *Before her ironing board.*
> *If maids be shy, he cures who can; but if a man be shy—a man—*
> *Why then the worse for him.*

The little blond head was still and the pale eyelashes were fighting to stay separated, so Bessie continued, pulling verse after verse of the Victorian favourite out of her memory, well past the time when Mary's ears, like the rest of her, had fallen asleep.

4

A Generous Offer and a Different Christmas

By the time October was well launched, Mod received a letter from Frank Starr, Hattie's cousin. He repeated his feelings of sympathy that he had previously conveyed and said since Hattie's death he had been thinking of something practical he could do, as a sort of memorial to his favourite cousin. After much consideration he thought sending Elizabeth and Gertrude to Edgehill School for Girls in Windsor, Nova Scotia would be something that would help the whole family, lessening the responsibility of five children for Mod and for Bessie and giving the girls a more varied education. Frank suggested that if Mod and Bessie agreed, they could start after Christmas. As soon as he heard from them he would be in touch with the headmistress of Edgehill to check on the availability of places. Edgehill had been established over a dozen years ago and was the best school of its kind east of Montreal.

Mod was dumfounded. He handed the letter to Bessie, who had to sit down to read it. They agreed not to tell the girls until the next day. They discussed Frank's generous offer thoroughly over cake and tea after all the children were in bed. They looked at the offer from all angles and could find no disadvantages of any importance. Of course the girls would be homesick, of course they would be missed at home, of course it would be a rush to have Miss Straight make their clothes in time, but the advantages to Elizabeth and Gertrude would greatly outweigh any minor negatives. Their education would be much more inclusive than that at the Gagetown Grammar School, though it had a good reputation. They would meet girls from more than acceptable backgrounds and generally their opportunities in life would be greatly enhanced. They stayed talking past their usual bedtime of ten o'clock, neither being able to desist from smiling and then smiling some more.

Bessie suggested the girls should be told at the family breakfast the next day, which happened to be a Saturday, so not the usual rush to get off to school. She thought their father ought to read Frank's letter out loud to them all. After porridge, boiled eggs and toast and marmalade were almost finished, Father announced he had a letter he would like to read to them all. Five pairs of eyes stared at the crisp, white paper that Mod pulled from his inside breast pocket. As soon as the lines were read, Elizabeth and Gertrude jumped up and hugged one another with an eggcup being knocked off the table in the commotion. No one paid any attention to the eggcup, its blue and white willow pattern now broken into pieces, except Trixy, the dog, who scuttled under the other side of the table. They all laughed at Trixy. Elizabeth and Gertrude then burst into tears, followed by Mary and Roger. Young Morris just said, "Well, lucky girls!" After that, Mary realized the letter seemed to hold good news so her tears dried and so did Roger's. Elizabeth and Gertrude's tears soon turned to laughter and they began asking questions.

"When will we know for sure? Can we come home for the holidays? What if we don't like the food? How will we get there? How long will the journey take? What if we lose our way? Will someone come with us? Will you all write to us? Will we have uniforms?"

On and on rolled the questions until Bessie said she would start to answer them. No one moved from the table for nearly an hour, except for bodily functions and then quickly returned. Bessie was able to assure the girls that Ayleene, the eldest of Frank's children also attended Edgehill, being a little younger than Elizabeth. It was likely they would all leave together for Windsor from Saint John on the ferry that crossed the Bay of Fundy. Elizabeth and Gertrude remembered playing with Ayleene two or three years previously on one of their rare visits to the big city. They found her to be shy but otherwise nothing to complain about. Bessie tried to provide the requested information as well as she could with additions from Mod.

Miss Straight would be contacted tomorrow about a date for her to take up residence, along with her sewing machine, for a few weeks. First though, Bessie needed a trip to Manchester, Robertson and Allison's store in Saint John for bolts of suitable serge for skirts and jackets, broadcloth for blouses and spring dresses and patterns for uniforms. Once a list of required clothes was received, action would begin. However, as young people's feet grew so quickly, she thought the girls would need to travel to Saint John in mid-December to fill their list of required shoes, slippers and boots plus any other items including classroom necessities such as note books, pencils, straight pens with extra nibs and ink, though perhaps that should be purchased in Windsor, to avoid the risk of spillage. They would not have to buy some items which would appear on the list, like a silver napkin ring, silver fork, knife, spoon and teaspoon, for each of the girls. Elizabeth and Gertrude thought it strange they would need to take some of the family silver to school, but could see the reason for it, and it would remind them of home.

Most of the rest of the day was absorbed by the news in that life-changing letter. The lucky girls sought their Aunt Bessie or father to answer more questions. Young Morris had mixed feelings. He would be glad to be rid of their silliness, but he knew he'd miss his sisters. Mary worried she would have to sleep in their room, leaving her dear Roger all by himself. "After Christmas" seemed a lifetime away to Roger so he felt everything would be the same for ages.

Bessie knew that once a confirmation of places came, Frank would write in more detail. There would be expenses, of course. Mod managed a thriving farm raising thoroughbred horses and selling them and also arranging for local farmers with not enough hay of their own to buy several acres of standing hay from him. He made a comfortable living for the usual expenses of a family with their considerable social standing, but not much overflowing for luxuries. This was one of those times when Bessie was particularly glad she had held out to be paid partly in stocks from the Curtis Publishing Company when her agreement was drawn up in 1890 to contribute monthly columns to *The Ladies Home Journal.* The magazine prospered. It now boasted the largest circulation of any magazine in the world. She was still contributing occasional articles so felt she was not only earning her monthly cheque but adding to the value of her stocks. Now she could easily sell a few, if necessary, though she would not act rashly.

Nearly two weeks passed before another letter arrived from cousin Frank. Providing the girls' school reports were adequate, two places would await them after Christmas. Future correspondence would be sent directly from the headmistress' secretary at Edgehill to their father at Meadowlands with details of their uniform list and all other requirements. In the mean time a copy of the girls' last report cards and a covering letter from the head teacher at the Gagetown Grammar School should be sent to the headmistress. Oh, and here is a little something to help with kitting out the girls. Mod looked in the envelope and found a cheque made out for two hundred dollars. Generosity itself! Hattie would have been so pleased Frank was being magnanimous toward her two young ladies, as she used to call them.

Bessie made a mental note of the three pairs of shoes—indoor, outdoor, gymnasium, plus slippers, rubber boots and leather boots, sun hats, felt hats, waterproofs, winter coats, dress gloves, undergarments, stockings, umbrellas, Sunday dresses, handbags, trunks, times two which would make a dent in the generous check but by no means exhaust it. Knowing how critical girls can be of one another she wanted to include two best dresses from a shop for her nieces, rather than have Miss Straight make them. Though she had never prepared girls for boarding school, Bessie had done her homework before writing about every necessity in her articles and books on the care of children in the 1890's. Requirements would not have changed by much. Even with such a long shopping list, Bessie knew it was unlikely she would need to sell any shares; they could stay put to accumulate more profit, sure to be needed for some emergency in the greater family.

Miss Straight and her sewing machine took up residence for the month of November once the list arrived and Bessie made a quick trip to Saint John to choose materials that were delivered the next day to the Gagetown wharf by riverboat. While she was in Manchester, Robertson and Allison's department store, she checked on the availability of all necessities so the purchases could be made in one day, with the girls, before Christmas.

Much trying on of partly finished finery kept the girls' excitement at a high pitch for the entire month, which prompted young Morris to wonder whether all the girls in that school were so silly. Mary and Roger were mesmerized by Miss Straight's whirring machine and grateful for bits of un-wanted material that they wrapped around their stick horses as blankets. Miss Straight had a habit of singing Irish tunes as she worked, which Mary, with her musical talent, picked up quickly. Though a spinster, the sewing woman had an affinity with small children. The sewing corner in the upstairs hall became a happy and favourite place for the little ones, especially as the weather was trying on winter.

With the two eldest girls being whisked away to boarding school before long, Bessie's original plan to keep the children together no longer existed. A more stimulating and exciting life than Gagetown and Meadowlands could provide awaited Elizabeth and Gertrude for the next few years. Bessie also considered that Mary should not be deprived of a life with a greater cultural and educational depth. Perhaps she, too, could attend Edgehill.

During the next evening tea and cake ritual with Mod, Bessie introduced the subject of a change for Mary. What did he think of offering Mary the opportunity of living in a larger community? Godparents were often called upon after the death of a parent, and indeed one was usually chosen with this possibility in mind. Would Mod think about the possibility of asking Mary's godfather, their cousin, John Robinson, and his wife, Sarah, to have Mary live with them in Rothesay? Though Mod had a sudden empty feeling and then a tightness in his stomach at the thought of not having his mischievous Mary with him, he knew it was best for her and voiced no objection to Bessie's contacting their cousins. Mod took a second slice of caraway seed cake while he and Bessie exchanged what they knew about the occasionally visited family branch. John Robinson headed a prosperous insurance company and with his wife, Sarah, had two little boys slightly older than Mary. It looked as though they would have no girls, so an instant daughter could benefit all concerned.

Without doubt, Mary and Roger would miss one another, but the little cousins would soon take his place, and Roger would be attending school next year, keeping him occupied. Mod suggested Bessie write the letter. She did, the next day, explaining that she was trying to make Meadowlands possible for Mod to manage, with just a housekeeper and domestic help, after she returned to nursing in September of next year. She pointed out that Mary was a bright child and adapted well to being away in New York for nearly a year when she was only five, so she thought she would not be overly homesick. The idea was to have Mary stay with them until she was old enough to attend Edgehill, though coming back to Meadowlands in the summer holidays, as would Elizabeth and Gertrude, when Bessie would also have her holidays from St. Paul's School. Sarah replied promptly on behalf of them both, saying she had always wanted a little girl and though the reason for her to have one was very sad, they would willingly take on the expected role of godparents. She also felt certain that Henry, nearly ten and Will, eight, would welcome little Mary.

Bessie responded with gratitude. Would delivering Mary in early January be acceptable? As Elizabeth and Gertrude would be in Saint John for a few days with the Frank Starr family before travelling to Edgehill for the beginning of the January term, Bessie suggested Mary could join the party leaving Meadowlands shortly after the first of January. All was settled except telling Mary. Mod decided he would read Sarah's letter to them all at the supper table, as he had Frank's, to put Mary's new life on a similar level as that of her sisters. Mod was rewarded with excited hand clapping and sparkling eyes from his little girl and general chatter about her future from all. Once Roger had taken in what January would bring, or more to the point, take away, Morris saw that his little brother was overcome with sadness at the thought of loosing his Mary, and cheered him slightly by saying, "You and I will be in charge of the farm, Rog."

Mary looked upon her stay with her godfather and his family as an adventure rather like Elizabeth and Gertrude's. She remembered New York was full of exciting new things to do and see and although she will never forget the day her lunch box fell open on the floor at kindergarten and out popped plain bread and butter sandwiches, with the crusts on, instead of animal crackers, like the others ate, mostly she had happy memories. She would go to a big school, be back for the holidays like her sisters and would write letters to Roger. He couldn't read well yet, but maybe her letters would make him want to learn. Aunt Bessie and Father must think she was grown up enough for this new life. She hoped she would not disappoint them. To begin with she would practice being good, at least until Christmas.

With Mary now also needing new clothes, Miss Straight was persuaded to stay on. Two navy blue serge skirts, two pinafores, one frilly blouse, two plain blouses, two petticoats, two nightdresses, and several underpinnings rolled off Miss Straight's humming machine. And then, partly because Roger was growing alarmingly fast, and partly to include him in the fun, Bessie requested a pair of winter trousers and jacket for him. The two were delighted that their happy time in the upper hall was extended. Their stick horses' wardrobes greatly benefited, as well.

*　*　*　*　*

A few days later, Bessie noticed Mary looked rather listless and feverish at breakfast, so told her she should go back to bed, where she would be given some light nourishment. Roger was kept away in case it was something serious. Bessie remembered the scarlet fever and was taking no chances. Mary was lulled to return to sleep by Miss Straight's sweet tunes drifting in from the hall accompanied by Roger's chatter to his well-blanketed horses.

When Mary awoke from her deep sleep, she drowsed a little letting her thoughts imagine Christmas, only two weeks away. "We're still in mourning. Father always wears a black tie and a black armband. They won't have extra people staying or even visiting for the day, probably. And anyway, with the three of them taking off a bit after the beginning of New Year's there was a lot to do, packing mostly and checking off lists, which Aunt Bessie was already doing.

"Whatever this Christmas brings, it won't be like the last one. Mother was having what Aunt Bessie called morning sickness and didn't feel up to the sleigh ride to and from the Jemseg church, but everyone else went, except Amelia. She was in the kitchen, already working up a room full of steam before we left. Let's see, Uncle Jack came from New York, but Aunt Addie didn't. She wasn't feeling well and luckily wanted bossy cousin Bess to stay with her. Big brothers, Charlie and Delancey were visiting some churchy friends so Meadowlands didn't have to share jolly Uncle Jack with anyone.

"A bit before Christmas, Uncle Jack told us all he's learned a great way to cook a turkey and hoped Aunt Bessie would let him be in charge of the immense, sad pile of feathers, soon to be plucked. She gave in after promises of perfection. He said friends in New York had tried it—'haybox

38

cooking' they called it. I think he said it would be 'succulent,' or something like that.

"For going to church, eight of us squeezed into one sleigh — the biggest one, black with thin gold lines drawn along the edges. Father drove up in front, of course. Uncle Jack sat next to him with me on his lap. Every now and then he tickled me until I could hardly breathe for laughing. Aunt Bessie, with her big sister voice, told him to stop. We'd had three light snowfalls and freezing weather so the shiny chestnut mare had no trouble pulling so full a sleigh. Father didn't believe in using the whip unless necessary, but Horsey, as Roger named her when she was born, seemed to sprout wings as she flew along the road to Jemseg, without any stinging whip.

"Why do horses have to do their poo poos in front of everyone? Maybe trotting makes them want to go. I feel embarrassed for them. Do they want to remind everyone who is doing all the work? The poos make a warm sweetness in the air, almost a-just-out-of-the-oven smell, but sharper. I can see yellow grain in the brownish poo before it drops to the pure white ground. I look back at the dark apples decorating the middle of the road, being lost in the distance.

"The church was filled with people in big coats and pink faces. We all just managed to sit in our usual front pew, right under the pulpit. In order to see anything of the vicar when he was preaching — mostly his chin and his hairy nose — I had to rest my head as far back as it would go on the back of the pew. But that day there was lots else to notice; green boughs tied together and wound around things, more choir than usual, even the hymns were carols that I learned in school so I sang as loud as I could like everyone else. Aunt Bessie, sitting next to me smiled, so I must have been doing something right.

"Father usually didn't bring his pocket watch out until the sermon had gone on for an hour. But that Christmas morning his tummy must have been rumbling, like mine, as he slid his hand under his jacket to reach his waistcoat pocket by the time the vicar was only just fully launched, in his sing-song voice, into what I feared would be an endless ordeal. When Father snapped the cover of his watch shut — his way of saying the sermon should finish soon — the vicar's head jolted, not expecting notice quite yet. He did his best to summarize several pages into a few sentences, give a blessing, and then, looking as though he'd taken a bite out of a wormy apple, announced a caroling hymn.

"I hung on to Roger's hand so he wouldn't get lost in the crowd leaving the church. Several came over to us to shake hands with Uncle Jack and

Father and to speak to Aunt Bessie. Finally Father fetched the horse and sleigh from a nearby barn and we all piled in again, well covered with buffalo robes. The bricks which had been heated in the oven and covered with straw still had some warmth left in them which my feet liked, especially as that too small wood stove in the church did little more than take the frost out of the air. Elizabeth and Gertrude started singing carols. The words from Uncle Jack's mouth, so near my ear, made it hurt so I twisted my head a little, and joined in. I was told in New York I had 'perfect pitch' which seems to please everyone. It just means I know how to sing. Uncle Jack must have it as well as we sort of sounded like one person with a double voice. Just as we turned off the road toward our house, the imagined smell of 'succulent' turkey hit my nostrils and my tummy growled again.

"Roger and I ran inside and I helped him take his boots off and put them in the boot box just inside the door. We slipped out of all our other layers and hung them up, part of being good I was working on. I suddenly knew I couldn't smell turkey, but guessed Uncle Jack's cooking did away with that. Aunt Bessie made sure that Amelia had everything ready in the dining room and the kitchen, including an especially big platter warmed for the turkey.

"Uncle Jack cleared his throat, as though preparing for a ceremony, and walked toward the cupboard where the turkey had spent the night in the haybox cooker. I managed to wiggle in to witness the miracle. He opened the box, removed layers and layers of hay, newspapers and cooking paper. But there, before my disappointed eyes sat a cold, purple-white, bare bird, almost embarrassing without its crispy, golden cover. Uncle Jack just about cried.

'What have I done wrong'? he asked Aunt Bessie who was by now also inspecting the disaster.

'Perhaps you needed to heat it up really hot before you put it in the hay box.'

'Hmm, I don't remember that in the instructions.'

"Aunt Bessie was good at handling disasters, probably from her nursing, like bringing people back to life when they were nearly dead. How would she rescue this turkey? She quickly ordered Amelia to put the largest frying pan on the stove with some chicken fat in it and for Father to carve the turkey in the kitchen. After a good frying, the turkey needed more chewing than usual and the gravy was a bit pale, but other than that Christmas dinner was as yummy as always. Uncle Jack pronounced his sister's brandy butter on the plum pudding to be excellent and he and Father afterward drank from glasses looking like little balloons, filled from the brandy bottle.

"Aunt Bessie changed the subject from the turkey disaster before the dinner was half over as she could see Uncle Jack was quite red from embarrassment. His red cheeks reminded me of Santa Claus. I rather wished I still believed in Santa Claus, but Aunt Bessie told me the truth when I came back from New York. When I asked her whether there was just one Santa, she said there was. How then could I have seen one on almost every street corner in New York, I wondered. She asked me whether I wanted to know the truth. Aunt Bessie was always very keen on the truth. I said I did. She said, 'There isn't a Santa Claus, parents bring the presents.'

"I said, 'Well there isn't a god then,' and went to my room, where I cried and cried, cross with Aunt Bessie for ripping my childhood from me. The same day she told me I was not to tell Roger, so at least I knew one bittersweet secret that was usually kept from little children."

All this remembering made Mary feel livelier. She opened her eyes to see Aunt Bessie standing tall beside her bed.

"Do you want a little lunch?"

"Heaps."

Both knew Mary had slept away whatever was bothering her earlier. She ate every scrap of food on her tray. But Bessie was not taking any chances. After his rest, Roger came in and they played for the rest of the afternoon with paper farm animals cut out from last year's catalogue, joined by the freshly robed stick horses.

*　*　*　*　*

Miss Straight's machine ran at a gallop until all her assignments won Bessie's approval. Threads, needles, measuring tapes, scissors and odds and ends moved with the seamstress to her next employer. Mary and Roger missed the lilting tunes and comfortable hum, but their stick horses had more than adequate wardrobes for the coming winter. Once school closed for the Christmas holidays, Bessie organized Elizabeth and Gertrude's buying trip to Saint John. Mod had been planning on taking the sleigh. Early December had been cold and snowy, but a sudden thaw had completely cleared the roads, making runners impossible. Young Morris hitched the chestnut mare to the carriage and handed the reins to his father. Gertrude wanted to sit beside him in the open, but Bessie and Elizabeth were pleased to snuggle under the hood out of whatever weather might be ahead. Morris promised to keep Mary and Roger out of mischief as they all waved the travellers off. Amelia was already busy in the kitchen beginning to sort out the many instructions Bessie had left.

Bessie originally thought they would stay overnight with cousins Lucy and Tom but, with winter around the corner, it was safer to be satisfied with a day trip. If they were on the road at eight o'clock, they should be back before dark. With her responsibilities lessened by three girls in the new year, she would not be so indispensable and looked forward to regular visits to the city of her childhood in the near future. As the sleek chestnut rhythmically jogged along, Bessie mentally scanned her lists for the day—the one she made and the one from Edgehill, both resting safely in her handbag for now to avoid the possibility of them being whipped out of her hand by an unexpected gust. The big department store, Manchester, Robertson and Allison was the first stop. If all needs were not met there, other shops along King Street would fill the gaps. This expedition would give her the first personal experience of outfitting girls for boarding school. Some items on the school list were already piled and waiting to be packed; new clothes from Miss Straight's sewing machine, silverware from the silver drawer, and still acceptable garments from the girls' wardrobes.

Bessie congratulated herself for already having ordered family Christmas presents in the form of suitable books from those recently advertised in *The Ladies' Home Journal.* They were offered at the fair price of thirty-five cents each plus ten cents extra for postage. She hoped they would arrive in time so she could read through those for the children. As she wrote in her articles and books aimed at mothers, knowing what the young in their care are reading is a role not to be shirked.

The girls were used to their aunt being occupied by her thoughts so were content to talk back and forth with the occasional comment from their father as they travelled. Before long, in spite of the hot bricks for her feet, and the buffalo robe over her knees, Gertrude slipped back between Bessie and Elizabeth, her chilled little body grateful for the combined heat. Bessie suggested singing, as a warming activity. They launched into Christmas carols despite the lack of snow and the bare, brown landscape. Soon Mod's robust baritone blended with the three sopranos and their combined voices seemed to bounce off the hills as they neared the city of Saint John.

Mod dropped "the ladies" off in front of MRA's and agreed to return in three hours, which Bessie thought ought to be long enough for all they had to buy. In the meantime Mod would spend time with cousins Lucy and Tom. He hoped for a small libation or two from their ample cellar.

The girls' cheeks were flushed with the excitement of the big city when, after trying on dresses, boots, shoes, raincoats, and all sorts of other necessities, the shopping party was picked up at the appointed time. Aunt Bessie had even asked for their opinions regarding preferences when the outcome was of no great importance. Two new trunks were stowed under the carriage's passenger seats and the collection of boxes and bags containing their purchases were tucked in under the buffalo robes.

Though they started their homeward journey in good time, Bessie knew any kind of weather might hit them in December and they were not prepared for an overnight stop along the way. Much of the return was taken up with the girls discussing their purchases and encouraging their aunt to tell them more about what to expect at Edgehill. To help combat a fierce wind that took hold a few miles from home, they again broke into robust caroling just when dusk was ripening into dark. Once home, Amelia's hot pork stew with dumplings went down well. A surprise rarity followed that Bessie could not resist buying — oranges! The three stay-at-home children were each given a small bag filled with ribbon candy and pink and chocolate "chicken bones"

*　*　*　*　*

With the loss of their mother, Christmas was now a different sort of day for the Scovil family, one of many to follow. In spite of the need to pay attention to the customs of mourning, Bessie concentrated on making the twenty-fifth of December as cheerful as possible. She even made sure Santa Claus left presents just inside the back door for Roger and Mary with their names printed on the brown paper wrapping. As Mary was tearing the paper off her carved wooden horse she looked up at her aunt who had her index finder over her lips, reminding her chatty niece not to spill the beans to Roger, who was speechless with delight as he uncovered his own "horsey."

Mod recited his usual blessing at the table; "For what we are about to receive, may the Lord make us truly thankful," but then slowed down and added, "and may we always remember our dear departed and our absent friends and family."

"Amen" was pronounced with more feeling than usual, which was followed by a definite hush, while they all thought of Hattie and her tiny baby.

A crisp, brown turkey with the look of being really "succulent" provided a welcome contrast to Jack's disaster last year. Uncle Jack was missed, however. The sleigh ride to and from church would not be as merry without his witty remarks. The brandy flames dancing around the base of the plum pudding produced the usual oohs and aahs. Mary's helping included the well-wrapped five-cent piece. Bessie's sharp eye and serving spoon just managed to include this prize in her portion. Mary had felt left out of the girls' shopping expedition, so this was a small compensation. Bessie was also feeling a little guilty about shipping Mary off to her godfather's soon after New Years. But she was trying to be realistic, thinking ahead to next September, by which time she would have engaged a housekeeper, and Mod with just the two children would be able to manage more easily. By then young Morris would be entering his sixteenth year and no longer a child. Roger would be starting school.

Bessie's choices of book presents appeared to be well received. She watched them all open her presents, one book for each. She was then completely surprised when Elizabeth presented her with a book shaped parcel from them all — *True Stories from Modern History* by Alice Strickland.

Now Bessie knew why Elizabeth took so long to "wash her hands" when in Manchester, Robertson and Allison's.

Some of the books had been devoured and others only tasted, when departure time for the three girls arrived. The need to make a list of every item put in the trunks bound for Edgehill was impressed on Elizabeth and Gertrude. Mary did the same in her halting, joining up writing. It made her feel part of their big adventure. She supposed hers would not be so thrilling, but Father and Aunt Bessie said her life would be more fun and she would come to know so much more. It would be like living in a little New York. It was not.

5

A Short Lived Option

Some Gagetown residents used the frozen river as a road at this time of year, but, with three children on board, Mod did not feel he could risk the possibility of thin ice. Harvesting blocks of ice from the river for summer use usually began in January and, with blowing snow, it was often hard to see exactly where locals had made a road. Yes, Mod thought, it would be better to travel on the land road though it was a little longer. And he would need the larger of his two sleighs, with double seats facing one another and a team to carry three heavy trunks and five passengers. At least there had been a two-inch snowfall in the last week, so the road should be packed and quite fast.

Bricks had been heating in the oven overnight. Morris brought them out and covered them with straw along with three kitchen warmed buffalo robes after he and a hired man had trundled out the trunks, stowed them under the seats, and tied them down. Before all the travellers settled into the sleigh, and when no one was watching, Roger and Morris hugged their sisters goodbye. The hired man held the restless horses. All the young were quite pink faced, and Roger was on the point of tears. Bessie organized the girls so that they took turns sitting with their faces to the wind and encouraged them to keep their well mittened hands under the buffalo robe. A short stop at the Evandale Hotel for the call of nature and hot drinks warmed them thoroughly. Soon, the hills of Saint John touched the horizon and they all burst into Christmas carols, always a warming occupation.

The enormous Starr house welcomed them all with the outstretched arms of cousin Madge, who organized hot drinks and cakes after heavy outdoor clothes were removed. Jovial cousin Frank hugged them all and shook hands with Mod. Ayleene, in between Elizabeth and Gertrude in age, had been well instructed to make them feel comfortable, especially as they would all be off to Edgehill the next week. Ruth was not much older than Mary, but more poised, taking the visitor's hand and leading her to a corner with two stools and a doll. Two little ones were scarcely more than babies, one walking, and both in the care of a nursemaid.

After a half hour or so of asking and answering questions, chiefly about requirements for school preparation that may have been overlooked, Bessie thought she and Mod and Mary should be on their way to the Rothesay Robinson cousins. Mary wanted to stay longer, hoping to put off saying goodbye to her sisters, knowing she would not see them again until the summer holidays, which seemed like ages. Cousin Frank's jovial manner made the separation less painful. He scooped up little Mary in his arms and announced that he felt sure the horses would welcome more exercise. Calls of "write soon" were exchanged as Mod climbed into the driver's seat as Bessie and Mary snuggled together behind him.

Bessie was pleased that a second bed had been put in Mary's room at the Robinsons so she would spend the first night away from home — the first without Roger — with her familiar aunt. This show of thoughtfulness on the part of Mary's new family promised a happy settling in period. Mod was in a comfortable room across the hall. Mary's first impressions were of a gruff godfather, two know-it-all boys a little older than she was, and a godmother whose smile quickly faded when she turned her head. But she wanted her father and Aunt Bessie to have a good opinion of her. She would try to fit in with life in this much grander house than dear old comfortable Meadowlands, where she knew every nook and corner like a rabbit.

The seven-year old was so tired over supper, which they called dinner, she could hardly keep her eyes open. But she was hungry, too, so managed to eat the mostly strange food on her plate. Mod enjoyed the opportunity of John's male company and talking politics. Sarah tried to keep the conversation general but failed and retreated to talking with Bessie about mutual relatives. As soon as dinner was over, Bessie suggested Mary should have an early night, which was not resisted.

After hearing Mary's usual prayer, "Now I lay me down to sleep...," Bessie slipped out of their room to join her cousins over coffee in the drawing room. The men had apparently exhausted Dominion politics and were now on the merits or otherwise of "Teddy" Roosevelt, the American president. Mod regularly combed the New York newspapers sent by Jack and Barclay and was well up on the subject, much to John's surprise. Bessie took the opportunity to point out Mary's favourable traits to Sarah, though not neglecting to mention she had a tendency to be headstrong. She would likely go through a homesick period because she was very attached to little Roger and life on the farm, but she should soon settle down.

Mary did not intend to hug her father and her aunt quite so hard before they left the next morning and felt slightly ashamed she could not easily let go. Her glistening eyes watched at a front window as the familiar sleigh, with Aunt Bessie the only passenger, became smaller and smaller, and finally, being reduced to a little dot, then vanished. Mary continued to stand at the window, feeling empty in her stomach. She became aware of Godmother's voice in the hall, speaking to the boys, Henry and Will. So far, they had not paid much attention to her. Now she heard Henry, the oldest, about ten, come up behind her and ask whether she would like to play a game. She tried to smile as she turned and said she would.

They went to the playroom at the back of the house. It was full of all sorts of toys, including two rocking horses. One was so big Mary was longing to climb on it, partly so she could tell Roger, but the game the boys wanted to play was "riddles," which was new to Mary. She would have preferred a doing game like the ones she played with Roger where you made up everything as you went along, but "riddles" seemed to be a thinking game. She would do her best.

"What's black and white and read all over?" asked Henry.

Mary's usually resilient brain could not imagine what was black and white but also red.

"A black horse with white fetlocks and a red blanket?" she asked.

"No!" The boys roared with laughter. "A newspaper."

Mary's confused state did not allow her to hear the next riddle. She blurted out the first word that came to her.

"A pig."

"No, you silly girl."

The boys rolled on the floor with glee. Mary could feel that hot tears were on their way, but she would not give the boys the satisfaction of seeing her cry so she dashed from the playroom with little dignity left, ran to her room and sobbed into her pillow. She wished she had announced that we don't play silly games in Gagetown, but didn't think of it in time.

Sleep dried her tears, but when Godmother bent over to say lunch was ready she felt she could not face the superior expressions of those rude boys. She said she was not hungry.

"I'll save some for you so you can have it later," Godmother responded.

When Mary was alone again she moved to the window seat covered in blue and white striped cushions. She found the carved horsey which "Santa Claus" had given her and set up the cushions to act like fences. A rush of longing for Roger came out of nowhere. Tears washed her eyes again. She stared out of the window hardly seeing mounds of snow and a dark green house with a white roof across the road, or was it a street? She imagined she could see Aunt Bessie and Father coming back in the sleigh, but of the few passing by, none took the turn to the house.

A short while later, Godmother, with a wrinkled forehead but smiling lips, came back carrying a tray of food under two overturned bowls.

"I'll just leave this for you in case you might like something to eat," she said as she put the tray on a little table and pulled a chair up to it.

"Do you remember where the bathroom is, just two doors away? I'll leave the door open a little. You will soon be used to everything, including the boys. They don't mean to be unkind. They don't know many girls your age. I'll be back again in a while."

A tiny "thank you" escaped from Mary's dry lips.

She then took little sips from the glass of milk until it was finished. She overturned one bowl and discovered gravy that was cold and slippery with globs of fat on top covering whatever was underneath next to something green and stringy. She welcomed the slice of bread and butter but the dessert was strange. It looked a little like Aunt Bessie's rice pudding, but instead of juicy raisins, there were slimy bits that she knew would make her throw up if she ate more than one spoonful.

The afternoon faded in daydreams of Roger and what he might be doing without her. Sometime later, the maid came in and removed the tray. Eventually Godmother, in a different dress, came to tell her it was time to wash and tidy for "dinner." This took longer than expected. By now Mary's hair needed a thorough brushing and a clean pinafore found to put on. Then, hand-in-hand with Godmother, she descended the dark wood stairway with the polished bannister, ending in a curved newel post, quite like Meadowlands, only with more steps.

At least grace was the same, with Godfather taking no more time to finish than did Father. Mary wished she were not sitting directly across the table from the boys. They smirked at her and crossed their eyes when they thought neither parent was looking. Conversation was mostly between the grown ups which was so different from Meadowlands where everyone had a say. Mary tried to keep her eyes on her soup which looked like tomato but had hidden, strange bits in it. One dropped on her white napkin. She watched the orangey stain expand then tried to pick up the bit with her spoon but it travelled to her knee and fell on the floor. She knew her face was getting red but was determined not to cry, concentrating on getting down more soup. After three mouthfuls, she realized everyone was waiting for her to finish.

Godmother intervened. "I think Mary has had enough, Edith, you can remove the soup bowls."

As the main course was being served, Henry asked his mother whether Mary could go tobogganing with them tomorrow on a nearby hill.

"Would you like that, Mary?"

"Yes, please", came the subdued answer.

The remainder of dinner was bearable, especially with the thought of tomorrow. When Mary and the boys were told they were excused and could go to the playroom, Will stuck his foot out and tripped Mary. She fell flat on her face, her teeth cutting her lip. Mary screamed. Godfather groaned. Blood flowed. It looked as though Mary had tripped over a chair leg so no one was punished.

"Take care of the child, Edith", ordered Godmother.

Edith took Mary to a bathroom washed the cut with something which made it sting and mopped up the blood still dripping on her recently clean pinafore. Edith took Mary to her bedroom and sat with her for a while trying to interest her in some children's books which the boys had outgrown. They were more to her liking than those horrid boys so she calmed down and made the best of being by herself before bedtime.

Mary's hot, cut lip ballooned worse than a cold sore. She thought about Meadowlands and what her sisters might be doing, not that many miles away. At least they would have one another and other girls. She dozed and then slept, dreaming that Roger had slipped under her counterpane to play farm animals with her.

Edith helped her dress for breakfast, buttoning her waist at the back and finding a clean pinafore. Godmother, after she saw Mary's puffy lip, announced she could stay at home with Edith while the others attended church at eleven. Edith said she could take a book into the kitchen while she prepared lunch. Edith was not as pretty as Amelia, nor as chatty, but she found a cookie and a glass of milk, which helped the morning pass. Soon the smells of roast beef, roast potatoes and baked onions drifted past Mary's nostrils. She closed her eyes and pretended she was back at Meadowlands about to sit down to Sunday dinner.

"Are you alright, child?"

Mary opened her eyes to reality, sitting in a gleaming white kitchen at a cold enamel table. Tears began flowing again.

"Cheer up, Miss, school will be starting soon and you'll make some friends. I hear you'll be tobogganing this afternoon and a little bird told me it's your eighth birthday on the tenth, so there's lots to look forward to."

Edith was kind. Mary tried to cheer up. Her tears stopped. The church-goers returned. Lunch tasted good.

It took a while to pile on enough clothes for tobogganing—two pairs of mittens, one under the cuffs and one over, the same with socks and leggings, her red woolly hat tied under her chin, and her scarf well tucked into last winter's coat.

Meadowlands was on interval land, completely flat, but Mary had tobogganed on a hill at the far end of Gagetown with school friends many times. She knew the routine. As many as three or even four could ride on a regular sized toboggan and more on a special long one. You must remember never to drag your feet, or a mitten, unless you want to change direction, on the left to go right or the right to go left.

The hill could be partly seen from the dining room window so the boys and Mary were told to have fun, but be careful. Henry and Will offered to provide themselves as a double team, if Mary wanted a ride to the hill. She took them up on their offer, thinking they at last wanted to be friends. She soon discovered their idea of fun was to try to tip her by slewing the toboggan this way and that not realizing their little cousin understood the knack of hanging on to the ropes at the sides and shifting her weight to compensate for the slew.

Their opinion of her went up a notch but not far enough to prevent them from tripping her several times on climbs up the hill. She pretended she had just slipped, not to give them satisfaction, and surprised Will, and herself, by successfully giving him the same treatment. The effects were a little more serious. As he fell, his forehead hit the edge of the toboggan, causing the skin to break and a small trickle of blood to ooze down his face. Will knew better than to complain about what a girl did to him so he put up with the cut without comment and the frosty air soon sealed the wound and numbed the hurt, but not quite his ego. He would get even when they reached the top of the hill

Mary was out of puff, which she disguised with an urge to make snow angels. Whenever there was freshly fallen snow she and Roger never tired of making whole families of angels. Just as she was putting finishing touches of the first angel's wings by patting her arms down for the second time, Will saw his chance to show his unwanted "sister" what he thought of her. He scooped up a mitt full of soft snow and thoroughly "washed" Mary's face in spite of her protests, especially when he included her sore lip. She hit him with her fists, which only encouraged him to stuff more snow into her mouth. Mary was small for nearly eight but living on the farm, with lots of exercise, had made her unusually strong. Her townie cousin backed away. Henry just watched, laughing a little.

Mary refused to cry, but stomped off in the direction of a little copse of spruce trees, where she coughed the snow out of her mouth and emptied it out of her collar. Her face had been "washed" before by boys at school but this was different; her assailant made no effort to make up and be friends afterward. She brushed the snow off a fallen tree and sat with her back to the sliding boys. In spite of what Aunt Bessie and Godmother had said, she felt these cousins would never accept her as a sort of sister. Will, especially, seemed to hate her. Perhaps he was jealous of the small amount of attention his mother had given her. It wasn't her fault she was a girl and she wasn't to blame for her mother's death. She knew she could not live like this day after day, the boys never wanting to be friends. Aunt Bessie said she should write a letter every week, like Elizabeth and Gertrude would be doing, telling of her adventures. She would ask to return home in her first letter and explain why.

The sun had sunk quite low in the wintry sky and was now behind a cloud. Mary felt an unpleasant combination of cold and damp from the exertions of her ordeal. She had sat on her log for a long while and was now feeling quite shivery. She knew it would be easier to slide down the hill than walk, so she made her way back to the sliding area and stood silently, waiting for the boys to turn the toboggan around. She knelt on the back, tucking her boots in and holding on to Will's horrible shoulders. They all knew it was the last run without anyone saying so.

When his mother asked Will what happened to his forehead, he answered without looking at her, "Just a bump," knowing a full explanation might cause Mary to tell all. She did not, even over dinner. A small amount of admiration crept into the boys' feelings about their cousin.

Mary fell asleep almost the moment she slipped between the sheets. The next thing she knew she was very cold, trying to pull her white nighty over her bare legs as she sat on the top step of the long stairway.

"Aunt Bessie, I'm cold", she called over and over.

A sleepy and startled Godmother came out of her bedroom, took Mary's hand and led her back to her bed. Mary scarcely opened her eyes. Godmother Sarah knew that sleepwalking was not uncommon among children, especially when they were undergoing some upset. John, her husband, was very annoyed at having his sleep disturbed, especially on a Sunday night with a busy day tomorrow. When Sarah returned to bed his frustration boiled over that they had agreed to take his motherless goddaughter. Assurance that the commotion would be short lived made little impression.

Aunt Bessie had given Mary three stamped addressed envelopes with two pages of writing paper in each, to encourage her to write. After breakfast Mary decided she must write, so she sat at the little table in her room and began with a pencil meant for school, with her best joining up.

She folded the paper the way it had been creased before, put it in the envelope and stuck it down, rubbing back and forth so it would not come unstuck. Mary found Godmother and asked her how she could mail it, adding that Aunt Bessie wanted her to write. Godmother smiled in a concerned way and said she would look after it. Two days later there was a lot of quiet talk between the grown ups at Meadowlands

The boys began school. There was no birthday party on the tenth, but Edith made a birthday cake that they all ate for dessert. A pretty doll with real hair, wrapped in a box, was sitting at her place. On the thirteenth, Mary was looking out her window. She could not believe her eyes. A sleigh turned into their drive and in it was Aunt Bessie and Father and Roger! Suddenly the sun shone for Mary as she dashed down to the front door. The "experiment" was over. A year and a half would pass before another was tried.

For the first few weeks after her return, Bessie was aware of how happy and contented little Mary was, hugging her aunt and her father more than she ever had in her whole life. Mod was delighted to have her back. There was a brightness in the house that was lacking in her absence. Roger wanted to be beside her all the time. Bessie supervised Mary's letter to thank her godparents for their hospitality, which was not a chore as her godmother, in particular, was really quite kind.

"As long as I don't have to thank those boys, I'll write anything," Mary offered.

January 10, Mary's eighth birthday, had come and gone. Now that she was safely back at Meadowlands, Mary told her family that the maid had made a birthday cake for the tenth and a hard doll with beautiful clothes and real hair was sitting on her chair at the dinner table, though in the excitement of leaving she forgot to bring it. Bessie thought a late family celebration was in order even though Godmother Sarah and Edith had given Mary's birthday special notice. In addition, hosting a party for Mary would lessen Bessie's feelings of guilt that she had put Mary through such an ordeal at such a tender age.

Two of the Caswell girls, Edith twelve and Frances ten, were invited for tea on Saturday to make the day special and somewhat filling the gap left by Elizabeth and Gertrude's absence. Mary thought she had never been happier in her whole life, sitting around the dining table with Roger and Morris instead of those scheming cousins, and two girls, even though not her sisters. The cake frosting with the same taste as the topping she devoured in the artichoke bed last summer brought back warm memories of mostly happy triumph.

The following Monday, Bessie read a letter from cousin Frank at the supper table. He wrote that he had safely delivered Elizabeth and Gertrude, along with his own Ayleene to Edgehill. The crossing of the Bay of Fundy had been surprisingly calm for January, no one was seasick and he left the three girls in good spirits.

Within a week, letters arrived from both Elizabeth and Gertrude full of their adventures. This was the beginning of years of obligatory Sunday letters home, none of which contained any criticism of their new life, or any spelling or grammar mistakes. Not until much later was it revealed that all their letters were monitored by one of the mistresses. Not only were incorrect spelling, bad grammar, and poor penmanship not allowed, negative comment about any aspect of life at the school was forbidden as well. Frequent rewriting was required to eliminate any of these unacceptable features.

Bessie had her suspicions about the letters; they were so perfectly spelled and punctuated and so unremittingly positive. She decided not to intervene at this early stage but rather to look for signs of unhappiness when the girls returned for the summer holidays. She had written in her book, *Care of Children*, ten years before, that children at boarding school should always be allowed to send uncensored letters home. This was useful as a way for the young to unburden themselves and to alert the parents to possible small problems before they became unmanageable. Bessie's disappointment with Edeghill's policy of forbidding open and honest communication with parents was tempered by knowing her nieces had one another to talk with and share problems. Not being able to write home freely was the price they paid for their new life and the opportunity to enrich their minds and prepare for their futures.

* * * * *

While Elizabeth and Gertrude were learning about pounds, shillings, and pence from their English born mathematics mistress, the Punic Wars from their English born history mistress, and the stories of Guy de Maupassant and elementary French from their Paris born mistress, life at Meadowlands appeared to continue much as it had been but with decided gaps.

No one had completely recovered from the loss of Hattie. Bessie thought of her whenever she looked at Hattie's favourite rocking chair. Mod thought of her when he glanced at her empty place at the foot of the table, a place no one could bear to occupy until he asked Bessie to do so. He found their bedroom so lonely, their bed unbearably wide without Hattie's soft presence. Young Morris always thought of her when he brushed his hair, as she had been keen on his keeping it tidy. When he looked in the mirror he saw her eyes looking at him. Little Mary missed her special smell, her pretty face and her gentle voice. Roger missed her soft lap and the way she rubbed his back with small, circular motions, when he was tired or not feeling well.

As if Hattie's departure were not enough, the family now had to adjust to the girls' leaving only four months later. With just a year between them, Elizabeth and Gertrude's relationship was more like that of twins. They giggled together, sometimes finding a joke so funny they could scarcely catch their breaths. They shared a bedroom and consequently confidences in a way that only girls on the verge of being twelve and thirteen know to be essential. Though they might be seen as almost a unit, they were also missed for their individual qualities. Elizabeth was patient and organized. Gertrude was more spontaneous and very determined. Mod especially missed their happy singing. Their weekly letters demonstrated an improvement in their penmanship and were poured over by the family. Bessie wrote every week so they would not lose touch with the reality of home. Mod always added a page and sometimes Morris a few lines about new farm animals. Mary, in her best joining-up style, often wrote her own page about what she had been doing. Roger sometimes printed his name next to her flourished signature.

Certainly for Bessie there was less to do with the eldest girls gone. She asked Morris more often now to keep an eye on Mary and Roger, though since Mary was eight and Roger nearly six she was not as concerned about the danger of them falling through the ice on the river as she had been. But she was well aware that such tragedies could happen at any age. The need to find a suitable housekeeper by September was never far from Bessie's thoughts. She continued to ask around at church, among friends and relations, and of course mentioned the need to the doctor from time to time, who needed to be reminded as he had the health of the whole community to occupy his thoughts.

* * * * *

Winter melted away. Spring floods were not as bad as usual with the water coming up just to the bottom step of the verandah and very little leaking into the root cellar or the basement. The promise of summer warmed the land. Seeding was not usually started until the twenty-fourth of May, Queen Victoria's birthday, but this year—except for the diehards—farmers started planting a good week before that because the soil was ready and the weather was warm.

One day after school, when June was well established and Roger was off somewhere with Morris, Mary wandered over to the big elms downriver from the Jemseg road. There was a beach-like place here where they would swim next month. Sometimes interesting flotsam found its way there, mixed in with the mud and the stones. Today she couldn't see anything more exciting than an old crate, with ropes at the ends for carrying it. She dragged it up on to the grassy bank thinking she would later ask Roger or Morris to help her take it to the barn. It would be useful for standing on to reach things.

As she ambled on, picking flowering weeds, she lost track of time until she realized she was nearly up to the groom's house. Jock was from Scotland and it was sometimes hard to understand what he was saying. His mother spoke the same way. His wife died three years ago leaving little Willie who was now looked after by his granny. Jock worked mostly with the horses. He knew how to braid coloured wool into their manes and make beautiful rosettes from wool to decorate their tails when they were shown at fairs, where Father often sold them. Father said there was nothing Jock didn't know about horses.

Mary hadn't seen little Willie for a while so she decided to look for him. She saw Granny on the other side of the house hoeing long rows into little hills, perhaps for early potatoes.

As Mary came nearer, she smiled at Granny and said, "Hello."

"Miss Mary," Granny answered, taking her corncob pipe out of her mouth first.

Mary spotted Willie sitting a couple of rows away, starting to cry. Granny skimmed the rows with her boots, put her pipe down on the warm earth, picked up Willie and noticed he had a bite on his wrist. She scooped up some dark earth, spat on it and rubbed it on the unhappy boy's bite.

At the same time he spotted Mary and started babbling to her. She sat down beside him in the trough between two rows. He picked up Granny's pipe, put it in his mouth and took a puff. Granny went about her hoeing. Willie put the pipe down. Mary, not to be outdone by a three year old, picked up Granny's pipe and felt it's warm bowl. She put it in her mouth and puffed, like Father did on his pipe.

She coughed a little and put it down. Granny looked up and smiled, at the same time keeping an eye in the direction of the big house, in case Miss Scovil came searching. She wouldn't want Jock to lose his job and a comfortable house and garden just because of a puff on a pipe. After playing a few games of stone towers with Willie, Mary's rumbling tummy told her it was nearly suppertime. She reluctantly got up, waved goodbye to Willie, left the garden patch, and wandered in the direction of home, hoping there was no smell of pipe smoke lingering about her.

6

A Season of Cousins
1904

Everyone at Meadowlands looked forward to the return of Elizabeth and Gertrude at the end of June. But then Bessie received a letter from cousin Frank Starr's wife, Madge, asking whether she and Mod would have any objections if the girls returned two weeks later. She would like the girls to accompany their Ayleene and the whole family to their summerhouse at Westfield for the first two weeks in July.

The letter mentioned that the three girls had become very close friends at Edgehill, and Ayleene had asked her mother to invite them. Madge added that if they needed any beach clothes or lighter garments, she would see they were acquired when she bought those items for fast growing Ayleene. When Bessie read the letter at the supper table, they were all disappointed to have to put off hearing tales of boarding school for another two weeks, but, when they talked about it, realized it was just part of the girls' changed lives.

No doubt there would be more changes to come. When Bessie and Mod discussed the new plans over tea and cake later in the evening, they agreed the girls would probably meet many young people from good families at Westfield, an area outside Saint John where the well-to-do spent their summers. Cousin Madge wrote that she would give notice of the girls' return. Frank and Ayleene wanted to accompany them on the riverboat. Bessie and Mod agreed they should ask them to stay overnight.

Bessie sorted the sleeping arrangements in her head; "The three Edgehill girls could sleep in the girls' room, Mary could vacate hers for Frank and she can sleep with me."

The Gagetown Grammar School closing did not produce the same degree of euphoria as it had last year. Miss Trenholm had married at Christmas and, of course, was then no longer allowed to teach. This meant no extravagant musical performance but instead recitations and readings from essays and poems the children had written. Two musical solos were performed. Morris sang "The Road to Mandalay" and the Kelly girl with the orange curls, who had a part in last year's musical, sang a song about daffodils. The Scovil family sat in the front row again and clapped enthusiastically, especially after Morris's offering. But they all missed Elizabeth and Gertrude, and had to accept they would never again be in the spring closing of the Gagetown Grammar School.

Once it was established that Elizabeth and Gertrude would not be home until nearly the middle of July, Bessie wrote to Addie, her sister-in-law in New York with whom she corresponded often, to see whether she and her daughter, Bess, would like to escape the heat of the city and visit for three weeks or so. Addie promptly wrote that she and Bess would be delighted to come as soon as school closed for the summer. Jack, Addie's husband and Bessie and Mod's eldest brother, would not be able to leave his position as an accountant. Charlie and Delancey, the family's older sons, would be at a church summer camp so would not be joining their mother and sister.

Bessie arranged for the visit to overlap for a few days with Elizabeth and Gertrude's return. Bess was fourteen, only slightly older than her first cousins and they would have much in common. The three girls got on very well three years ago when Addie and Bess came for a visit. Bessie hoped this time Mary would be included more often in the older girls' activities and conversations, and that Bess might have outgrown her need to be overly bossy.

With only two days between the school closing and the arrival of the New Yorkers, Bessie had Amelia air and thoroughly clean the spare room, wash the curtains, make up the beds, and put a vase of mixed flowers on the dressing table. She wanted a warm welcome for Addie and Bess. Hattie and Addie were the nearest Bessie had to real sisters in her entire life. It was always a sadness for her that three sibling sisters had not survived babyhood. Now that Hattie was gone, Addie was even more precious.

By the time her Aunt Addie and cousin Bess had a day of recovery from their journey, Mary was already resenting the big fuss Aunt Bessie was making over their visit. There was more interesting food, for which Mary had no objections, but every little whim of the guests was attended to. Bess sensed their power and began bossing Mary around. With seven years separating them, the Yankee cousin felt she had a right to be the authority. Mary wished Elizabeth and Gertrude would come home to occupy the attention of the big city know-it-all, but she knew that would not happen for at least two weeks.

Mary's envy at the visitors' red carpet treatment and her general annoyance with Bess was reaching the boiling point when one day Aunt Addie threw down an unkind remark as she was standing next to Mary observing river traffic from the bank.

"There's a scow load of monkeys coming up the river for Mary," she quipped, which set off an explosion.

"There's a big brat in our spare room," Mary replied without thinking.

"Do you mean me or your cousin Bess?" Aunt Addie asked with some feeling.

Mary was not up to making that distinction. She was already in hot water, so she ran off somewhat gleefully at having let out a large quantity of stored venom. Bessie quickly realized that Mary was not happy and not getting on well with her cousin. She asked Morris to spend some time with Bess, who was only a little younger, in an effort to take the pressure off Mary until Elizabeth and Gertrude returned. Though a chasm of experiences and interests divided them, Morris did his best, suggesting Bess might like to see the latest colt frisking in the pasture next to the barn.

As Morris and Bess walked toward the barn, she tried to protect her New York black patent leather shoes from the worst of the barnyard muck. Morris put a handful of grain in a bucket and shook it, hoping to attract the colt to the fence so Bessie could pat his nose. He thought it would be a good first step toward getting to know the horses. At the time, Bessie was in the kitchen making a cup of tea before returning to her writing. She looked out the kitchen window and was pleased to see Morris, acting on her request. Addie was resting on the verandah.

Bessie saw Morris rattle the bucket with the desired effect. The chestnut colt trotted warily over to the sound of food, carefully watched by her mother. With the colt's head down in the bucket, Morris began to rub between her ears. Bess did the same but then reached farther down the colt's forehead. She was surprised at the feeling the soft surface over the hard bone at the same time. The experience was so odd and exciting, she drew in her breath in a quick gasp. The startled colt raised her head, whinnying and snorting in Bess's face, before galloping off.

Aunt Bessie, watching from the kitchen window and ignoring the boiling kettle, saw Bess lose her balance and fall backward into the muck of the barnyard, which was churned up twice a day by the cows coming into the barn for milking and then going back out to pasture. Bessie's first instinct was to rush to the scene and comfort her niece, but then saw she should not make the move. It was quickly obvious by the way Bess got up and was walking that no serious damage had been done that could not be removed with soap and water, except, perhaps, to her pride. Bessie was amazed to see Bess smiling and laughing instead of bursting into tears, which was her usual way of dealing with frustration. Morris must have come out with one of his funny quips, which no one could resist. Bessie pushed the well-boiled kettle off the hot spot, made her tea, and walked up the back stairs to her writing nook before anyone or anything else could distract her.

She silently congratulated herself on not interfering with the young now confident Morris who could handle the situation. Bessie heard them changing out of their clothes into their swimming costumes and robes. Shortly afterward, she saw them from the window of her upstairs nook at the front of the house, walking to the wharf. Mary and Roger had gone with Mod by carriage to Jemseg where he wanted to see a man with a reputation as a hard worker. Elizabeth and Gertrude would not be home for a few days, so, with luck, Bessie thought, she could finish her article for the August issue of *The American Journal of Nursing*, as long as Addie was happy to repose on the verandah.

Two more warm July days passed with everyone finding a corner or two of interest until Elizabeth and Gertrude returned accompanied by cousin Frank and Ayleene, who stayed over night as planned and returned to Westfield on the morning riverboat.

The next day for a special homecoming meal, Amelia served a roast chicken with crisp potatoes and new carrot thinings. As they all sat around the dining room table, Elizabeth and Gertrude were pelted with question.

Morris started off by asking, "Can you speak some French?"

The two girls whispered together briefly, then with big smiles replied in unison, "Le chapeau de ma tante est noir."

Their big brother was impressed.

"Je suis en accord avec vous les filles. Tres bon," added Bessie as her own school days came rushing back to her

All eyes moved from the boarding school girls to Bessie. No one had any idea she could speak French. Even Mod had no inkling of his sister's mastery of the language. He had been too young at the time to appreciate Bessie's struggle with French verbs. He joined the young in his astonishment. Bessie beamed, offering to keep the girls' French alive over the holidays by speaking a little every day with them.

"We'll sing you some French songs, after supper," suggested Elizabeth.

"That's a good start," agreed Bessie.

Mary wanted to know whether they could always find their own knives and forks, and what did they do if they couldn't? She asked if their clothes were warm enough? Were they cold at night? Did all the girls sleep in one room? Did they have any detentions? Were other girls mean to them? Morris wondered whether they played any team games? Did they put on plays and sing in choirs? What was the worst part? What did they do at

Westfield with the Starrs? Roger asked whether they were ever smacked for being bad and what was it like being in a big ship? Bess asked if they had special friends they liked better than the others? The questions went on and on. Mod listened. Addie observed. Bessie presided.

By the time half of these questions were answered with pauses to allow food to be chewed, the celebrities said their jaws were getting stiff. However, Amelia's snow pudding, a tangy lemon sauce poured over a fluffy white mound of cooked egg whites and sugar, seemed to revive them and they were able to continue. Bessie suggested they take turns answering questions, allowing the other to eat, which worked remarkably well, except for occasional disagreement about the answers.

As Bessie hoped, cousin Bess gravitated toward the returned schoolgirls and she was pleased Morris had found his Yankee cousin better company than he originally thought she would be. So after Morris finished his daily chores, the six young ones spent the next two weeks in a little gang. Mary wanted to hear every detail of her sisters' lives away from home and Roger tagged along. Trixie, the border collie, trotted along with them on picnics and splashed and yapped when they went swimming, which was almost daily.

Mary and Roger were beginning swimmers making progress toward conquering the art. Rumour had it that a surefire method of learning to swim was to be shown what to do with your arms and legs and then thrown off the end of the wharf into deep water with a rope tied around your waist so you could be hauled in if you didn't learn to swim the first time. Mary thought this seemed more like a trick and decided she could learn to swim on her own. For now, Roger was content to splash about in the shallow water.

Once she got the hang of it, Mary could swim quite well for the first minute or so while her navy serge bloomers and long sleeved blouse plus hair covering cap and bathing shoes were still filled with air. When they became sodden with water, she thrashed her arms and legs the best she could but her buoyancy had been lost and she could barely drag herself out of the water. She noticed her sisters and Bess were able to go further, even with soaked bathing suits. She carefully watched how they moved their arms and legs and improved her technique with good results. Mary often wished she were a boy. They wore hardly anything for swimming, just sort of navy blue underwear with short sleeves. No heavy wool serge to drag a body down.

Bessie and Addie, always well hatted, would sometimes have chairs taken down to the riverbank to keep an eye on swimming activities. When Addie acidly confided to Bessie that she did not want to look like a field hand when she returned to New York, a large sunshade was set up to protect her from getting a suntan.

With their Aunt Addie and cousin Bess staying on until the end of July, Elizabeth and Gertrude, as well as their three siblings, continued to enjoy more planned activities and more interesting food than would have been usual. All this was directed by Bessie's desire to be certain the New Yorkers thoroughly enjoyed their country experience. This also allowed the Edgehill girls to readapt slowly to family life on an isolated farm after the busyness of school and the many amusements of the Starr household.

7

The Search for a Housekeeper Resumes

During the time Bessie had been concerned with the New York guests she had neglected her writing. Now, much needed to be accomplished if she were to maintain her reputation of never being late for deadlines. Right after dinner, the day Addie and Bess left, she placed her left hand on the mahogany banister and climbed the stairs to her writing nook, hoping to complete the article she had started for the September issue of *The Ladies' Home Journal*. The word "September" echoed in her brain. It was nearly August. She had less than two months to find a suitable housekeeper so she could return to St. Paul's for the autumn term, beginning in late September. She and the Coits exchanged occasional letters so she was up to date with St. Paul's news. They were expecting her at least a day or two in advance of the student's return.

As soon as she sat down at her walnut desk with the tassel-like brass handles, she wrote a note in her diary to inquire, again, in Gagetown about housekeepers. As before, she would speak with the rector, with shopkeepers, relatives, and anyone she met causally. She would also visit the Peters family, who were very pleased with their housekeeper, to see whether she had a friend looking for work and a good home. She would ask Mod or Morris to take her over to Gagetown on the following day. With that decided she set about to finish an article and then read some medical journals to choose selections for her next "Notes from the Medical Press" for *The American Journal of Nursing*.

Over their tea and gingerbread before bedtime that night, Bessie told Mod of her intention to spend some time the next day in Gagetown, making inquiries about a housekeeper for September. Mod looked down at his teacup, stirring in the sugar, yet again, unnecessarily.

"I'll take you over. I want to find a replacement for Jim. His lungs aren't good so he's not able to help with the haying."

Mod took two sips of tea, though it was still rather hot. He needed time to collect himself faced with the thought of Bessie's leaving.

Once breakfast was finished the next morning, Elizabeth and Gertrude were occupied making up verses in French and planned to collect flowers for pressing after that. Morris said he would keep an eye on Mary and Roger, and Amelia assured Miss Scovil she would have dinner ready for all the young shortly after twelve o'clock. Bessie expected they would be back mid-afternoon but as it was nearly nine thirty before she and her brother finally pushed off from the wharf, considered they might be later.

"Why don't you turn up at the Peters' around twelve?" Bessie suggested as Mod swung the rowboat into the side of the Gagetown wharf.

"I can think of no reason why I shouldn't," he replied, licking his lips and smiling in anticipation as he tied a round turn and two half hitches.

Mod arrived at the Peters' before the grandfather clock finished striking the noon hour, to find Bessie had already arrived. As expected, they were asked for dinner and used the time to good advantage for catching up on village activities and for Bessie to underline their need of a competent housekeeper after the youngest three of the six children were excused from the table.

Mrs. Peters urged Bessie to have a word with their "treasure," which she did. The housekeeper could think of no one competent enough to take over the household but would ask around among her friends. There were no positive answers from anyone Bessie contacted that day, but they all said they would ask others. Although disappointing, she did not expect the perfect solution to suddenly appear on Front Street, complete with suitcase, ready to move in. Mod was luckier. Old John Chapman was selling his hay as it stood this year so he could spare his son, Elias, during the haying season.

The relative tranquility of life for Bessie since she had returned to Meadowlands over fourteen months ago was very helpful for her bad heads. She now rarely had the severe headaches and eye pain she was prone to. Occasionally, when she did, they were less apt to be accompanied by nausea, bright flashes, and uneven vision. However, that evening, as she was eating her last cake crumbs, she was aware of that tight feeling in her forehead, which always preceded a migraine. She told Mod that she was going to bed a little early, after her busy day, but she knew her old "friend" was back again because of her worry over the housekeeper issue.

Bessie lost no time in finding the paper packet of powdered analgesic that she kept in the drawer of her bedside table. She shook the contents into a half glass of water, stirred it up and swallowed it, knowing quick absorption sometimes meant a lighter attack. She prepared herself for bed, cutting short her formal prayers but asked for guidance in helping her find a housekeeper. The powder did its work, nibbling away at the pain until sleep chased away Bessie's worries.

The next day was one like many that August, sunny and warm in the day, occasional rain at night with cooler temperatures. The Scovil family attended church at Jemseg on Sunday mornings and if the weather were dry, Gagetown in the evening. Bessie was gratified to hear both Elizabeth and Gertrude singing all the hymns with practiced voices, evidence they were getting a thorough Anglican grounding at Edgehill. Attentive as she normally was to religious service, Bessie allowed her thoughts to wander one Sunday evening during a sermon that was put together in an especially poor way.

Her brain kept returning to the problem of finding a housekeeper and the fact that no possibilities had surfaced. She went over and over in her head how she could lessen the workload for a potential housekeeper.

"Mary is over half way through her eighth year. Nine and a half would be old enough for her to join her sisters at Edgehill. My shares have been doing especially well recently. There will be no need to drop hints to cousin Frank who is already a most generous relative, though I know the profits from his coal empire are unimaginably high. Mary will have no problem being accepted by Edgehill as she may well be the smartest of all the children, and the school gives preference to sisters.

"In a month Mary will start school at Gagetown, travelling with Morris, her place at the little Porter school being taken by Roger. After a year in a proper school setting, with more discipline than the one room school, Mary should be ready for boarding school, especially with her sisters there. Then, when I am not there during term time, there will only be the two boys at home, and Morris is nearly independent. The right sort of woman should fit in well, but where is she?"

The rector's voice began to take on that "I'm nearly finished tone," which brought Bessie's wandering but helpful thoughts back to the present. As all bowed their heads for the post-sermon prayer, Bessie decided to talk about Mary's future with Mod that evening, over tea and cake.

*　*　*　*　*

"I hope we hear from a suitable housekeeper soon," Bessie said, as she passed Mod his tea. "Have you asked Amelia whether she knows of someone? She would presumably stay on."

"Yes, I've talked with her about her role. She said she'd fit in. She'd be the housemaid if the housekeeper wanted to do all the cooking or vice versa. Amelia likes being here, but realizes someone needs to be in charge when I go."

Mod sank his teeth into a square of moist gingerbread made special with a little yellow cream poured over the top, which was small compensation over his worry about Bessie's departure.

"I was thinking," Bessie began again. "In a year's time Mary should be ready for Edgehill, which would really mean only Roger for the housekeeper to mother during term time. And, of course, I will be back in the summers. It might be an incentive for a woman who believed two young children were one too many. She'd have about eight months with two, then the summer holidays, then only Roger. Morris now needs more of your company than mothering."

"What about all the expense of uniforms and tuition?"

"I'd prepare Mary's trunk for school next summer. My stocks have done especially well recently so I would be happy to foot the bill."

"That's generous, Bess. What would this family ever do without you?"

8

A Riverboat Trip & Saint John Shopping

Elizabeth and Gertrude began begging Bessie to take them to Saint John for a day of shopping so they could choose some store-bought clothes. Besides the fact they had both grown considerably during the year, they absolutely had to have dresses, jackets and coats that had not been made by Miss Straight. Her blouses and skirts were passable, but please, please, the girls begged, not so many homemade clothes. All of the other girls had the very latest fashions from big city stores. They sometimes felt like country bumpkins in front of the others, though they pretended they didn't mind.

"There are more important things than clothes," Bessie at first replied but then softened her response as she remembered her resolution about making sure the girls had all the social advantages that an education at Edgehill could provide.

"Alright, let's go to Saint John the day after tomorrow. Mary can come too."

Bessie's hastily assembled plan now included buying Mary some new clothes for the coming school year, though she was growing into Gertrude's castoffs so wouldn't need much. She was also trying to include her youngest niece in thoughts of attending Edgehill, which she decided to introduce on the riverboat trip to Saint John. When there, Bessie knew she had to stock up on enough material for blouses, skirts, petticoats and nightdresses for the coming school year. Miss Straight and her sewing machine were already engaged to be in residence on August 10th, and to stay for as long as it took to replace the outgrown and worn out garments.

The riverboat trip was always full of excitement for the girls. Even Bessie enjoyed the luxury of sitting in the dining room, watching the countryside slide by while being served a well-cooked meal. If they caught the early boat, leaving the Gagetown wharf at nine, they could have a leisurely day in town, returning on the late afternoon run. A large evening meal would be served up shortly after they boarded the riverboat for the homeward journey. Bessie packed a little picnic they would eat before arriving in the city. In spite of her swelling bank account, she could not shake the inheritance of the need for frugality.

Once the party of four crossed the gangplank, a different world greeted them. Though a seasoned world traveller, the motion of the riverboat always gave Bessie a little thrill. The day was still cool and fresh, so Bessie installed herself in a comfortable chair in the sitting room with a good view of the passing landscape through low windows.

"I want to explore," announced Mary.

"Alright, if the three of you stay together. Tell me what you've discovered in half an hour."

This left Bessie enough solitude to delve into two medical journals she needed to investigate. She made some satisfying progress before the girls bounced back, all talking at once until she suggested they take turns.

"I talked to Sadie Slipp. She is going to a dentist in Saint John. Her tooth has been aching all week," Elizabeth reported.

"I peeked through the window into the kitchen and saw a cook licking her finger after dipping it in a pudding," admitted Gertrude.

"I sat on a big coil of rope and it was almost as comfortable as an easy chair," Mary chimed in.

"Try another half hour and report on the animal life you see on the shore, wild or domestic," their aunt suggested.

Bessie congratulated herself on thinking of a mind training activity for the girls that would also give her enough time to make further, needed selections for her medical reporting in *The Ladies' Home Journal*. After the second half hour had elapsed, the girls came rushing back with tales of spotting numerous animals. Mary was sure she'd seen a moose, but Elizabeth thought it might have been a horse. Bessie knew her leisure was finished so suggested lunch. By now, the day had warmed enough for a comfortable picnic on deck.

When not a crumb was left, Bessie steered their thoughts to clothes and material selection.

She opened the conversation by saying, "Mary, keep an eye on what the girls choose as with luck you might be joining your sisters at Edgehill in a year."

All six eyes flew to their Aunt Bessie's face, to see whether she was being serious.

"You should be given the same advantages as Elizabeth and Gertrude, dear. You will be able to take music lessons, do gymnastics and learn all sorts of things Gagetown doesn't offer. I plan to go back to nursing once I have found a suitable housekeeper, so things will not be quite the same, except during the holidays, when we'll all be together again.

"At least there won't be any bullying boys," Mary reassured herself.

Elizabeth and Gertrude looked at one another, but said nothing.

"We'll talk about it more, nearer the time, but you'll have a whole year and a bit to get used to the idea."

Manchester, Robertson and Allison's department store was consistently reliable and Bessie saw no reason to shop elsewhere. Mary began to think of Edgehill in glowing terms when she saw the mounds of clothing her sisters were accumulating. She knew she would be wearing Gertrude's castoffs for several years, but now, at least, she would be allowed one brand new, store-bought winter dress. She picked out a red tartan with ruffles over the shoulders and tried it on. It was a little big, but just the way Aunt Bessie liked new clothes to fit.

"Room to grow," she observed.

Bessie had concerns about it standing up to repeated washings without the colours running. The sales assistant said they had received no such complaints about the quality of their dresses.

Since today was the unofficial introduction of Mary into the lives of big girls, Bessie wanted her to have only happy memories so the red tartan dress was added to the purchases. It was put in its own box and tied with string. Mary carried it all the way back to Meadowlands, glued to her side.

The trip home was much occupied with reviewing the purchases of the day, the older girls wondering whether they had made the best choices. Mary was sure she had. She patted her box from time to time, almost as though it were alive. Elizabeth and Gertrude each carried one parcel but most of their purchases would come up on tomorrow's riverboat along with Bessie's bolts of navy and gray serge and lengths of light material for Miss Straight's skillful hands to turn into wearable, though perhaps not fashionable, clothes. "Serviceable," Bessie called them.

There was only a short wait after boarding the homebound riverboat before the dining room was ready for all to take their seats. Bessie made sure they had a table by a window. There were no menus. Instead, a red faced waitress, engulfed in steam, burst through the swinging door and sailed by all the tables, repeating in a nasal voice, "Ham, lamb, roast beef or salmon, ham, lamb, roast beef or salmon." She completed a circuit and disappeared into the waiting steam.

She returned in a few minutes, hovering at each table for decisions.

"Could I have ham and lamb, please?" Mary asked in her best grown up voice, when it was her turn.

"Well, Miss, that's not usual, but since you asked so polite like, I'll give you a half 'n' half."

"That's very kind of you," Mary smiled, still in her straight-backed, adult mode. "I like one as much as the other."

Gertrude wished she had thought of that ploy, but she had become used to accepting rules without trying to get around them, so had opted for lamb. Elizabeth chose roast beef and Bessie salmon. After the waitress moved on to the next table, Mary remembered she had said nothing about vegetables.

"I hope she comes back so I can tell her I hate parsnips."

"Everyone has the same, usually mashed potatoes and one or two other vegetables. There won't be any parsnips, not until after the first frost," Bessie advised.

Four plates arrived, each with the selected choice but all with generous servings of potatoes, carrots, cabbage, and gravy and egg sauce for the salmon. Dishes of butter, pickles, and fluffy white bread were on every table. After all this came bread pudding with hidden caches of plump raisins and strawberry jam, topped with pouring cream from little white jugs. Cups of tea followed. The girls were allowed cambric tea: ninety percent milk, ten percent tea, with sugar.

When the shoppers arrived home, there was no discussion about what to do. After showing the purchases they carried to the stay-at-home "men," the girls were ready for bed. Bessie made sure Mod had his tea and cake, but she only sipped on tea. His feelings were mixed when Bessie reported that Mary raised no objections to boarding school next year.

9

Aunt Bessie Makes a Decision

By the middle of August, Bessie was thoroughly worried over the chances of finding a suitable housekeeper. Amelia had discovered two possibilities from Young's Cove, well beyond Jemseg. They were both friends of her sister, but clearly too inexperienced and not capable of giving instructions to Amelia. For two minutes one day, Bessie even considered promoting Amelia to being in charge, but then quickly dismissed the idea. Amelia did not have the education, religious background, or the ability to direct the children, partly because of her youthfulness. Amelia had just marked her twentieth birthday.

Bessie knew St. Paul's was expecting her before the end of September. Dr. Coit was relying on her. She must write to him.

Meadowlands, August 15, 1904
Dear Dr. Coit,

In spite of leaving no stone unturned, my efforts to find a suitable housekeeper have yielded none. Unless I am very fortunate, indeed, I will not be with you for the beginning of the school term.

You have been so understanding and accommodating in the extreme, which makes me doubly sad that I have had to disappoint you with regard to my returning. Previously you have said that nurse Rideout has been satisfactory. She should know of my circumstances so she will not entertain thoughts of leaving, as by now she must feel the power of being in charge and wish to continue in that mode!

As much as I hate to actually write it, I suppose this is a letter of resignation, as I cannot keep you suspended any longer.

With my best wishes to you both,
Elizabeth Robinson Scovil

After placing her straight pen back in its holder, Bessie stared out of the dormer window over her desk and through the elm trees on the shore of the river. Her eyes did not register the scene. She saw only a blur and realized tears had come to her eyes. She removed her spectacles, cleaned them with a little cloth she kept for that purpose in her desk drawer and returned them to her permanently pinched nose. The interval gave her time to dampen her emotions and return to reality. This letter certainly marked the end of her professional working career, for which she started training when she was twenty-nine. And what a career it had been! She had no regrets. She was glad of her choices, but she did regret letting down Dr. Coit. She would miss their interactions. He was a soul mate. They would still correspond occasionally, but that was limiting. Family must come first, she knew. She could not possibly walk out on Mod. She could not leave him with just Amelia.

Bessie comforted herself with the thought she still had her columns in two nursing journals and could still write for *The Ladies' Home Journal*. Her occasional articles were always welcomed. "My organizations often want my input as well," she thought. "The VON in Saint John has just asked me to give a series of lectures on home nursing, that I will now accept. I will probably continue to write books. I will be asked to speak at conferences. My professional career is not really over, just taking a different turn. Yes, I have done the right thing by sending my resignation to Dr. Coit but that does not mean I'm put out to pasture."

Dr. Coit replied by return mail. He appreciated Bessie's concern but graciously accepted her resignation and then added, "If at any time in the future you are able to make satisfactory arrangements, your old position will be waiting for you here at St. Paul's, with whomever is in charge then, being your assistant."

Bessie read this with some emotion. "Well, a return is an unlikely possibility, but the opportunity is still there and that's gratifying to know.

That evening, over tea and caraway seed cake, Bessie told Mod of her exchange of letters with Dr. Coit.

"Does that mean you'll stay, for a while, at least? He clearly has a high opinion of you, Bess."

"I will continue inquiring, dear, but I think you're stuck with me." Bessie smiled at her brother.

"My dearest wish." Mod's face radiated relief and joy, as he drained his cup and asked for another.

*   *   *   *   *

When it became clear to Bessie she was unlikely to return to St. Paul's, she decided she should renegotiate her arrangement with the editor of *The Ladies' Home Journal*. After so many years of continuous monthly columns, a page of advice to mothers, as well as long articles elsewhere in the magazine on such subjects as nursing as a career, Bessie thought she was on firm enough ground, especially as an "Associate Editor," to ask for a concession. She did, and her suggestion was accepted. The arrangement was to continue the column, which she would send in two months before publication. She would also continue answering reader's questions on a monthly basis.

The Editor wrote a fulsome letter, putting great value on her reputation in the nursing world and as an expert in childcare. In the early 1890's, when the magazine was establishing its eventual preeminent position in the world of magazine publishing, young women who could afford the ten cents would buy it chiefly for Miss Scovil's page dedicated to advice for mothers. The current editor seemed every bit as appreciative as did Mr. Bok, the one who engaged her originally, so long ago.

Bessie was also listed as "Associate Editor" of *The American Journal of Nursing*, for which she wrote a monthly column called, "Notes From the Medical Press." This was chiefly a matter of selecting and paraphrasing information from several medical journals she thought readers of *The Journal* ought to know about. The publication was launched in 1900 with Sophie Palmer, a friend from nursing school days, as the editor. Sophie had asked Bessie to help, and her two or three page contribution every month had received enthusiastic support. No remuneration was offered at the time and there was still none, but Bessie's dedication was based on her fondness for her old friend, plus her desire to help educate younger nurses, and, she had to admit, keeping her name in the public eye. She had every intention of proudly continuing with her contribution as "Associate Editor" for as long as Sophie was in charge.

With the three girls away for much of the year, she would now have flexibility in spending more time reading medical journals and selecting material for her column, and in accepting speaking engagements on behalf of the Victorian Order of Nurses, which she helped Lady Aberdeen establish in the 1890's. And there was her work for the National Council of Women of Canada and for the international section, both started and presided over by her friend Lady A, when her husband was Governor General. Her obligations involved attending meetings and responding to speaking invitations.

Now, on the twenty-third of September, with Morris and Roger at school until late afternoon, Mod at Jemseg for the day discussing the sale of a horse, and Amelia making cucumber pickles in the kitchen, Bessie looked forward to an uninterrupted few hours of putting together a page for the December issue of *The Ladies' Home Journal*.

Taking a cup of tea, Bessie walked to the front hall, put her left hand on the swirled mahogany newel post, and slid it slowly up the polished bannister, savouring the touch of warm skin on cool wood and noting the prevalence of liver spots on her arm, the appearance of which the effect of the summer sun had made more prominent. She smiled, thinking of her mother's usual comment about these signs of aging, "Proof of experience and wisdom," she had said. "Let's see how wise I can be this morning," mused Bessie, as she sat down at her little walnut desk with spiraled legs and numerous useful cubbyholes.

To refresh her memory regarding her article for last December, Bessie extracted her copy of that issue from her bookcase. Ah, yes, it was entitled "The Children on Christmas Day," one hundred and fifty words on how to make Christmas a happy time for everyone, but especially how to make it a fulfilling time for small children while avoiding over-indulgence. With some satisfaction she noted that at the bottom of the column there was the usual encouragement to readers to digest her columns and ask questions:

"Miss Scovil will continue, during the coming year, her talks to mothers about children three years old and upward. She will answer all questions either in *The Journal* or by mail if stamps are enclosed."

Large envelopes containing several dozen letters arrived every month from the Curtis Publishing Company. Bessie answered them on the company stationery provided, resealing the large envelope, so they could be placed in a Curtis envelope. After all these years — now fifteen — there was rarely a question that required more than a moment's consideration. She had seen and read them all, over and over again, but realized they were new and pressing for the writers. Stay with the question at hand? Well, I need a new topic.

While part of her brain was thinking about that, her eyes were flitting over the advertisements on either side of last December's column, many in keeping with her article. Four games were advertised:

> *Parchesie, the Royal Game of India. The best Game ever published, price $1.00.*
>
> *The Spelling Board. One of the best educators have ever seen, price $1.00.*
>
> *Pin the Tail on the Donkey, on cloth, price 25 cents.*
>
> *Fascination, consisting of a top, eight marbles, and a board, price 25 cents.*

These games were all appropriate for Christmas. They are available from good stores or directly from Selchow & Righter, the New York company that made them or distributed them.

There were also the usual advertisements for baby wardrobe patterns, cribs, children's waists, stocking supports, and for two twenty-eight-inch swaths of human hair for $4.00, or $1.25 for twenty-two-inch lengths. Bessie thought of the impoverished women who sacrificed their treasured locks to pay for some medical necessity or family crisis, as Louisa Alcott had depicted in her famous book, *Little Women*. Ah, it suddenly came to Bessie; that's my Christmas topic—books for children. She immediately set to work. This is where the New York papers sent by brothers Jack and Barclay and those from cousin Lucy in Saint John were invaluable.

She paused at the thought of Barclay, her youngest brother. The papers he had sent were now several years old. He had been lured by the slogan, "Go West young man, go West," and he did just that. He went to Calgary, Alberta. He had become disenchanted with the noise and dirt of New York City. After seventeen years working as an accountant with an import/export firm on Broadway, Barc, at not quite thirty-five, radically changed his life. With a feeling for the rural life still alive, he had secured a position riding on horseback over the Hay River area paying treaty money to the Indians.

Bessie had a feeling of some regret that she had not been able to steer her brother into an occupation that would make use of his considerable intellect. She always enjoyed seeing an envelope addressed to her in his superb handwriting and knew there would be an unusually intelligent and interesting letter inside.

With a scolding thought, Bessie returned her concentration to the matter at hand. She might be out of the swim here in rural New Brunswick, but she took pride in not being out of date. She pulled her file of clippings from the last year and sorted out those with information on books for children she could review and recommend. She divided her choices into five categories: "Children Six to Ten," "Girls Twelve and Over," "Books that will Please Boys," "Fact with Fiction," and "For Boys and Girls Alike." Now, with that organization of the subject, she was ready to put it all together.

Bessie started with the title to her column, "Good Books for the Young" by Elizabeth Robinson Scovil. The first sentence struck the right note—"All children love a good book." Then she devoted one or two dense paragraphs to each title, working in Canadian books when possible and giving three of Miss Louisa May Alcott's creations her blessing in "For Girls of Twelve and Over." Any parent looking for a suitable Christmas present should find an inspiration somewhere here. Bessie was most satisfied with her last paragraph, "For Boys and Girls Alike," which she reread:

The Story of Joan of Arc, *as told to a party of nephews and nieces, none older than eleven years, is fascinating.* In the Days of Queen Elizabeth *is a charmingly written account of the times of the great Queen.* Camps and Firesides of the Revolution, *containing extracts from documents written at the time described, gives many interesting details of the lives of our ancestors.* Ancient History for Beginners, *intended for High School pupils who have not studied history before, is written in a most interesting manner and filled with pictures.* A Little Captive *is a graphic story of the times of Cromwell.* The Other Boy *came into a family of boys and girls to their mutual satisfaction.* Topseys and Turveys *is a book of comic pictures by Peter Newell, which when turned upside down presents a set of entirely different pictures.* Bird Portraits, *by Ernest Thompson Seton, has much interesting information about twenty birds.* The Bible for Children *is the text of our familiar version arranged in a continuous narrative. The book is fittingly illustrated with choice reproductions of famous paintings.*

After a few minor changes, Bessie sat back and viewed the morning's work with satisfaction but then realized her breakfast had long since been used up feeding her brain; she needed to stretch and take some nourishment. She picked up her teacup and saucer, decorated with purple and yellow pansies. Without thinking, she looked into the cup and noticed the damp tea leaves on the bottom arranged every which way. She knew some people put a great store in "reading" tea leaves for fortune telling. "That's alright for a party game," Bessie mused. "But not something to be taken seriously." Nevertheless, she wondered what that little leaf near the rim might mean. She dismissed the thought and descended the back stairs to the kitchen.

The kitchen smelled strongly of raw onion. Amelia had been peeling and chopping them for much of the morning, which, along with sliced cucumbers, were going into a huge kettle for making pickles. She took the drooping slice of white bread out of her mouth that she had placed there to absorb the eye stinging onion juice as it was released into the air and addressed Bessie.

"I've made you a cold beef sandwich with horseradish and put it in the larder, Miss Scovil. This work makes a girl hungry, with that onion smell and all. I couldn't last beyond noon," Amelia explained.

"Thank you, Amelia. Would you make me a fresh pot of tea and put both on a tray for me while I take a short walk outside to freshen my brain for an afternoon at my desk?"

"Yes, Miss. I'll carry it up for you."

"Good, thank you," Bessie replied as she opened the double doors off the kitchen and found her nostrils hit by the barnyard smells being carried on the wind now coming from that direction. She turned away from the farm buildings and started for a little stroll along the Jemseg road, glad she had brought a jacket, as the day was cool. The thought came to her how surprised her readers would be if they knew their much followed author lived on a simple farm, heavy with the odours of onion juice and manure, miles from anyone apt to read her book recommendations.

Both brain and appetite were invigorated by her exercise. On returning to the house, Bessie set about satisfying the latter first. Amelia knew just the right amount of their homegrown and homemade horseradish sauce to spread on a beef sandwich to add interest but not submerge the flavour of the meat.

After finishing her sandwich, she started on her "Notes," first absorbing useful information from her stack of the latest medical journals. Before reading very far in *The Medical Standard*, one article stood out as a must for her nurse readers. She paraphrased it:

> *E. J. Kemp reports in* The Medical Standard, *a case of a girl suffering from spontaneous dislocation of both knees, who was pale, emaciated, weak and loose-jointed, with a slight hacking cough and exaggerated respiratory murmur over both lungs. The family history was tuberculosis. After six months' treatment with general massage and unction with cod liver oil the patient recovered perfectly. Another case of acute tuberculosis recovered under the same treatment, as did a third, a girl suffering from hystero-epileptic attacks following several bites by a dog.*

She wanted to encourage nurses to try simple methods first, without worrying about the possibility of neglecting their patients. Her aim was to give thought provoking snippets that would encourage further reading rather than one long, exhaustive article that would fill the usual two pages. As Bessie's eye ran over the index of *The Medical and Surgical Journal* out of Boston, she noticed another possibility. "Burning With a Hot Water Bag," which told of a certain Miss Helen Ward, sister-in-law of an ex-judge, who had an operation performed on one of her legs while a private patient in St. Vincent's Hospital. While there, "a nurse carelessly allowed a hot water bag to remain in contact with the limb, in consequence of which, it was claimed, permanent injury had resulted." At the first trial the case was dismissed; the second resulted in a disagreement of the jury; on the third Miss Ward secured a judgment of ten thousand dollars. An appeal reversed the outcome on the grounds that the hospital was not bound to provide a patient, even a private patient, with its best nurse, and ordered a new trial, which resulted in a verdict in Miss Ward's favour and a settlement of $19,420. Having an ex-judge for a brother-in-law probably did Miss Ward no harm. Nurses must absolutely read that report. Bessie set about making the details as succinct as possible.

Afterward she chose to summarize an already short snippet, though she knew it would be slightly out of date by the time it was published:

> *THE WORLD'S DEATH-RATE - The death-rate of the globe is estimated at 68 a second, 97,921 a day or 35,740,800 a year. The birthrate is 70 a second, 100,800 a day or 36,792,000 a year, reckoning the year to be three hundred and sixty-five days in length.*

She then added a summary of an article about "Non-Alcoholism in Greece" from the *Greece Medicale,* which stated that alcoholism is "practically unknown" in Greece because of the purity of the wines. At this point, Bessie knew she was half way toward completion. After another twenty minutes of perusing journals, she decided on two somewhat connected articles, "The Vital Importance of Detection and Relief of Eye-Strain" from the *New England Medical Monthly* and "Headache as a Symptom" by a Dr. Ellis, from *The New York and Philadelphia Medical Journal.* There was so much material in each she had trouble summarizing them, but she knew full well that her difficulty in keeping it brief stemmed from her intense interest in both subjects, having suffered from eye strain, migraine and bad heads most of her life.

Bessie's hand was beginning to feel cramped with so much writing when she heard the voices of Morris and Roger wafting up through her slightly open window from their rowboat, as they tied up at the wharf. She replaced her straight pen in its holder and secured the top of her bottle of Waterman's Ink. When Bessie descended to the kitchen, Amelia was counting her jars of pickles, "twenty-eight, twenty-nine, thirty." When Morris and Roger burst in they both said "phew" in unison and held their noses, but were more than happy to taste a little from the bottom of the preserving kettle. Morris hinted, with a grin in Roger's direction, "that a nice slice of bread and butter would help take away some of the sharpness."

10

Cousin Frank's Motorcar

When a letter arrived from Miss Smith's office at Edgehill, seeking confirmation of the Scovil girls' intention of returning in mid-September, and including an up-to-date list of requirements, Bessie knew she must now reorganize the girls' trunks. Miss Straight's recent productions needed to be checked and a decision made over which of Elizabeth's clothes would fit Gertrude and which of Gertrude's should be set aside for Mary. Their recently purchased finery from Manchester's was tried on and admired, yet again, before having name tags sewn on and being added to the piles of clothes to be transferred to the cavernous steamer trunks. Mary and Roger had outgrown their desire to cover stick horses in blankets from Miss Straight's snippets, but invented a new game with the leftover fabric pieces. They took them to the verandah and then spent hours cutting them in different shapes and fitting them together in arrangements they called "quilts."

Though Edgehill did not begin until the middle of September, Elizabeth and Gertrude were again asked to stay at the Starrs in Saint John a few days before that. All was in order by the eighth for departure the following day. Bessie decided the recent trip to Saint John by riverboat had been such a success they should repeat it rather than taking the road. Mary ought to come too so she can absorb the flavour and excitement of the journey she will probably be taking in a year.

One of the hired men loaded the trunks on a wheelbarrow, trundled them down to the wharf, and helped Morris ease them into the rowboat. They were so heavy the men decided two trips would be sensible. Mary offered to travel with Morris and Father and the trunks for the first run. Everyone, including Roger who had slipped into the second boat trip, was eventually waiting on the Gagetown wharf when the riverboat tied up. Elizabeth and Gertrude were not able to control their tears as they hugged Father, Mary, and little brother Roger. They gently hit Morris on his arm and he on theirs in gestures of affection.

"Don't be too good," Morris shouted to them as Bessie and the three girls stood at the railing, all waving while the boat backed up before turning out into the main channel of the river and starting on its way.

Bessie and the girls were expecting cousin Frank to be at the Saint John wharf with a sizeable carriage and perhaps a driver. He was indeed there, with a driver, but not with the usual conveyance. Instead, there stood a black horseless carriage—a motorcar! While Bessie and cousin Frank exchanged greetings, the children stared at the shiny creation until prodded into politeness by allowing their eyes to be diverted for a few moments to their welcoming host.

"So you like my horseless carriage, do you?" Frank said to no one in particular. "Ayleene wanted to come but I thought there mightn't be room, so she is jumping up and down waiting for you at home."

Porters soon secured the steamer trunks to a luggage rack at the back of the vehicle. After helping Bessie and the three girls into the covered back seat, Frank climbed into the front seat. Before any movement began, the driver walked to the front of the motor with an L shaped rod in his hand that he applied with a circular swinging motion of his arm, which produced a loud noise and considerable shaking of the vehicle. Mary, wedged in between her aunt and sister Gertrude, grabbed both their arms and hoped she would be safe. All four passengers were holding on to someone. Cousin Frank, noting everyone's worried expressions, assured them this was usual and they would soon be on their way. And then—with speed beyond imagination—they were!

Bessie prided herself on being quite familiar with modern inventions, especially those related to the care of the sick. She had travelled on ocean liners and on many conveyances in the United Kingdom, the United States and Canada and was at ease in most new situations. But, as they sped along, narrowly missing carriages, horses, pedestrians, bicycles, and carts, she had to admit she had never been exposed to such a mixture of noise, vibration, speed, and exhilaration. Once the girls noticed Bessie was smiling, they gradually loosened their clutching grasps on one another.

"That's better," said Frank as he turned around and noticed their changed expressions. "It's a great invention. Mr. Ford is a genius. In another twenty years the streets will be full of them and there won't be a horse left."

"I hope your Mr. Ford will think of a way for motor cars to use hay, otherwise, with no horses, farms like Meadowlands will be doomed," Bessie called back to Frank, her composure and quick wit having been restored.

"There'll always be a need for some horses, I imagine," said Frank trying to reassure Bessie as realistically as possible, though his expression told her the opposite.

The girls' reunion was a hugging and laughing one, though they had been separated for only two months. Ayleene gave Mary a good-sized hug, too, which made her feel part of the clique of older girls. Cousin Madge had organized light refreshments for all, which she knew would be appreciated, especially by Bessie and Mary, soon to return on the reverse run of the riverboat. The grownups had time to renew their knowledge of family matters in between cups of tea, little sandwiches, and cakes. The young were all led to the day nursery by Ayleene to have theirs and to play with the little ones, supervised by the nursemaid.

Mary had a good look at the nursery rhyme tiles around the fireplace, which she remembered seeing before. She was surprised at the brightness of the colours of her namesake's blue dress, and her lamb's pink bow, just as though they had been painted that morning. She recognized several others, including a realistic looking spider next to Miss Muffet, she supposed. There was a shiny brown piano in the far corner that she longed to sit at and try to play a few notes, but as she was walking toward it Elizabeth reminded her to eat her snack, as she would have to leave soon.

Mary hoped there would be time for both. In spite of downing smoked fish sandwiches, animal crackers, and pretty little frosted cakes as quickly as she could, time flew by and cousin Madge and Aunt Bessie soon came into the nursery to announce the motor was leaving in ten minutes for the wharf. A wistful glance at the piano was as near as Mary came to playing even one note. Quick visits to the nearest of the seven bathrooms was all there was time for.

The usual round of hugs and damp eyes accompanied Bessie and Mary's departure. The exciting contraption was noisily waiting for them at the bottom of the front steps. This time, as his chauffer piloted them to the wharf, cousin Frank sat with the two passengers so he could talk without shouting.

Once on the boat, Bessie and Mary found a sheltered spot out of the early autumn breeze where they could identify landmarks on the shore and spot the first colours of September. Mary did not feel such an urge to explore the now familiar boat without her sisters, but she did want to ask her aunt about life at Edgehill. There were lots of little questions that her sisters either did not know the answers to or provided less than adequate explanations. When asked a question, Bessie was careful to either admit ignorance when she did not know the answer or to hold back when she thought it best. Her aim was to sow seeds of enthusiasm for attending Edgehill in the mind of her little niece without raising concerns. The questions that continued to tumble out of Mary's well of curiosity suggested Bessie was succeeding.

The wide river around them presented a busy and interesting scene. Scows of cattle were being ferried to fresh island grass; others laden with logs headed toward a sawmill and still others, loaded with lumber, were returning from the mill; small boats with noisy engines sped by and a few rowboats with children out for some fishing floated quietly on the water. Mary was not distracted. Her questions continued.

"Will I be able to stay a few nights at cousin Frank's and play the piano in the nursery?"

"You will be able to do more than that, my dear. At Edgehill you will be able take piano lessons once or twice a week."

"Oh, I can't wait!" Mary replied with delight.

"I started to learn when I was about twelve and loved it, especially when I could play tunes I knew," Bessie continued. "Of course, I had to practice every day, otherwise my playing would not have improved."

Just then Miss Featherstonehaugh came into view and settled herself on a bench beside Bessie. Mary knew that was the end of conversation with her Aunt Bessie, as Miss F. loved to talk.

Mary decided to amuse herself by waving at the people who she occasionally saw standing on the shore of the river and was much gratified when they waved back. As they passed various wharves, she garnered a multitude of waves. Soon, the Gagetown wharf came into view. She could just make out Morris and Roger standing near some freight and Mr. Fox, a local apple grower. The boxes were probably apples from his farm bound for Fredericton. As Miss Featherstonehaugh droned on and on, Mary turned, caught Aunt Bessie's attention and pointed to the wharf. Mary waved and waved until her brothers saw her and both waved back.

At the supper table that evening, a review of the day brought thorough descriptions of cousin Frank's latest acquisition.

"Terrifying to begin with, like a roaring animal about to eat you and then lovely and exciting," exclaimed Mary. "And oh, we went faster than anyone. Everything went by like lightening."

Roger's eyes opened wide with wonder. "Are you making that up?" he asked in partial disbelief.

"No, no, it's true. Horseless carriages are real and so noisy they are almost scary," added Mary.

Bessie expanded in detail, not disputing Mary's account and ended by saying, "I was very impressed. They will be everywhere in a few years, I expect."

Bessie and Mod spent much of the rest of the meal discussing the inevitable loss of hay sales once horses are less in demand.

"Cows will need hay, and no machine will take over their job," Mod wisely offered. "And I'm sure there will always be a need for horses, especially on farms."

Morris was absorbing the new information in his usual thoughtful way. "Maybe the same sort of motors will be put in different machines to pull plows and harrows and other farm machinery," he suggested.

"Perhaps, but that won't happen for a very long time," his father said, in an effort to reassure himself and his son.

I I

"Island" Life

Life without Elizabeth and Gertrude seemed strange all over again. The obligatory Sunday letters from each, properly spelled and beautifully written (several times, probably), were dissected by all at meal time and then more thoroughly by Bessie and Mod over tea and cake in the evening.

There were other changes. All the children now attended school. Roger started at the one room Porter school, directly across the river and up the hill. Mary graduated to the Gagetown Grammar School, which she soon started calling "the Grammar." Either Father or a hired man rowed the three children across the river, a fifteen or twenty minute trip, depending on the direction of the wind. For the first few days after school started, and until he felt bold enough to go on his own, Mary and Morris hurried Roger along the road up to the little school. After Roger was delivered, Mary and Morris climbed back into the rowboat. Morris liked taking up one of the oars, especially when his father manned the other one. If the morning were breezy, they hugged the shore for the final stretch to the Gagetown wharf.

At the end of September, Roger brought a note home addressed to his father.

> *Dear Mr. Scovil,*
>
> *For the last week, Roger has been at least a half hour late for school every morning. He needs to be brought here.*
>
> *Yours truly*
> *Sarah Innis*

Mod thought a good discussion about this would be appropriate over supper, especially as Morris and Mary were experts on the subject of the little school. Since there was much to be talked over, not a scrap of the beef stew with fluffy dumplings — one of Amelia's recent additions to her repertoire — was left. However, not all had been said, even following second helpings. Then came Yankee Toast for afters, fried bread blanketed with a sticky, bubbly, warm covering of molasses and butter. By the time the meal was finished, many memories of Porter School had been aired and everyone had had his or her say on the matter of Roger changing schools.

Mod had always thought that some of Mary's Porter School experience had been very unfair. She had suffered at the hands of the previous teacher, Miss Sharp, when Mod and the teacher's father were in a dispute about Scovil cows wandering into a Sharp hayfield. When Miss Sharp's father was eventually defeated in the matter, the teacher took it out on little Mary. This resulted in misbehaviour by Mary whenever her sense of justice was sufficiently ruffled. This included an episode when Miss Sharp bent over to give her a slap on the head and Mary pulled on the beaded cord that was attached to the teacher's pince-nez. The beads went flying all over the schoolroom floor. Mary made sure each little bead was retrieved, which took a good half hour and then it was time for recess. She looked back at the episode as being doubly satisfying.

Morris said his two years there were ancient history to him; lots of fun with his friend Kenny is what he remembered most.

"Have you been walking slowly to school, Rog?" Mod asked his son.

"Yes, I try to be late. I don't like school. It's boring. The teacher makes me stand in the corner for ages if I don't have my work done on time. It makes me feel sad. I feel like crying, but I don't."

Mary said there were ways of having fun. She and Frankie often volunteered to get a bucket of drinking water, making sure they spilled some on the way back so they would have to go for a second trip later. Then, before replacing the tin dipper so it floated on the water in the bucket, they would each take a long drink that made sure they would have to be excused for trips to the out house within a half hour. And that could take quite a while. If you put up two fingers when you stuck up your arm, that meant you had serious business to do, which the teacher accepted would take longer than just getting rid of excess drinking water.

"That's enough of that," said Bessie, gently chastising Mary for mentioning bodily functions at mealtime.

Morris quickly added with a smirk, "We used to do all that too," which earned a frown from Bessie.

Mod had a soft spot for Roger, his youngest, deprived of his mother so young, and perhaps not as creative as Mary.

"What would make school better for you, boy?" asked Mod softly.

"I'd like to go to school with Mary and Morris."

Mod and Bessie's eyes met, which was a sign the subject needed further discussion over tea and cake.

"We'll think about that and see if it's a good idea," Mod replied.

"That will cut fifteen minutes off the rowing. We can go direct to Gagetown on a catty-corner line instead of on two sides of a triangle," added Morris, showing off his geometry.

"You'd like Miss Bates. She even laughs sometimes," offered Mary.

After discussion later that evening, Bessie and Mod agreed that the reason for starting the children off at the one-room school—to give them a gentler introduction to education—was not working for Roger. Since children were allowed to begin at the Gagetown school if they were age six before the end of the year there was no reason Roger should not join the other two, especially as the first three grades were in one room and Mary would probably be in the next row.

Bessie and Mod each had another piece of Victoria Sponge cake to seal their agreement. It was Friday so nothing would change until Monday when Mod said he would take the three children to school and have a word with Miss Bates and the Principal. On the way back he'd drop in on the Porter school and explain his son's future absence. Roger had never been happier. Mary was determined her little brother would be able to print the alphabet before Monday and Morris was pleased his breakfast would not have to be downed in such a rush.

*　*　*　*　*

Getting to school by the time the heavy hand bell was rung was not always possible at any time of the year. Unhelpful winds and storms often slowed down the Scovil children. But they were not marked "late" if they were tardy, nor "absent" when the river was freezing over or breaking up. The first showing of skim ice or the warning signs of the spring thaw prompted their teachers to assign home work for three weeks, which was entrusted to Morris in a sealed envelope addressed to his father. Mod passed the papers over to Bessie. She happily took over supervising home schooling in the mornings and, as a reward for concentration, gave her charges free afternoons. During river freeze-up and break-up they were stuck on the Jemseg side of the river, relying on the little Dykeman store in the village for any provisions needed, or doing without.

These two seasonal periods of staying put was a time for starting projects, tidying cupboards, shoeing horses, or planning the next spring planting. "I'll do it when the ice goes out." was a well-worn form of procrastination. No mail could move. Morris, especially, missed his village friends. He announced one morning that his daily essay assignment, which finished off the three hours of home schooling each day, would be titled, "Life On An Island." Mary asked if she could write a long letter to her sisters for her exercise. Bessie thought they were both good choices. Roger practiced his joining-up penmanship.

Bessie tried to maintain a happy atmosphere with special treats in the afternoons or evenings. Making molasses taffy was one of them. Everyone took part, even Mod who was a dab hand at pulling out the long ropes of the slightly cooled mixture of boiled molasses, sugar, water and butter. He taught Mary and Roger to fold it all back on itself before it fell to the floor, then, with well buttered hands, pull it out again, fold and pull, fold and pull, until it had cooled enough to twist, rest, and cut into bite sized pieces.

There was no snow that year as the river was freezing and there was little wind, so the ice was marble smooth with millions of tiny bubbles imprisoned beneath the surface and only the occasional crack to avoid. Once the ice was thick enough, skating became the mode of transport for those of all ages who enjoyed the sport. Father sharpened all the skates the weekend he announced the ice was safe. Morris decided, come Monday, he would pull a sled to school so Mary and Roger could hop on when skating was too much for them. Mary was quite adept at skating but Roger had not yet perfected his glide. Morris made sure they all had their blades fastened on to their boots properly so he wouldn't have to freeze his fingers fiddling with them in mid-river. He strapped their book bags on to the front of the sled and they all set off with mixed feelings about giving up home schooling, but looking forward to the first skate of the season and seeing school friends.

After a week of these perfect skating conditions, heavy snowstorms covered the ice. Well-shod horses and sleighs were now common on the river. Mod was happy to drive his children to school. Bessie made an arrangement with the Caswells that if a heavy a storm came up late in the day the children could stay with their aunt and uncle and cousins. They were told that if their father was not at the school by the usual time, they were to go to the Caswells for the night. If he arrived late, he knew where to find them.

Early December brought cloudless skies and brilliant sun that bounced off the snow and was agony for Mary's eyes. Bessie had inquired from an optician in Saint John about dark glasses to fit a child and learned that none were available in the city. Every sunny day, on returning from school, Mary complained of sore eyes, in spite of her squinting and pulling her hat down to her eyebrows. In desperation, one evening over supper, Mary looked from her Aunt Bessie to her father and announced, "I'm going to write to Uncle Jack and ask him to send me a pair of dark glasses.

I remember there is everything you can imagine in New York so I'm sure there'd be a pair to fit me."

"That's a good idea," Bessie responded. "If he's too busy, Addie can look. Why not address it to both of them?"

"I'd sooner write to just Uncle Jack," replied Mary, thinking of the heated words she and her Aunt Addie had exchanged on her last visit.

"You do that," said Mod, and immediately found her a sheet of writing paper and an envelope, along with Jack's address for her to copy.

> *Meadowlands,*
> *December 5, 1904*
>
> *Dear Uncle Jack,*
>
> *I hope you are all well. We are accept my eyes feel like little needles are shooting into them when the sun shines on the snow. There are no dark glasses to fit someone who will be nine in a little over a month, not even in Saint John where Aunt Bessie has looked. Would you go to a little shop that sells specticles and ask for a pair that will keep the sun out of my eyes, please, and send them to me.*
>
> *I wish you were coming for Christmas. Elizabeth and Gertrude will not be here either. They are too far away to come in the snow.*
>
> *From your neece,*
> *Mary*

Mary knew better than to expect the glasses any time soon, but she could not help having a good look at the mail whenever it was collected from Gagetown. They regularly received magazines and newspapers from New York sent by Uncle Jack and Aunt Addie, or sometimes by Uncle Barclay that were read by Aunt Bessie and Father. She remembered being shown the big building on Fifth Avenue where Uncle Barc worked as an accountant when she had lived in New York the year she was five. Uncle Barclay did the same work as Uncle Jack. The building where he worked was on a street called Broadway. Uncle Barc came to Uncle Jack's quite often while Mary lived there, especially for meals. He lived by himself but in a house with lots of other people who were not married. He was happy to play games with her and knew lots of make-believe stories, but he didn't laugh as much as Uncle Jack.

As always happened with Christmas around the corner, there were little secrets around the coming of the mailbag. Sometimes Aunt Bessie would quickly grab a small parcel before anyone else could look at it. One day, as her aunt was casting her sharp eye over the contents of the bag, she spied a little parcel addressed to Mary that she quickly passed to her. Mary's heart leapt into her throat. In the upper left hand corner was Uncle Jack's address. It seemed to take an age to unwrap all the layers of protection, and then, in a little cardboard box—a pair of dark spectacles! She put them on her nose. They fit perfectly. She looked out the window at the sun bouncing off the snow. There were no little needles attacking her eyes. She danced around the dining room table where the mail was being sorted, thrusting her be-speckled face into everyone else's. No one minded. They were all happy for her, knowing how she suffered from the glare of the sun.

"There was no point in waiting for Christmas," Bessie said. "You need them now, dear. What a good fit."

A little wave of guilt for not being at home when Mary's eyes were damaged hit Bessie, but the sight of the glasses on Mary's nose chased it away.

School closed for vacation a week before Christmas with recitations, songs, and little skits. All three Scovil children took part. It was not as elaborate as in the summer, but enough to produce a good crop of parents and grandparents. Mary sang a solo—ironically about the delights of snow. Morris was the mainstay of the choir and Roger did his best to remember the words.

Christmas brought lengthy letters from Elizabeth and Gertrude along with sachets and bookmarks they had sewn and painted. Amelia was surprised and pink faced with joy to receive a sachet from each of the girls. Bessie counted twenty-two Christmas cards from relatives and friends. They included some from St. Paul's School, including the Coits, some from the Newport Hospital, and several from old classmates she had been in training with at the Massachusetts General Hospital, now scattered all over the United States, but who she still heard from every year.

As usual, Bessie had thought ahead, ordering books for everyone from those offered by *The Ladies' Home Journal,* and getting two off to Edgehill in good time. Mary had no money for presents but since her teacher said she had a "gift" for drawing, produced pictures, which she painted, for everyone. Roger was allowed to sign his name at the bottom beside hers, if he did it in a neat joining-up way. Sewing, especially fancy stitches, made her eyes hurt, but drawing and painting were fun. She spent hours perfecting a horse's head for Roger. She hoped he would like it. Morris had an artistic eye, too. He copied Mary's idea for presents and turned out pleasing little snowscapes with a touch of colour for everyone.

In an effort to make the holidays more festive between Christmas and the New Year, Bessie invited the entire Peters clan for afternoon tea and games aimed at young adults, though there were still two of the six who could be considered children. The men talked politics and smoked their pipes after eating. The two women played guessing games with the children and other skill testing ones organized by Bessie that required pencils and paper.

Once all was going well, she and Mrs. Peters withdrew to a quieter corner to concentrate on exchanging news. Though Bessie had resigned from St Paul's on paper, in her heart she had not entirely given up. Mrs. Peters had nothing helpful to report on the subject of available housekeepers. The women in the village who wanted daily work—house cleaning and cooking—had their own families and could not live in. Bessie began to think she must stop holding on to the thinnest possibility.

In the late afternoon, the Peters sleek chestnut horses were brought from the barn by Morris and Jock, the groom, and harnessed to their two sleighs. The family piled in and started for home on the path across the river ice. Bessie and Amelia cleared away the tea dishes. The day had been a success, with lots of laughter and conversation. All the sandwiches and cakes, large and small had vanished, except for one piece on each plate that was required to be left for "Miss Manners." Morris quickly offered to "tidy up," so they too disappeared.

I 2

Winter Horse Racing on the River
1905

With the progression of winter, the jars of preserves gradually diminished on the cold room's shelves in the cellar and Bessie made a mental note to put down more strawberry jam next summer. In order to combat that shut-in feeling that mid-winter brings, she donned her snowshoes when the wind was not too fierce and set out for a half hour's trudge along the road to Jemseg, or at least where she remembered the road being before drifting had erased it. But mostly she wrote her articles, her letters to Addie and Jack and Barc, and to other scattered relatives. She faithfully wrote a weekly reply to the letters of Elizabeth and Gertrude and all the others signed their names at the bottom. Sometimes Mod wrote to the girls, as well or instead.

Once the January thaw had passed and cold weather returned, the annual explosion of village activity began. Horse racing on the ice attracted devotees from miles around. The owner of one of the two general stores put up a horse for raffle. Tickets were on sale at his counter for weeks before the meet. Hundreds were sold at ten cents each; the chance of winning a two-year old mare for a ten-cent outlay was too much for any man to resist, even if it meant less food money for his wife.

On the Saturday of the races, the Scovil family all set off mid morning for the site equipped with buffalo robes, heated bricks covered with straw, and a basket of food. Someone would be selling hot drinks and perhaps soup heated on a fire in a three-legged metal container the village blacksmith had designed and made. The day was perfect — blue sky, bright sun, completely calm, and nicely below freezing, which kept the ice firm. Mary was happy, wearing her sun spectacles.

The owners of the different classes of horses had to pay to enter. The total of the entry fees for each race was the prize money pocketed by the winner. If more than eight horses were signed up for one race, there were heats, with the final winner being the only one in pocket. Not a lot of money changed hands, though there was also some unofficial betting. The day was

93

a social gathering as much as anything, an excuse to make the effort to see friends and relatives, to have some expansive conversation, for men to talk politics and horses, for women to discuss domestic matters and illness, and children to play tag where they didn't annoy the grown ups.

Cheers and hand clapping rang up and down the frozen expanse as winners were proclaimed and received their prize money. To allow everyone to reach home before winter's night set in, an announcement was shouted out around three-thirty that the winning raffle ticket was about to be pulled. Mavis, the plump twelve-year-old daughter of the owner of the mare, stepped up with a cardboard box that was well covered to keep the wind from whipping away the contents.

Looking out over the crowd, her father selected Mr. Dingee, a landowner of note in the village, to pull a ticket stub out of the box. Mr. Dingee made sure the cover was tight and then shook the box with gusto. He removed the cover, pulled out a stub, and called "8269" in a voice that must have been heard in Saint John, Mod thought as he checked his number. It was not his. Heads were bent, checking numbers. Then, all eyes were suddenly fixed on the owner of the mare who waved a ticket in the air proclaiming it to be number 8269. Mr. Dingee gave the stub a close inspection. Being a religious man, he did not want to be associated with anything dishonest. Yes, no doubt about it. This was the right number. Some of the crowd congratulated the winner, but some mumbled they smelled a rat. The old and new owner of the mare was also the master of ceremonies so he thanked everyone for coming and said he'd see them all next year.

"Has that ever happened before?" Mary asked her father on the way home.

"No, and it seems mighty odd to me."

"The only way for it to be rigged is if all the tickets in the box had the same number," Morris observed.

"That's unlikely," added Bessie, who wanted the young to think well of their elders.

Conversation and gossip on the subject of number 8269 buzzed about in the community for weeks, until signs of spring changed the focus. With heavy rains, the river ice broke up quickly and the freshet brought flooding a little higher than comfortable, but not catastrophically high. Only a foot or so of water covered the dirt floor in the cellar at Meadowlands, and it soon drained away. There was no need to grease the iron stove, or to tether a boat to the verandah. Skating, snowshoeing and sleighing gave way to rowing and thinking about the delights of summer.

13

Cousin Sophie Arrives from Boston in Her "Motah"

School closing ran its usual course. Bessie made sure she obtained a report on Mary's school year, which she would need to send to the Edgehill headmistress. Mary's progress was more than satisfactory, and in some areas, outstanding, so Bessie was sure she would be accepted for the autumn term. Roger just managed to be promoted to the second grade. Morris, already fifteen, slipped easily into the senior room. Soon all their routines would be reshaped with the arrival of Elizabeth and Gertrude. Once confirmation of Mary's acceptance at Edgehill had been received, along with an up-to-date list of requirements (though she doubted the list had changed much), Bessie vowed to start early on filling a trunk for the new boarding school student. She was glad there were no more nieces to deplete the silver drawer. She must remember to include Mary's initialed silver napkin ring with her knife, fork and spoon.

Bessie was pleased the two girls had made so much progress with French and again offered to speak a little each day with them, which they happily accepted, wanting to show off their skill. Not only had their French improved, something else changed. They each had acquired a nickname. Gertrude's was "Trudy," not unusual, but Elizabeth's was "Wowsie" just because another girl, a chum, once called her that. Mary thought using their new names would make her more part of their lives, though Bessie, Mod and the boys were not immediately won over.

"A lot of the girls have very different names," said Wowsie in defence of hers. "Not even nicknames. There's Troyte Bullock, who's usually called 'Trout' because she has freckles, and Raynsley Hensley, who's my best friend, and Emma Retta Randall."

"Oh, and Mathole Wokam, who's my best friend," added Trudy. "When I asked her where her first name came from, she said her parents made it up. She thought they wanted something different to go with their strange last name."

In late June and early July, the strawberry bed was especially generous, so not only did they appear as an every day dessert, but, remembering her

95

resolution, Bessie made sure that Amelia had enough time to put up twice as much jam as she had last year.

A boat trip to Saint John was on the horizon for filling Mary's trunk with whatever was needed that Miss Straight or Meadowlands cupboards could not provide. Replacements for worn out or out grown clothing for the boarding school veterans were also on the expanding list for purchasing in Saint John. Bessie calculated the riverboat journey to the city should wait until after mid-August to allow for the expected summer growth of the children, especially their feet. Children's toes seem to put on a half inch every time the wind changed, Bessie thought to herself, as she added "boots and shoes" to the list she kept in one of her desk cubby holes. In order to buy footwear for Morris and Roger, she would have them trace their feet on paper—an easy way to buy shoes and boots that fit well when fashion was not important.

Everyone was looking forward to the usual summer activities of swimming, picnicking, fishing, visiting friends and cousins in Gagetown, and having them over for a meal. Then, in the mailbag, Bessie received an unexpected letter. It was from cousin Sophie Robinson, a well-off distant cousin who lived in Boston. Bessie visited her several times while in training and rather liked this flamboyant and humorous woman. Cousin Sophie's letter said she was planning a little motoring trip northward and hoped to visit some of her late husband's relatives. She much appreciated hearing from Bessie every Christmas, hoped she was coping with her nephews and nieces, and was looking forward to meeting them. She intended to set out with her chauffeur at the beginning of the last week in July. She would send Bessie short letters along the way and try to give her a definite day of arrival.

When Bessie read the letter at the supper table, the whole family was excited at the prospect of having a motorcar parked at Meadowlands, especially Morris and Roger, who had not experienced the thrill of cousin Frank's horseless carriage. Cousin Sophie was not a blood relative, Bessie explained. She had married a much older second cousin of Bessie's mother's. He had made a great deal of money in "business" before he died. Bessie was careful not to mention that no one ever knew exactly what kind of "business" it was in which he made so much money.

By this time, the raspberries, picked earlier in the day by assorted children, had disappeared from the table and Bessie excused herself to reply to cousin Sophie's letter. Directions were needed and a description of Meadowlands, so rustic and simple compared with the extravagance of Boston. She did not want cousin Sophie's expectations to be unrealistic. Bessie also saw the need to give advice, pointing out the necessity to wear dusters because of the dirt roads and to be aware of the lack of places to eat and acquire gasoline or other motorcar requirements along the way. It was a very long way from Boston to Meadowlands. Had cousin Sophie made inquiries about putting the motorcar on the train as freight as far as the Maine border or even McAdam, New Brunswick? Bessie also wanted to know how long Sophie would like to stay. She quickly penned her warm welcome to Sophie because she needed to spend the evening working on September's articles for *The Ladies' Home Journal*.

As Bessie climbed the stairs to her writing nook, she wondered where she would put cousin Sophie's chauffeur. Sometimes a hired man, who could not reach his home in Jemseg because of bad weather, would sleep in the hayloft in the barn, but that would not be suitable for a chauffeur. The second room in the attic, across a little hall from Amelia's was the only possibility. He was probably a chatty Irishman, which would lessen Amelia's anxiety as she was of Irish extraction and she did have a lock on her door. He could eat his meals in the kitchen with Amelia. With all that somewhat sorted out in her mind, Bessie now felt free to concentrate on the job at hand.

By the end of July, letters were arriving every two days with short accounts of cousin Sophie's progress. James, the chauffeur, was a resourceful driver. Before departing Boston, he had mapped their entire journey in keeping with his employer's wishes, including not only the visit to Meadowlands, but also to Saint John, Fredericton, and perhaps Nova Scotia. They obviously did not look into the possibility of placing the motorcar as freight on a train. Bessie was relieved to read they sometimes spent two days in one town if the previous day's progress had been particularly arduous. Food and drink to last until evening was procured before setting off each morning. So far, pleasant places had been found for midday picnics—by a lake, on top of a hill with an entrancing view, near a farmhouse surrounded by flowers, etc. There had been only one rainy day when they did not travel. The chauffeur's seat, in particular, was not well protected on the sides, though they both had rain repellent costumes, if required.

As they drove along country roads and through villages and towns, they were always a point of great curiosity. James kept the new Model B Ford, with its brass and wooden fittings, in gleaming condition with daily polishing. Since leaving Boston, they had seen not more than a dozen of Mr. Ford's creations, and all those were the 1903 Model A design. All the occupants waved to one another as they passed, as though belonging to an exclusive club, and in a sense they did. Cousin Sophie's letters became longer and longer, filled with glowing details of her adventure through the Boston States and into Maine. There was scarcely a complaint, except for the difficulty of obtaining suitable hotels. Once they had to stay in a large farmhouse as a poor road had impeded their journey to the intended town.

Whenever a letter arrived, Bessie read it out loud at the supper table to give everyone an idea of what their remarkable relative was capable of doing, once she had made up her mind. When the day dawned for cousin Sophie's arrival in mid-August, she had grown into almost a mythic being. Bessie thought no one would be surprised if she appeared on Pegasus, touching down on the Meadowlands' lawn. The Yankee relative had already spent three days in Douglas, near Fredericton with Robinson cousins, so could now manage the journey to Meadowlands in half a day, with no difficulty. Sophie wrote that the motor could travel as fast as fifteen miles an hour on a good road. She was hoping to arrive around four o'clock.

The three girls had all been sleeping in Mary's room for two nights, to give Amelia a chance to summer clean what quickly became the guest room. The room in the attic was also made ready. Bessie composed careful menus for three days, which is all the time cousin Sophie thought she should allow for Meadowlands. After visiting Rothesay and Saint John, they needed to return to Boston before the chilly days of September.

The morning of the great day was overcast, but by noon the clouds had vanished and there was a perfect blue Canadian sky with a windless day to welcome the American relative. Keeping occupied until arrival time was almost more than the children could manage, so Bessie assigned them various chores that filled the time without wasting it. They were almost grateful. At three-thirty the girls put on clean pinafores and pulled up their sagging stockings. Roger, still wearing short trousers, yanked on his long, black stockings as well, smoothing out the accumulated ridges around his ankles. Morris had been working in the barn. He needed vigorous hand and face washing, plus a change of boots.

An air of tension gripped all the children by four-fifteen. Mod was busy with a sick horse so Bessie could not ask his advice, but suggested the young start walking along the road to Jemseg and wait at the Mound, where their old pet horse, Nelson, had been buried, and where they now frequently picnicked. They had been gone not more than fifteen minutes when Bessie heard the noise of the motor in the distance. It steadily increased, grew quieter for a bit, and then started up again. A cloud of dust hovered over the Jemseg road and through it came a horseless carriage filled with laughing children and a round-faced be-hatted woman swathed in a duster.

But most notable of all was the chauffeur. He was the colour of good quality dark chocolate, as was his livery and the motorcar, all now slightly muted by a layer of road dust. Bessie stood and walked slowly forward to meet her guest, not knowing exactly where the machine would come to a stop. As the contraption came nearer, the driver's face lit up with the biggest smile Bessie had ever seen, showing a mouth full of perfectly arranged gleaming teeth. The machine halted and the noise stopped. The chauffeur nimbly stepped on to the running board, then to the ground before opening the door behind him, spewing out children then a laughing cousin Sophie. The women embraced.

"Welcome, cousin Sophie. You are a marvel!"

"James is the marvel," Sophie replied, turning her head toward the chauffeur who was already unloading boxes and cases from the dust and waterproof trunk fastened to the ledge under the back seat.

James touched his fingers to his peaked cap and smiled again, in the direction of his employer. Bessie was used to Negroes as there was a well liked and respected family in Gagetown, the Hectors, and others who lived in Otnabog, a few miles away, but they were all normal in size. James must be six feet four inches or more, thought Bessie and then remembered the bed in the attic, comfortable for ordinary size people like the short Irishman she had been expecting.

Bessie quickly decided it would be best for the luggage to be placed in the kitchen and then sorted out. As James and Morris began carrying cases toward the kitchen door, Amelia opened it, intending to assist. Seeing the enormous, dark brown chauffeur coming toward her was so unexpected she uttered, "Lordy," and tripped on the step. Before she could catch herself, James deftly caught and steadied her with his free arm. Her shock evaporated as he beamed his dazzling smile in her direction.

"I'm... I'm Amelia and I've come out to help."

"I'm James and I'm trying to help, too."

"I'm Morris and these boxes are as heavy as lead," Morris quipped, and all three broke out in laughter.

Amelia was more than a foot shorter than James. When she looked up at him as he laughed, she could see the roof of his mouth, pale pink, like the inside of a seashell.

While the baggage continued to pile up in the kitchen, cousin Sophie turned to the Scovils still lingering near the motorcar and asked, "What do you think of my big brown motah?"

The sound of her Boston accent made cousin Sophie seem even more exotic. They all agreed, her "motah" was almost magical.

Mod appeared and warmly welcomed their guest. He wanted to know about the mechanical details of the motorcar. Sophie said that James could tell him what he wanted to know once he finished unloading. The girls hovered around the machine, agreeing it was even more splendid than cousin Frank's and hoping they could go for a longer ride in it. Their eyes turned to James as he came out of the house and collected another load. He looked even grander since he had shaken the dust off his uniform. He was the tallest person they had ever seen and with such a soft, musical sounding voice and such beautiful, straight, white teeth.

Before Bessie could shepherd her guest into the house via the front door, the much-travelled relative removed her ankle length duster and her silk scarf holding her wide brimmed hat in place. She banged them together and shook them vigorously, which produced clouds of road dust.

"I'll spare your house a souvenir of my travels," announced Sophie, as she rolled her bulk through the screen door, held open by Mod.

Though by now it was already five o'clock, Bessie decided to go ahead with a light afternoon tea with just sandwiches. They would keep the cake and cookies for later. The children almost forgot to eat as cousin Sophie captivated them with tales of her travels. As she paused to take a bite of a moist cucumber sandwich or quench her thirst with Saint John packaged Red Rose tea, she was pummeled with questions from all five children. Mod intervened, embarrassed that this sophisticated cousin would think ill of his parenting.

"You'll have three days, so let your cousin eat in peace."

Sophie did not seem to want to eat in peace. She elaborated on her journey with the children's questions in mind. Each comment inspired another question, which the young reluctantly stored away for another time. Amelia felt more in control of her kitchen, once James sat down, though still bewitched by his smile. She could not remember when she had enjoyed eating sandwiches and drinking tea quite so much. She had no idea chauffeurs knew how to dry dishes so expertly.

Time flew by. On the second day Morris talked with Mod. Mod talked with Bessie, then she asked cousin Sophie whether James could take the children for a drive to Jemseg with a picnic at noon on the way back. Sophie was enthusiastic, promising she would insist that James go as fast as the speed limit allowed, all of fifteen miles an hour, but at least a man did not have to walk in front anymore, waving a flag as was the law back in the '90s.

With the children occupied, this was a good time for the adults to visit Gagetown. With Sophie in front and Bessie in back, Mod rowed the boat smoothly across the river. There were no Robinson relatives in Gagetown for Sophie to meet, but she was curious about the Scovil's nearest centre of community life. Dinner with the Caswells and a visit with the Peters were as entertaining for Sophie as it was for the hosts.

"Such charming and educated people," Sophie commented as Mod rowed back to Meadowlands, grateful the wind was with him.

By the time Mod tied up at the wharf, and the two ladies were safely landed, the clatter of the big bown motor reached their ears mixed with the last bars of "Carry Me Back To Old Virginny." The children, pink faced from speed and singing tumbled out of the motorcar, thanked James for the adventure and then cousin Sophie. Morris asked his father whether he could teach James to row, after supper, as a "thank-you" for the drive.

"That's thoughtful," said Mod. "Better clear it with cousin Sophie, though."

Everyone regretted the day of departure, but, as Sophie said, "Summer is running away and we have a long way to go."

James reloaded the baggage in the motorcar, including a sizeable picnic carefully and regretfully prepared by Amelia. Morris helped the chauffeur polish the brass and wood trim just before leaving, though they both knew it would again be covered in dust by the time the motor reached Saint John. Hugs and handshakes were enthusiastically given and returned. Waving continued even when only dust could be seen rising from the road to Jemseg.

The house felt very empty the next day. Everyone was subdued, as though something valuable had been lost. Wowsie and Trudy agreed that the only good thing about the day was that they had their room back and did not have to share any longer with wiggling Mary.

Halfway through the morning, Bessie realized the deadline for her "Notes from the Medical Press" for *The American Journal of Nursing* was due in two days. She devoted almost the whole afternoon to making selections for the column, occasionally lifting her head to see the five children, through the trees, swimming and playing near the wharf—a good occupation on an unusually hot day in the third week of August.

As soon as Bessie licked the stamp and ticked off "A.J.N." on her list of things she must accomplish, her eyes fell on the notations that read, "Edgehill Trunks" and "trip to S.J." She had given Miss Straight a few days off to spare Sophie the constant whirring and singing, and to leave the attic room free for the chauffeur. Miss S. was returning the next day for the final push toward finishing the necessary clothes. The seamstress's familiar presence filled the last days of summer, while Bessie scrutinized the school lists and made one of her own.

                              *   *   *   *   *

The riverboat trip to Saint John for the three girls and Bessie was even
more enjoyable than last year. When they were all seated on the deck,
Bessie turned to Mary and asked; "Mary dear, would you like to have your
hair cut quite short? There will be no one at Edgehill to take out the snarls
and you don't like plaits. You can keep your bangs and have a Dutch cut,
straight at the sides and tapered at the back."

"Oh, lovely," Mary responded. "Anything to have no snarls."

The three girls left for a discovery walk around the boat while Bessie
thought more about this expedition. She remembered the entreaties of
Elizabeth and Gertrude for the purchase of at least one good dress, rather
than have Miss Straight make them all, and she determined to save Mary
some of the embarrassment her two older sisters had suffered. Bessie
calculated the required number of shoes for indoors and out, for weekdays
and Sunday, and boots for snow and rain would all make a considerable
stack. Fortunately for the remainder of Frank's bank account, Gertrude
had grown into all of Elizabeth's footwear so only two complete sets had
to be purchased. Trudy was used to Wowsie's hand-me-downs. She had
grown up somewhat in her sister's shadow, but, most days, would not have
changed the arrangement even if she could. Her older, self-assured sister
looked out for her and was her confidante.

Once the shoppers were back home, there was the usual trying on of
the contents of the parcels and the consumption of treats by the stay-at-
home boys. As the days progressed into September and the trunks were
nearly filled, Mary could not resist inspecting hers frequently. She could
hardly contain herself when she imagined what her new life would be like,
actually having piano lessons and being able to play a piano, and having
lots of friends. When her excitement made her feel almost on fire she
found Roger and asked him to play "statues" with her outside. One would
whirl the other around with outstretched arms, then let go all of a sudden,
with the whirler calling out what he or she wanted the whirled to look
like when frozen. Then the whirler would slowly count until the "statue"
moved. Then the whirler and the whirled would change places. Mary and
Roger were happy to play this for an hour, finally lying on their backs in
the warm grass, making up stories about the clouds, deciding which were
animals, or odd looking people.

I4

Mary Goes to Edgehill:
An Ominous Beginning

The Starrs wanted all three Edgehill girls to spend a few days in Saint John before the trek across the Bay of Fundy and on to Windsor. Early in the second week of September the travellers and their trunks set off from the Scovil Point wharf in two rowboats. A smaller one had been recently acquired so one person could row easily and more quickly to Gagetown if necessary. Morris took command of the small boat with Mary and her trunk and Roger as cargo. Mod took the oars of the big boat, which had been relied on for years. Bessie stepped carefully on board, followed by giggling Wowsie and Trudy. Jock, who had trundled their trunks to the wharf, helped Mod load them into the boat and the whole Scovil family pushed off for Gagetown.

As a means of travel to Saint John, the riverboat was preferred by all in the summer over the less exciting and more tiring road trip. Bessie made sure they left home in time to be well organized when the riverboat tied up at the Gagetown wharf. The usual hugs, half hugs, and moist eyes accompanied good-byes. Extravagant waves continued until those on the wharf looked like pins and those leaning on the railings of the boat blurred into the background. For a few moments Mary's excitement left her, as she was stricken with the idea of life without Roger—for months and months. Wowsie noticed the sudden sadness of her little sister. Mary stood with her eyes glued to the fading wharf, the corners of her mouth turned down, and her thumb perilously close to being sucked.

Cheerful cousin Frank met them with his chauffeur-driven 1903 Ford, still shiny and splendid, though after the experience of cousin Sophie's "big brown motah" the girls did not gape at the sight of it. They were more than happy, after their aunt was seated, to pile into the back seat covered in beige leather. They saw two other Fords on their way to the Starr's house. The idea of horseless carriages must be catching on.

The five days at the Starr house with its seven bathrooms were full of adventure, especially for Mary. She sometimes played dolls with Ruth and

103

guessing games with the five who were old enough, including Ayleene, but no riddles, she was relieved to discover. Connie and Penniston were still very young and were usually looked after by their "nurse." Mary decided to lose no time, so at the first breakfast, after she succeeded in neatly cutting off the top of her boiled egg, she asked cousin Madge; "Please could I try to play the piano in the day nursery, and when would be the best time?"

"Any time, dear, but be sure to close the door," Madge replied with a smile.

As soon as she was excused from the table, Mary climbed the two long flights of stairs to the top of the house and made her way to the back room. She went in and closed the door. She knew she was in the right room; there were the nursery rhyme tiles around the fireplace she had admired when she was here the last time. And there was the dark, shiny, giant in the far corner. No keys showed but she discovered they had a cover that she could roll back. She sat on a stool capable of twirling around. She made two complete revolutions and then thought that wasn't the reason she was here. She gently put a finger on one creamy key near the middle of the row, then another and another. She found she was making up a little tune and played the six notes over and over so she could remember them. Then she chose six different notes until they sounded right to her ears and added them on to the first. She did the same twice more, playing her collection of twenty-four notes over and over, humming in tune with the sounds. Mary knew that musical pieces had names. She named hers, "Music of the Stars," and smiled to herself about the double meaning.

Wowsie suddenly opened the door telling Mary to hurry as they were going for a walk to meet cousin Frank who would drive everyone back for lunch.

"Let me play you my tune."

"Later, we have to hurry."

"Wait, I should cover the keys."

The days were so full of unusual excitements, Mary forgot to think of Roger, until she had said her prayers and was climbing into bed, on the second day. I wish Roger were here. He would like it as much as I do. If Edgehill is anything like this, I'm sure to like it.

*   *   *   *

The Bay of Fundy, often raging like a mad genie, was as calm as a pond for the crossing to Digby, Nova Scotia. The rough weather brought by the September Equinox had not yet arrived. Cousin Frank made the trip even more fun for the four girls. He pointed out the dolphins swimming in coordinated teams, as if showing off; and in the distance, whales leaping into the air and lashing their tales like big, flat whips.

The arrival of the ferry at Digby was timed to catch the train running north up the Annapolis Valley to Windsor and beyond. There were no motors at the Windsor station, so cousin Frank hired a large carriage to accommodate them all and the luggage. Ayleene, Wowsie and Trudy were all looking forward to seeing their friends after the long summer break. Mary was wide eyed with surprise at the length of the drive leading up to the school. She thought it would never end. Cousin Frank knew the ropes. He reported the arrival of his charges to the headmistress, Miss Smith, an imposing, well-corseted lady with a plummy English accent. She welcomed the three back and paid special attention to Mary, telling her she would find it strange at first, but after "settling in" was sure she would be happy.

Wowsie, Trudy and Ayleene were in the senior dormitory and Mary, being the youngest in the school, was in the junior dormitory. As they went their separate ways, Wowsie said to Mary, "Be good," and smiled at her little sister.

"See you tomorrow," said Mary.

"Maybe," replied Wowsie, now out of Mary's hearing.

As Mary was unpacking her nightclothes and sponge bag from her trunk, which was placed at the end of her bed, the biggest girl in the junior dormitory came up to her.

"What's your name?"

"Mary, what's yours?" Mary replied with a quick smile, thinking she had already found a friend.

"You'll know, soon enough. By the way, if you go to sleep tonight, something terrible will happen to you, especially since you have short hair," said the nameless girl.

"Why?" asked Mary in shock, her eyes suddenly enlarged with fright like a terrified horse. The girl smirked, turned her back, and walked away.

Mary's bed was the last in a line of beds that filled the dormitory room. There were no belongings on the bed next to hers, no one unpacking. Beyond were a group of girls talking and smiling and looking in her direction. Though she had no idea what they might do, she knew she had as much right to be there as they had so she undressed discretely, the way Wowsie and Trudy did. With her nightdress on and her dressing gown well tied, she wiggled her feet into her slippers and walked past the girls to the bathroom, giving them a little smile. No one spoke. All the other girls had long hair. When she returned from her ablutions, Mary had to walk again uncomfortably near the posse of unfriendly girls. She put her nose slightly in the air and tried not to give the impression of being terrified. As she reached her bed, a tall woman walked in announcing she was Miss Rice and would be in charge of the dormitory for this term.

"Everyone in bed in fifteen minutes. I will be back then to read prayers."

The gossiping girls scattered to their own spaces while Miss Rice strode toward Mary, who was beginning to put away her sponge bag and find her hairbrush.

"You must be Mary Scovil. Why is your hair so short?"

"My aunt thought it best to have it short." Mary replied. And remembering Wowsie's instructions added, "Miss."

"Oh! We are a jolly, happy family here. Hang up your uniform tonight for tomorrow. I will awaken you at seven o'clock. Wash and dress and go to breakfast by eight. Come back to your dormitory afterward, make your bed, clean your teeth and make sure your bowels move. Then go to chapel, next to the headmistress' office, then class. Here is your timetable. Ah, your first class is arithmetic with Miss Marsh. Her room is next to the dining room. Remember to take an exercise book, a pencil and a rubber. Oh, the bed next to you will be occupied soon. Helen Heaney is attending a family funeral today."

With that long list of instructions and news, Miss Rice smiled briefly, handed Mary her timetable and departed. Poor Helen, thought Mary. I hope it isn't her mother. A flash of her own mother's face appeared in her brain as she began to unpack. The navy serge jumper dress was a lot longer than she was used to wearing. She laid it out on her bed and added one of the three middy blouses, neatly folded by Aunt Bessie, then the navy jacket, just in case all the other girls were wearing theirs tomorrow. She finally managed get them neatly on hangers and then stuffed the hanging clothes into her small closet, all the while making little glances in the direction of the others, but they were all busy as well.

At least there would soon be another girl as a buffer between her and the bully girls. If only Miss Rice had asked if she had any questions. She wanted someone to explain what terrible thing would happen to her if she fell asleep. Instinct told her it wasn't a good idea to ask, even if there had been an opportunity. As she was looking for her new, long, black stockings to wear tomorrow, she suddenly thought of Gerald and Will, her bullying cousins in Rothesay. These girls were like them.

She had some safe time to think about the terrible thing before any chance of sleep. What could the girls possibly do to her? They could hold a pillow over her head so she couldn't breathe, but Miss Rice wouldn't be pleased with that and neither would their parents. No, they probably wouldn't kill her. She would stay awake and just pretend to be asleep; then she could watch what they were up to.

Miss Rice blew back into the room and commanded: "Down on your knees, girls." She read several prayers and finished with, "And may God watch over you."

Mary's long ago conversation with Aunt Bessie about Santa Claus popped into Mary's mind. If there was no Santa Claus why should there be a god? If there happened to be one, up in the sky probably, how could he hear Miss Rice directing him to look after them? But if nothing terrible happened tonight, maybe he was on duty after all.

Before Miss Rice left the room, Mary slipped deftly into her bed, stretched out on her right side, facing the other beds with her eyes almost closed, but not quite, on guard. At least the room was not deep black because of the light from a lamp in the hall, just like at Meadowlands. There was enough light to see anyone coming toward her bed. Even so, her heart was pounding. She kept awake thinking of Wowsie and Trudy—at least under the same roof—and of Meadowlands with Roger and Morris sound asleep, and perhaps Aunt Bessie and Father eating cake and drinking tea and reading those newspapers from New York sent by Uncle Jack.

For the longest time Mary managed to watch the other girls, through her nearly closed eyes. They all seemed to be sleeping. She wanted to lay on her other side, but knew she had to remain facing the enemy. She tried closing her eyes completely and opening them quickly. No one was moving toward her. She tried again and kept them closed longer. Still no one moved. She relaxed a little more and closed her eyes again. The next thing she knew, light flooded in through the windows.

15

Learning the Ropes

"Good morning, girls. Everyone up," commanded Miss Rice in a voice loud enough to shake eleven girls from their dreams. Mary pinched herself. She had survived the night, though maybe she had been infected with the plague, which wouldn't show for a few days. Aunt Bessie is sure to want to nurse her at home. A light dose of the plague would take her away from her misery. She hoped for it.

Somehow Mary managed to remember Miss Rice's instructions and even brushed out three snarls — such a change from long hair. Having short hair seemed to surprise everyone, perhaps that's what made the others so mean. It can't be a crime to be a little different, and for a good reason. Maybe the others were jealous. No, that was unlikely.

Breakfast was sticky oatmeal porridge, flabby toast and marmalade, and cambric tea. They sat at tables for twelve with the dormitory mistress at the end, making sure they all bowed their heads for grace and used their own cutlery and napkin. Mary noticed the familiar Kings pattern on her spoon and knife, like a shell, and her initials on her napkin ring. Cousin Frank must have given them to the headmistress. She tried to see Wowsie or Trudy or Ayleene sitting somewhere in the sea of senior girls at the other side of the dining room. The place assigned to her on the bench put her back toward them, but she turned her head as often as possible, searching, until reprimanded by Miss Rice. Mary was almost sure she caught sight of Wowsie's long blonde hair as everyone at that senior table stood up to leave. If only Wowsie could have smiled at me, she thought.

When Miss Rice decreed, everyone at the table stood and walked single file to their dormitory and completed the list of morning requirements. chapel was next, with the headmistress, Miss Smith in charge. She wore a pince-nez, like the teacher at the Porter school, which made her appear very cross. But when she smiled, which she did twice, she seemed almost beautiful, even though her hair was pulled back into a tight bun. Mary was sure her corset was laced too tightly. She could see the outline of the whalebones through her dress and her chest was pushed up very high. She began to feel sorry for Miss Smith, but was forced to concentrate when required to stand and sing "All Things Bright and Beautiful," which she did in a loud voice without looking at the words. If a god were on duty, surely he would hear her and be pleased and look after her. She saw Miss Rice look down the row at her, smiling slightly; perhaps surprised she knew how to sing. But she had the misfortune to be standing next to the bully, who tramped hard on her foot, so Miss Rice's approval was diluted with a wave of pain and fear for the future.

The arithmetic class was another surprise. Miss Muir, the mistress in charge, like all the others Mary had met so far, spoke with a clipped English accent. She said, to Mary in particular, as she was the only new junior girl, that they would use the English system of money—pounds, shillings and pence. Mary must see her after class about a special lesson so she could catch up. Mary thought she would tell Miss Muir that she lived in Gagetown and was not going to live in England so could she please use dollars and cents, but she knew she would not have the courage. (Little did either of them know that Mary would, in fact, well past middle age, live in England for twenty-five years, where the knowledge of pounds, shillings and pence came wafting back from the past.)

History class came next, which was about an early English Queen, Queen Boudicca, and then gymnastics. As the day was warm, the class went outside on a not very green lawn where the girls were all given a pair of Indian clubs made of pale, smooth wood. The gym mistress, Miss Foote, with curly, blond hair and the largest nose in the world, told Mary, new and short, to stand in the front row so she would be near for correction. Miss Foote showed them simple swinging movements that the girls all copied; they were meant to be good for posture. She then showed them more complicated motions. Much to Miss Foote's surprise, Mary did not require correction. She followed the instructions almost perfectly, until excessive enthusiasm caused one Indian club to fly out of her hand, and, fortunately, land in some bushes, so no real damage was done, except to Mary's feelings of accomplishment.

Miss Foote explained to them the need for a good grasp of the clubs at the top of the small end. They copied her. They stood still and swung their clubs over their heads, then walked about the field in single file, swinging them like long arms. Mary was aware that breakfast was far in the past, her tummy beginning to make empty noises. Relief came when they heard the bell being vigorously rung by the meal duty mistress, whose name Mary had not quite grasped. The mistress had red hair and walked as though she had sore heels, putting her weight on her toes as soon as she could, after each step. As instructed, all eleven girls marched single file by a big, wooden box, just inside the door, where they were told to gently place their clubs. Ten minutes was allowed for hand washing and hair brushing in their dorm and then off to the dining hall for lunch.

The girls walked to the end of the room where they picked up their own eating utensils, each in separate piles according to patterns. If more than one girl had the same pattern, they had to tie coloured thread around the handles so the kitchen staff would sort them properly. Mary tried to find a place at the table as far away as possible from Bully Girl. Although not on her side of the table, Bully Girl managed to sit directly opposite Mary. As only two places separated each of them from Miss Rice, Mary thought she would be safe. She hadn't counted on Bully Girl's long legs being able to reach her shins with a painful blow. Mary winced just as Miss Rice's eyes met hers.

"Try to maintain a tranquil expression while eating," commanded Miss Rice. "To improve digestion."

Mary's lips had almost formed "But ..." when she remembered Wowsie telling her she must never be a tattle tale; that was the best way to make enemies. Instead, she concentrated on finishing her plate of stew with dumplings — not as fluffy as Amelia's but edible — and looking forward to what seemed like rice pudding on the sideboard. Mary ate every gooey grain while listening to the other girls' conversations, trying to decide who might be friendly. She kept her legs well tucked under the bench, just in case. After lunch, it was time for French class.

Mademoiselle Guigon wore her very black hair in a loose bun falling off the back of her head, with wispy bits hovering around her eyes, which she often tried, unsuccessfully, to push behind her ears. She had a heavy accent that Mary struggled with. She said everything twice, once in French and once in English. Mary could hardly understand the English and certainly not the French. Suddenly, she realized a question was being directed at her.

"Marie, have you studied the French language before?"

"No, Miss."

"You must call me Mademoiselle. It is 'Miss' in French. No? Madem ... mo ... selle. Come to me after class and we will arrange catching up time, Marie."

"Yes, Madem ... mo ... selle."

Mary wanted to tell the teacher that her name was not "Marie" and never had been but knew this was not a good time. By the end of the hour, after repeating the correct pronunciation of a list of words and their meanings, Mary quite liked this class, like a game. Next came music class, singing really, but not just any old songs. They were going to learn to read music, read all those black notes having different sounds. Mary thought she would just like to sing, but she listened to what the headmistress said. Afterward, Miss Smith came up to her and said she was to have piano lessons and the first one is now with Miss Steel.

"Come with me," Miss Smith said as she walked down the hall followed by a now tired Mary, wishing she could play with Roger. The sound of a piano being played behind a closed door boosted her energy. Miss Smith gave a curt knock as she opened the door to a little room. The piano mistress stopped playing and stood.

"Miss Steel, this is Mary Scovil, the new girl. She has a good singing voice so may well pick up the piano quickly, though she has not had lessons before."

Mary had been looking forward to this day for so long, her enthusiasm brought up new energy and overcame her weariness. As Miss Smith strode into the practice room, Miss Steel moved to a little table and began flicking through some sheet music. Mary smiled at Miss Steel whose lips stretched just a bit in return. They each said, "Good afternoon."

The teacher motioned for Mary to join her on the piano bench in front of the shiny, black monster that took up nearly half the space in the practice room. Miss Steel put her fingers on the keys and played a little tune, saying it was called "Bobby Shafto's Gone to Sea."

"The notes on the page tell us what notes to play on the piano, but before you try you have to learn and practice scales to make your fingers ready to learn as well as your head."

The rest of the lesson was all about "e-g-b-d-f" and "f-a-c-e." Mary was given work to practice at 4 p.m. on Tuesdays and Thursdays and would have lessons at 4:30 on each of those days. It was already Tuesday, so she could not touch the piano for two days. The thought disappointed Mary.

"Write that down in your exercise book, so you will not forget. Every practice and lesson is important," said earnest Miss Steel. "Off with you now to the dining hall for tea and a biscuit, then to your classroom for homework prep."

As Mary wiggled into a place on the bench for tea and biscuit, she made sure she could see over the great divide in the direction of the senior section. She and her sisters had been under the same roof for nearly a day and a night and they had not spoken a word to each other, nor had their eyes met. As she sipped on her cambric tea poured by Miss Rice, and waited for the plate of thin cookies to be passed to her, Mary definitely saw Trudy sitting at a senior table talking with another girl, but they had their backs toward her so there was no hope of exchanging the slightest smile. Even so, just seeing the back of her sister's head and the special way her hair fell, made Mary feel less alone.

The girl sitting next to her with large blue eyes passed her the plate of biscuits. Mary knew she must hold the plate while the girl took one, then she should pass it to the next girl, on her other side, who would hold it for her. After the little ritual was over, Mary gathered her courage and turned to the girl with the sky-blue eyes.

"What's your name and where are you from?"

"Louise, and I live in Montreal. What about you?"

"I'm Mary and I come from Gagetown."

"Where's that?"

"It's about half a day's trip on a river boat from Saint John."

"Is that near here?"

"No. It's …"

Miss Rice stood and announced, "Tea is over. Go to your classroom for your prep."

Mary tackled her piano prep first. Miss Steel had given her sheets with lines on them that she was to decorate with notes for f-a-c-e and e-g-b-d-f and other exercises listed at the top of the page. She wished she could soon really play the notes for "Bobby Shafto." She liked the tune. Next came Mme. Guigon's ten French words to learn, special ones to help her catch up, and ten more for everyone, which took a long time. Mary was relieved to discover some words were quite like English. Then she had to write a paragraph about the life of Queen Boudicca. The mistress in charge of prep moved from her desk to walk between the rows of girls and stopped half way down by Mary. She bent down and spoke in a soft whisper.

"You must be Mary Scovil. My name is Miss Rutherford. I was new last year. Do you have any questions about prep?"

Mary wanted to ask about the terrible thing but she knew that had nothing to do with prep. "Can I practice Indian club swinging for prep?"

Miss Rutherford smiled and said that all the practice for that was done during class. "But, if you are on the demonstration team for the end of the year, you have special practices."

"I'd like to do that." Then, sensing Miss Rutherford's kindness, she quickly added, "When can I see my two sisters who are in the senior school?"

"The two sides mix every Sunday for a half hour after chapel."

Miss Rutherford continued walking along the rows, stopping now and then. Mary went back to Queen Boudicca, forcing herself to stop thinking about next Sunday, five whole days away. She had to hurry with the last sentence after Miss Rutherford stood and said to return the homework to their dorm. Then, for a half hour before dinner, she said, they were to play catch with old tennis balls kept in a box just inside the door leading to the playing field.

After putting her prep in the drawer of her bedside table and making a quick trip to the WC, which, she discovered was the name for the bathroom, she picked up a worn tennis ball and hoped for a friendly partner. She stood at the side of one of the groups, but no one threw a ball to her. After a few minutes she took her ball, wandered off a little to throw it as high as possible before catching it. She was well practiced in this skill and was pleased when she caught most of her high tosses. After a while, the girl who said her name was "Louise" came over to her.

"That looks like fun."

"Yes, it's quite easy."

Just then Miss Rutherford rang a bell and Louise scampered back to her chums. As Mary brushed her hair before dinner, she again silently thanked her Aunt Bessie for having her hair cut short. Some of the girls braided their own hair or tied it back, especially for exercises, but she hated that pulled feeling and was grateful for her recently acquired freedom from major snarls, even if it meant she was a freak because of it. She might look as though she came from Mars, so she would just have to prove she was normal.

At the evening meal — her first at the school — Mary was determined to catch a glimpse of Wowsie or Trudy or Ayleene so she again sat facing the senior section. Sure enough, there was Wowsie walking toward her bench place, looking in her direction. Mary wanted to wave both arms above her head and call out but knew she mustn't. Instead, she followed Wowsie's lead, smiled, and wiggled her fingers at shoulder level in the tiniest wave. Wowsie knew her sister well, so just to make sure there was no verbal greeting, she put her index finger to her lips, hoping another smile would satisfy her lonely sibling until Sunday.

Miss Smith, still wearing her too tight corset, stood on the slightly raised platform at the far end of the hall while she waited for all the girls to be seated, then bowed her head and said the very same grace Mary had heard her father recite for as long as she could remember. At the thought of the rest of her family gathered around the Meadowland's dining table, Mary's eyes began to cloud with tears. She kept her head down for a few seconds after the "amen" trying to banish the urge to cry; she was not helped in this by Bully Girl sitting across from her, looking fierce. Generously decorating her baked potato with butter from a dish on the table, Mary managed to encourage the overflow to improve the overcooked cabbage. Following the meal, each girl was allowed up to two slices of bread with strawberry jam. They could choose water or cambric tea, or both. Mary was thirsty so she chose both.

After dinner, the junior girls could spend over a half hour in the little library, reading whatever they liked. Miss Rice made a note of the books selected for reading. Mary noticed a book titled *Black Beauty*. Knowing it was about a horse, she took it off the shelf, hoping to bring back happy memories of Meadowlands. Well before the library session was finished, however, it was clear this was not a cheerful book. But Mary was gripped by the story and knew by the time the library session ended that she had to continue reading whether it made her sad or not.

As the girls clattered up the staircase to their dorm, Bully Girl squeezed Mary into the bannister and whispered in her ear.

"Don't forget… one of these nights, something terrible…" hissed the much taller girl, with snapping brown eyes.

Mary's heart started thumping in her throat. She wanted to say something, but couldn't think of anything that would help. She tried to walk faster but another girl was in the way. She pretended she was deaf and had not heard, looking straight ahead. Bully Girl vanished among her friends, leaving Mary with the threat whirling around in her head.

She lost no time completing the going to bed routine, hoping to exchange a few words with Louise on her way back from the WC, but that was not possible as the only friendly girl had her head in her trunk and looked busy. Miss Rice popped in briefly to say she would be back in ten minutes for prayers. Mary was ready, so she took her homework out of the drawer and reviewed it, sitting on the bed trying to look occupied; but her thoughts were with the terrible thing.

When Miss Rice's readings and prayers were over, she walked down to Mary's bed.

"Helen Heaney is expected to arrive tomorrow, so you will have someone sleeping near you."

"Oh, good," Mary exclaimed. She wanted to blurt out why she was so pleased but knew she would have to explain and that would mean being a tattletale, which would make everything worse, so she just left her reply to those two words. She survived one night, so maybe she would another, especially if this God is on duty looking after them all as Miss Rice asked.

Mary tried the same approach as the previous night—facing the other beds, with her eyes almost closed, but not quite. After a long while, she saw the dark figure of a girl get out of the third bed beyond Helen's. She put on her dressing gown and slippers. Mary froze, but managed to sneak her thumb into her mouth to calm her fear. The girl started walking toward the door and probably the WC. Maybe on her way back… but no, it wasn't Bully Girl. The figure returned and quietly slipped into her bed. Mary rubbed her sweaty back dry on the sheets and resumed her vigil through half closed eyes. Her heart gradually calmed down and the need for sleep conquered her fear. Suddenly Mary realized she had pulled through a second night as Miss Rice threw back the drapes.

16

A Cruel Lesson

The second day, Wednesday, was not as daunting for Mary as Tuesday had been, though there were still many mysteries. She studied her schedule, discovering that English would be the first class, taught by the same mistress as History. Each week, two days of the English class would be for grammar and two for literature, with no class on Tuesdays. There were even classes scheduled for Saturday mornings. Saturday afternoons were for drama and sport. On Sundays, the boys from Kings School at the other end of the same property joined the girls for an hour-long chapel service. After chapel, the girls were required to go to their classroom, write a letter home, submit it for correction, and rewrite it if necessary.

As Mary was brushing her hair before lunch, Miss Rice came to her end of the dorm with a strange girl beside her.

"Helen, this is Mary Scovil, who is new this term. Helen has been here a year so she will be able to answer any questions you might have about the school. We must all help to cheer up Helen, as she has had a sad loss in her family."

The girls said "hello." Helen flushed with the reminder of the reason for her late arrival. A strong looking man with a big, black moustache and beard brought up Helen's trunk and set it at the bottom of her bed. Miss Rice suggested Mary wait for Helen to change into her uniform before they both went down for lunch.

Mary sat on the edge of her bed as Helen opened her trunk and spread out what she needed.

"I'm sorry you've had a funeral in your family," Mary offered as a friendly opening to possible conversation.

"Thanks. My mother died last week. I miss her so much. She was sick a long time," Helen answered as she wriggled out of her traveling clothes.

"Oh, mine died two years and two weeks ago and I still miss her. That's partly why I'm here, I think, to make less work for my aunt, though it's supposed to be to give me a better education."

"I came last year. My mother had TB and was in a tent in the garden quite a lot of the time. They were afraid I would catch it because I spent so much time with her."

"I was sent to New York for nearly a year when I was five because someone was in a tent in our garden."

"Well, we have at least two things in common," observed Helen, as she poked her head into her serge jumper dress. "How old are you?"

"I'll be ten in January," replied Mary.

"So, you're only nine. That's young to be away from home. You must be the youngest girl in the school. I came about a month before I was ten. I was homesick for ages. When's your birthday? We'll be the same age after that. Mine is the tenth of October"

"That's funny. My birthday is on the same day, the tenth, but in January, and I'm homesick already. The other girls are not friendly and one is beastly which makes it worse."

"I bet I know which one," Helen responded sympathetically. "We'd better hurry. Miss Rice will be having kittens."

Mary trotted beside her new friend, almost daring to feel happy. As Helen and Mary slipped into the two vacant places across from one another, they exchanged glances as if to say, "we'll talk later." Helen and the girl next to her then began catching up. Mary studied the cooling, grey soup; it looked almost delicious. Though Miss Rice had already spent a few minutes with Helen in the dorm, she now made a more general welcome.

"We are pleased to have you back with us, Helen."

"Thank you Miss Rice," Helen replied knowing the routine—always brevity and appreciation when replying to a mistress. Though Mary knew the welcome was certainly not meant for her, she could not help feeling a tiny bit included in the warmth of Miss Rice's voice.

Since this was the beginning of term, the English grammar class was mostly a review of parts of speech, how to use them and what they do. Mary had always found adverbs and adjectives a little confusing, though she knew one was telling more about a verb and the other about a noun. Miss Woodly gave them a helpful hint, for which Mary was grateful and remembered ever after—adverbs often ended in "ly." For prep, Miss Woodly dictated five sentences that needed to have six parts of speech underlined in different ways. Miss W. strongly believed more was learned if effort were concentrated so she had the class complete the assignment, then, to save herself work, told them to hand their scribblers to the girl in the seat ahead for marking. Mary thought she would like Miss Woodly.

The rest of Wednesday ticked along without much drama. The prep completed on Tuesday was accepted and a time was set for catching-up in French on Friday afternoons. Swinging the Indian clubs was the highlight of the day for Mary, along with a distant view of Wowsie, Trudy, and Ayleene at dinnertime. Mary was really looking forward to her piano practice and lesson at the end of Thursday afternoon, but Wednesday night had to be endured first. As they were getting ready for bed, Mary and Helen had a good talk about missing their mothers. Mary then had a strong urge to tell Helen about Bully Girl, but that would be tattling, so she decided to wait. Just having Helen next to her diluted her fear. But what if Helen didn't wake up when Bully Girl put a pillow over her face and held it there?

Mary used her so far successful technique of slipping into bed and half closing her eyes after prayers. No talking was allowed after that, but Helen turned in her direction and mouthed the words, "Good Night." Mary did the same, and they both grinned. Little did Helen realize that Mary was afraid she might be dead in the morning. After carefully keeping watch through her half-shut eyes, Mary again saw a girl creep out of bed and go to the WC. She stayed on guard, absorbing every sigh, cough, and sound of someone turning in their bed, until her little body surrendered to the need for sleep.

As soon as Miss Rice again welcomed sunlight into the dorm, Mary remembered this was Thursday and the day for her late afternoon piano practice and lesson. After a bearable day, helped by chats with Helen, practice time came. She had already gone over her piano prep three times and was now ready to put her fingers on the keys. Mary arrived five minutes early and occupied the chair just outside the music room. Miss Steel soon opened the door and told Mary to go in and practice for a half hour, after which she would have her lesson. Just sitting alone at the piano was a thrill. Her fingers ran up and down the keys, playing the "scales," as Miss Steel called them. How exciting to make music! Then she tried "Bobby Shafto" from the sheet music on the piano and thought she did quite well, once she figured out which keys to press. When Miss Steel came back, she had a long, wooden yardstick in her hand. She complimented Mary and asked her to play "Bobby Shafto" again. In her enthusiasm to show Miss Steel how well she could play, Mary hit a wrong note, but kept going. Whack! Down came the yardstick on the backs of her fingers, which hurt and surprised her so much she shouted, "Ouch" at the top of her voice and burst into tears.

"Quiet. When you hit a wrong note, never proceed. Always correct the note and go on. Try again from the beginning."

Mary knew there was no way out so she tried to do as she was told. She managed two lines before making another mistake, but quickly found the correct note. Her anxiety now caused her fingers to tremble. She had to go back and repeat those two lines until they were perfect the first time and then on to another and another until the end. The tune was in Mary's head so when the note was wrong she immediately knew but was terrified she wouldn't get the correction made before another whack. Her prep before next Tuesday was to practice the piece until it was perfect the first time and to work on the scales that were set out in sheet music.

The knuckles on Mary's hands were red and swollen, matching her flushed cheeks as she left the practice room. She was frightened, disappointed, and confused. She had expected learning to play the piano would be a happy experience. It was now tinged with fear and pain. If only Miss Steel weren't so strict! She confided her misery to Helen as they were brushing their hair before dinner. Helen said she wasn't at all musical and neither were her parents so they didn't say she had to learn the piano, but she had heard that Miss Steel lived up to her name and was not at all forgiving of mistakes.

"Your knuckles look sore. Maybe you should soak them in cold water".

Any suggestion sounded good to Mary so she did just that for a few minutes, and reported a small improvement as they headed for the dining room.

Mary was quick to wiggle in to occupy the place next to Helen on the bench. When Miss Rice lifted her head after grace, her eyes settled on Mary's red knuckles, then on Mary's red eyes. Mary knew Miss Rice knew. She wondered whether she would be punished for being punished.

After dinner, it was back to the classroom for homework and then a blessed hour outside on a warm, mid-September evening. Mary could see the senior girls being given tennis lessons at the far end of the playing field, too far to spot anyone. The juniors were taught the finer points of croquet and supervised while they played in two teams. The team not playing was required to watch and think how they might have played differently, or to applaud a good shot. Helen kept an eye on Mary to make sure she was paying attention, but that was hardly necessary as Mary was never far from her one friend.

Bedtime loomed. Mary was hopeful of another night on this earth, but she knew if she became too relaxed Bully Girl might strike, so she followed what had become her nightly routine—staying awake as long as possible. Thinking about what her first Friday would bring would be helpful. She knew that in order not to overtax the hot water system, two students in the junior dorm were assigned to have baths each night, except on Sunday. She and Helen were both assigned for Friday night. Mary remembered that on Friday she would have her first catching-up French lesson with Mademoiselle Guigon, who did not seem too strict. She had learned how to smile and practiced quite often, unlike some of the teachers. Mary got a happy feeling about her catching-up lesson and tried not to think of next Tuesday's piano torment. She thought more about the usual routine of classes, homework, and meals, about the possible pleasures of French, and about a nice, long bath on Friday night.

All this was swirling around in Mary's head, as she lay facing the row of sleeping girls. As her eyelashes started to flutter with the need for sleep, she accidentally brushed the knuckles of her right hand across the rough blanket, sending a shot of pain up her arm. She quickly put her knuckles to her mouth, warming the joints and taking away some of the pain. Miss Rice's god was not looking after her very well, but at least no pillow had been held over her face. Not yet. Prompted by her hurting knuckles, Mary's thoughts turned to the horrible Miss Steel who had not only hurt her but had turned her beautiful piano lessons into a misery. How would she survive next Tuesday afternoon? On Sunday when she wrote to Aunt Bessie and Father she would tell them. Composing that letter in her head kept Mary awake for another half hour or more, and then, it was Friday morning.

17

Hiding the Truth

When Miss Rice opened the curtains, Mary felt she had only just fallen asleep but automatically went through the getting up routine. Though her knuckles hurt when she bent them, she managed to fasten all her buttons in time to go down for breakfast with Helen and the others. She pushed herself through the day, determined not to fall asleep in class, though it was a near miss during adverb spotting. Her catching-up French lesson found Mary so agitated about the need to stay awake that she caught herself each time she started to nod off.

She left Mademoiselle's room clutching a long list of vocabulary to learn before the next Friday and headed directly to the library. At last, for forty minutes before dinner, she could plunge into reading *Black Beauty* with no questions asked or answers expected. After dinner it was back to homework prep. Mary devised a way to stay awake while doing homework. She propped her head on her bent left arm. If she started to fall asleep her arm would flop down, her head would jerk and she would wake up. She survived without reprimand for her homework, though she knew it was not her best effort.

A half hour before bedtime, Helen and Mary, accompanied by Miss Rice climbed the stairs in preparation for their baths. The white porcelain tub, surrounded by curtains, sat on its substantial lion claws at one end of the bathroom. Six basins lined the opposite wall. The water closets were in the adjoining room with separate cubicles for each one. Miss Rice, noticing the dark circles under Mary's eyes and her still red knuckles, suggested she bathe first.

She told Mary to undress at her bed and, wearing just her dressing gown and slippers and carrying her nightdress, to come to the tub with her towel and face flannel. Miss Rice directed her to go behind the curtain, pass her robe out, as the hook was too high for Mary to reach, climb into the bath and complete her ablutions in five minutes. Once Mary was settled into the comfortably warm water, Miss Rice said she would be just outside the room in case Mary needed her and to keep other girls from entering. Hair was shampooed only once a month.

Mary was less than a week from home-washed hair so a little cap was provided to keep it dry on this occasion.

The warmth of the bath so relaxed Mary that when she returned to her dorm she slipped into her bed and fell fast asleep. She was oblivious of Helen retuning from her bath and of the others preparing for bed. Miss Rice walked down to Mary's bed to find out why she was not kneeling for prayers. There was no response when she called Mary's name. Miss Rice did not have the heart to rouse the tired and bruised little girl, so left her to nature's healing medicine.

Five nights and I'm still alive, thought Mary, as Miss Rice's "Good Morning, girls" roused all twelve. Saturday might not have regular classes, but it was no day to be lazy. Once they were through the usual skimpy attention to ablutions, dressed in games' clothes — voluminous navy serge bloomers, and middy blouses — breakfast, bowels, and prayers attended to, Miss Smith, the headmistress, addressed the students. "She is so *upright*," thought Mary. "I wonder if she sleeps in her whalebone corsets. Perhaps that's why she is in change of everything; she is straighter than everyone else. It makes her look as though she holds the answers to all questions."

True to form, the headmistress announced her instructions for the day's activities. "As the weather is dry, there will be outside activity for the juniors in the morning and for the seniors in the afternoon consisting of tennis lessons, croquet, Indian club swinging, and races. There are two grass tennis courts. Four girls can be instructed at one time for fifty minutes while the others will participate, under supervision, in the alternative activities, until it is their turn for tennis. Meanwhile, the seniors will remain in the hall for drama. After lunch the two groups change places."

Mary spotted Wowsie, Trudy, and Ayleene, across the great divide. As she caught their attention, all three gave the tiniest of smiles, which she interpreted to mean, "We'll talk tomorrow."

Though her fingers were still a little stiff, Mary enjoyed most of the morning. The tennis racquet was heavy for her small wrists but she usually hit the ball, though serving was not always successful. Indian club swinging was even more fun than last time. The mistress with the big nose encouraged Mary saying she was very good at that form of exercise. Croquet took patience and not too much energy. Since her legs were shorter than all the other girls, Mary did not expect to do well in races, but she applied what she had learned at the Gagetown Grammar and made sure she got off to a good start and to put on a spurt near the end. Bully Girl, with her long legs — like a heron — won every race she was in. Though unlikely, Mary secretly longed to beat her but then realized her life was worth more than winning a race.

The afternoon drama class was taken by the headmistress who introduced the session by telling the twelve juniors they would be working on *Alice in Wonderland* for the end-of-term play. They would all have parts. But first they would need to learn something about basic acting, such as how to project the voice, how to whisper and yet be heard, how to cry, to laugh, to fall without hurting and a dozen other tricks. Mary forgot Miss Smith's whalebones as she concentrated on her instruction and practiced with Helen when partners were needed. The two hours flew by and then tea and biscuits and back to *Black Beauty*.

As Mary walked from the WC toward her bed and prayers that evening, she realized her knuckles had not bothered her all afternoon. A warm feeling of happiness came from somewhere and she smiled a little. Just then Bully Girl looked in Mary's direction, her frown as black as a thundercloud. Again, she whispered, "Don't forget, one of these nights …" After a quick glance in the bully's direction, Mary pretended she had not heard, but by the time she reached her bed a knot in her stomach had replaced the smile on her lips. At Miss Rice's signal for prayer-time she knelt by her bed and found herself silently praying, "Dear Miss Rice's God, please do as she asks and watch over us and keep Bully Girl from killing me. Amen."

The sixth night went much the same as the others, a huge effort to stay awake and then succumbing to the need for sleep. Sunday was different from the other days; boiled eggs plus toast and marmalade instead of slimy porridge for breakfast. Mary neatly sliced off the top of her egg with one blow, a trick that was her specialty. She thought the cook could use a lesson from Amelia, who knew how to make boiled eggs slightly firm but not rubbery like this one. However, she quickly told herself not to complain about a bullet-hard egg when she should be pleased with another night's survival.

Chapel was a grand affair, lasting more than an hour. The boys from Kings School took up one side. There were a lot of them, maybe fifty or more. They were all wearing dark grey suits with different sorts of ties. Mary moved her eyes but not her head to watch them as they shuffled over the hardwood floor to their benches. She noticed one boy with ears sticking out more than most, and a body which had not caught up to his large head. How surprised she would have been just then if someone said, "This is the boy you will marry."

Three masters came with the boys and sat on the ends of the rows. The headmaster, who looked like a sort of rector, wore a white "dog collar" beneath his pink, round face. He stood at the front with Miss Smith, who, in her very straight way, towered over him. It all began to sound like Matins in the Jemseg church on a Sunday morning. Mary thought of her family at home in the front pew listening to the same words, hoping the sermon would not be too long. She thought about Mr. Hatheway standing in the pulpit in Jemseg and tried to turn the headmaster into him by squinting. In spite of them seeming to have the same need to give a long sermon, no transformation took place. But they had another thing in common; Mary was never quite sure just what Mr. Hatheway was trying to say. The headmaster was perhaps a little clearer, but just when she was almost able to latch on to a thought, he would shift to something else. She wanted to ask questions, but of course could not. At least she knew all the words and tunes to the hymns and sang lustily.

Chapel was over. The boys left and the time finally arrived for the great divide to be breached. After nearly a week of only distant glances, Mary could at last talk with her sisters and cousin. She hugged each of them so tightly and for so long they protested a bit. Mary was afraid if she let go they would disappear.

"Save some for next Sunday," Wowsie suggested.

"I have to talk to you about things. Let's sit down over there."

Mary led the three seniors to an unoccupied out of the way corner. Out poured Mary's misery. Bully Girl's threats and her whacked knuckles were at the top of the list, followed by the slimy porridge and only five minutes in the bath.

"I'm going to tell Aunt Bessie and Father in today's letter. Will you, too, so they will know I'm not making it up?"

"We can't and you can't," shot back Wowsie. "All the letters are checked for spelling and grammar mistakes and anything bad that happens at school. If you write anything bad about school, you'll have to rewrite the letter. They say it's so families don't worry about us."

Mary was astonished at Wowsie's words. She tried to argue back but was speechless.

Trudy quickly changed the subject. "Have you made any friends?"

"One. Helen. She's over there with her back to us. She sleeps in the bed next to mine. Her mother died, too. She says everyone knows Miss Steel is strict."

Trudy lowered her voice and replied; "There's a rumour that Miss Steel's father gave a lot of money to the school, so Miss Smith has to keep her on. You can't give up piano until the end of term, so you'll just have to put up with it, and make sure you don't hit any wrong notes."

Wowsie had one more bit of advice. "If your knuckles get very sore, you can ask to see the nurse who comes on Saturday after lunch, every other week. Maybe she will give you some salve to help. You could ask her to bandage them, which might make Miss Steel think twice or at least it would be like a cushion."

"The way to get along here is never to be a tattle tale, except about something good," added Ayleene.

"I haven't even told Helen about Bully Girl."

"Best not to; it would complicate things," Wowsie advised.

Nothing very cheering had come out this conversation that Mary had so been looking forward to and the half hour was rapidly dwindling. Mary shifted to questions.

"Have you heard from Meadowlands yet?"

"No, we aren't allowed letters until we have sent one, so sometime this week we will have news."

Suddenly, a mistress rang the hand bell indicating the half hour had truly vanished. Again hugs all around, and then Mary watched the three girls disappear, their long hair dancing over their retreating pinafores. She stayed in her chair, digesting what she had been told. She now realized she was basically on her own in spite of the nearness of her sisters and cousin. She could not prevent her eyes from welling up and sending a tear down each cheek as she stared at a distant window.

"Cheer up, Mary, at least you have family here," Helen said as she walked over to her friend and sat down.

"I can't believe I'm not allowed to write the truth home."

"Telling them might mean they wouldn't let you stay. If everyone did that there wouldn't be a school. It gets better after you've been here a while. You'll see. Let's go and wash our hands or we'll be late for lunch. I smell roast beef."

Helen's encouragement helped Mary feel a little better, but she wondered what would happen to the school if one of the juniors were found lifeless with a pillow over her face. Indeed, Helen's nose was accurate. Roast beef and Yorkshire pudding made deliciously soggy with gravy, along with carrots and fluffy potatoes with only a few lumps, followed by treacle tart awaited the ever hungry, growing girls. Sunday lunch helped to soothe the frustrations of the morning. Directly afterward, came letter writing in the junior classroom, supervised by Miss Rice. The process was so frustrating for Mary that it almost obliterated the joy of the yummy lunch. She decided to try to do her best, not telling the whole truth, but not lying either and trying hard to spell words correctly.

Miss Rice quickly reviewed Mary's letter and circled three spelling mistakes that needed to be corrected. After making sure she knew the right spellings, Mary carefully re-wrote the letter, grateful that Miss Rice had not tried to get rid of the little hints of misery. Mary had known for a long time, well before Edgehill, maybe since New York when she was five, that the best way to be happy was not only to enjoy the good parts of what she was doing now, but also to have something to look forward to, even something quite small, like mashed potatoes without lumps.

As she handed in her letter home and had it finally approved, including the envelope addressed to "Morris Scovil, Esq." (which is the way Miss Rice said was correct), Mary immediately pressed her happiness button, looking forward to a reply. Wowsie said there might be one this week. She needed something to overcome the disappointment still rattling around inside her of not being able to write about Bully Girl or Miss Steel's yardstick.

Aunt Bessie was always so keen on telling the truth. Surely she would be upset if she knew. Was not telling the whole truth the same as telling a lie? She knew even grownups did not always say the whole truth. If they did, other people would be cross or sad. Ah, that's what Wowsie said about not writing any misery stories home. They would make Aunt Bessie and Father cross and certainly sad. The school didn't want parents cross and sad. They would certainly be cross and sad if she died from a pillow over her face or broken finger bones; oh well, look forward, always look forward.

*　*　*　*　*

Both Bessie and Mod were feeling anxious about Mary settling into boarding school life. Being high strung and opinionated were not the best attributes for happiness in a communal setting. Bessie reminded Morris to be sure to collect the mailbag before he rowed himself and Roger home from school on Wednesday. Perhaps the girls' Sunday letters would have arrived.

All the remaining Meadowland's family gathered around the dining table when Mod opened the bag. Mixed with medical journals, newspapers from New York and a copy of the latest *The Ladies' Home Journal* were three letters, all postmarked "Windsor, N.S." As they were read, Amelia found an excuse to enter the dining room, watering the potted plants on the table by the windows. Mod picked up Mary's and gave Bessie, Elizabeth's and Morris, Gertrude's. They all sat down, including Roger, who waited impatiently to hear his sisters' words. Mary's were the ones they all wanted to hear first. Mod read the perfectly spelled few sentences from his youngest daughter whom he missed more than he would ever admit.

"What 'not nice' things happen when Mary makes a wrong note?" Roger
wanted to know.

"Probably the piano teacher shouts at her," offered Morris.

"I'm glad to hear she has made a friend in the first week," Bessie said,
changing the subject. She had experienced something of bad tempered
piano teachers in her youth. She knew Mary would feel very disheartened
that her much anticipated music lessons were flawed.

"It looks as though Mary is missing your cooking, Amelia," Mod said
to the plant waterer, who looked pleased and said, "Oh, the dear girl."

Elizabeth and Gertrude's well-practiced letter writing was also perfectly
spelled and, of course, only informative about their school work, drama
class, tennis progress, friends. Each letter had two positive references
to Mary.

"Let's all write this evening after supper so the boys can take them over
tomorrow," Bessie suggested. "They might be at Edgehill on Friday." Poor
Mary is obviously missing home, Bessie thought without saying it.

Three well-filled envelopes were handed to Morris before bedtime.
He would make sure they got into tomorrow's mail. He would not be to
blame if they didn't arrive at Edgehill by Friday. He missed his sisters, but
especially his little one and wished she had not gone away. But he knew it
was best for her, once she got used to it all.

Bessie was struck by how much life at Meadowlands was simplified
with the three girls away at school. There were no female moods, no flying
into unreasonable annoyance, no pouting, no one saying, "I'm going to the
garden to eat worms," though none of this happened often. Lacking his
heroine, Roger had transferred his need for company to Morris who found
more of interest in his baby brother than formerly. Rowing to and from

school did more than enlarge Morris's biceps. Their chats reminded him of his own way of looking at his small world nine years previously and he vowed to educate his little brother in ways that grownups did not seem to bother with. Sensing this, Roger constantly asked questions, which Morris did his best to answer.

18

Moments of Triumph

One evening a week, usually Saturday, Miss Rice was relieved of her duties as head of the junior dormitory by Mademoiselle Guigon, which turned out to be lucky for Mary. Early in the term, Miss Rice informed the girls she expected attention to manners and good behaviour. The rules were posted on the wall by the dormitory door. If, during any week, there were two broken rules by any girls, everyone had better be careful because a third misdemeanour in the same week by anyone would mean all the juniors would go to bed an hour early on Saturday evening.

During her third week at Edgehill, now with permanent dark circles under her eyes and perpetually sore knuckles, Mary ran up the stairs after her Thursday piano lesson. Her intention was to soak her fingers in cold water and hold a cold face flannel over her eyes and cheeks to cool the red blotches. Unfortunately Miss Rice was coming down at that same moment.

"Mary, no one is allowed to run on the stairs. It's dangerous."

"But..."

"I have to give you a detention. You're the third this week, so you won't be popular, I'm afraid, but the rules have to be obeyed."

"Yes, Miss Rice." Mary knew this was all she should say.

Detentions were posted on the dorm wall next to the rules, so by Saturday morning, when Mademoiselle Guigon pulled back the curtains, all the girls knew that the punishment—the first of the term—was Mary's fault. While Mary was brushing her blessedly short hair, the girl who slept next to Bully Girl came down to the miscreant's bedside.

"You might get out of your detention and free us all if you give Mademoiselle Guigon a postcard for her nephew in France. He collects them; do you?"

"Of course. I'll try. Thanks."

Mary quickly dug into her belongings in her trunk at the bottom of her bed and found her least favourite post card, one with rather pale flowers and bent corners. She picked it up and approached the mistress who was sitting at her small desk at the end of the dorm near the door, making sure the girls behaved themselves.

"Mademoiselle Guigon, do you think your nephew in France would like this postcard for his collection?"

A wisp of black hair fell over M's forehead. She pushed it behind an ear, trying unsuccessfully to restrain it, while she studied the pallid card. She turned it over and over and, with a little frown, said, "Non Marie, it is not goot. The edges are broken."

"Oh," Mary acknowledged.

Quickly returning to her trunk, she replaced the rejected card and selected the prize of her collection. She thought it was gorgeous. Deep purple flowers embossed with velvet stood out on a lush green landscape. It was her latest acquisition. Cousin Sophie sent it on her trip back to Boston. But, if she must, she must.

"Do you think your nephew would like this one?" asked Mary as she placed her favourite postcard in the mistress' hand.

"Ah, yes, leettle Marie, I think he might. Thank you."

Mary looked into Mademoiselle Guigon's eyes for as long as she dared, pleading, but said nothing more. As she turned and took two steps, the mistress stopped her.

"Wait, Marie, as you have been so kind, you can be excused your detention."

She stood, walked to the crime sheet and drew a line through Mary Scovil's name. Mary's walk back to her bed was a mixture of misery and triumph. Several girls gave her sly smiles of approval. Most of all she treasured that Helen, with her back to the rest of the girls, gave her a big grin.

After quick ablutions, discretely donning her night dress, evening prayer, and a private entreaty to Miss Rice's god for protection (she assumed Mademoiselle Guigon's god was the same or at least related), Mary slipped into bed, hopeful for a good night's sleep. But the thought crept into her mind that if she relaxed too much, this might be the very night Bully Girl would strike, especially since there was no smile of appreciation for her sacrifice on BG's face along with others. So Mary stuck with her routine, eyes just slightly open for as long as she possibly could, trying to remember French vocabulary, words to songs, composing a letter home for tomorrow, or anything that would keep her brain awake and the ability to fly out of bed if BG came creeping in her direction with a pillow.

Sunday morning arrived without mishap during the night, then the rubbery boiled egg, toast and marmalade, and chapel, before a too brief talk with her sisters and cousin. Mary regaled them with the details of the surrender of her best postcard in order not to have all the girls mad at her.

"Isn't that called bribery?" Mary asked Wowsie.

"Yes, but we don't use that word when it applies to a mistress. It's called negotiating when we do it with them."

* * * * *

After gymnastics on one cool but sunny afternoon, Miss Foote said, "Mary Scovil, please stay behind after class."

Mary reddened with surprise, but when she saw the mistress was smiling, her anxiety nearly vanished, but not quite. Boarding school life was full of unpleasant twists, so Mary did not abandon all her apprehension.

"Don't worry, Mary. It's not a detention," Miss Foote said and smiled again.

Mary relaxed.

When they were alone, the gym teacher asked, "Would you like to lead the school in Indian club swinging at Sports Day in two weeks?"

"Yes, please, Miss," replied Mary. "But won't a senior girl do that?"

"No, I want you to do it. You have a special ability. We'll work out a routine. You can practice with me and then with the whole school before the Sports Day."

The gym teacher knew the school governors, other local dignitaries, and parents who lived nearby and would attend the ceremonies would be impressed by this tiny girl and her unusual athletic ability. A senior might be as expert technically, but Mary's whole body responded to the drill, which greatly enhanced the routine. Miss Foote was a young teacher and she could see Mary was not the happiest of girls with those dark circles under her eyes and her fiery red knuckles, obviously a victim of piano lessons. Mary reminded her of her little niece, back in London, with her corn silk hair and delphinium blue eyes.

As Mary walked off the games field, she wished she didn't have to wait until Sunday to share her good news with her sisters and in her letter to Aunt Bessie and Father; at last, something that made her happy and would probably make them happy as well. She knew, however, that Bully Girl would be jealous.

* * * * *

Bessie, Mod and Morris were more than happy that the tone of Mary's letters changed for the better. Roger was confused. Why was swinging pieces of wood in the air making everyone so pleased?

"It's like being chosen to recite at a Christmas concert," Mod offered.

Roger understood his father's explanation. Mary was always good at anything that was bouncy and hiding in small places like a worm, so maybe

133

being wiggly made her the best with those clubs. He was pleased for her if that's what she wanted to do, but knew he would not be chosen to recite in front of the whole school, ever. He certainly hoped he wouldn't.

*   *   *   *

Miss Smith looked out of her office window at 9 a.m. on Sports Day. Mistresses were marking off tracks and putting up signs on little posts. The sun came and went behind scudding clouds. Would the day be rainless? Mid-October often was wet. Holding a version of Sports Day inside was a disappointment five years ago, when it rained so much Noah would have felt at home. She knew it was somewhat blasphemous to pray for a dry day, but before she could dwell on its proprietary, she did just that, as she walked out onto the field to encourage her staff and to make sure they were setting up correctly.

On the previous Wednesday, Mary asked Miss Foote, if she could be excused her piano lesson on Thursday. No explanation was needed. Both Miss Foote and Mary knew it was easier to swing Indian clubs if her knuckles were not sore. Miss Foote said she could be excused. By Friday, Mary was so excited she slept even less than usual. She noticed that Bully Girl had been frowning at her a lot lately. Surely BG would not deprive her of her moment of glory the night before the great day. Worrying about the possibility deprived her of much needed sleep as well.

Indian club swinging was to be the finale — the whole school on show. Mary donned her gymnastic clothes — a clean middy blouse and navy serge bloomers that came nearly to her knees. She was careful no slimy porridge fell on either and the same with the "light lunch" of sandwiches and cambric tea.

When guests had assembled on dining room benches and classroom chairs under a row of maple trees at the edge of the playing field, Miss Smith welcomed them all, announcing the order of events. She encouraged the guests to walk around the edge of the field should they wish a better view. Bursts of sun prompted Miss Smith to feel that her childish prayer might be answered after all but she noticed that most visitors pessimistically carried umbrellas.

The afternoon was filled with perspiring girls, trying to be first or at least to perform their best. Shortly before four o'clock, Miss Foote told Mary, who was in a huddle with Helen, that the finale would take place in five minutes directly in front of the guests. In spite of all the practice sessions, Mary felt a little nervous but knew she had mastered the routine. At least she had her back to the visitors, except when she turned around, at the end, and with the whole school would bow slightly and try to remember to smile. (Miss Smith had decided that curtsies in serge bloomers would look absurd). When the grand finale was performed, Miss Foote was right about tiny Mary Scovil endearing herself to the governors and parents.

Extended clapping followed the almost perfect performance. From her position off to one side, Miss Foote noticed a senior girl in the back row being a little late with one movement. The headmistress announced the first and second place winners in all sports, then added, "Thank you girls. You had better run to your reward in the dining room."

The guest's umbrellas flicked open in response to a few drops of rain now penetrating their leafy canopy. Before Mary could dash to shelter, Miss Smith put her hand on Mary's slim shoulder and steered her toward the Chairman of the Board of Governors and his wife. They congratulated her on her performance and shook her hand. Mary smiled, said, "Thank you," and curtsied out of habit in spite of the bloomers.

"You'd better run along, Mary," smiled Miss Smith who had now raised her umbrella ready to share with any members of the Board who needed protection. Mary flew across the open lawn through the cloudburst but was thoroughly soaked by the time she dripped puddles on the dining room floor. Having been called over to meet the Chairman of the Board and his wife, she was the only girl to be so drenched. Miss Rice appeared with a towel, dried Mary's hair somewhat and tried to blot the moisture from her shoulders. There was no suggestion of changing just yet, as it was usual for the guests to speak with the girls, partly as a learning experience for the students in making conversation with adults. After tea and biscuits for the visitors and lemonade for the students, a number of guests sought out the little, wet, Indian club swinging expert for congratulations and conversation. Wowsie, Trudy, and Ayleene had also performed well and were among the winners. They especially excelled at tennis. They compared achievements with Mary and praised her performance, which warmed her chilled body just a bit.

"You look as though you've been swimming," Wowsie told her little sister. "You'd better change."

Just then Miss Rice noticed Mary's shivering, drowned rat appearance, and told her to go and completely change out of her wet clothes and, after a good dry-off, put on her regular uniform.

"Then come join the juniors in the library until dinner," she added.

Mary was happy to return to *Black Beauty* again, now able to relax knowing she had done as well as she could. She was pleased with the afternoon. Even Bully Girl followed her lead with the Indian clubs but did not smile at the end as they were told to do. In spite of her long legs Bully Girl did not come first in any of the races. She would probably frown more than usual.

Never mind, she thought, I'm safe for now—back to *Black Beauty*. The next she knew was hearing Helen whispering in her ear, "Wake up Mary, you've fallen asleep."

Once in bed for the night, Mary's shivering body did not allow her the release of sleep until she added her dressing gown on top of her long nightdress. When Miss Rice pulled back the curtains to show a drizzling day, Mary's first sensations were a scratchy throat and a hot head. It was Sunday, so there wasn't the scramble of a weekday since breakfast was a half hour later than usual. The hard boiled egg did not bother her, but the crisp toast, even with marmalade, was rough on her increasingly sore throat. She was looking forward to writing home about yesterday and talking more with her sisters and cousin. There was an hour long chapel service before any enjoyment, though she usually quite liked singing hymns, especially if they were familiar and reminded her of sitting in the front pew at their Jemseg church. Later, back in the junior dormitory while Mary was brushing her hair before lunch, she noticed Helen looking at her in a strange way.

"Mary, are you feeling alright?"

"No. I have a sore throat and a hot head. Aunt Bessie would send me to bed, but I'm not sure what to do here."

"Tell Miss Rice. She's just in the corridor. I'll come with you."

Miss Rice could see little Mary was not well, and feeling guilty about allowing her to mix with the guests yesterday before changing her wet clothes, the mistress quickly responded by taking Mary's temperature. It was nearly 102 degrees, quite high enough to be sent to the infirmary.

"A senior is leaving the Infirmary this afternoon, so nurse will be on duty. Helen, go with Mary and make sure the nurse sees her immediately."

19

Relapse

Bessie, Mod and the boys received no news from Mary that week, but they did get a detailed account from her sisters of how she led the whole school in Indian club swinging, and about their prowess at tennis and other sports. They also received a short note from Miss Smith notifying them of Mary being admitted to the infirmary with a sore throat and a temperature brought on, no doubt, from the unfortunate weather of the previous day. The headmistress always followed school rules, informing the parents whenever a girl developed an abnormal temperature and was admitted to the infirmary. She added that she would keep Mr. Scovil and Miss Scovil informed of any changes in Mary's condition, and a quick recovery was expected.

"Miss Smith takes her duties seriously, I'm glad to see," Bessie said to Mod that evening as she poured his tea. "This session in the infirmary shouldn't last long. In my experience children develop illnesses quickly but often recover just as quickly, unless it's serious, of course."

"Hmm. You're the expert. Let's hope it's a simple cold," Mod added before taking a second bite of a particularly tasty pound cake.

"If we write to Mary this evening, we can catch tomorrow's mail," said Bessie, remembering how her past charges suffered more from homesickness when they were ill. She had already put the boys' contributions from last evening in an envelope. Morris drew a little pencil sketch of Trixie, the family border collie as she was sleeping in front of the stove and Roger produced his version of a horse's head, copying Morris's words underneath, "GET WELL SOON".

* * * * *

Mary certainly had all the symptoms of a heavy cold. She sneezed and shivered for two days and nights.

"Here's a "pig" to keep your feet warm," the nurse said as she came toward Mary's bed.

"Oh no, not another crazy boarding school thing," thought Mary as she braced herself to accept a live pig in her bed. She smiled with relief when she saw the nurse was carrying a pottery jar, with an opening at one end shaped like a pig's snout.

"It's full of hot water. You'll soon be as warm as toast. Careful you don't stub your toes on it, Mary. This "pig" can bite," the nurse joked.

She seemed to be in a good mood, so Mary summoned enough courage to ask for another blanket. The combination of "pig" and blanket at last gave her enough warmth for an hour's sleep, in spite of a completely stuffed nose and open, dry mouth.

Mary's third night in the "sicker," as the girls called it, was restless, like the other two, with the usual nose blowing and need to sip water. She did not feel at all hungry, but the nurse urged her to consume three bowls of broth during the next day and a scrambled egg with fingers of bread and butter. Helen visited her every day, bringing her current gossip and news about class work, but was made to stand at the door. Miss Rice, still feeling responsible for Mary's chill and resulting cold, dropped in two or three times every day. Miss Smith also made a daily visit but mostly talked with the nurse, who informed her the patient's temperature had not decreased. Miss Smith gave Wowsie and Trudy permission to visit briefly. Like Helen, they stood at the door for a few minutes. It was a treat for Mary to see them. She felt more alive when they visited, as though they pumped some special family medicine into her as they chatted in the door way.

Half way through the fourth night, Mary began to cough. The dry hacking woke up the nurse who produced a half spoonful of thick honey for Mary to lick and swallow gradually, soothing her rough throat and calming her cough for a while. The nurse refilled the "pig" with hot water and gave the patient another pillow so she would not be lying so flat. She placed a little kidney shaped enamel dish on a stand by the bed for spitting.

"At least my knuckles will be pleased I'm in the 'sicker,'" thought Mary as she realized that Thursday, the usual day for dreading her piano lesson, had now arrived. There was another advantage to being sick—Bully Girl was far away. The nurse plumped up a third pillow so her coughing would not be such a strain. Before breakfast, nurse produced a spoonful of warmed honey with a little saucer underneath to catch any drips. Mary licked it slowly to prolong the pleasure and relaxed against her pillows. A freshly filled "pig" at her feet added to her comfort.

Miss Rice's first visit of the day brought homework—mostly history and English reading and some new French verbs to master. A coughing spell coincided with her placing the books on the bedside table, increasing her feelings of responsibility for this little girl's misery. As she looked down at the pale child, Miss Rice knew without a doubt that Mary's lowered resistance greatly hampered her ability to throw off her cold. She was aware that Mary was not sleeping well and lived in fear of the piano mistress. It was troubling to her that boarding schools can be cruel and uncomfortable places for some children. She told Mary she would be back after lunch.

Mary's cold dragged on, settling into bronchitis, though the headmistress was able to inform Meadowlands that her temperature had dropped to a little over one hundred degrees. A doctor from Windsor was called in. He recommended daily poultices on her chest and back, an abundance of nourishing fluids, sitting up in a chair for an hour at a time and three five minute walks around the room each day, but no return to the dormitory.

The doctor came back in a week and announced the patient could sit in a chair all day, except for a rest in the afternoon; she could get back to her studies but remain in the infirmary to prevent any infection from spreading. Regular meals were brought to her on a tray. Helen came whenever she could and Miss Rice brought and collected her prep. Wowsie and Trudy continued to look in daily. One morning the nurse discovered that her charge's temperature was normal and continued to be so that evening. She still had a cough, but it was now loose. When Miss Smith visited before bedtime, the nurse said she thought Mary was no longer infectious and could return to the dormitory. Her occasional cough was not apt to disturb the other girls, but perhaps she should not attempt gymnastics or outdoor exercise for a few days. Miss Smith had confidence in the nurse. After nearly three weeks in its protective cocoon, the little patient vacated the "sicker" with mixed feelings.

Getting back to a busy routine was not easy, but in a few days Mary's usual energy returned. Helen reminded her of schedules which had leaked out of her brain. Bully Girl continued to frown at her so Mary knew she still might attack. The security of the "sicker" vanished giving way to the usual wakefulness far into the night.

Around the middle of November, Miss Smith announced to the school during assembly that the governors decided the interior of the school should be upgraded and completely painted during the Christmas holidays, which would last for a month, from the 10th of December until January 10th.

Miss Smith then added; "This means that all girls and staff will vacate the school for that period. Anyone who cannot return home will be accommodated in a house in Windsor made available by the governors. Letters will be sent to all parents and guardians this week."

Mary could not believe her ears. Christmas at Meadowlands! Though this arrangement made for great inconvenience for many parents — collecting their children and returning them in winter weather—the governors made this decision because the painters and other workmen gave reduced rates during this time. Redecorating would still entail considerable expense but not having any girls to feed during the holidays would pay for some of it. Mistresses who did not have a home in Canada could stay in Windsor along with several girls, whose parents were abroad, but that expense would be negligible, especially since a wealthy governor was lending a house to the school free of charge.

20

A Reprieve

Broad smiles covered all faces when Mod read Miss Smith's letter aloud at the supper table. Everyone had an idea about how to make the holiday more than special. In two days, cousin Frank's distinctive writing appeared on one envelope when the mailbag was emptied. He said he would collect the Scovil girls along with his Ayleene on December 10th and bring them to St. John for a couple of days, if Mod could pick up his girls on the twelfth or thereabouts. They were welcome to stay longer, but no doubt they would want to join the Meadowlands family as soon as convenient.

"The twelfth it will be," said Mod immediately.

That evening, Bessie and Mod discussed the unexpected but welcome news over their tea and cake. Bessie had prepared a new recipe for Mod's taste buds—"Fruit Tea Cake." It was perhaps a little heavy for so late in the evening, but she was anxious for his opinion of this unusual recipe. It called for five different dried fruits to be chopped and soaked overnight in strong, warm tea. Two tablespoons of Seville orange marmalade were added to give a tart, but sufficiently sweet flavour. One mouthful assured the cake a place in the kitchen's repertoire. Bessie decided she must teach Amelia how to make it. While they were both indulging in seconds, Mod reached for the New York papers that had arrived from Jack in today's mailbag. Bessie began planning for the girls' arrival though still a month away. Tomorrow she would check on books available from *The Ladies' Home Journal* this year and order six, one for each member of the family.

With the passing of two years since Hattie's death, the family's period of mourning was over. Though they would never stop remembering that sad September in 1903, they could now have parties without eyebrows being raised. Perhaps she would invite the Caswells and the Peters and their children. She would ask the girls whether the idea appealed to them. After all, it would be mostly to add gaiety to their holidays. Bessie wanted them to have happy memories of home life in their early years, as she had from her youth in Saint John.

Meadowlands lacked the glamour of the Starr mansion, with its seven bathrooms, massive chandelier in the entrance hall, endless rooms and electricity everywhere. But she liked to think all the children would look back at their Meadowland's days with the affection that comes from intimacy and the occasional celebration, always touched with sadness, of course, having been deprived of their mother so young.

As ideas came to her, Bessie jotted them down in her little planning book, which had a small pencil tied to the binding and was usually kept in her dress or skirt pocket. Before she and Mod had quite finished their evening ritual, Bessie had written "chocolate balls" beside "Christmas Party?" She remembered how popular they had been the first time she made them, years ago. She closed her little book, but immediately reopened it remembering to note that she must finish writing articles for January's *Journal* and other magazine deadlines, and perhaps make a start on February's, all before December twelfth. Her habit of easily finding solitude for her writing would be disrupted with three lively girls in the house.

As Mod was neatly folding the papers to continue his perusing of them tomorrow, he guessed what she was doing and said to his sister, "I wouldn't worry too much about entertaining the girls. They'll want to reconnect with the boys and all the things they used to do,"

"Perhaps a little party with the Caswells and the Peters if the children would like that," his sister replied. "I'll ask them before I plan much. We'll see. Good night, dear."

"Good night, Bess. That was, indeed, delicious cake."

Sister and brother each carried a kerosene lamp with them as they climbed the front stairs to their respective bedrooms. Amelia removed their tray to the kitchen and put away the remains of the cake in a tin with a tightly fitting lid, but not before she had tasted the tiniest sliver and smiled. She had already carried two jugs with hot water up the back stairs, placing them on washstands in the two bedrooms for 10 o'clock, now past by ten minutes.

*　*　*　*　*

After a busy three weeks and a bit, pleasantly punctuated with three letters every Wednesday describing the allowable details of school life, December twelfth arrived. As the twelfth was a Saturday, Morris asked if he could go with his father to share the driving and help with the trunks, which they had been informed would be accompanying the girls in order to make redecorating and renovations at the school easier. Mod agreed, pleased his elder son was taking on family responsibilities. Roger wanted to go too but Morris told him there was not enough room on the way home. With three sisters, three large trunks and probably three hundred bags, which girls always seemed to carry, there wouldn't be a square inch.

"Rog, if you came, you'd have to sit on my head," teased Morris.

Recent, generous snowstorms, now well packed on the road to Saint John, ensured the runners of the sleigh had smooth travelling and the horses easy pulling. Morris helped the hired man harness a double team to the large sleigh. He added buffalo robes and hot bricks that Amelia had kept in the oven overnight. A layer of clean straw insured there would be at least a modicum of warmth on the way home. As the hills of Saint John appeared, Mod allowed the reins to go a little slack as the horses had found their comfortable pace and needed no urging.

As they approached the city, Morris spoke up; "It'll be great to see those silly sisters of mine. Edgehill seems to agree with Wowsie and Trudy. I wonder about Mary."

"We'll discover that before long," his father replied.

Mod passed the reins to Morris as they entered the city.

"You need some experience driving in traffic, son."

Morris took the reins with a mixture of pride and terror as the horses navigated their way through carriages, wagons, and carts of all kinds pulled by an assortment of horses, some neglected and some well-groomed. A motorcar careened by on the snow packed street at a crazy speed, causing the Meadowlands horses to shy. Morris tightened the reins and controlled them through their fright. After that excitement the young driver was on his toes, while urging the team up the long hill from King's Square to Carleton Street.

The front door of the Starr house was on a side street as the shape of the lot and the architect were at odds when it was built. Morris steered the team into the side driveway where a groom came forward to take care of the horses. Mary had been watching from a window seat to the left of the door. When she spied those familiar horses, and then the sleigh and her father and brother, she called out, "They're here," in a voice so loud it surprised her and caused the girls to hurry down two flights of stairs and to be there when Frank and Madge opened the door and greeted their country cousins.

Mary grabbed her father's hand as he bent down to kiss her cheek and couldn't let go. Mod was shocked by Mary's thinness and pale face but thought the contrast of outdoor and indoor light might be the cause. Wowsie and Trudy's rosy cheeks quickly eliminated that explanation, as he hugged and kissed them all. Without thinking, Morris wrapped arms around little Mary, lifting her slightly off her feet. When he set her down, she clung tightly to her big brother and then reluctantly released her grasp. Morris caught himself in time to just give his older sisters the affectionate little punch on their arms, which was their custom, and a big smile.

Before long they all gathered around the Starr's long, mahogany table for a hot lunch of beef and vegetable soup, roast lamb and a beautiful Apple Charlotte for dessert. Mod and Morris, now well warmed from their travel, enjoyed listening to the girls' chatter, interspersed with cousin Frank's witty appreciation. Madge soon reminded them the day was running away and the Meadowlands cousins needed to prepare for their trip home. The trunks were already in the hall. A version of those "three hundred bags" Morris had spoken of seemed to be there as well. The groom brought around the fed and watered horses. Morris helped him with the trunks. Hugs and "see you in January" were exchanged by the schoolgirls. Wowsie and Trudy thanked cousin Madge and got bear hugs from jovial cousin Frank. The men shook hands all around. Morris was pleased to be included in that masculine custom.

*   *   *   *   *

Dusk was beginning to shut down the day as Morris drove the sleigh up to the back door of the Meadowlands' house so the trunks could easily be taken into the kitchen. Bessie hugged her smiling and laughing nieces and they all grabbed Roger for a communal embrace. Then, even before she removed her winter coat, Mary slumped into a chair.

"At last, I can sleep!" she said so forcefully and with such relief in her voice that everyone stopped talking.

"What do you mean?" her father asked.

"I mean, I don't have to stay awake at night to make sure Bully Girl doesn't do something awful to me."

"What *exactly* do you mean?" Mod asked again as he examined his daughter's pale face and sunken eyes.

"I mean like smothering me with a pillow. She said the first night that if I fell asleep something terrible would happen to me. I stay awake for as long as I can every night."

"So you haven't been sleeping well since term started?" asked Bessie, horrified by what Mary had just said.

"I mustn't, or Bully Girl will get me."

After a long pause, Bessie broke the silence; "We'll talk about this later, dear." She bent over and gave little Mary a reassuring hug as best she could, considering her niece was still sitting down.

144

Then, recovering her presence of mind, Bessie straightened up and announced, "Supper is nearly ready. Take off your outdoor things and tidy up. We'll eat in fifteen minutes."

The girls scampered up to their rooms with Roger close behind. Morris hung about their doorways, savouring the excitement of his sisters' homecoming. Bessie beckoned Mod into the sitting room, leaving Amelia beaming in the kitchen, trying to refrain from peeking at her dumplings, nearly cooked, like fluffy clouds on top of her perfect pork stew.

"I won't have Mary returning to that nightmare," Mod announced quietly but with an intensity and authority Bessie had rarely heard in her brother's voice. "The child has lost weight, she has dark rings under her eyes, and is clearly miserable."

"The worst is probably over, Mod. There's often a little bullying that goes on for a while in boarding schools. Mary's short hair is enough to set her apart. Let's hear the whole story before we decide what's best. Elizabeth and Gertrude are clearly flourishing. The school is unlikely to be seriously flawed."

"They were much older when they started," Mod replied. "They were in the senior school from the beginning. Mary seems to be the youngest girl in the whole school, a target for those who enjoy making others unhappy. Her health is suffering. We do, indeed, need to hear the whole story."

Bessie was taken aback by the tone of Mod's reply. His reference to Mary's health cut to the quick; it triggered Bessie's feeling of guilt over her previous inadvertent neglect of her niece's health.

"Lets have a cheerful supper and then try to obtain a complete picture," Bessie offered as they heard Amelia ringing the old school bell to tell everyone her meal was ready. With the tension broken, brother and sister exchanged smiles as they heard the five children laughing and all talking at once as they scooted down the stairs, school rules left behind, taking their usual places at the dining room table.

Mary could not remember when she had ever been happier. Even during Father's usual galloping "For what we are about to receive," she wore a broad grin. She ate every morsel on her plate and asked for a second dumpling with gravy. Wowsie and Trudy also had good appetites, leaving nothing on their plates, and not just because they were used to obeying school rules. The boys appreciated Amelia's food as well, though they lacked the girls' contrasting experience of the school's less palatable menus.

Bessie had no difficulty steering the conversation toward agreeable subjects. What did the girls do at the Starr's for the day they were not travelling? All three spoke at once, saying cousin Madge took them Christmas shopping. Wowsie put her index finger up to her lips to be certain Mary wouldn't blurt out just what they had bought for everyone. Mary covered her smiling mouth with her hand. Morris brought his sisters up to date about the Gagetown young. Trudy wondered why no one asked about Edgehill so she described Sports Day and how expert Wowsie had become at tennis and Mary's leading the whole school in Indian club swinging. Wowsie said that Trudy's tennis had improved a lot, too; she just needed to work on her serve.

As tiny remnants of second helpings of snow pudding were being cleared from bowls, Bessie decided, after a certain look from Mod, that now was the time for the darker side of Edgehill to see the light.

"So what do you think of your first term at Edgehill, Mary?"

Though Mary knew her words would not be censored, she was so used to holding back the truth that for a moment she was confused. Her face was suddenly flushed with emotion and from the effort to contain her tears; then, the dam, building up for three months, burst.

"You'd better tell us about it," Bessie said as she gently put her hand on Mary's arm and passed her a folded handkerchief.

Out tumbled all the misery brought on by Bully Girl's hissing comments and Miss Steel's yardstick. Mary stuck out her hands. No one doubted she was telling the truth. Morris and Roger's eyes were glued to their sister's red knuckles, some with scabs. Everyone could see her sunken eyes, which gave credibility to Mary's account of Bully Girl's behaviour. Everyone stayed seated around the table. No one felt like abandoning Mary.

"Why didn't you tell us?" Morris asked Wowsie and Trudy, who were sitting together feeling uncomfortable.

"There was no way we could. Our letters are censored too with the excuse they should have good grammar and spelling. Lots of seniors suffered from Miss Steel's yardstick when they were juniors, so we expected Mary's knuckles to be red. We had less than a half hour every Sunday for mingling time and it wasn't at all private. But we told her not to tattle on Bully Girl as a tattle-tale is hated by everyone," Wowsie offered as an explanation of their inability to be helpful.

"There wasn't anything we could do. We weren't allowed into town without a mistress, so no chance of sending a letter without someone knowing," Trudy added.

They all looked at Mary with a mixture of admiration and pity. Bessie broke the silence; she asked Mary whether she liked anything about Edgehill.

"Oh, yes; Helen, my friend. Her mother died, too. And gymnastics, especially Indian club swinging. Miss Foote is nice, but just thinking about

Miss Steel makes me shake. I wish I didn't have to go back. If I could sleep all night it wouldn't be so bad."

Mod looked at Bessie, who gave an almost imperceptible nod.

"You don't have to go back if you'd sooner not, Mary," Mod said slowly and deliberately.

Mary jumped up from her place, ran down to the end of the table, and hugged her father with all her strength. Then smiling and laughing, ran to hug her Aunt Bessie at the other end, all the while saying "thank you, thank you, thank you" over and over as though she had been granted a magical wish from a story book.

"I'll be good, I'll be good. I'll even try to be nice to cousin Bess the next time she visits."

"You weren't sent to Edgehill because you didn't behave, Mary, but so you would have a better education and meet more interesting girls," Bessie explained. And then in the silence of her thoughts, added, and because I wanted to lessen the load on your father, should I go back to nursing.

"Now that you've said I don't have to go back, I can say I did learn a lot, much more than at the Grammar. I read all of *Black Beauty* in the library and French was sort of fun."

"Maybe, when you're older, you can go back for a while," Bessie suggested.

"Not if Bully Girl and Miss Steel are there, please."

Bessie brought the conversation to a close; "Help Amelia clear the table, children; we've held up dish washing with all our chatter."

21

Aunt Bessie Makes Peace with the End of Her Nursing Career

With the excitement of a long and strenuous day behind them, a general sense of tiredness and a wave of yawns swept through the family. Amelia's more elaborate than usual homecoming meal and Mary's great relief brought the day to a satisfying close. Even Bessie and Roger, who could not blame the hours of travel, were affected. Bessie suggested an early night for all, which no one objected to. When the house was quiet, Bessie took a little tray into the sitting room where Mod was settling into his favourite chair.

"Just tea tonight, dear, unless you have room for cake. I haven't."

"Amelia did herself proud. I don't have room for another crumb either."

Bessie poured a cup of tea with just the preferred amount of milk and sugar for Mod, then one for herself. She inhaled the familiar relaxing aroma and gave a little sigh.

"Is something troubling you?"

"Well … yes. It's lovely having the girls back, but poor little Mary has had such a hard time. She was really too young. I shouldn't have been so selfish, wanting to make it easier to return to nursing. I blame myself for putting my career ahead of family."

"You did what you thought was right at the time."

"My problem is that I so enjoy nursing. It is what I was meant to do, including everything that has flowed from it like writing, speaking and helping Lady Aberdeen start the Victorian Order of Nurses and her Women's Council. And I would never have had all those opportunities in England or have gotten to know Florence Nightingale if I hadn't taken up nursing. And the regular money is not to be despised."

"And don't forget, having tea with Queen Victoria," Mod added.

"That was unforgettable and so unexpected. A great honour, but at the top of my list is my hours of conversation with Miss Nightingale, even though her mind was not as sharp as it had been."

"You should write your memoirs."

"I have written long pieces for publications about different adventures. Sophie Palmer took one for *The American Journal of Nursing* on my visits to Miss Nightingale. I think I read it to you, the one about her not wanting to sign the photograph of her I took, but giving in by putting her signature on my Birthday Book, which I still have, of course."

"I remember. That's a treasure. You can keep on writing and speaking; instead of doing nursing you will be teaching the art, which you have been for years anyway. There's always a chance a good housekeeper will appear and you can go back to nursing."

"No, I think I must finally write to Dr. Coit. Perhaps there is no one out there who would have the qualifications necessary for being an appropriate housekeeper. The good rector has only three years to go before he retires. I daresay my assistant will see him out. I would not feel comfortable if you and Meadowlands were not well looked after. From now on, Meadowlands is my only home. Opportunities will no doubt come my way to help in the greater world."

"I can't imagine you twiddling your thumbs, Bess."

"I'm not sure I ever learned."

As Mod drained his teacup he stood and announced, "I'm going to turn in. That double drive took the stuffing out of me."

"I expect it did. Good night, dear."

Bessie walked over to tidy some papers on a table by the front window. The light of the full moon bounced off the frozen river. Before she knew what she was doing, Bessie recalled a poem her mother used to recite. A cloud passed over the moon, which interrupted her reverie, but she stayed, watching the night, imagining her mother's soft voice speaking familiar words.

> *The Lady Moon came down last night,*
>
> *She did you needn't doubt it,*
>
> *A lovely lady dressed in white,*
>
> *I'll tell you all about it.*
>
> *They hurried Len and me to bed*
>
> *And Auntie said, "Now maybe*
>
> *That lovely moon up overhead*
>
> *Will bring you down a baby!"*
>
> *We didn't quite believe it true,*
>
> *'Cause Auntie's always chaffing.*

The cloud moved on, leaving that sharp whiteness Bessie remembered seeing from her bedroom window when she was young, long before her father's financial troubles. She remembered leaving the heavy draperies open so she would feel the full brightness on her face as she fell asleep, like a friend watching over her.

"I remember," mused Bessie, "asking Lady Moon what my life would be like, wondering whether it would be similar to my mother's, with all those babies dying in a few days or weeks, but hoping for something different. I was special because I lived and I should pay back for that blessing. I remember telling Lady Moon I really wanted to help other people in some way rather than marrying. It was a secret between the two of us. I could not even tell dear Mother, as she would expect me to be unhappy in such a life. I could not tell Isabel, either; though my best friend, because she would sometimes let secrets escape. I am glad I resisted the overtures of those desperate schoolmasters at St. Paul's who brought me bowls of violets at Easter and oranges directly from Florida. They were hoping to be asked for tea. There were so few women about. One master invited himself to tea. I remember he talked about himself and of his saintly mother the entire time. I could not spend my life with such a self-centred, opinionated bore. Really, Lady Moon, I have not met a man, ever, who inspired a desire to be subjected to his advances. Dr. Coit comes the nearest, but even if he were not married I would not wish to be his wife, though I love his intellect. Yes, I escaped being absorbed into the identity of a husband legally owning me and my time and any money I made from writing.

"Oh, yes, Lady Moon, I'm glad I remained true to my decision. What a life I have had! I must accept that my days as a working nurse are probably over. But I will not suddenly unlearn all I know about my profession. I will try to put it to good use. Mod's children will benefit. What a mercy I don't have a dozen of my own! I'll write more books, perhaps. They last longer than magazines and journals, though I'll stay with dear Sophie as long as she wants me."

*   *   *   *   *

With less than three weeks remaining before Christmas Day, the entire household took on a happy frenzy. That first day included a sleigh ride to the Jemseg church in the morning with complimentary comments directed at Bessie and Mod regarding the growth, obvious health and general demeanour of the two eldest girls, in particular. Though Mary had one good night behind her that was not enough to improve her sunken eyes. However, she was so pleased to be able to hold Roger's hand after the service was over, and he hers, that their smiles of happiness insulated her from any slights.

A blustery wind came up in the afternoon causing loose snow to swirl about the river. Mod decided that since the evening would probably be moonless, and, with poor visibility, evensong at Gagetown should not be contemplated. They were all still a little weary from the day before, and the three girls from spending much of the afternoon unpacking their trunks and hanging up all that need not be washed.

Mary's feelings were mixed as she unpacked her trunk. She regretted missing the chance to learn to play the piano. I have so much music inside me, just waiting for a chance to get out, she thought as she hung up her navy serge tunic. Her slightly soiled middy blouse lingered in her hand before she threw it on to the laundry pile. It represented her triumph with the Indian clubs. Perhaps the Grammar would buy some and she could teach a class how to use them. Wouldn't that be fun! She returned the cutlery and her napkin ring to the silver drawer. At the bottom of her trunk was the piece of paper Helen had thrown in with her Ottawa address on it. Mary had done the same so they could write to one another over Christmas. She would have to tell Helen they might never meet again, though they could freely write when Helen was on holidays. As Mary finished putting everything away, Aunt Bessie came in and sat on the end of the bed.

"Edgehill has taught you to be more tidy, I see."

Mary just smiled, happy to be in her old room.

"In case you change your mind, I will wait a few days before informing Miss Smith you will not be returning. After several nights of good sleep and your knuckles are no longer sore, you might feel differently. I feel badly you had such a hard time. Do you think your short hair had something to do with your misery?"

"It probably did," Mary replied. "There was some talk about it. Everyone else had long hair. But I was glad for short hair. I couldn't have kept the snarls out."

As Bessie stood to go to her writing nook, Mary, with her eyes on the floor, quickly said, "I'm sorry that it didn't work out, Aunt Bessie, but I was scared."

"I know, dear. The rules were hard on you and the bullying made it worse."

*　　*　　*　　*　　*

The Grammar would not close for another five days, so the next morning, after a quick breakfast, Morris and Roger, with Jock in charge of the reins, took off in the sleigh for Gagetown.

Through his last mouthful of cocoa, Morris said to the girls, "Be sure you have a look at those twin foals. You won't recognize them!"

"We will," they chimed in.

After clearing the table, they bundled up and made tracks through a small layer of fresh snow that had fallen in the night. As they passed through the harness room, they noticed the big scraper used for clearing snow leaning against the wall.

"If we can get the scraper down to the river, we can start clearing a skating space," Trudy suggested.

"If we tie a rope around the handle the three of us can drag it and maybe put it on the toboggan," Mary put in.

Wowsie and Trudy agreed but first they all went into the barn to admire the sleek chestnut foals and pat them on their heads. They had grown considerably larger in the few months the girls had been away at school.

"Let's name this one Star Bright," Wowsie suggested, as she gave the foal with the larger white star between its eyes an extra rub.

"And the other one Star Light," added Mary.

The three grinning girls recited the well-known wish that inspired the names: "Star light, star bright, the first star I see tonight, I wish I may, I wish I might, have the wish I wish tonight."

Trudy was impatient to put her idea into practice. "Let's find the toboggan and put the scraper on it and a couple of those snow shovels."

Morris or Roger must have been using the shovels, as they were all near the door of the tool shed, having been taken down from summer storage on a platform near the roof. By the time the scraper was more or less on the toboggan and the tin shovels stowed on board, the sun was dancing on the snow and torturing Mary's eyes. On the way down to the river, she made a detour into the house to pick up her sun spectacles and tell Amelia where they would be spending the morning, a habit from Edgehill where any deviation from the expected had to be reported.

When the little band with their tools reached the frozen river they agreed on a plan to test different places until they found smooth ice. They dug four holes through the snow before they found an area of smooth black ice showing the tiny bubbles of air trapped underneath. They took turns; one threw away the top layer of loose snow with a shovel while the other two followed close behind pushing the scraper.

After an hour, Mary announced she'd had too much cocoa for breakfast and headed for the outhouse. Wowsie and Trudy kept working but then realized Mary was taking far too much time. She was quickly forgiven when she returned with three large cookies that Amelia had just taken from the oven. After the cookies, fresh snow by the mouthful diminished their thirst enough to keep them at their labour, but with increasingly frequent rests on the toboggan until they heard Amelia vigorously ringing the dinner bell.

*　*　*　*　*

With Morris and Roger at school and the girls tied to their project, Bessie installed herself in her upstairs nook planning to write a few remaining Christmas letters. She sipped her cup of post-breakfast tea as she looked through the leafless trees at the girls just starting their ice-clearing project. Now that Mary did not want to return to Edgehill, the thought of giving up her active nursing career was always lurking just behind Bessie's conscious thoughts. Being at the end of her career, reminded her of the beginning. As she looked at the frozen river through the frost edged window, her fuzzy reflection reminded her of the expression on her mother's face when she confided her decision to take up nursing.

"'I would sooner you became a housemaid,' Mother said to me, looking directly into my eyes. I knew she was in earnest, but I had made up my mind. I wasn't exactly a headstrong child. Gracious, I was twenty-nine and more than ready to stand on my own feet, especially with dear Father not able to secure another position after his bankruptcy. I must not be a burden on the family for the rest of my life. My application papers from Massachusetts General needed both Mother's and Father's signatures, which they reluctantly gave after much discussion behind closed doors.

"Can twenty-five years have passed since that train trip to Boston for my interview? Such preparations — visiting the dressmaker in Douglas who was unexpectedly adept at making patterns from magazine pictures; Velma was her name and her sister, Viola, was a milliner. They seemed out of place in the country, after learning their trades in Boston, but both parents became ill so they returned to their roots. I had been saving my money from occasional teaching positions for a noble cause and this was it!

"Mother refused to splurge on a new suit for the trip to Boston, but accepted Velma's suggestion to place fresh black velvet insets into the front of her jacket and Viola's for new black taffeta ribbons on her brimmed felt hat. I indulged in a new light wool suit, black of course, with decorative buttons on the cuffs and the bodice with a slightly flared waist.

154

Viola convinced me of the persuasive powers of a new hat, the latest style she said, somewhat perched to one side over my forehead with a black ribbon containing white flecks forming a bow just over my chignon. I wore that outfit for years! Mother and I both owned white blouses with a little lace at the neck, which were perfectly suitable.

"Mother wore her favourite cameo broach at her neck and I a silver medallion that Father had given me on my eighteenth birthday when we were all still living in Saint John, more than ten years earlier. Father did not feel well enough to accompany us. We had both made that train journey to Boston before. It was becoming more and more common to see ladies travelling together, without a father, brother or husband. And now, what a change, we go where we like though heeding good advice about not having conversations with lonely men. Boarding the train in Fredericton and then on to McAdam Junction and crossing into Maine at Vanceboro was trouble free. That was before dining cars, so we took packed lunches. But we did have a sleeping car designed by a Mr. Pullman. I, of course, gave Mother the bottom bunk while I climbed a little ladder and settled on the top one. Eventually the regular clickity-click acted as a sleeping draught, which gave us both quite a decent sleep. At least I had sleep enough to enable my wits to suitably answer questions from the Ladies' Acceptance Board at the hospital. After a rumbling night and somewhere well into the Boston States, the train stopped at a station with a busy restaurant where we ate a hot breakfast.

"By way of celebrating my successful interview, Mother and I took tea and cake at a nearby hotel restaurant, then a hansom cab to cousin Sophie Robinson's for a three night visit, stretched from the intended one night at her insistence. And then there was the over two months of anticipation until I made the journey again by myself. I won the argument with Mother by pointing out that, as a nurse, I would have to learn how to talk with strange people, even men. A little practice would not hurt. When I boarded the train in Fredericton in late August, Mother looked at me as though she did not expect to ever see me again, her hungry, parental eyes wanting to remember every wisp of my hair."

Thoughts of that emotional scene made Bessie lower her head and search her pocket for her handkerchief. Spying her half-full teacup, she took a sip and found it cold. She checked her little clock and at first thought she had forgotten to wind it. More than an hour had passed in idle musing. She really must write some letters, at least one to Addie. But her active brain would not pull away from her reverie. As she looked through the frosty window, she took comfort in seeing her three nieces happily dedicated to clearing the snow from the river ice so the reunited siblings could enjoy holiday skating together.

"I am so fortunate," she thought; "a profession and five children without the bother of a husband. But for a long time Mother wished I had chosen differently. After I had been training for a year, she began to warm to my decision and to consider the nursing profession had some merit. That was in 1879, after I wrote that article on "Nursing as a Profession for Women," which *Youth's Companion* published. Mother was as amazed, as was I, when it brought over a thousand applications to the training school and a letter of thanks from the chairman of the board of directors of the hospital. She realized I would not have received a letter like that if I had been a housemaid.

"I remember about the same time, *Scribner's Magazine* printed my paper on "Domestic Nursing." Oh, the thrill of receiving a substantial cheque from them, close to my thirtieth birthday! That encouraged me to offer a series of seven papers on "Home Nursing" to the *Christian Union*. My name became known as an expert on nursing before I actually worked professionally. The urge I had to share my knowledge of nursing was nearly as strong as wanting to study it. What would I have written about if I hadn't decided on nursing as a career? I could also have written on nutritional cooking. *Good Housekeeping* was keen to use anything I sent them in the way of meal preparation and recipes. But that was after 1890 when my name was already established in *The Ladies' Home Journal* as an Associate Editor and in charge of a page that was mostly advice to mothers."

Amelia's spirited ringing of the dinner bell brought Bessie back to the present. "Good gracious," she admonished herself; "not a letter written. Never mind, I enjoyed that peek into my past—curiously fascinating."

22

The Joy of Skating

The dinner bell turned Amelia into a veritable Pied Piper, with the girls running up from the river, Mod coming in from the barn where he had been discussing with Jock which horses to take to the Winter Fair in January, and Bessie skimming down the mahogany stairway into the dining room where steam was rising from bowls of orange and carrot soup. This appetizer was followed by a vegetable marrow stuffed with minced beef and onions, then a creamy rice pudding well dotted with fat, sticky raisins, and anointed with yellow cream. In addition, a pile of sliced, white bread from yesterday's baking, which Amelia placed in the middle of the table, gradually shrank, as did the dish of Meadowlands homemade butter. Mod and Bessie listened attentively as the sisters described the fine points of clearing the ice, pleased they had learned so well the art of co-operation for a common goal.

When Mod thanked Amelia for such a good repast, she said, "I'm trying to put a little flesh on the girls' bones, especially Mary's."

"I feel fatter already," Mary grinned.

As the three girls helped Amelia clear the table, Mary made a proposal; "Let's do more ice clearing and surprise the boys so we can all have a skate before supper. It's not big enough, yet."

"Alright," Wowsie agreed, "but let's do a jig-saw puzzle first while we rest up. I can hardly bend."

"Very sensible, Elizabeth," commented Bessie, as she picked her cup of tea and prepared to return to her writing nook.

Trudy quickly fetched a boxed puzzle from the shelf where they were kept. Neither of the older girls would admit to being too tired if Mary still wanted to clear more snow. Doing a puzzle while resting up was a compromise all accepted. They had all worked on this complicated flower garden puzzle many times before and so finished it in not much more than a half hour. They retrieved their snow clothes from where they had been thawing and warming on a clotheshorse beside the stove. After wriggling into them, buttoning up, and tugging on their boots, they headed out the kitchen door.

When they reached the river, the cleared space seemed to have shrunk so they set about with even greater determination to enlarge the skating area. They followed the same arrangement of sharing the work as the morning's ritual. Two hours of shovelling and pushing passed, until Mary announced she needed to use the outhouse again. Her sisters quickly agreed they did too, and they all felt the need of a hot drink. When Amelia spotted them dragging their feet toward the back door she put a saucepan of milk on the stove. By the time they stomped snow off their boots, brushed some off their clothes with a corn broom and opened the storm door, three white enamel mugs with dark blue rims were about to be filled with girl-thawing cocoa.

"Unless you're freezing, better not come in."

All three knew Amelia was right. Those hidden troughs of snow would melt and trickle down their necks, their wrists and their ankles after five minutes inside. As they stood in the sun and drained their mugs of the sweetened, hot chocolate, they hatched a little plan.

"Any cookies?" they laughed in unison as they returned the mugs.

Amelia caught their merriment, produced three cookies of the morning's vintage, and, with mock formality, gave a little bob of a curtsey.

*   *   *   *   *

As Bessie sipped her still hot tea, about to begin a letter to Addie, her eye fell upon her pile of *The Ladies' Home Journal* that had become less than tidy, perhaps because of Amelia's enthusiastic dusting. One issue, half way down the pile, was sticking out of alignment. Bessie pulled it out, in case the cover was bent. It was dated January 1901, nearly six years ago. "How my life has changed since then. I wonder what I wrote for that issue." She took the copy over to her desk and started turning the pages. Her name, as Associate Editor, was on the title page as usual, along with all the familiar content, laid out like a delicious meal on a buffet table. She turned to page eight; "What May Happen In The Next Hundred Years" by John Elfreth Watkins, Jr. "Ah, yes, I remember this, but not the details. I'll just read the introduction."

> *These prophecies will seem strange, almost impossible. Yet they have come from the most learned and conservative minds in America. To the wisest and most careful men in our greatest institutions of science and learning I have gone; asking each in his turn to forecast for me what, in his opinion, will have been wrought in his own field of investigation before the dawn of 2001 — a century from now. The opinions I have carefully transcribed.*

Bessie's eyes scanned the headings of the twenty-eight prophetic paragraphs: "The American will be Taller," "Ready-Cooked Meals will be Bought from Establishments," "Photographs will be Telegraphed from any Distance," "Trains One Hundred and Fifty Miles an Hour," "There will be Air-Ships," "There will be No Wild Animals except in Menageries," "Man will See Around the World," "Telephones Around the World," "Vegetables Grown by Electricity," "Strawberries as Large as Apples," "Peas as Large as Beets," "Black, Blue and Green Roses as large as Cabbage Heads," and on and on with these fantastic predictions.

Bessie could not resist fully reading several that especially wrested her attention.

> *Few drugs will be swallowed or taken into the stomach unless needed for the direct treatment of that organ itself. Drugs needed by the lungs, for instance, will be applied directly to those organs through the skin and flesh. They will be carried with the electric current applied without pain to the outside skin of the body. Microscopes will lay bare the vital organs, through the living flesh, of men and animals. The living body will to all medical purpose be transparent. Not only will it be possible for a physician to actually see a living, throbbing heart inside the chest, but he will be able to magnify and photograph any part of it. This work will be done with rays of invisible light.*

"Can that ever be? My, how that would revolutionize medicine and nursing. Perhaps the 'wisest and most careful men' who produced these ideas just have very active imaginations. However… And here's another I vaguely remember reading, 'How Children will be Taught.'"

> *A university education will be free to every man and woman. Several great national universities will have been established. Children will study a simple English grammar adapted to simplified English and not copied after the Latin. Time will be saved by grouping like studies. Poor students will be given free board, free clothing and free books if ambitious and actually unable to meet their school and college expenses. Medical inspectors regularly visiting the public schools will furnish poor children free eyeglasses, free dentistry and free medical attention of every kind. The very poor will, when necessary, get free rides to and from school and free lunches between sessions. In vacation time poor children will be taken on trips to various parts of the world. Etiquette and housekeeping will be important studies in the public school.*

"Well! Governments will have to be more philanthropic than they are now, but what a blessing free medical attention would be to the poor. It would save so much unnecessary misery. And what's this…"

To England in Two Days? Fast electric ships, crossing the ocean at more than a mile a minute, will go from New York to Liverpool in two days. The bodies of these ships will be built above the waves. They will be supported upon runners, somewhat like those of the sleigh. These runners will be very buoyant. Upon their undersides will be apertures expelling jets of air. In this way a film of air will be kept between them and the water's surface. This film, together with the small surface of the runners, will reduce friction against the waves to the smallest possible degree. Propellers turned by electricity will screw themselves through both the water beneath and the air above. Ships with cabins artificially cooled will be entirely fireproof. In storm they will dive below the water and there await fair weather.

"My fellow travellers who turned green in bad weather will be glad to hear about this, if only for their grand children. It all seems like magical absurdity, but so would the motorcar in 1801. Hmm … just one more before on to letter writing. Here's one I should show Mod, but perhaps not.

Automobiles will be Cheaper than Horses are Today. Farmers will own automobile hay-wagons, plows, harrows and hay-rakes. A one-pound motor in one of these vehicles will do the work of a pair of horses or more. Children will ride in automobile sleighs in winter. Automobiles will have been substituted for every horse vehicle now known. There will be automobile hearses, automobile police patrols, automobile ambulances, automobile street sweepers. The horse in harness will be as scarce, if indeed not even scarcer, then as the yoked ox is today.

"No, I will not recommend this article to Mod. He would be saddened by the demise of his beloved horses. Of course, there still might be some kept for the enjoyment of horse back riding. I cannot imagine the English enjoying fox hunting in automobiles. But in another century there might not be any foxes as one of the other articles prophesies.

"Before I tidy this away I must look at what I wrote in this issue. There I am, on page 46, under "The Child and Its Mother," answering a dozen questions sent in by readers, everything from how to make a bassinet quilt to a list of games suitable for the young to play indoors in the winter.

The advertisements are at least as informative as my column. "Do Not Stammer," "Artistic Stationery," "Dunlop Pneumatic Tires For Bicycles, for Carriages, for Automobiles," "Metal Doll Heads," and, surprisingly, one for a "Safety Hammer Automatic Revolver" for $4.50, with an illustration of the gun hiding under a gentleman's pillow. As usual, there are a number of requests to order patterns for children's clothes."

As Bessie slipped the magazine carefully back where it belonged in chronological order and reached for her writing paper, she was aware of a growing darkness in spite of the dormer windows surrounding her nook on three sides. Perhaps the sun had gone behind a cloud she mused. But craning her neck a little so she could see the girls still at work on the ice, she discovered to her amazement that Mod and the boys were sifting across the river at great speed, rapidly approaching Scovil's wharf. "Can it be so late?" she thought. "Perhaps they were let out early." She looked at her clock. "No, already four! My, how delving into the past eats into leisure—but what a pleasant 'meal.' I must go down and welcome the boys."

*   *   *   *   *

After a day of being penned up in school, the boys paused for only a handful of Amelia's cookies and glasses of milk, found their skates, and ran down to the cleared ice, eager to join their sisters and take advantage of the lingering daylight. It was one of those unforgettable experiences of childhood, remembered for years afterward; so unexpected for the boys, so gratifying for the girls and so much fun for all. Once they were all gliding, they formed a fast moving whip, practiced their Dutch Roll, skated arm in arm, and scrambled back up after crash landings. Roger's technique was not up to the others, so Morris went to the carpentry shed and brought back an old kitchen chair that he could use as a stabilizing support for pushing over the ice as he practiced balance and strokes. They could also use the chair as a resting place for tiring ankles, or to get a second wind. The sun came out from behind a cloud, which brightened the evening before finally setting and giving that red promise of a "a sailor's delight."

Bessie insisted that Amelia make supper an easy one. As always this time of year, Amelia had spent the afternoon preparing traditional food of the season. She had made mincemeat and a white fruitcake, which needed less time to cure than the dark ones and the plum pudding, which were now ageing since being prepared this past Sunday. She served baked potatoes, glazed ham out of the brine barrel, and little pickled beets, all farm produced and most satisfying to everyone, especially the hungry, flushed cheeked young. They knew what the dessert would be; after baked potatoes

161

in their jackets, it was traditional to have baked apples stuffed with dates and raisins floating in their own cinnamon spiked juice.

The exuberance of the children, all together again, made Bessie think of how proud Hattie would be to see them maturing. Affecting the lives of five children may not be as important as the health of hundreds, but when they are part of your own family, the satisfaction is somehow greater. And then there's Mod, she thought, seeming relieved with her decision, even chuckling a bit at the end of the table over Morris's latest witticism. Bessie's feeling for the man who was once her little brother welled to the surface. "I have no right to burden him further. He's still not recovered from losing Hattie."

*   *   *   *   *

Friday came with the predictable Christmas closing at the Grammar: recitations, carols, mentions of excellence, and congratulations from the Principal. The girls renewed friendships with old classmates, talking and laughing together in the small hall over mugs of hot cocoa and cookies. Then it was holidays for all, with an effort made to keep the skating space open, and even enlarged. Bessie wrote to Miss Smith and the Starrs that Mary would not be returning to Edgehill after Christmas, but possibly some time in the future when she was older. She said that Elizabeth and Gertrude were very happy there and she felt that Mary would have been except for her immaturity. There was no point in going into detail, in case Mary later wanted to return.

Christmas day threatened a heavy snowfall, but by the time Mod and Morris tied Horsey in the Jemseg church horse shed even flurries had stopped. As usual, the Rev. Mr. Hatheway's sermon was far too long and Mod had to brandish his pocket watch and threaten with a loud click of the cover to emphasize the passage of time. Anticipation increased as the singing of carols through the crisp air on the way home whetted appetites even further. As soon as the door opened, there was no doubt that Amelia had lived up to expectations. Never again would they encounter Uncle Jack's hay-box "cooked" turkey, as they did two years ago. Forever afterward it was always mentioned as Amelia's tawny, crisp-skinned perfection appeared and surrendered to Mod's razor sharp knife.

Bessie's effort to select books that appealed to all was moderately successful, as usual, but the new feature of this Christmas was the results of the girls' afternoon of shopping with cousin Madge. Mod received a notification of a subscription to the *Saint John Monthly*, beginning in January. Bessie was given a beautifully embroidered handkerchief trimmed

162

with Brussels lace. They had selected a jackknife for Morris and a box of Crayola crayons with eight different colours for Roger. The three sisters were all smiles when they saw the happy reception of their carefully guarded secrets.

During Christmas week, Bessie arranged for the Peters to come for a party of high tea and games, as the suggestion was thought to be a good one by the girls. She planned to invite the Caswells as well, but a nasty cold was running through the family, probably caught by the doctor from one of his patients. The DeVebers invited the Scovils over for a dinner and afternoon games for both grown-ups and the young.

The days fled as though being chased. Soon it was time for Bessie to make sure the two trunks returning to Edgehill were properly filled with clean and pressed clothes and all the other necessary paraphernalia. Mary and the boys reluctantly returned to the Grammar, leaving Wowsie and Trudy singing their French songs while they kept the ice clear so they could all skate at the end of the each day.

Mary paid attention to every word her teacher spoke at school. She slept like a newborn baby every night, except for the occasional dream when Bully Girl's mean face appeared. Her knuckles were no longer red and no longer painful, except when she removed her mittens and they were over-exposed to the cold. They reminded her of her torture and that she would probably never learn to play the piano. But she chose no-misery and no-piano over misery and piano, and, sadly, no Indian clubs, of course. But she was sure she had made the right decision. She might never have survived another term. That pillow could have landed on her head and stayed there. A dead girl can't play the piano anyway.

"Mary, dear, would you like to go down to the Starrs with the girls? They're leaving on Saturday, the day after tomorrow. Cousin Madge wants them to spend a couple of nights before the 10th. You would come back with Father the same day."

"Yes, please, but it's not a trick to get me back to Edgehill, is it?"

"Of course not, Mary! You decide when you want to return."

"*Jamais!*" It was one of words in Mary's French vocabulary with a musical sound, which she will always remember.

23

A Grave Injustice at Gagetown Grammar
1906

January 1906 progressed without special drama. Bessie continued to write for publication and family letters, especially to Addie and Jack. Wowsie and Trudy's envelopes arrived on schedule, with acceptable bits of information they thought would interest Mary, especially messages from Helen. Juniors were not allowed to send to or receive letters from friends. Mary replied to Helen through her sister's letters and so kept in touch with her friend. Roger came back into her life again as her chief playmate, though she could see that he and Morris were closer than they had been before she left. In the evenings, after homework, Morris thoughtfully suggested things to do which the three of them would like and sometimes succeeded.

February was different. Up until the twentieth, life for the Scovils was generally predictable: heavy snowstorms, days of flurries, brilliant sunshine, almost frozen fingers, evenings of making twisted molasses candy, missing Wowsie and Trudy, sitting around the Franklin stove, listening to Bessie read a book she thought the young would like and asking them to take turns. But Tuesday, February twentieth, shook the serenity of Meadowlands and, up to a point, the village of Gagetown.

Morris would be sixteen on July fourth, so he was in the senior room at the Grammar with eight others. Their last names were Otty, Dingee, Reid, Brooks, Belyea, Kelly, Gilcrest, and Biddiscombe, the last three being girls. Maizie Biddiscombe had wheat coloured curly hair with a tint of red and a face covered with freckles. Morris's jokes always made her toss her head back in laughter, and sometimes holding her sides to stop the ache from laughing so hard. He thought of her without embarrassment as a friend, as much as a boy of fifteen can have a friend who is a girl.

Maizie was smart, but because of her family responsibilities her homework was not always completed or even started. At 11 o'clock, Tuesday morning, February twentieth, the senior room teacher, Miss Jones, discovered that Maizie had not done her assigned homework. Miss Jones could not contain her fury over this disobedience. She called Maizie to the front of the room, took the strap from the long drawer in her desk, and told Maizie to hold out an up turned hand. The other seven students sat rigid in their seats. Girls were never strapped. Miss Jones pushed Maizie's sleeve up, exposing her tender wrist. When the strap descended, it lashed her wrist, which hurt far more than it would have on her housework toughened hand. The second lash of the strap with Miss Jones' full might behind it on Maizie's inner wrist brought an involuntary scream of pain from the girl.

Morris's eyes were less than three feet from Maizie's arm which he could see already becoming red and welted. He could not bear the feeling of the hot pain from this beating of Maizie's body and the terrified look in her eyes that had replaced their usual happy twinkles. He knew he would try to stop the beating of a dog or a horse. The beating of a girl shocked Morris into instinctive response. He stood up, grabbed the strap from Miss Jones' hand as it was descending, and accidentally knocked off her glasses, which fell to the floor where they shattered. Maizie stumbled back to her seat, crying. The astonished teacher yelled at Morris to sit down. He did so, having completed what he had to do, but still holding the strap. Miss Jones' feet clicked rapidly to the back of the room where she vanished through the door, only to return in short order, accompanied by Mr. Millage, the Principal, earnestly pushing his round, wire-framed glasses up on his nose. Mr. Millage, ignoring Maizie's red and swollen arm, her tearful face, and gentle whimpering, ordered Morris to go to the office, which he did.

There are always at least two versions of a drama like this. Miss Jones said that Morris tore the strap from her hand and assaulted her with it, knocking off her glasses and breaking them. He should be expelled. Morris said that he could not sit there and see a girl's wrists being beaten so hard that she screamed. She was not guilty of any bad crime. He had never seen a girl strapped before. He would not stand by and see a dog or a horse beaten. Maize didn't deserve to be beaten. How could he have just watched and done nothing to stop it. He didn't mean to touch Miss Jones with the strap or break her glasses. He was sorry. He just wanted the strapping to stop.

Mr. Millage had been Principal for only a year and a half. He did not know how to deal with this. Miss Jones was a good teacher. She was strict, but she got results. Morris came from an influential family, the largest landowner in the area, one that often help purchase scarce school supplies. He was a good student, sang well at closings and was generally co-operative and popular with everyone. Mr. Millage was in a dilemma. He took the problem to the Queen's County Educational Committee. Morris was given homework and told not to attend school until a decision was reached. It took two weeks. Morris was expelled.

Mod sent a note to Mr. Millage with Mary, asking for a meeting that was granted two days later. Mod drove Mary and Roger to school that day. Mr. Millage, nervously pushing his glasses up on his shiny nose, explained that the decision was not his. The Committee believed their decision was best in the interests of maintaining school discipline and order. Miss Jones was highly rated as a teacher. A teacher's authority must not be undermined, the Committee members agreed. Morris was a bright lad and would undoubtedly do well eventually, if he learned to control himself.

Mod measured his words carefully; "Mr. Millage, a grave injustice has been done."

He did not shake Mr. Millage's hand, but simply stood, turned, opened the office door and left, red faced and barely able to contain his fury. He stood outside on the school porch trying to cool down. Instead of walking to the shed where he had tied Horsey, he walked down the road to the river and along Front Street toward the DeVeber's at the far end. Gabe DeVeber was a good friend with a sensible head on his shoulders. Mod knew a half hour with Gabe was the best medicine, especially as it was not a good idea to return home still simmering. Bess was already upset and he needed to be rational when giving the news to Morris.

Gabe was surprised but pleased to see his old friend, so early in the day.

"I need to talk to you Gabe. You're the most sensible man in Gagetown. I need that just now. Morris has been expelled from school for unfair reasons. I'd appreciate your advice."

Mod told the whole story, from Morris's point of view and the teacher's, and what Millage did and did not do. Gabe curled the ends of his mustache and puffed on his pipe. Mod sipped on his tea that had been brought in by Lily, the maid. It was too early for something stronger, which is what he really wanted. Mrs. DeVeber was visiting in Saint John.

"You should be proud of your son, Mod," Gabe began. "He acted out of common decency and kindness. No teacher should be allowed to strap on the wrist, or girls at all, for that matter. Too bad in the excitement he accidentally knocked off her glasses and hit her with the strap. That's where the school has some leverage. Unfortunately, they'll take the teacher's word against Morris's intentions. I caught wind of this a few days ago. People are hungry for gossip this time of year."

"So you don't think I should send a letter to the County Council, appealing the decision of the Education Committee?" Mod asked.

"Oh no, send a letter strongly objecting to their stand and telling them what yours is, maybe even saying you are proud of Morris for showing himself against unnecessary cruelty, exercising Christian principles, that sort of thing. You might offer to pay for the broken glasses, so the two parts of the problem can be separated, the accidental and the intended. The County Council is unlikely to back down unless Millage presses them and he hasn't the guts to do that."

"Thanks Gabe. That makes sense. Even if they let him back, it would be hard for everyone. I don't think he's learning much this year, anyway. He's too old to start at Kings. He'd have too much catching up to do. The girls are learning French and quite advanced History at Edgehill. I expect it's much the same for the boys. He's very good with the horses, but he needs to learn things I can't teach him. Thanks for listening to me. I'll send a letter to get it out of my system. I'd better get home. Bess will be wondering why I'm so long."

The two old friends stood and walked to the front hall, where Lily produced Mod's coat, hat, scarf and mittens, all warm enough to keep out most of the perishing wind that would be pushing him across the river.

"Wait a minute," Gabe interjected, "I've just remembered something. I was talking with Will Law last week and he told me something you might want to check on. He read in a newspaper that there's going to be an agricultural college in Truro—a two-year course, and perhaps more, starting in September. He's always looking for lads who know something about orchards and hopes to get a fellow from the college one day. Might be something your Morris could tackle. He'll be sixteen soon won't he? That should be old enough. I remember when he was born."

"Hmm… I'll have a word with Will. Yes, in the summer, he'll be sixteen in July."

Mod left the DeVeber's in an entirely different mood from when he arrived. He walked up to the horse shed and quietly apologized to Horsey for taking so long by giving her an affectionate rub on her nose. Mod was surprised his pocket watch told him the morning had nearly gone.

*　*　*　*　*

Morris spent the morning dealing with his mixed feelings and anxiously waiting for his father's return. He kept busy in the barn and was currying a horse when Mod arrived back at Meadowlands. Morris pummeled his father with questions as they unhitched Horsey.

"Millage wouldn't budge," Mod explained, "but I had a talk with Gabe and he gave me an idea or two. You did the manly thing, son. Your classmates know what happened. A mean teacher never comes out well. Let's go in to dinner and we'll talk more."

Bessie was watching from the dining room window and guessed the outcome when she saw the two walking from the horse barn with no expressions of jubilation.

"Oh, my darling boy." Bessie took Morris's cold hands in hers for a moment and wanted to hug him but knew that fifteen-year old boys found that too emotional for comfort. Amelia carried in a casserole of scalloped potatoes and a platter of sliced cold beef left over from Sunday's joint. Her bread and butter pickles were already on the table along with her horseradish sauce and a loaf of yesterday's bread, to be cut as needed. After Mod said grace at his usual rattling pace, there was complete silence except for the sound of cutlery on china and the ticking of the wall clock. It was the family practice not to discuss issues of importance until the meal was over, or at least well advanced.

"I think our digestions will be improved if we break the rule, this once," Bessie offered. "What did Mr. Millidge say, Mod? I can see it wasn't in Morris's favour."

"Millage is a coward. He took it to the County's Education Committee and then disowned the decision, which is now probably written in stone," Mod replied.

"I would do the same again," Morris interjected, "but I'd be careful not to knock that woman's glasses off her ugly nose. They don't seem to believe that part was an accident. I bet she wouldn't like her inside wrists strapped."

"It's hard to be blamed for an unintentional crime," Bessie sympathized but said no more. She knew that order had to be maintained in a school so decided not to comment on the use of the strap, though, in this case, she felt it was entirely a misuse, especially as Maizie's family were trying so hard to keep her in school.

"I'll tell you what Gabe said," Mod continued. "I called on him for his advice. He made sense. He didn't think we'd get anywhere if we asked for an interview with the Education Committee—even supposing they'd give it—but not to be put off writing to them, disagreeing with their decision and saying Morris was doing his Christian duty to protect Maizie from the cruel and unjustified action of the teacher. And further, I should underline that the broken glasses were an accident and offer to pay for them."

"It might make them think twice if a similar case comes up," added Bessie. "The Committee should have interviewed Morris for his side of the events."

"I wouldn't go back, even if they'd have me. I wasn't learning a lot from her anyway and it would be zero now."

After a pause, Mod replied, "That's understandable, son. I think you're right. But Gabe told me something else; he said there's news of something coming up in September that may interest you. Will Law saw an article in a newspaper about a new agricultural school starting over in Truro, a two-year course, probably for students at least sixteen. You're a natural with horses, but with professional training and a college certificate between your fingers you'd do a lot better with Meadowlands than I have. I'll go over to see Will and find out what else he knows about it. I'm sure Bess can suggest books for you to read to keep your brain working. And you can help the hired men for part of the day. What do you think of that?"

"It's lot to take in, all at once," Morris replied. "Wouldn't Truro be expensive?"

Bessie, pleased with this news, quickly intervened. "My stocks have been doing well lately. I'll look after Truro."

"Oh, thank you, Aunt Bessie. Everybody should have an Aunt Bessie!" Morris exclaimed. "What a relief I don't have to go back. This last couple of weeks I've been wondering how I could stick with it. I can take Mary and Roger over and collect them and see my friends for a bit after school. There's only four months until the end of June, anyway. Wowsie and Trudy will be surprised."

"Let's wait until you're accepted at Truro, dear, and then tell them," Bessie cautioned. "Their letters are apparently read by a mistress and depending upon which one, they may be made to feel some negative impact. You can give your sisters all the details in June."

"I don't know which school is crazier, theirs or mine! I'll leave around three to collect the squirts and try to see Maizie, see if she's alright."

Partly to deal with his frustration over failing to get Morris reinstated in school, and partly to give his son an immediate goal, Mod tracked down Will Law the following day after he took Mary and Roger to school. Will was in his apple storage shed sorting out apples that had gone rotten.

After the usual greetings, Mod came right to the point; "You've probably heard that my Morris has been expelled from the Grammar for trying to help a Biddiscombe girl. Gabe told me you mentioned that Truro is starting an agriculture college in the autumn. Would you happen to still have the newspaper with that story?"

"It was only last week, so it should be here," Will replied.

He walked over to the pile of papers in the corner that he kept on hand for using between layers of apples when he put them into storage. He found the correct paper, opened it to the right page, and passed it over to Mod. Mod gave it a quick read and discovered everything he needed to know and handed it back to Will.

"Keep it," Will offered. "Your lad might like to see it."

24

Young Love and a New Name

Morris found himself in limbo. He had already finished the assigned homework and spent time every day trying to be useful in the barn. He felt in his bones and his heart that the decision to expel him would never be changed. He wasn't sure it would make any difference even if it was, except it would show the world that girls shouldn't be beaten on their inside wrists for something not their fault. He liked helping around the farm but was not at all sure he wanted to spend the rest of his life being a "gentleman farmer" like his father, employing others to do most of the work. Maybe the agricultural college at Truro was the answer. Perhaps he would learn how to grow especially good apples along with other things he knew little about.

While waiting for Mod to return, Morris took the scraper down to the cleared patch of ice, deciding to improve on it so he could have a skate with Mary and Roger after he collected them in the late afternoon. As he came to land, Mod used the momentum of the sleigh to pull up on the little hill close to where Morris was preparing the ice. He was saddened to see his clever, half-educated son just filling in time, waiting for news that might change his life for the better. Morris dropped the scraper and hopped on the sleigh's runners for the last spurt to the barn. As father and son unharnessed Horsey and Morris gave him a little rub down, Mod pulled Will's newspaper out of his pocket.

"Have a look at this. They'll take boys of sixteen with a good school record."

"But I don't have that."

"I'll get Millage to concentrate on your marks and usual behaviour. He owes us. Let's see what your aunt thinks. She's good at reading between the lines."

Dinner was on the table as they walked through the kitchen door. Bessie read the report in the paper and the three of them began dissecting the possibilities as they began their meal.

Bessie started out on a positive note; "If Truro offers suitable courses, perhaps you could travel with the girls and cousin Frank to Windsor.

I know there's been a train connection from there to Truro for the last five years or so."

"That's supposing Truro will take me."

"There's only one way to find out, dear. If you write for an application form to the address in the newspaper, saying you will be sixteen in July, you should hear back in a week or so."

Morris was glad to have something constructive to do. He immediately wrote the letter and showed it to Bessie, who approved and gave him a stamp from her supply. There was a good half hour before Morris needed to harness Horsey again for the afternoon drive across the river. He vigorously used the time improving on his morning's effort putting the ice in a decent shape for an after school skate. With the envelope, which might change his whole life, well wedged in his inside pocket, he coaxed Horsey into a trot over the snow road across the river, now well outlined with small spruce trees stuck in the snow every so often and with a trail of frozen horse dung. The runners slipped smoothly and easily over the temporary winter road.

Maizie was talking with Mary and Roger on the Grammar's steps when Morris arrived. She went immediately to the sleigh, her freckles standing out on her blushing cheeks.

"I'm ever so sorry, Morrie. I'll never forget what you did for me. I couldn't have born much more."

"I'd do it again," Morris replied, a bit overcome with the feeling of seeing Maizie again. "But I wouldn't knock her glasses off next time. I think that's what's really got me into trouble."

Maizie stepped close to the sleigh and reached out, putting her hand on the edge of the seat; "But there'll never be another time for two reasons: you've been expelled and Miss has come over all nicey-nicey with me. She wants me to sit for a scholarship so I can learn to teach."

"Are you going to?"

"It'll mean Myrtle will have to do housework out, Mum says. She's only thirteen and so small and skinny. I hate to think of it. Anyway it won't be until September, if it happens, after I'm seventeen."

"But you graded every year."

"Yes, but I was sick and the doctor said I mustn't start until I was seven."

"I hope you get that scholarship, become a famous teacher, and show that old witch."

With that, Maizie laughed and, in her usual way, tossed back her head so her curls bounced. Morris was glad to see her laugh again and was momentarily spellbound with feeling.

"What will you do, help on your farm?"

"Father's working on something."

"You'll be alright," Maizie said with confidence, looking straight into Morris's eyes.

She stepped back from the sleigh and added, "Mum wants me home. I've got to go. Bye."

Mary and Roger tucked the buffalo robe around their knees and ankles while their feet found the usual heated bricks under a layer of straw. Morris geed and hawed Horsey back onto the road, keeping an eye on Maizie's curls until his neck could turn no further in her direction. The young ones were chattering between themselves about school, which, as he trotted the mare across the ice road, left Morris's thoughts free to roam over the side effects of being expelled. For one thing, he would not be spending five days a week in the same room as Maizie any more, the realization of which gave him a kind of pain. "With luck," he mused, "we might meet for a few minutes like today, but in six months or so we'll likely have gone in different directions. If I hadn't tried to protect Maizie, none of this would have happened—but couldn't help it, I had to!"

The "squirts" more than just appreciated their brother's efforts at ice maintenance. They wanted to give him a hug, partly for his effort and partly to cheer him up. They had noticed how quiet he was on the drive back to Meadowlands.

After quickly swallowing glasses of milk and sampling Amelia's cookies, Mary and Roger booted up and were ready to shake off the restlessness that being in school produces. Morris took time to give Horsey a proper rub down after he hung up the harness and they all three headed for the river. Morris went through the motions of skating but his thoughts were elsewhere. Even while giving the young ones tips on turning corners and how to suddenly stop without falling, he could not get that last view of Maizie's bouncing curls out of his mind. He decided he wanted to be called "Morrie," Maizie's name for him.

Later that evening, when the family was half way through Amelia's crispy fish cakes and carrot casserole, Morris announced that from now on his name would be "Morrie." He explained that it was his school nickname but he didn't reveal who had given it to him or why this was so special. No one said it was a silly idea. After all, the nicknames "Wowsie" and "Trudy" had been readily accepted, though Bessie and Mod often forgot to use them.

It seemed to Mary that nicknames were something you were allowed when you were at least twelve or older. She wondered what hers would be. She didn't like "Mary." She knew she was named for her grandmother,

Mary Eliza, Father's mother, who died the year before she was born. The real reason she wasn't keen on "Mary" was because the memorial stained glass window to her grandmother in the Jemseg church, just by their pew, showed a woman in a long dress with the folds falling in a silly way; it made the upper part of her leg seem far too long and the part between her knee and her ankle too short. Mary knew she had a "good eye" for getting her drawings right, which had been confirmed by her teachers at school. It was a nuisance and made her uncomfortable to look at a picture that wasn't right. But she couldn't redraw the stained glass window, so she just disliked the name of the person it was meant to remember, which meant she had no choice but to dislike her own. She hoped her nickname would not be "May." May was the name of an unfriendly girl at Edgehill.

Roger was satisfied with his name, especially since his Aunt Bessie had told him that "Roger Morris" was the name of a famous man who lived in a big house near New York a long time ago. But he did like being called "Rog" by his brother, so he supposed that would be his nickname.

*　*　*　*　*

Aunt Bessie was right. Eight days after Morrie sent his letter to Truro, an application form arrived, which he filled in after checking with the grown ups. A reference from the most recent teacher or principal and marks from the last examinations were required. Mod could not bring himself to ask Millage, face to face, for a reference, and certainly not Miss Jones. He was afraid he would not be able to keep his temper in check. He decided to discuss it with Bess over tea and cake that evening.

The lemon and caraway seed cake Bessie made that morning when Amelia was concentrating on a pot of soup turned out exceptionally well. A little sliver tasted before serving assured her that she had not put bicarbonate of soda in it instead of sugar as she had with that icing a few years ago. That notable lapse from her usual careful attention to such things still haunted her; she had not repeated it. Mod pronounced the cake "moreish," which was always good for a chuckle and set the tone for their little ritual. Once Bessie had passed Mod his cup of tea, he brought out what had been swirling around in his head all day.

"What ideas do you have about this reference business, Bess?"

Bessie finished her first bite of cake, savouring the caraway seeds as their full flavour opened to her chewing and combined with the tartness of the lemon. She then sipped slowly on her tea, a sure sign of serious thinking.

Bessie began with carefully chosen words; "If Morris is soon to be launched into the world, making his own day-to-day decisions, I think he should handle the request for a reference. If the outcome is unsatisfactory, we can intervene, but let's give him a chance first."

"Do you think he should go over and ask Millage or write him a letter?"

"Let Morris decide. His hurt is not healed, so he may have trouble responding to any negative reaction from Millage without anger, which would not help the outcome. Let's see what his thoughts are. He certainly has excellent marks and there is nothing against his behaviour before he stopped Maizie's strapping. Face to face would give Millage an opportunity to make peace, but he might not be up to that yet."

"You're always so wise, Bess. All those years of nursing and dealing with the young and their problems… But you always had a level head on your shoulders."

"If that's so, it's probably because I was the oldest child and without siblings for so long; the poor little mites all died so early. I had more to do with grown ups, dear Mother, especially. She was wise in spite of her deafness. She taught me to look at all angles of a problem."

"Yes, we had good parents," Mod added. "It's so sad about Father's disaster. It was a bad time for banks in the '60's. Three went down in New Brunswick in the same year. Mother was wonderful. I never heard her complain through all those years of diminished circumstances at Douglas."

"She had happy memories of growing up there," Bessie explained, "so that helped coat the pill. Our grandparents and great-grandparents had the highest standing in the community so anyone living in Pine Grove had a certain cachet about them. Have another slice of cake, dear. This recipe was one of Mother's favourites."

*   *   *   *   *

When Morrie returned from taking Mary and Roger to school the next morning, his father and aunt suggested a chat. They asked him which road would he like to follow, a face-to-face request for a reference or asking in a letter?

"I was wondering about that, driving back this morning," Morrie replied. "I can't decide, exactly. If Millage gets nasty, I might not be able to bite my tongue and that would ruin everything. If I write and he sends a poor reference, I don't have to use it. I could then ask the old witch."

Bessie set the stage for a discussion; "No one can dispute you have always had very good marks and have taken part in school activities. Your father and I talked about this last evening. You clearly have two possibilities, a face-to-face request or a letter. Let's think about both."

The three discussed the topic until it was threadbare. Morrie finally made the decision to write to the Principal for an official copy of his marks in the last examinations and for a reference suitable for an application to the new agricultural college at Truro.

"Morris, you seem to have this well in hand," Mod finally said to his son in a tone of admiration. "I told Jock I would meet him about now, so I'll leave this to you two."

Bessie smiled as she could see this fatherly expression of confidence was not lost on her nephew. Mod got up, struggled into his heavy barn coat hanging just inside the kitchen door and went to meet Jock. Morrie assembled pen and paper and started immediately on the first draft of his letter.

As Mod walked to the barn, he was thinking ahead to the Kings County Fair in Sussex. Though it was now only early March, it was not too soon to plan for the September Fair. Mod wanted to talk over with Jock his plans for preparing Meadowlands' display of horses and whether he would need more supplies. While watching him work on the horses for the winter fair, Mod noticed that some colours in the wool supply were running low.

Mod had complete confidence in his groom. Jock was an expert horseman who took great pride in his work. He was particularly skilled in preparing Meadowlands horses for public events, which was important for the farm's business. The young Scot was a marvel at making eye catching rosettes from coloured wool like no others to place at the top of the horses tails, and for weaving into their manes. Mod knew some farmers came by just to look at Jock's latest artistic effort, but he also knew it was maintaining the basic quality of his horses that sold them, and this was Jock's main area of expertise. He hoped the fellow would see him out.

Though his wife died when their son, Willie, was small, Jock's mother was there to look after the domestic side. She seemed to rule the roost so it would be a special girl who would take on Jock for a husband, already with one child. It was rumoured, he had his eye on Amelia's younger sister. Mod smiled to himself as he looked forward to hearing that old country burr in Jock's voice. When he opened the barn door to the harness room, where they always met, Jock was putting the finishing touches on a list of his needs for September including which colours of wool and the number of hanks of each.

Bessie busied herself with next week's menus at the other side of the dining room table from Morrie. She was conscious of the bond between Mod and his eldest son, especially since Hattie's death. Mod was aware of the gap losing his mother made in his son's life, as was Morrie. At first, both made an effort to become closer, knowing Hattie would want it, and then it came naturally, which Bessie was glad to see. She was careful not to usurp Mod's role as a parent, but she was also aware how much she loved her eldest nephew with his quick wit and optimistic outlook. It was almost as though she had given birth to him herself. She so hoped this recent bump in his life would have no lasting negative effect and might even be an advantage if handled well.

Morrie was not entirely satisfied with the first draft of the letter. As he prepared to make a second draft, his mind wandered. He glanced at the chair at the end of the table and remembered his mother sitting there—the chair where his aunt now sat during meals. He often thought of Hattie, his pretty young mother. His strongest and dearest memory was of the days during her last August when they all would gather on the verandah, drinking lemonade, looking for cool breezes from the river in the late afternoon. Aunt Bessie could never replace her, but he and all of them were lucky to have her. He hoped she would stay and make a stepmother unnecessary.

Morrie shook himself out of his reverie and went back to his drafts. Finally, he completed a third version, which ended with the sentence; "As my examinations results will be those ending before last Christmas, I hope your reference will end then, as well." He studied each version again before lifting his head and sliding the papers across the table to Bessie. She read them all, thinking the last one was most suitable until she came to the final sentence. She thought, though did not say it, that if Mr. Millage was so lacking in self-confidence that he had to ask the School Committee for a decision, he could well take umbrage at being directed on how to do his job by a supposed miscreant. Morrie's suggestion might result in a less positive reference than he would write otherwise.

"I like the last version," Bessie responded, "but I would leave out the final sentence. It could do more harm than good just now. Mr. Millage might not like so much direction. Just make a good copy and sign it 'Respectfully, Morris A. Scovil' and see what happens. We can intervene if his reply is unfair."

Morrie concurred, made a new copy, and gave the letter to Mary as he dropped her and Rog off at the Grammar the next morning. There was no sign of Maizie on the road from her home, so he tickled the whip across Horsey's rump in order to be quickly on his way and lessen the chance of being spotted by the Principal or Miss Jones. Mary felt important, being trusted with what seemed liked a special mission. She knocked on the Principal's door and handed over the sealed envelope.

"Thank you, Mary," Mr. Millage said in a formal voice, from behind his glasses. Her Aunt Bessie had taught her to always say, "You're welcome," on such occasions so she did, and then turned toward her classroom, walking at a brisk pace, but not running, which she knew from her Edgehill days was an unforgivable sin.

Millage assumed whatever was in the envelope must have something to do with Morris, but this was a busy time of the day, so he put it to one side, in spite of his inclination to open it immediately. Several times during the morning, the Principal's eyes rested on the envelope but others were always in the room. He wondered if the Scovil family had decided to go to the law. He knew Miss Scovil was a clever woman, had travelled a lot, published many books, and even had tea with Queen Victoria. She could well have information he did not. This letter might contain facts that would complicate his life and perhaps cause him to be dismissed from the position he worked so hard to obtain. He must open it when he had some time to himself. All the children, except five, including the two Scovils, went home for dinner, but teachers often wanted to discuss something with him when they had finished their sandwiches, so even the noon hour would not be a good time to see what the envelope contained.

At the end of day, Mr. Millage finally slit the envelope with the metal letter opener decorated with an open book etched onto the handle, a present from his mother when he became Principal. He was completely alone in his little office. To show himself he was in charge of his emotions, he took off his glasses, puffed his warm breath on each lens in turn and polished them with his pocket handkerchief. Only after completing this ritual, did he remove the letter from the envelope.

As he read the letter, Mr. Millidge released the tension that had been building up in his chest, and which now came out as a sigh of relief. The letter, which he could see was written in Morris's hand, was straightforward, but he read it twice to make sure there was no hidden reason to feel uncomfortable. His worry was unfounded. His hunched shoulders relaxed to their usual position and he smiled. "Of course I will compose a letter of recommendation and will do so in very positive terms, not mentioning the recent and unfortunate episode. It was all too bad. Morris would have stayed on for at least another year and been a good influence on the younger boys. The Scovils were one of the few families that could afford to keep a boy in school after the age of fourteen. But Miss Jones had been adamant. Her highly respected uncle was on the County School Committee. She would have been hard to replace in mid-year if she had resigned, as she threatened, and that would have been a black mark against me in the Committee's eyes. What's done is done, but I'll do my best for the boy with a good reference."

Two days later, Morrie suddenly felt his heart beating in his throat, as Mary passed him an envelope while she and Roger were climbing into the sleigh for the trot home. He managed to get as far as the frozen river before his anxiety and curiosity combined to allow Horsey a short rest. There, on two pages were exactly what he hoped for and needed—a record of his Christmas examinations and a "To Whom It May Concern" letter saying nothing but nice things about him. Morrie carefully placed the papers back in the envelope, then slipped it into his coat pocket before letting out a whoop of relief that startled Horsey into a trot. Mary and Roger wanted to know why their big brother had gone crazy.

"That envelope has exactly what I need," he explained.

"Can you go back to school?" Mary wanted to know.

"I'm going to Truro—maybe."

Conversation on the subject began the moment the three opened the door and continued all through a supper of potato scallop, salted pork, along with Amelia's special bean pickles and treacle tart for dessert. After supper, Morrie settled into writing a short letter, advised by his aunt, to accompany the application form and the two documents from the Principal. Even before Mary and Roger had finished their homework, Morrie's puffy envelope was sealed and ready for posting.

For the next few days, the topic of acceptance and the result of that were often discussed by Mod and Bessie over tea and cake in the evening and by all of them at mealtime. Mary's eyes teared up at the thought of losing Morrie the way she had lost her sisters. Roger became very quiet. Morrie stared out of the window. The snow bank beyond the verandah was skimmed over with a fresh flurry of blowing snow and he could see Trixie chasing her tail, looking for a companion. Mostly he imagined what Truro would be like. He tried not to think about being rejected. That would lead nowhere.

Morrie scarcely looked at the mail for the first four days, and then it was Sunday. By Monday, when there was still nothing for him, he tried not to feel disappointed, but he was. Bessie recognized that look on his face, one that cheerful, joke-cracking Morrie rarely wore.

"Truro won't be very well organized yet, dear, so best not to expect a quick reply."

Morrie saw the sense to his aunt's remark and tried to busy himself with more than just taking and collecting the "squirts" to and from school. He shovelled wider paths to the pigpen, henhouse, barn, and outbuildings.

He kept the skating area free of snow. When Mary and Roger were busy with their homework he sat at the table with them, occasionally helping, but mostly properly reading last Christmas' book. He'd only it skimmed at first. *The Last of the Mohicans* by James Fenimore Cooper was heavy going, but soon, the fascinating story became something he gravitated to more and more often. He found it easier to deal with the unknown in 1757 than with the unknown of 1906.

25

The Art of Horse Show Grooming

The world continued to turn on its axis. Now that they were well into March, the sun rose noticeably earlier and set a little later every day. The usual letters arrived from Wowsie and Trudy with messages for Mary from Helen. Other envelopes in the mailbag were from Addie and Jack in New York and from Barclay in Calgary. Magazines and newspapers from various relatives arrived, as did the journals to which Bessie subscribed for keeping up with her profession. Correspondence from Bessie's friends and colleagues far and wide came in, but nothing for Morrie.

On the next Friday, after he returned from the school run and warmed himself near the stove, Morrie gently loosened one of Amelia's molasses cookies from it's moorings, though it was yet too hot to handle. As he was cooling it in his hand, Amelia wagged her finger and said, "Tut, tut." He just smiled back without saying anything, which was unusual for him. He was too preoccupied to come up with a response that would make Amelia laugh.

Bessie suddenly appeared in the kitchen door, having come from her upstairs writing nook to pour a new cup of tea. Morrie turned to his aunt and spilled out what had been eating him both ways across the river.

"Do you think I ought to write another letter to Truro? Maybe mine got lost. It's been more than ten days."

"I know it's hard to be patient, dear. But, as I said before, the college is just starting and they won't have a full office staff. The decision maker will be overloaded. I'd wait three weeks before you write again."

"If I can." Morrie replied with a mock groan.

Mod, lured by the rattling teacup and the smell of baking, came into the kitchen on his route to the parlor to read the latest New York Times from Jack.

"I expect Jock would teach you the fine points of decorating the horses tails and manes. They won't put up with just anybody doing it. Horses seem to take to you, son. Do you want me to ask him?"

"Yes, OK; I'd like that. It seems complicated, but I guess I could learn," Morrie responded, his face brightening.

"Learn everything you can about anything and store it away. You never know when it might be useful," Bessie added as she withdrew, mounted the stairs with teacup in hand, and returned to her writing nook to work on her articles.

"I saw Jock walk into the barn a few minutes ago. I'll go up and ask him now."

"Thanks. I'm clearing the paths again, after I steal a couple more of Amelia's specials. She knows they melt in my mouth."

"Oh, you do go on, Master Morris." Amelia replied without blushing.

"With reason, Amelia, with good reason! You ought to enter those in the Kings County Fair. You'd come back with a red ribbon."

"Oh, I wouldn't have the nerve. King's County's full of women who've been baking all their lives — ten times better'an me." Amelia paused and then added, "But your aunt told me a secret something to add, so maybe I would have a chance."

"And what's that?"

"Can't tell. Wouldn't be a secret then, would it?" Amelia laughed and went back to dropping spoonfuls of molasses and butter-rich dough on to the baking sheet.

Morrie walked out into the cold sunshine, picked up a shovel and set about reclearing the path to the barn. His head was down, thinking about what Truro would say, when suddenly his father's feet appeared just where he was about to scoop up the next load. As he straightened up he looked directly into his father's blue eyes.

"Jock would be glad to show you what he knows. After dinner today for a first lesson, say about one thirty."

"Good, that's an hour and a half before I harness Horsey for getting the kids. That should work."

Decorating a horse's tail and mane was much more complicated than Morrie imagined. It was not just straightforward braiding. Wowsie taught him how to braid Trudy's long hair when they were all young. That was easy, and once he learned, he never forgot. For the horse's tail, Jock chose three clumps of hair at the top, not the whole tail, combed them and started braiding, incorporating three strands of stout string called lobster marlin. It was just the colour of the horse's hair. Jock explained there was a good reason for the string besides making the braid stronger. When he came to the end, he pushed the tip of the braid through the middle of the braid at the top of the tail and tied it around itself to make a bun. It reminded Morrie of the bun at the back of the head of a chatty Gagetowner, Miss Featherstonehaugh, but larger.

With the bun firmly in place, Jock began showing Morrie how to decorate it. Using a huge version of one of Bessie's darning needles, he threaded it with bright green wool, soon producing what looked like a cluster of leaves at the top of the bun. He repeated the same leaves at the bottom, then changed the wool to yellow, which quickly became flowers growing out of both clusters of leaves.

"Now you try, on Horsey."

"Thanks, but I'd better do it tomorrow. It must be after three. I'm not trying to get out of it; I'm collecting the kids. Is tomorrow OK, at the same time?"

"Aye, lad."

The groom and Morrie smiled at one another, having both enjoyed the afternoon. Jock helped with harnessing Horsey, which is always easier with two. Morrie could tell by the sun it was well past three, but he dropped into the house to check and to tell someone he was crossing the ice. That was a rule. Someone else must always know when you planned to cross the ice, especially now that April was not far off.

Morrie became engrossed in the second session with Jock even more than the first. Mod's plan to provide a new learning experience for his son seemed to be working. For well over an hour and a half, patient Horsey put up with the novice's attempt to decorate her tail, just as Jock had with the big Clydesdale, Prince. He chose the same colours, trying to copy every detail.

"Pull the wool a little tighter, there, so the flowers don't droop."

"Like that? I don't want to hurt her."

"She'll let you know, if you do. Well done, lad. Do you have time for her mane?"

"Better not. I was almost late yesterday. Would tomorrow be OK?"

"Fine with me, unless your father wants me for something else."

"It was his idea, so I'm sure he won't."

Jock again helped Morrie harness Horsey, who flicked her tail more than usual, probably from discomfort, but Morrie could almost imagine from pride. He wasted no time crossing the ice, hoping for a chance to exchange a few words with Maizie, but when the sleigh pulled up at the school, he just caught a momentary view of her before she turned off the road; a glimpse was better than nothing. As Mary and Roger were approaching the sleigh, they spotted Horsey's decoration.

"Father's not going to sell Horsey, is he?" Roger asked, looking worried.

"No, no; I've had lessons from Jock! I did all that. Not bad, eh?"

"Looks like Jock did it," Mary declared.

"Thanks, sister. I'm braiding her mane tomorrow."

On the trot home, Morrie realized he had not thought of Truro all afternoon. Now with the mail bag, which he'd picked up from McKinney's store, safely stowed on the floor of the sleigh, he was wondering again. When they were back in the house and the mailbag's contents had been shaken out on the table, Morrie remembered the expression, "a watched kettle never boils." He wasn't superstitious, but he tried not to look as the sorting began, but couldn't resist sidelong glances.

The usual items tumbled out and sat on the table, until claimed. Most of the mail was always for Aunt Bessie along with a few items for Father. Hanging on to the possibility of good news, Morrie poked at the letters, making sure none were hidden. An envelope addressed in Aunt Addie's hand was not lying quite flat. He lifted it, and there was a small envelope addressed to "M. A. Scovil, Esq., Scovil's Point, Queen's County, NB." He picked up the cream coloured envelope and turned away from the rest of his family, not sure how he would react to rejection. He need not have worried. As soon as he grasped the content, he wheeled around and announced,

"Truro says 'yes'!"

The dining room shook with happiness. Morrie accepted his Aunt Bessie's hug and kiss. Mod clapped him on the shoulder. Mary and Roger danced around the table. Everyone read the letter. The mood had not faded when Amelia, who, of course, had heard everything, brought a celebratory tray of tea and the usual after-school milk and cookies for the young.

"They're lucky to have you, Master Morris, I'd say."

"I'll tell them that, Amelia!"

The acceptance was dissected over the late afternoon refreshments. The letter was brief. Term would begin September 16, 1906. A letter would follow with lists of required and optional clothing and supplies. A curriculum for the two-year course would be sent at the same time along with a breakdown of tuition fees per year, ten percent of which needed to be paid a month before classes commenced. A diploma in agricultural sciences awaited those who completed the program satisfactorily.

"Now can I tell Wowsie and Trudy?" Morrie asked, turning to his aunt.

"With such a happy outcome, I should think so, wouldn't you, Mod?"

"I can't see why not."

Mary and Roger usually played outside for a while after being tied to their desks most of the day, but this day was different. They wanted to stay close to their brother who would be taken from them too soon. Morrie settled to write to his sisters at Edgehill, sharing the drama of being expelled, and then accepted at Truro. Mary took out her homework, joining

Morrie at the dining room table. Roger found his as well and settled in a chair next to his brother.

The next morning, Horsey again sported her recent adornment across the river after her "flowers" were tightened a little when Jock and Morrie harnessed her. They confirmed their previous arrangement for the afternoon. But first, Morrie needed to talk to his father about what to expect at Truro. He found Mod seated at the side of the Franklin stove in the sitting room, devouring the most recent New York Times from Jack, a week old, but all new.

Mod freely admitted he had to guess what the agricultural college in Truro would be like. He explained that he and Jack attended school in Saint John until their bankrupt father had to leave the city. They finished their formal education at Douglas when they were each seventeen, Jack went into the reserve army and received a certificate saying he was qualified to "command a Battalion," but before there was a need to do so, departed for New York and a career as an accountant, a milder profession than that of army officer and to which he was better suited.

"When I finished school," Mod continued, "I thought I might also join the reserves. But by that time Meadowlands had become our family's haven. I learned how to operate a farm. My father was an intellectual and a city person, but even so, provided some good guidance in his declining months. My only schooling in farming came from observing grandfather Robinson organize his considerable acreage and watching his hired men at work; occasionally, I was allowed to assist.

Morrie listened to all this with great interest. He had never before thought about how his father had become a farmer. This was a revelation. He was filled with admiration at the way his father, just a few years older than Morrie was now, took on a big challenge and learned what he had to learn to be successful.

"We'll just have to guess," Mod offered, "but we'll know better once they send the curriculum. Having lived all your days on a farm and being so good with horses you won't have any problem. And you've always been good at school and know how to study."

There was a confidence in his father's voice that warmed Morrie's heart.

Morrie ate a second slice of Amelia's apple pie made from those sad looking disks of dried fruit that hung on strings at the back of the stove all October, now miraculously transformed. By the time he digested an article from *The New York Times* Mod put in front of him, which was about experiments with increasing the size of fruits through cross breeding, the dining room clock told him it was nearly one-thirty and time for his lesson.

Jock knew Morrie carried good news the second he walked into the harness room. The groom waited until the boy shared what produced such a bonny grin. With such a happy start, the mane decorating lesson went smoothly, though not without the need for mastering intricate moves. It was basically braiding all the mane hair with narrow plaits incorporating a strand of coloured wool with each of the three handfuls of hair and a neat finish of knots. At the top of each braid rested a "flower" similar to the ones created for the tail but different enough to require extra concentration.

"They might not know how to do this in Truro," Jock mused with a twinkle in his eye. "I learnt it as a lad in Sterling. You can teach 'em!"

Morrie took Jock's remark as a joke, but then began to think he just might know more than some of the others. He carefully watched Jock complete one side of Horsey's mane then tried the other, and with some pride in the result.

"If you're still here for the county fair, perhaps you'd help me get the horses ready, aye?"

"I go the week after, I think. Sure, I'd like that though maybe the horses wouldn't!"

After the session, Morrie immediately set out on the ice road for Gagetown. He urged Horsey to a fast clip in an attempt to arrive at the Grammar earlier than usual. Maizie was buttoning her coat on the school steps as the cutter stopped just in front. They smiled warmly at one another.

"Looks as though you're off to the fair," Maizie said as she noticed Horsey's colourful mane.

"Not yet, but I've been learning how to do it," Morrie replied as he jumped down from the cutter. "I do have some good news, though. I've been accepted at the new agricultural college in Truro for a two year course."

Maizie completely forgot herself and threw her arms around Morrie in a spontaneous hug of happiness for him and a lessening of guilt feelings over his changed circumstances. Morrie had been imagining a hug from Maizie for some time, and now, for a magical moment, they held one another in a tight embrace and then separated with hot, red faces, both laughing, both pleased it had happened.

"It was worth getting into Truro just for that," Morrie quickly joked, covering their slight mutual embarrassment but also showing his true feelings.

Mary and Roger tucked themselves under the buffalo robe, stowed their book bags so they wouldn't bounce out, and waited for their brother to finish talking with Maizie. They had seen the hug and knew something special had happened.

Maizies's freckles stood out on her flaming cheeks in a way that made Morrie want to kiss them, but the moment was broken when she announced: "I must run. Dr. Caswell's coming to see Mum. I have to look after the little ones. He's your uncle, isn't he?"

"Sort of. His wife is my mother's sister."

"That's why you're not a bit like him. He's so gruff."

"He's kind inside. When people are really sick he knows what he's doing."

Maizie finished buttoning her coat and hesitantly backed up a few steps. Morrie reached out, touched her arm and said, "I hope you'll be the next one with good news."

"We'll see. Bye."

"Bye."

"Hi squirts." Morrie at last greeted his siblings as he climbed on to the driver's seat. But he didn't immediately click his tongue against his teeth or pull on the reins to start the homeward journey. He waited until Maizie turned and waved just before disappearing around the curve in the road that led to her home.

26

"We're an island again."

The ice went out earlier than usual. After a mild spell the second week in March all movement across the river temporarily stopped—except for the most foolhardy or desperate. Then came a cold snap that again allowed the usual toing and froing. With that warning, Bessie made a list of foodstuffs for Morrie to buy at McKinney's in Gagetown to tide them over. There was always Dykeman's store at Jemseg, but they did not have the variety offered by McKinney's. Mary and Roger were laden with homework for three weeks, as it was likely the ice floes would make the river too dangerous for manoeuvering boats for at least that long.

There was something about the spring breakup that was a special time for everyone. Bessie had a little notebook in her desk drawer she called her "Breakup Book" in which she recorded preparations for this annual event. She now referred to it again and added new suggestions. Bessie had already sent two months of contributions to her journals and magazines and had written letters to her regular correspondents explaining her unexpected silence so they would not be worried or think her remiss. They would all write longer than usual letters to Wowsie and Trudy, reminding them of the spring breakup.

Roger and Mary liked the changed routine with their aunt supervising their schoolwork and adding her own wisdom. But they missed their friends and the twice daily adventure behind Horsey jogging over the ice road. With no school schedule this spring, Morrie asked Bessie if he could do the supervising of Mary and Roger's studies some of the time.

"Of course, dear. I would be grateful. That's thoughtful of you. You remember how it goes—three hours in the morning seems to be enough, with two or three breaks. An essay at the end of the morning is a good way to finish. Change it as you think best as long as the work is covered, and add more if you like. Try some reading in the afternoon. I'll give you some books to choose from. Read for a while until they are interested in the story and then have them take five minute turns. Mary reads well, but too long makes her eyes ache. I think she might need glasses. Roger definitely needs practice, which should also help with his spelling. I'll usually be at my desk if you need me."

For the next few mornings, Mod checked the thermometer then walked down to the river before breakfast to look for signs of what was coming—a slight melt where the ice meets the land or that indefinable something, a feeling of heaviness in the ice. After all these years, Mod had a keen sense of reading the ice just before breakup. Every few years, news of a fatal or near fatal accident on the river at breakup reached their ears. Usually it was boys daring one another to go out on the ice.

By Friday of a week that began cold, but moderated, Mod made up his mind.

"We're an island again," he announced over supper.

The sleigh might have crossed a few more times, but Mod was not prepared to take risks. His family had born more than enough sadness. Mary caught Roger's eye over the tomato scallop and ham. They silently smiled approval of Father's decision, which meant freedom from teacher's frowns.

Along with the enforced isolation of the breakup, came the possible disruption of usual life because of flooding. One of the topics at meal times now—bad floods of the past—fascinated the young, but was tinged with a little anxiety. Mod's tale of the most dramatic flood he remembered silenced them all, though he told it every year at this time. He stroked his moustache with his index finger and thumb on his right hand as he started.

"It was when your dear mother was still with us and three little ones under six. Spring was freakish. When the ice started moving, the rains came and didn't want to stop. In addition to the rain, there was more than the usual amount of snow still on the ground, especially in the woods. So when all that started melting way up in the woodland streams, the runoff poured into the river and the St. John flooded higher than we had ever seen it.

"Everything made of iron on the ground floor that we couldn't move had to be coated in grease, especially the kitchen stove. We used pig fat as we had lots of that. We set up a little makeshift stove on the second floor landing and could use the same chimney. A corner of the upper hall was turned into the pantry and all the furniture had to be moved upstairs. The bedrooms were full of extra furniture. Just as the water started seeping under the front door, Hattie remembered all the boots in the boot box in the front hall, so they were rescued. Do you remember helping to carry them up the stairs, son?"

"Sort of," Morrie answered. "Might be because I remember you telling us about it."

"It was sad to see our polished birch hall floor completely under water. And that's why the ceiling of the cold room is covered in sawdust."

"Tell us," said Roger. "I like this part the best."

"You know we bank all around the edge of the house every autumn with sawdust as an insulator against the cold and then put boards around it to hold it in place and evergreen boughs for extra insulation. Well, when the water surrounded the house, it poured into the basement and to the bottom floor, carrying some of the sawdust with it. When the water receded, some of the sawdust stuck to the cellar ceilings. It was mostly cleaned up but some was left to remind us it could happen again.

"When the water left the front hall — it had been a good foot deep — we hoped the floor would flatten out and waited until it pretty much dried, but it stayed buckled, warped. We had to bring in a carpenter. We even tied a rowboat to the verandah that year, so I could check on the animals and take the hired man some food. He stayed with us and slept in the barn to make sure we were all alright, the animals included."

Everyone was quiet for a few minutes wondering what Morrie then put into words.

"Any chance of that happening this year?"

"I don't think so. The snowfall has been normal. The water will probably be up to the verandah, some in the cellar, as usual, and over the lower fields, but I'll be surprised if it does more than that."

After a few days, high water made them an island and life settled down to the twice yearly rhythm of independence from the rest of the world. Everyone made an effort. Bessie tried to plan more interesting meals and Amelia took special care with new recipes. Mod encouraged his children to rise to worthy conversation at mealtime. Morrie suggested to Bessie that during their fifteen minute morning recess he take the young ones down to the bank to observe how the ice was going out. Bessie agreed. What they saw and heard changed each day. On the first few days, there was a grinding and growling of ice floes against each other like fighting animals, then, as the days passed, less ice and more water, running quickly.

"Look!" screamed sharp-eyed Mary, "There's a hen! Poor thing, she's all by herself."

Indeed, sailing from up stream was a lonely hen, apparently resigned to her fate, perched on a tree branch next to some barn boards firmly frozen into a sizable ice floe.

"Can we save her?" asked Roger.

"How?" his brother asked. "Do you want me to swim out to get her? I'd last about one minute in that water, don't you think?"

"Could Father take the boat out?"

"Too dangerous," Morrie replied. "Even if the boat didn't get crushed, how could the hen be coaxed into the boat? You know how nervous hens are. That's a Barred Rock. They don't much like to fly. Too bad it's not a Black Sumatra. They're good fliers. She'd be off that ice in no time."

The three siblings stood on the bank watching until the marooned hen was barely a speck in the downriver distance.

"Let's write our essays about it; maybe about what the hen is thinking." suggested Mary as they tramped back to the house, blowing clouds of warm breath into the frosty air. And so they did, all the while regaling their aunt and father with details of the homeless hen—a conversation that continued over dinner.

"Let's hope there's an ice jam further down so Miss Hen can hop to dry land," offered Bessie, looking for a happy ending for the hen so the children would not have bad dreams about her fate.

* * * * *

Bessie decided to take full advantage of Morrie's willingness to oversee the children's schoolwork, spending most the mornings in her writing nook under the eves. Though she had made the decision to cut back her contributions to *The Ladies' Home Journal* to "occasional," she had an urge to prepare something for next Christmas, which should be in the November issue and that would mean being in their hands by September, as she promised. "Last year's was popular so I will have the same theme, children's games, and suggest they publish it in November again, ready for Christmas parties. I'll just find that issue and make sure I don't repeat myself. There it is, page fifty-four under 'Old Games that Children Love.' I've paraded those old favourites: The Gooseberry Bush, Fox and Goose, Little Sally Waters, My Lady's Toilette, Oranges and Lemons, Oats, Peas, Beans and Barley Grow, I Sent a Letter to my Love, Hunt the Squirrel, Post Town, and Puss in the Corner. I have lots more up my sleeve, enough for this year's page—probably the last."

Bessie hummed the tune to "Oats, Peas, Beans" while she looked for her box with "LHJ Ideas" printed on the cover. She knew she was usually a little off key, a little flat, but no one could hear her, most of all Mary with her perfect pitch, who couldn't help remarking on her aunt's failure in musical matters. "Jack is my only brother who can sing well. But Hattie had a sweet voice, which must be where Mary's came from."

Inside the box, filed alphabetically under G, were pages of children's games, with ticks and dates beside those already used. She browsed through the others and selected several—A Menagerie, Birds in the Nest, Peter in the Bramble Bush, and The Dukes of Marlborough. She took out a full sheet of paper, dipped her pen in her inkpot and began an introduction to what she decided to call "Merry Frolics," suggesting age groups and occasions for each game. The Dukes of Marlborough was by far the longest. She read it carefully to see whether it was too complicated, decided it was not, and wrote a little preamble:

"Judging from its name this game must have come to us originally from across the Atlantic. Two children, a boy and a girl, if possible, are chosen to represent the Dukes. The Dukes advance toward a line of participants, singing:"

> *Here come two Dukes of Marlborough,*
>
> *With a ransom, tansom, tismal, tee.*
>
> *Here come two Dukes of Marlborough,*
>
> *With a ransom, tansom, tismal, tee*

The line responds, singing:

> *What is your will with us sirs,*
>
> *With a ransom, tansom, tismal, tee?*
>
> *Our wish is to be married,*
>
> *With a ransom, tansom, tismal, tee.*

The line:

> *Will any of us do, sirs,*
>
> *With a ransom, tansom, tismal, tee? etc.*

The Dukes:

> *You're all too black and brown, sirs,*
>
> *With a ransom, tansom, tismal, tee, etc.*

The line:

> *We're good enough for you sirs,*
>
> *With a ransom, tansom, tismal, tee, etc*

The Dukes:

> *We'll take the fairest of you,*
>
> *With a ransom, tansom, tismal, tee etc.*

The Dukes each choose a child from the line and then advance again, singing:

Here come four Dukes of Marlborough, etc.

"The verses are repeated again and again until all are chosen or the game palls."

Bessie finished with a fulsome paragraph hoping her readers would enjoy incorporating at least some of these games into their holiday repertoire etc. etc. In keeping with her lifelong habit, she would make a second copy just in case the postal service failed her or some other catastrophe prevented delivery. The second copy was usually the neatest and the one to be sent. She kept the original in her file. But this morning's effort would have to wait until later before a copy could be produced. Bessie had no wish to argue with Amelia's dinner bell; quite to the contrary, the morning's activity had given her an undeniable appetite.

When the last fat raisin and the last morsel of Queen-a-Pudding had been consumed and the dinner chatter about river breakup had wound down, the young cleared the table for reading aloud time. Bessie excused herself, taking a cup of tea up to her nook while Mod retired to the Franklin stove supposedly to read, but everyone knew there would soon be contented light snoring escaping through the open doorway.

Bessie started to make a good copy of her morning's work. Perhaps it was a little long, even for the fourteen by eleven inch LHJ. That had not made any difference in the past. The editor accommodated her article by changing the format—making the print smaller or larger as required. Sometimes it almost needed a magnifying glass, but the printer's ingenuity saved Bessie a great deal of trouble. An Associate Editor's contribution, with her reputation would not be chopped. Within an uninterrupted hour she produced a blemish-free copy.

As Bessie reread it, she found herself giving the lines in The Dukes of Marlborough more thought than she had when first selected. What would be the reaction of the Hectors or other Negro persons to the lines, "You're all too black and brown sirs?" They would never read it, of course, and neither would most Negro people in the States. There might be a maid in a comfortable household who would see a copy her employer had thrown out, but her reading abilities would probably not be advanced.

Bessie paused to reflect: "When I nursed Mrs. Tufts II, at her home in Newport, Betsy, a Negro maid, had one of the sharpest minds I had ever encountered. Cousin Sophie's chauffeur, James, was clean, personable and had mastered that complicated automobile inside and out, and was able to read and write. Lack of education and opportunity has kept Negro people in low positions. But who will clean out our outhouse if and when Sam's grandson goes to school, learns to read and write, works in an office? That won't happen in my time, but it probably will, one day. The potentially accomplished Negro maids of this world will grow tired of cleaning up after the dull minds of the Mrs. Tufts. Many think it is God's will that Negro people should serve white people. I cannot believe He would consider any of his people to be inferior to any others. Oh, well, this is only a children's game."

Bessie finished copying her clincher paragraph, wrote an accompanying letter to the present editor with her suggestion that her article be placed in the November issue, as was done last year with great success. She added that it could be her last but was not prepared to place that in writing and would like to carry on as she last suggested. She went on to say how much she had enjoyed her many years — since 1890 — of being associated with the prestigious magazine. After sealing the envelope, Bessie dropped it in the basket accumulating outgoing mail until it was safe to cross the river by boat.

As the envelope slipped from her hand, the sound of general movement and chairs scraping came up to her, signaling the end of story hour. Nicely timed. The day was still bright. Bessie slipped down the stairs.

"Would any of you like to come for a walk along the road? My brain needs some fresh air. How about yours?"

"I will," said Mary, always ready for a possible adventure.

"Me too," echoed Roger.

Although he had already spent four hours with the "squirts", something prompted Morrie to say, "I'll make four."

With the rapid melting and occasional rain, as much earth as snow and ice was now underfoot. Rubber boots were the order of the day. Bessie had a pair that fitted over her shoes and almost touched the bottom of her skirt. The others pulled on warm socks and slipped into their Wellingtons. Mod came in for a cup of tea just as they were ready to leave.

"Bess, can you spare your assistant tomorrow? I think he should come to Jemseg with me. Good experience. I'm going to be talking with a couple of men about summer work."

"Sure, I can go, can't I Aunt Bessie?"

Morrie lifted his head from taking a lump out of his boot.

"Of course, dear. You've already been a great help."

Before the four started on their walk, they all gravitated toward the river to check on the size and speed of the floes.

"There might be another hen," said Roger.

"I hope not. Poor hen. You wouldn't want to be on a piece of ice with no way to get home, would you?" Mary's soft heart had not allowed her to abandon the image of the stranded animal.

"The water's up only about a foot or so isn't it?"

"Looks like it, dear. It's running quite fast so maybe the flooding won't be too much of a nuisance."

The road to Jemseg was a mixture of mud ruts, snow ruts, puddles and icy patches.

"Give me your arm, Morrie. This is more slippery than I imagined. I don't want to break my old bones."

Morrie offered the crook of his arm to accommodate his aunt's hand. As they made their way up the Jemseg road, he felt comfortable knowing he was moving, almost imperceptibly, into adulthood a little more each day. Mary and Roger ran ahead, cleared a rivulet, unbanked a little dam, and crushed ice crystals with their heels. Once out of hearing range, Bessie quizzed her "assistant" about the children's progress. He answered as best he could, the role of "teacher" being so new.

The early part of the walk, up to the Mound where old Nelson was buried, was mostly open, bordering on some of the five hundred acres of hay producing fields. Then trees became more numerous until a small, dense forest of mixed conifers and deciduous stands took over on the higher ground. Both Bessie and Morrie knew this little forest extended only as far as the lake so they were not concerned when the two young ones disappeared to explore on their own. Laughter and twig snapping indicated they were not far away.

"This wind is getting rather fierce. If we turn around it will be at our backs."

As Bessie spoke, Morrie stopped and looked into the woods for Mary and Roger. But what he saw were two black balls high up in the branches of a tree, like squirrels' nests. But these weren't nests, they were moving, they were bear cubs! Morrie knew, as did everyone over the age of five who lived in the country, that getting between a mother bear and her cubs was not a healthy place to be. With a shudder, he realized that could be just where his little sister and brother were right now.

Morrie did not wait to consult his aunt, or even to tell her what he saw. He called out in as loud a voice as he could summon,

"Get out of the woods, right now. Bear cubs up a tree."

A few seconds passed; no children appeared. Morrie called again, and then the two tumbled out through the bushes at the edge of the woods running like scared rabbits, looking behind them every little bit. When they reached the safety of the road, they looked back and saw the cubs, safe in their swaying tree. There was no sign of the mother.

"Let's move," Morrie said with some urgency, as Mary and Roger broke off the hugs Bessie was giving them, their two small bodies still shaking from fear.

"You took a while. Could you hear me bellowing the first time?"

"Yes, we ran as fast as we could, but my legs seemed to be tied to the ground. That never happened to me before," Mary panted.

"Did you see the mother?"

"I saw something big and black," said Roger, holding tightly to his brother's hand.

"It might have been a rock," Mary offered. "There's a big one in there."

"The main thing is you're both safe," Bessie said, accepting Mary's hand for the entire walk home.

"I'm proud of you, dear, the way you took charge."

"Just seemed to be the thing to do."

From time to time, they all turned to make sure they were not being followed. But with the wind at their backs, their scent was also being pushed away from the bear. They soon felt clear of the danger.

"We were nearly chased by a bear, Father," Mary exaggerated as they all sat down to tea, milk, and cookies. Mod listened attentively to various versions of the adventure. Bessie caught Morrie's eye and they both smiled.

27

Mary Befriends a New Student

The rain that spring was not excessive, nights remained cool, and the days too. The three weeks passed without more drama and the river was once gain safe for boating. Mary and Roger returned to school feeling they had missed nothing except the companionship of their friends. Morrie rowed over and back from Scovil Point to Gagetown twice every weekday. The exercise strengthened his arm muscles, which he could see were taking on a manly appearance.

He and Maizie talked a bit when their paths crossed, as they did when Morrie arrived a bit early, before school let out. But their chats were brief. Maizie was always in a rush to get home to help her mother. Dr. Caswell told Maizie that her mother had tuberculosis, must rest more, and could not go out to do housework in other people's houses until she was completely recovered. Maizie's thirteen-year old sister took over their mother's paid housework. There was no alternative if the family of four were to eat. Morrie knew the situation. Their father died about five years ago, leaving nothing but bills. The two little boys were too young, at six and seven, to bring in more than pennies from McKinney's store, where they did odd jobs on Saturdays.

The promised envelope arrived from the agricultural college at Truro with all the details needed, including a list of six books recommended as background reading. Mod and Bessie, with considerations from Morrie, chose two as the most useful for a young man who was already familiar with farm life. Bessie promptly ordered them from a recommended bookstore in Halifax. With the outline of the courses in hand, Morrie had a better idea what to expect from Truro, which now began to look like something he could handle. "Truro," rather than being just the name of a town, now took on a shape, a feeling, a sense of a new life, a challenge. When the books arrived, he made a point of reading some every day until they were both more or less digested, sometimes with a little help from Mod, when asked.

*   *   *   *   *

A new girl had been added to Mary and Roger's schoolroom in their absence. Her name was Magnolia, but she was called Maggie. Her family had moved from the Otnabog settlement, a few miles away, to a little house on the outskirts of Gagetown. Her father had secured a full time job working at Reid's sawmill.

Mary was familiar with the pale brown, grown-up Hectors, and their two small babies, but Maggie was different. Her rich brown skin and wooly hair were exotic. It was a change for Maggie as well. Everyone in her previous school was like her, but here the students were all different. She was a month younger than Mary, both ten. Mary had never talked to a Negro girl her own age. She was fascinated by Maggie's broad smile that showed off her perfect teeth. Mary tried to think of things to say that would make Maggie smile so she would show her teeth—so much more beautiful than hers. Mary's lower teeth were pitted because she had scarlet fever when they were growing in. Mary always noticed and envied perfect teeth. She liked Maggie and made sure she was included in the games at recess time.

One warm day in late April, Mary appointed herself to select someone to be "it" in a game of tag. She collected a circle of girls around her. She started pointing at each girl in turn, "Eeenie, meenie, miney, moe, catch…" Mary was suddenly aware she would point directly at Maggie when she said "nigger," Maggie was just two girls away. She knew she must not do that. She quickly said, "Oh, let's have 'one potato, two potato' instead." The other girls instantly put out their "potato" fists in front of them and Mary continued, "One potato, two potatoes, three potatoes, four, five potatoes, six potatoes, seven potatoes, more," with the elimination of one "potato" on "more," until only one person was left, who was then "it."

Mary wasn't sure whether Maggie knew why she had changed the selection method; the others must have been aware but no one said anything. They all just got on with playing tag until the bell rang. Mary felt she owed Maggie. She knew she had nearly insulted her new friend. She hadn't really, but so close. Maybe Maggie hadn't even noticed but Mary remembered how she had felt at Edgehill, trying not to show she cared about a hurtful remark. Maggie was probably used to being called a "nigger," so maybe it wouldn't have mattered if she hadn't changed to "potatoes." It was confusing, but Mary's conscience bothered her, so she made sure Maggie was included in all the games, smiling at her when she won.

One day, just as recess began, Mary and Maggie were the last two in the "coat line." The other students were already out the door. As Mary was hurrying to button her coat, Maggie came up to her and placed a kiss with her pretty pink lips on Mary's right cheek.

"I lub you, Mary."

"Oh ... that's nice," was all the astonished Mary could manage. She was pleased, in a way, but at the same time a little uneasy. Kissing was something that happened in families, or at least among relatives. It was a stage beyond hugging. Maggie had jumped that custom. Schoolgirls did not hug or kiss one another at Edgehill, though a hug seemed to be allowed if someone was hurt and perhaps crying, but not always. Mary decided she would not tell her family all the happenings of the day. She would leave out the recess kiss. It was too special, too unusual, and the grown ups might not understand.

*   *   *   *   *

April grew into a sunny May. Morrie took over the kitchen garden. A hired man plowed and spread manure as soon as the tilth was right. Mod and Morrie spent an afternoon together deciding what should be planted and where, rotating from last year to take advantage of what certain plants gave to and took from the soil. They paid a visit to McKinney's store, which had all the seeds needed, including onion sets. They had their own potato sets from last year's crop. Morrie was keen to plant. Mod complemented his son's enthusiasm but advised caution. He explained the unwritten Victoria Day rule—no seeds in the ground until the twenty-fourth of May.

The old Queen had been dead for five years, but, in New Brunswick, her birthday was still a good date for gardeners to mark and start their planting. Before Victoria Day, the soil was often still too cold for good germination and soaking rains rotted seeds and sets. Some gardeners gambled with earlier planting and were occasionally lucky, but usually it was not worth the risk of losing seeds and effort and then replanting. Experienced gardeners knew that seeds planted when the soil was fully warmed up, even if they waited until early June, would rapidly germinate, quickly grow into strong plants, and yield a good crop.

Sure enough, Mod's words were prophetic. On the seventeenth of May it started in with a heavy cold rain—the kind that bounces off the ground when it hits. This weather continued off and on for four days. The ground was soaked. By the twenty-sixth, and after three days of sun, the soil was warm and dry enough to plant. Jock came by to admire Morrie's first day of planting just as he was covering the potato sets.

"You might want those spud sets a little nearer the light. They'll go blind down there."

"A couple of inches deep?"

"Try three."

"OK, thanks."

Morrie went back over the uncovered row, raising each potato set so it would be covered to the depth recommended. After a full day of planting, he complained over supper that he would never be straight again.

"There's a secret, son. Don't stay bent too long, straighten up completely and stretch and then go at it again," Mod advised. "I should have mentioned that."

"There has to be a secret," Morrie quipped, "otherwise farmers would all be bent double by the time they were thirty."

"What about the orchard pruning you did last March? You seemed to take to that."

"Arms are tougher than backs, but I need more arm muscles, too. If I had my own mixed farm I'd soon be fit or dead from starvation or overwork!"

"When you finish the planting, Jock has agreed to teach you everything he knows about horses, even making horse shoes."

"I'd like that. I'm a horseman, I think, but I need to try everything. Perhaps I don't have to go to Truro."

"You'll learn a lot of theory at Truro. There's a science behind farming. With the practical stuff in your head and your muscles, you'll have something to hang it on."

"You might even want to teach there one day," added Bessie thinking of the teaching role he had taken on with Mary and Roger. "You have a capable head on your shoulders."

28

A Trip to Atlantic City & "New Eyes" for Mary

In early June, Wowsie's and Trudy's letters announced an invitation would arrive from cousin Madge soon, asking them to spend two weeks in Westfield at the Starr summer house, as they did last year.

"I hope there is no reason why we cannot," Wowsie wrote in her best hand, fit for passing the mistress' censoring. "It will be such a good chance to improve our tennis. Ayleene says we will have lessons. We are looking forward to being with you all at Meadowlands, of course, but that will be delayed only until the second week of July. Also would it be possible for Ayleene to return with us and stay for a week or so? Cousin Frank would accompany us from Westfield on the riverboat."

The same mailbag brought the letter from cousin Madge.

"Jammy humbugs," Morrie exclaimed. "I hope they don't get too stuck up, playing tennis with those rich kids. Ayleene is so quiet, but she started to come out of her shell last summer."

Bessie responded more positively; "It's so good of Madge and Frank to take such an interest in the girls. The least we can do is have Ayleene here for a week or so."

*　*　*　*　*

The Grammar's closing in the third week of June included a choir with Mary and Roger in the front row — Mary because she could sing and was short and Roger chiefly because he was short. Morrie decided he had been away long enough that he could return with his father and aunt as family. His desire to talk with Maizie, to hear the outcome of her examinations, was greater than his fear of possible embarrassment if Mr. Millage or the witch said something to him he didn't know how to deal with.

Morrie wondered why he had recently missed connecting with Maizie even when he came early to pick up Mary and Roger. When he asked Mary about this, she said Maizie was sometimes in school and sometimes not. Surely, she would be at the closing. She was not. Nora, a friend of Maizie's, told him her mother was too sick to leave alone, but she'd passed her examinations and would probably get a scholarship. He was disappointed not to see those bouncing curls and have a chance to talk with her, but he was glad to know that at least she would likely not have to earn a living doing other people's housework.

Both Mary and Roger's report cards indicated progress but Mary's teacher commented on her difficulty seeing clearly what was on the blackboard and her inability to read for any length of time without her eyes tiring. This confirmed her aunt's recent suspicions that Mary must have her eyes tested. Bessie herself had worn glasses for many decades, having first acquired them when she was a nursing student. After trial and error, she eventually found a young man, a Dr. Hindsmith in Atlantic City, New Jersey, who had the reputation of being "the best refractionist in the United States." He had diagnosed her rather difficult eye problems, which led to successful treatment with glasses. Over the years, Bessie had regularly returned to Dr. Hindsmith for continuing care and updating the prescription for her glasses, though she had not done so since coming to Meadowlands, three years ago.

Bessie decided that Mary must have the best eye care as well. Guilt still nagged at Bessie for not being there to care for Mary during the later stages of scarlet fever. At that time, Hattie was pregnant and not well and Elizabeth wanted to take a photograph of the whole family sitting in the sun in front of the Meadowlands' house. Had Bessie been there, she would have kept Mary in bed, in her darkened room, rather than having her eyes exposed to the bright sunlight.

Bessie had a word with Mod about Mary's eyes. He wondered about the expense. She assured him she would look after it. With her brother's gratitude and acceptance of her plan, she went straight to her desk and wrote to Dr. Hindsmith for an appointment for her niece and for herself in the near future. After that, she composed a letter to her cousins at Douglas and another to Addie and Jack in New York, asking to stay with them while on this journey. Four days later a reply came from Dr. Hindsmith's office, suggesting Thursday, June twenty-ninth at 2 p.m. "Splendid!" thought Bessie. "We'll be there and back before the girls arrive home. Mary will love Atlantic City and it's boardwalk along the ocean beach. I could do with a little American air again as well." The same mailbag brought welcoming replies from Douglas and New York.

Bessie shared the news over supper.

"Will my eyes stop aching when I read, if I have glasses?"

"They should, dear."

"How will we get there, to Atlantic?"

"Atlantic City, it's called. We'll go by riverboat to Fredericton, stay the night with the cousins in Douglas, take the early morning train, and, after making several connections, arrive in Atlantic City where we'll spend two nights in a hotel in case you need a second appointment. We'll then take the train to New York and stay with Aunt Addie and Uncle Jack for two nights. Do you remember being there when you were five?"

"Quite a lot of it," Mary replied. "I went to that kindergarten where rich children took animal crackers for their lunch and I just had bread and butter sandwiches. Uncle Jack laughed a lot and had a red face. Cousin Delancey was mean. He'd walk me to kindergarten but almost ran. I had to hang on to his little finger and just about flew or he said he'd leave me behind. I was always scared on those walks that he would really leave me and I wouldn't be able to find my way back. But it was fun singing at that big hotel, the Waldorf something. I wore a heavy black wig as I was supposed to be a Japanese. It made my head hot and itchy."

"Yes, you were one of the 'three little maids from school.' All the cast was from private schools in New York, mostly those specializing in music. I think the owner of the kindergarten knew the organizer and told him of your good singing voice. You were the only one from your little school to be in the play."

Mary smiled, thinking of what it had been like looking out at the audience in that fancy hotel, remembering when to sing and not to scratch her head.

"Will I have to put up with Bess and what about Charlie and Delancey?"

"Charlie is studying to be ordained and Delancey is starting this autumn so I expect they will be away as councelors at an Episcopal summer camp, and perhaps Bess too. She is nearly 17."

Bessie thought about all the fees she had quietly paid for those three children to attend summer camps in order to take them away from the noise and dirt of the city.

"What's Episs …?" smirked Roger.

Bessie ignored her nephew's attempt at off-colour humour. "Episcopal is the word Americans chose for their Anglican Church, once they became independent of England.

"Bess is so stuck up," Mary said as she pointed her nose in the air. "She thinks her buck teeth give her the right to be superior."

"She's not used to farm life. She's alright after she stops feeling strange," Morrie added, thinking of how well they got on when she visited last summer, laughing when she fell into the cow muck.

"I should tell you," Bessie added, "your Uncle Jack does not have a full time position as an accountant anymore, not since the President closed the Trust company where Jack had worked for nearly two decades. He occasionally obtains part-time work. I'm telling you this, Mary, so you don't ask him why he is not going to work, or make any reference to it."

Mary nodded in response.

The evening was still sunny and warm. After supper, Mod took his cup of tea to the verandah, the young went outside looking for adventure, and Bessie climbed the stairs to her writing nook with tea in hand, continuing to think about poor Jack, poor in more ways than one, she knew well.

"I send him a cheque every month to cover the rent for increasingly smaller apartments, though I would not be surprised if some of the money were used to purchase intoxicating beverages." Bessie mused. "Alas, it's an unfortunate habit he may have picked up when training to be an Officer in the Reserves in Fredericton before he even left for New York, or perhaps cousin Bev and his fast crowd in the big city lured him into imbibing. Jack and Addie were such a handsome couple with the promise of a happy life, but has each fallen short of that—Jack losing his position and Addie being robbed of her health by her father. Bess was a difficult birth. Addie should have had extensive repair work done, but Dr. Barker, her father, confident she would not have to lift anything heavy in her affluent life, wanted to spare her the discomfort of complicated stitching with the greater chance of infection. I received a request from Addie for $200 to pay for an operation to have her prolapse corrected. I sent it by return mail with details of what she might expect in the way of convalescence and with cheerful comments about how much better she would feel. Alas, I could have restrained my enthusiasm. The operation never took place. It was "postponed" several times and then the money vanished to pay bills. That dear Jack put Addie up to the ruse, if that's what it was, is not an idea I like to entertain. We were all brought up to be honest. I must concentrate on thanking the good Lord I am able to help those badly in need. He directed me toward the best path for me—no husband, but instead a good career in nursing and writing which has meant I can help others. In return, He has allowed me to enjoy Mod and Hattie's children as though they are my own and perhaps help them along satisfying paths. Enough musing. I must make a list of clothes Mary and I will need, and, oh yes, write to that nice little Traymore Hotel on Illinois Avenue in Atlantic City, near the doctor's office. There's no time for a reply, so I'll ask them to contact the hotel next door if they are full, and for a room with two beds so Mary's tossing won't keep me awake. Gracious! We must leave the day after tomorrow. We'll take the early train from Fredericton so there's no need for the Pullman car. I'll treat us to two meals in the dining car. Mary will like that. Let's see — we'll be back in eight days: a night in Douglas each way, two nights in Atlantic City, two in New York and two days on the riverboat."

The deep frown that had taken over Bessie's expression as she ran over the vexing past in her mind now softened as she chose a piece of paper, dipped her pen in the ink bottle, and began a letter to the Traymore Hotel.

While Bessie was thinking and organizing, Mary was writing to Helen. Now that school was over, they could exchange letters. "I have so much to tell her — the stranded hen, the bear cubs, and especially the trip to Atlantic City. It's silly I can't write to her at school. I still have her Christmas letter. I'll reread it."

A feeling of weepy sadness crept up on Mary when she was half way through Helen's letter. For a few minutes, Mary wished she were returning to Edgehill with Wowsie and Trudy in the fall, chiefly to see her friend but also to swing Indian clubs and to learn so much every day. But she knew she would have the underlying dread of Bully Girl. She looked at her knuckles, now entirely recovered from the piano teacher's yardstick, and the agony she had endured flowed back. If she couldn't sleep properly and was always scared, that was no place for her, in spite of having to give up Helen, almost. They could be pen pals in the holidays, and perhaps when they were older could visit one another. Meadowlands and Gagetown might be quiet and slow but at least she could relax, feel safe, and be herself.

*　*　*　*　*

When Mary and Aunt Bessie returned from their journey to Atlantic City and New York, Mary talked almost non-stop for two days. She declared these two cities were the most exciting in the world — the noise of horses hoofs, of engines, of trains, of metal wheels on cobble stones, and of so many people all talking at once created unimaginable excitement. She went on and on about the tall buildings almost blotting out the sky, such colourful clothes, bright store windows, and people selling food on the sidewalk. Over supper the first night, when everyone was well launched into their bowls of fresh strawberries and cream, Morrie asked Mary what the two best things were about the trip.

She thought for a minute, then said, "Three: the eye doctor finding the trouble with my eyes, cousin Bess being away, and eating in the dining car on the train. Oh, yes, and skipping along the boardwalk by the ocean in Atlantic City. That's four."

Bessie laughed at Mary's selection, though she was pleased her eyes came first.

"It turns out," Bessie explained to the family, "that Mary has extreme astigmatism, which means she has trouble making both her eyes look at the same letter or word. This is why reading tires her eyes so much. It also appears that some of the pigment—the colouring matter in her eyes—has been destroyed, probably when that photograph was taken when she had scarlet fever. That's why the bright sun bothers her. The doctor will send spectacles that should get rid of the first problem, along with a new pair of sun glasses to replace her old ones, which are a little small now."

"It will be like having new eyes," Morrie added with a note of happiness for his sister. "Looks like that trip was well timed."

"Yes, and Aunt Bessie had her eyes checked too."

"No change for me, luckily. Mary's should have been tested before. Her "new eyes" will be here in a few days."

Indeed, within a week a little packet arrived for Miss Mary Scovil. The family gathered with anticipation. The prescription spectacles, snuggled in a firm case, immediately landed on Mary's nose and stayed there. She walked around the house, examining first one thing and then another with delight, reading a few lines from a book, smiling, and laughing. She then went out doors, walking around examining leaves and flowers.

"Oh, oh, oh!" she exclaimed over and over. "Oh, thank you, Aunt Bessie. This is the best present I've ever had! I must be seeing like other people do! And my new dark glasses fit much better than my old ones."

Mod had moved to the sitting room and was reading *The New York Times.*

"Come here, Mary," he called. "Let's see how your eyes feel after reading this."

Mary skipped in with her silver-rimmed, owl-eyes sparkling on her nose and sat on her father's lap. He selected a column about the care of horses in New York City, choosing a paragraph near the beginning, before the less than pleasant details were revealed later. Mary flew through the paragraph, stumbling only on one word, and then hugged her father after announcing, "My eyes don't have that pulled feeling any more. This is like a miracle! This is so lovely!"

29

Creating a Tennis Court

Mary was looking forward to surprising her sisters and cousin Ayleene with her changed appearance. They were due to arrive in two days time so that meant a flurry of cleaning and airing their bedroom and moving in another bed. Bessie spent a little extra time planning meals for the following week, making sure some of Wowsie and Trudy's favourite dishes were included, assuming Ayleene would like them as well.

"I'll make a little note to include food related activities—making ice cream and pulled molasses candy and perhaps divinity fudge. The girls might also enjoy preparing a meal. It's unlikely that Ayleene knows more culinary arts than how to boil water, if that, so the novelty might appeal. We might as well promote the rustic pleasures that Meadowlands has to offer. This is part of its charm for city dwellers."

As soon as the three girls walked down the gangplank, Morrie knew it would be a different sort of summer. Each girl carefully carried a tennis racquet in a press under one arm. Morrie had rowed one boat. Jock, with Mod as a passenger, had rowed another to the Gagetown wharf. But three girls, two trunks, and Frank were more than two row boats could handle. Knowing this in advance, Mod had arranged to borrow one of the Caswell's boats, which would make the journey more comfortable and safer, in case the water were choppy. Frank had a little overnight case with him as well. Bessie had invited him to stay at least a night. She did not often vacate her bed for a visitor, but Frank had been so generous, ascending to the second attic room for one night was the least she could do. The alternative was to oust Mary from her bed, but it was on the narrow side for a body as substantial as Frank's.

Bessie, Mary, and Roger were already at Scovil's wharf when the three boats could first be spotted making the return trip. There were times when Mary forgot she was wearing spectacles, but this was not one of them. Even before it was at all sensible to wave a welcome to the travellers, she rearranged the glasses several times on her nose. As the boats came closer, she began to wave and call out. Roger joined her. All three girls called back and waved. Then they were at the wharf and climbing out as the men steadied the boats. Hugs, big smiles, and laughter accompanied everyone's chatter along with Trixie's welcoming barks.

The girls immediately noticed Mary's new adornment and commented on how smart the glasses looked. They were aware that glasses were sometimes the cause of unkind teasing and wanted Mary to be proud of them. They were quickly reassured when Mary bubbled over with enthusiasm for what the glasses had done for her eyes. Roger's extra inches of height did not go unnoticed. Everyone could see he was in a growth spurt and was no longer a little boy. All three Edgehill girls had gained poise, height and womanly figures. Morrie noticed that Ayleene's eyes were the palest blue he had ever seen.

As the group began moving toward the house, Morrie and Jock transported Trudie's trunk by wheelbarrow and carried it together up the front stairs, as the back stairs were too steep. They repeated the operation with Wowsie's trunk, adding Ayleene's valise. The riverboat dining room had provided an ample meal less than three hours earlier, so Bessie had arranged for them all to have glasses of this season's raspberry cordial and small cakes on the verandah.

As they relaxed in the pleasure of being family, the two generations seemed to meld. Wowsie and Trudy described the highlights of the trip from Westfield, their unforgettable week there including five days of tennis lessons and how they hoped to make a tennis court at Meadowlands, with Morrie's help. Mary held everyone's attention as she described the highlights of Atlantic City, New York, and the train trip. Frank caught them up on the latest development in Saint John, which especially interested Mod. Morrie had already written to Wowsie and Trudy about being accepted at the agricultural college in Truro, but they wanted to know more and this was news to Frank. Bessie watched her growing family with pleasure and satisfaction.

The next morning, after a leisurely breakfast, they all walked down to the wharf to say goodbye to cousin Frank. Wowsie and Trudy properly thanked him for a splendid week with the Starr family, and he, in return, thanked them for what he termed was a touch of "real life." The expansive Frank hugged all the girls, shook hands with Mod, smiled and nodded to the boys, and, with a remark of appreciation, bowed to Bessie.

While Morrie and Frank boarded the Scovil boat, Mod took up the oars of the Caswell boat for its return. They pushed off for Gagetown where Frank would catch the riverboat back to Westfield.

As Morrie pulled on the oars, Frank called out to his daughter, "See you in a week at Westfield."

"Eight days," corrected Ayleene, which was the time she and the girls and Bessie had determined would be convenient.

"Right; that's a Tuesday, isn't it?"

"Yeeeeeesssss," the three older girls dragged out the answer and waved, as Morrie's strong rowing picked up momentum.

By the time Morrie and Mod delivered Frank to the wharf, saw him off on the riverboat, returned the Caswell boat, did a little shopping for Bessie at McKinney's, and rowed home, dinner was almost ready. Meanwhile, Bessie enlisted the young in making strawberry ice cream. It was going to be a hot, sunny, July day and ice cream would be a hit. They started by picking strawberries right after breakfast, hulling and slicing them, retrieving ice from the ice house, and crushing and packing it around the canister that held the cream and strawberries in the ice cream maker. Then came the big task of turning the crank that rotated the paddle inside the canister until the contents froze into ice cream. Morrie was tired after all his rowing in the heat of the day, but he volunteered to take a turn with the cranking every few minutes to insure uniform freezing.

Much to everyone's satisfaction, dinner consisted of a cold meat pie with a pastry, accompanied by freshly cut cucumber and tomato slices, along with Amelia's freshly made bread and butter. Mary commented that the pastry was "as light as a butterfly's wing." The strawberry ice cream dessert surpassed all expectations, not least because everyone had had a part in producing it, including Mod, in a way. He had supervised the replanting of the strawberry runners of the previous two years, insuring the good crop they were now harvesting. The huge mound of new ice cream was served in the cut glass bowl taken from the china cabinet for this occasion in Ayleene's honour. They all had seconds. Only the tiniest of pink pools of melted cream remained in the bottom of the bowl.

Before all the young helped clear the table, Wowsie requested everyone's attention and presented her plan for a tennis court at Meadowlands.

"Tennis is such fun. The teacher at Westfield gave us a little book with the court measurements in it and an old net with a few holes they were going to throw out. I brought it home in the bottom of my trunk. "

"I wondered what made it heavy as lead," Morrie quipped.

Wowsie wrinkled her nose at him and continued; "We thought we could make a tennis court on the stretch of grass on the far side of the house, on the way to the orchard. There's plenty of room."

Trudy burst in: "Morrie, if you could hitch a horse up to the mower and cut the grass as close as possible a couple of times, the rest of us could pace it off, tie strings to pegs and paint white lines with whitewash."

"Oh, let's," said Mary and clapped her hands.

Everyone looked at Mod.

After a pause, he nodded his head, smiled and said, "I don't see why not. I've thought of enlarging the orchard there, but that can always be done in the future."

"What a good idea," added Bessie, knowing this would keep all the children happily occupied for days.

Ayleene, feeling at home in this relaxed and informal family of cousins, chimed in, "I'll help too. I'm so glad to be here."

*　*　*　*　*

And that is exactly what happened. Later that afternoon, in spite of already having had more than enough exercise, Morrie cut the grass with the mower on its lowest setting. But first, since he seemed to be in charge, he ordered all the others to pick up and clear the area of all sticks and every stone larger than a five-cent piece. He pitched in and helped. Mary had the bright idea of using a hand rake to remove big stones and small sticks. The raking worked well but was so tiring they took turns. They began to wish tennis courts could be a little smaller. After two hours of raking and hand picking in the sun, Amelia appeared with a tray of fresh lemonade with ice bits in it.

"Amelia to the rescue! We won't die after all," quipped Morrie as they stretched out around the tray while Wowsie filled the glasses. After another hour of labour, Morrie announced the grass was ready for cutting.

"But let's have a swim first. I'll cut it after supper when it's cooler."

No one argued with that. Wowsie told Mod, who was keeping an eye on things from the verandah, they were going swimming, which was one of the few Meadowland rules — always tell an adult when you go swimming. Bessie, who had been writing in her upstairs nook, which was as hot as an oven on this breezeless day, heard the announcement through her opened windows and decided to join Mod on the verandah partly to keep an eye on the progress of the swimmers. Out they soon trotted, the girls in their navy serge short-sleeve tops, voluminous bloomers, little serge mob caps, long black stockings, and laced-up swimming shoes. The boy's swimming costumes were much simpler, little more than short-sleeve, navy blue underwear down to their knees. Boys learned to swim rather than just playing in the water, which was considered more appropriate for girls. But if girls stuck with instruction, they too could become strong swimmers in spite of such encumbering costumes.

During the previous week, the three girls had competed in perfecting their swimming strokes at Westfield, even after their suits became heavily sodden. The result was a definite improvement in their swimming abilities, which they proceeded to show off to the boys and the adults, who they knew were watching. Not to be outdone, Mary, who could already swim, switched to the sidestroke, which she saw her sisters and Ayleene were using, and found it easier than the breaststroke. Morrie and Roger did the same. Morrie's rowing muscles allowed him to easily outstrip his eight-year old brother. He slowed down, once the girls saw what he was capable of. He then helped Roger, showing him how to make his legs cut the water like scissors.

Swimming cooled them all and revived Morrie to the point that he was willing to harness a Clydesdale to the mower to see what they could do toward turning the designated area into a tennis court. Changing was simple for Morrie and Roger. They stood by the clothesline, well out of anyone's view, slipped off their dripping suits, hung them on the line, and, wrapped in bathing towels, dashed up the back stairs to get dressed. The girls continued to laugh and splash about in the river, but once they saw Morrie lead the toffee coloured workhorse toward the future tennis court, they came ashore and headed to the house. Bessie caught them before they entered, making sure they shook like wet dogs, squeezed out their dripping costumes as much as they could, took off their bathing slippers, and dried their feet on a towel that Amelia produced. Only then could they run upstairs to change.

After hanging their swimming clothes on the line, they joined the adults on the verandah where a tray of raspberry cordial and cookies awaited them. Bessie persuaded the girls, despite their excitement over the tennis court, to sit while they ate and drank. Mod asked them about their swimming progress. All the while, Morrie's geeing and hawing of the Clydesdale and the clatter of the mower up and down the tennis court area could be heard around the corner. Morrie's voice, the clinking of the harness, the noise of the mower, and the horse snortings combined to make the girls drink and eat as quickly as Miss Manners would allow and then excuse themselves. The Clydesdale shied a little as the four girls suddenly appeared from around the corner of the house in their white skirts and blouses, but, under Morrie's calming hand, soon became used to the observers. He walked behind the horse and a little to the side of the mowing machine, gently holding the reins, with Roger helping.

"Do you want to take the reins, Ayleene?" Morrie called out thinking to enlarge his cousin's experience of farm life. "Come, I'll show you."

Trudy pushed Ayleene forward. "Go on!"

"If you walk beside me."

Morrie put the reins in Ayleene's hands, just so and placed his own on top until she had a firm grip. The smell of her hair, sort of spicy, reminded him of Maizie but he quickly put her out of his mind in order to concentrate on the task at hand.

"Just say, 'walk on' and make a little clicking sound with your tongue against your teeth, like this."

The Clyde obeyed. Morrie stopped the horse so Ayleene could direct him, but her "walk on" was so soft nothing happened.

"Louder," Morrie advised.

"Walk on," Ayleene shouted and clicked her tongue as loud as she could. To her amazement the horse walked forward the whole length of the future tennis court with grass flying from the mower. She laughed, hardly believing what had happened. This was all so new and exciting. The others took turns as well. In spite of the interruptions, the entire surface was cut and the horse returned to pasture before Amelia rang the supper bell.

Conversation over the supper table was livelier than usually as the accomplishments of the afternoon events were being relived.

"There's a bag of whitewash in the tool shed which just has to be mixed with equal parts of water. That will be good for marking off your tennis court," offered Mod. "You'll need to peg string down where you want the lines to go."

Wowsie took the little booklet on tennis court measurements from her pocket and read, "A tennis court has to be seventy eight feet long and at least twenty-seven feet wide and the centre line and the net at thirty-nine feet from the serving line."

"Let's start after supper," Mary piped up enthusiastically.

When not a single strawberry or streak of cream of their dessert was left, Bessie and Mod prepared to take their cups of tea on to the verandah where the slightest of breeze was playing.

"You can use the kitchen ball of string, if you like," offered Bessie.

A huge ball of string, made up of many small pieces tied together, had long been kept on a kitchen shelf

"It will be covered in whitewash. Is that OK?" asked Morrie.

"Yes, dear, it's hardly ever used. Saving string is a habit from leaner days. And there's plenty of it."

The young all assembled on the recently mowed grass, together with two pots of whitewash, paint brushes, the kitchen ball of string, a supply of forked sticks cut by Morrie and Roger, and a tape measure. But first, they had to rake off the cut grass. Wowsie fetched two rakes and they all pitched in, taking turns. Next, the measurements were made, the string staked out and the whitewash liberally applied. After more than two hours of work, much laughter, and high expectations, a tennis court took shape.

"Now, Trudy observed, surveying what they had created, "we need two big stakes to hold the net."

"I'll find them, point the ends, and dig the holes in the morning," Morrie replied. "We've done enough for today and the whitewash has to dry. I'm done in."

Variously patterned with whitewash, grass stains, and smudges of dirt, the tennis court makers all flopped on the verandah.

"You must have used up most of your supper," Bessie commented. "Your father and I were about to have tea and cake. Amelia has left a tray in the kitchen, but she has gone up to her room. Elizabeth, dear, would you do the necessary? The cake's in the nearby tin and there's a jug of milk in the larder.

As Wowsie got up from her perch on a step, Ayleene did the same, "I'll help," she offered.

When they left, Morrie said he thought Ayleene was coming out of her shell, especially pleased how she took the reins and seemed to enjoy it all.

"I hope so," Bessie replied. "She's a dear girl and her parents have been so kind to us."

"We'll make a country bumpkin out of her before the week is out," Morrie added.

Even before breakfast the next morning, the "workers" all examined the "court." The dew was beginning to dry and there had been no rain overnight to diminish the whitewash. Today was the big test. Would the tennis balls bounce enough on the grass?

"You will put in the stakes for the net soon, won't you?" Mary urged her brother.

"Don't be a slave driver. I need to eat my breakfast first," Morrie shot back in good humour. He realized with a feeling of satisfaction how much they all depended on him.

Immediately after breakfast, the well-worn net was laid across the middle of the rectangle measured to the inch to make sure the net would be in the right place. Morrie found two cedar poles in the woodcutting yard that had not yet been cut into fencepost lengths and pointed their butt ends with an axe. Roger helped dig two deep holes. Together, the brothers worked the pointed ends of the poles deeply into the subsoil and then filled holes with rocks and dirt, packing it all tightly around the poles. They finished by tying up the net between the two poles. Wowsie, Trudy and Ayleene had been watching from the house and now appeared with their racquets and a tube of tennis balls.

"You can all have turns," Wowsie said to Morrie, Mary, and Roger, "but we three will show you how it's done, and whoever isn't playing can collect stray balls. OK?"

A pang of envy hit Mary as she realized she would never be the one who was the expert at tennis. Would it be worth going back to Edgehill for that chance? A vision of Bully Girl wiped away that thought. I'll learn by watching and practicing and try not to be jealous, she thought. Roger became "ball boy" at one end and Mary at the other. Morrie took the side toward the orchard. The house would stop balls on the other side. Trudy and Ayleene took one side of the court with Wowsie taking the other. They began to serve and return the ball. They were all surprised and delighted at how well the ball bounced.

We'll just practice until everyone has had a turn," Wowsie announced. "It's only fair, after all that work everyone did."

The novices were shown how to hold the racquets, how to throw the ball just so when serving, and how to hit a backhander. Mary had the advantage of having watched the girls at Edgehill, and had even had the opportunity to hit a few balls, so she knew she could do it. Morrie's extra muscle power allowed him certain advantages, but Roger's wrists were a little weak for the heavy racquet, so he was encouraged to use both hands for returning the ball, with occasional success. As the heat of the day advanced, energy flagged in spite of enthusiasm for the venture. When Amelia came out with a tray of raspberry cordial and cookies, she found all six sitting or lying on the grass, in the shade, talking and laughing, tennis balls and racquets scattered around them.

Every day following saw all six on their tennis court, Morrie less than the others as he had garden work to attend. Ayleene suggested they all help him with the weeding so he'd be back playing sooner. For the city girl, with no experience of gardening, weeding had an exotic appeal. Her country cousins saw it differently, but through her eyes it became part of the fun of having a visitor. Morrie wasn't sure whether so many feet and hands swarming over his garden were an advantage, or not, but Ayleene's wanting to help touched him.

Tuesday came far too quickly for everyone. Other than a day in Gagetown, visiting the Peters and the Caswells, whom Ayleene had met the previous year, all the time was spent at or near Meadowlands. They fed horses oats from a bucket, curried Horsey under Jock's supervision, helped the hired man bring in the cows for milking, played with Trixie, walked part way down the far field to talk with Willie and Granny, and often went swimming. One day they took one of Amelia's famous picnics to The Mound and afterward walked further toward Jemseg where the Scovil children knew they would find turtles covered in green algae in a little creek to show Ayleene.

Mary wondered if she couldn't persuade Wowsie and Trudy to leave their tennis racquets at Meadowlands since there were lots at Edgehill. If not, she would ask for two racquets as a combined Christmas and birthday present. She hoped there might be lighter weight racquets that would help Roger play with one hand. She wanted him to like it so they could play together. You can't play tennis by yourself. In spite of still being short, Mary was able to return many balls; she seemed able to guess where they would land. Wowsie called her a "natural" and took pleasure in giving her pointers, partly to make up to her little sister for not being happy at Edgehill. As it turned out, the net and the racquets with their presses remained. Mary was jubilant and made both her brothers promise to play with her.

Bessie suggested they all join their visitor on the riverboat trip back to Westfield, where she and her family would spend most of the rest of the summer. Mod decided he too could do with the cooling breezes promised by a river trip. The day was calm, so Mod pronounced that four per rowboat would be safe. There were no big trunks, only Ayleene's valise for the week and her own tennis racquet. The Scovils would not be staying the night but return on the late afternoon boat, so no need even for toothbrushes. Madge and Frank were waiting near the wharf in their shiny motor. They set out a little picnic tea, which all enjoyed during the half hour before the returning boat arrived. There was hugging all around, on arrival and departure. Ayleene was now the second girl Morrie had hugged, except for sisters. He understood why it was such a popular activity.

"I can't imagine a happier visit," Bessie summed up the last week after their paddle wheeler left the wharf. Everyone agreed.

They all waved and waved as the riverboat began churning upriver and the three Starrs and their motor receded into the green distance. Mod's pocket watch said seven-thirty when he and Morrie slipped the rowboats to the side of Scovil's wharf. They all appreciated the light, evening breeze, but the day's heat still lingered and the delicious cold supper Amelia had waiting for them was perfect.

Once they all sat down and Mod had rattled through "For what we are about to receive ..." and passed the potato salad to Bessie, Morrie spoke up; "Too bad Ayleene doesn't live nearer. She seems to like country life."

"She said she did when we talked at night," Trudy confirmed.

As he helped himself to three slices of their own pickled pork, Mod asked, of no one in particular, "Do you think if we had a proper tennis court made in the spring — leveled, rolled, and seeded — you would all use it next summer?"

"Yes," they all answered in enthusiastic unison, and laughed.

Such a good idea, Mod," Bessie offered; "a little strange for a farm, but why not with so many young people to enjoy it?"

Much discussion followed about the location — the same as now or somewhere else? Could they get a new net, spare racquets, a lighter one for Roger and on and on? The subject followed them on to the verandah where, after a while, Bessie suggested a piece of cake and tea for anyone who wanted it. Only the grown ups wanted tea on such a hot day, but all spoke up for cake. It happened to be a traditional favourite, gingerbread with a bowl of cool whipped cream for topping.

"Yum! My system demands cream," joked Morrie as he covered his cake with two large dollops.

Now that their guest had left, life returned to a more practical level. Bessie went through the girls' school trunks with them, deciding what needed to be replaced, what Wowsie had outgrown and could be worn by Trudy, what should be put aside for Mary to wear in a few years if she grew tall enough. "She does seem to have inherited the Scovil tendency to be short," Bessie mused, but thought better than to mention it. Meanwhile, Mary was bouncing in and out of her sisters' room, looking nostalgically at the familiar uniforms and other necessities of life at Edgehill, but then stopping because it made her eyes hot with a sort of longing.

Bessie engaged Miss Straight the seamstress to come on August first so there would not be a last minute rush and to stay as long as need be. She wrote to Manchester, Robertson and Alison in Saint John and ordered a bolt of navy serge and another of grey, which would be delivered by riverboat in a few days and kept at McKinney's store in Gagetown until collected. A trip to Saint John after mid August would allow for necessary purchases, such as middy blouses and especially for shoes and boots for everyone. And, for the first time, a trunk for Morrie, which also would need to be filled with everything required for his life at Truro.

*   *   *   *   *

The summer progressed with many sunny days. Three foals were born and much admired every day by the entire household. Morrie was justifiably proud of his garden. It produced early and abundant crops of beans, peas, lettuce and new potatoes and grew lush with the promise of the later vegetables. Every two or three days he presented his Aunt Bessie with a generous bouquet of sweet peas, which he had planted at her request. He thoughtfully presented Amelia with similar bunches of the fragrant flowers. He roped Roger into helping with the garden work, hoping he would take over some of it next spring.

Bessie often picked up her mending basket after dinner and encouraged the girls to join her for an hour on the verandah with their needlework. It was a Meadowlands' rule to wait an hour after eating before swimming. Wowsie and Trudy were embroidering little blue, mauve, and pale pink flowers on huckaback guest towels, with the help of stiff rings to hold everything flat and smooth. Now that Mary had glasses, handwork did not make her eyes hurt as it had previously. She was determined to master smocking, though she had trouble preventing it from puckering in the wrong places. She could not keep up the concentration for more than a half hour at a time, and then waited impatiently for the next half hour to pass, when they could all go for swim.

Morrie sometimes brought the book he was reading to the verandah and occasionally read aloud a few paragraphs he especially liked. Roger whittled on pieces of softwood with Morrie's jackknife, though it was never obvious what the finished article would be. Mod joined them with his tea on these occasions, just to be near his growing family and to hear their conversation. With a mixture of happiness and sadness, he imagined how proud Hattie would be of their five surviving children. He tried to imagine which of his girls would grow to look the most like Hattie, and thought it might be Elizabeth, though none had Hattie's distinctive nose — straight with somewhat flared nostrils.

The whirring of Miss Straight's sewing machine in the hallway at the head of the stairs soon dominated the house. She sang while she worked. Her Irish tunes and strong musical voice blended with the sound of the sewing machine and could be heard in every corner of the house, especially when she was working on a long, straight seam. She ate her meals with Amelia, a little vase of Morrie's sweet peas decorating their kitchen table. As a way of complimenting her companion's cooking, she declared she always put on weight when working for Miss Scovil.

The now familiar routine of following Bessie's list, ticking off completed items one by one, proceeded through August. New and renovated articles of clothing were tried on, adjusted and pronounced wearable. Wowsie's out-grown garments always had to be taken in a bit for Trudy. At fifteen, Wowsie had already developed a considerable bosom, generally thought to be the result of her drinking large quantities of milk. Bessie tried to limit her niece to one glass at a time, but Wowsie always craved at least two. Trudy's development took a more normal path.

The expedition to Saint John was complicated by the need to spend time in the young men's department. Morrie was outfitted with his first store bought suit. The girls each chose a ready-made dress. A new dress for Mary was not strictly necessary as there were always her sisters' out-grown frocks waiting for her, but Bessie still felt guilty about Mary's suffering at Edgehill and a new dress helped ease her conscience. Bessie systematically ticked items off her list as middy blouses, shoes, leather and rubber boots, slippers and various necessary odds and ends were selected. The money Frank had provided for the girl's education covered the cost of their uniforms and other necessities. Bessie's shares in the Curtis Publishing Company were continuing to do well, so the rest of the considerable expense was not a noticeable strain on her purse.

30

Kings County Agricultural Fair

Like last September, the Starrs asked Wowsie and Trudy to spend a few days in Saint John before cousin Frank delivered them and Ayleene back to Edgehill. Bessie, Mary, and Roger made the riverboat trip with them and their freshly filled trunks. Two rowboats were needed to make the river crossing to Gagetown. The rowers, Mod and Morrie, were glad for a calm day with only ripples and no threatening waves. Wowsie and Trudy were chatty with departing nervousness and anticipation of returning to Edgehill. After seeing the riverboat travellers off from the wharf, Mod and Morrie decided to spend the day in Gagetown visiting the Caswells, the Peters, and the DeVebers and then meet the return riverboat in late afternoon. Halfway through their visit with Gabe DeVeber, Morrie excused himself, explaining he wanted to see how Maizie and her family were getting along.

"Don't stay in the same room with her mother; TB is catching," Mod advised as Morrie stood to leave.

*   *   *   *   *

Madge had invited Bessie and the two young ones to stay in Saint John for a few days, but Bessie declined. She needed to complete the filling of Morrie's trunk in preparation for his going to Truro, the Kings County Agricultural Fair was coming right up, and the Grammar began next week. Mary and Roger should really be there for the opening days because, with the annual trek to Sussex for the Fair, they will miss Thursday and Friday. Bessie knew that attending the Fair would be more educational than two days in school. With their sisters off to Edgehill, it gave Bessie great satisfaction to see Mary and Roger excited with anticipation for the trip to Sussex for the Fair. She had arranged for them to stay with second cousins, the son and family of her father's brother, near Norton. They had only two children and their rambling farmhouse and barns could easily accommodate an influx of relatives and their horses for a night or two. On Friday and Saturday they would stay in a boarding house in Sussex.

221

Bessie sometimes forgot how different her life had become since she had given up her active nursing career, a vocation that sometimes had required interacting with dozens of people every day. She was thoroughly looking forward to the Fair's little splash of rural excitement, a completely new experience for her, though Mod had talked about it in some detail when he and Jock returned last year. The year before that, the fair was just after dear Hattie's departure, and the year before that Bessie had been in a different life hundreds of miles from New Brunswick and Meadowlands.

The King's County Agricultural Fair was the first of its kind in New Brunswick, and, in fact, in the whole of Canada. Mod had explained it was first held in 1895 and had grown in size and importance over the past eleven years. The Fair now drew huge crowds from a large area. The more Bessie heard about the Fair the more interested she became.

"If I'm going to live on a farm for the rest of my days, the least I can do is embrace rural life," she thought. "Entering my pickled beets, sweet mixed pickles and gingerbread in the home cooking display at the Fair would be a start; perhaps more to prove to myself that I am capable of changing than for winning accolades. If I did place, it would prove something, I suppose. *Good Housekeeping* and *The Ladies' Home Journal* thought my recipes were worth publishing. Who knows? Anyway, participation is what makes the world go 'round, not the prizes."

After just three days of school, Mary and Roger felt privileged, which of course they were, as they climbed into the carriage, while Jim, the hired man, and Jock, the groom, made sure Horsey's harness straps were as tight as they should be, having checked the same on the team of shiny black Percherons. By six o'clock on Thursday morning, with a slight haze over the river that often precedes a warm day, the little procession was on the road to Jemseg. From there it would be on to Cambridge Narrows, the Kingston Peninsula, and their cousin's farm near Norton.

The team of Percherons, splendidly decorated by Jock and Morrie, their manes and tails braided and embroidered with colourful wool rosettes, would know the way. They pulled a hitch-wagon—a real boneshaker—that would be used in team competitions. Mod, who would share the driving of the team with Jock, looked proudly over the backs of the workhorses with their polished silver pieces holding the well-oiled leather harness; altogether a superior turn out. Behind them, tied to the wagon, two high stepping chestnut colts seemed to catch the general excitement. They were also the recipients of Jock's and Morrie's artistic decoration, Mod could easily sell them locally but he knew they would bring more at the Fair auction on Saturday, where concern about a lost bargain always drove up the price.

Following the colts came dependable Horsey with her splendid decorations, hitched to the carriage. Her mood seemed especially good as if she was still under the effect of Morrie's calming hands and soft words in her ear when he had slipped on her gleaming harness earlier that morning. Morrie held the reins as his aunt, sister and little brother settled under the carriage hood and Amelia, with a big smile, took her position on the jump seat facing them. She'd been smiling since she carried the picnic baskets out and wedged them carefully among the over-night valises and the box of Miss Scovil's precious entries for the cooking competition. This was a new adventure for Amelia and she was pleased to be included.

Morrie covered the luggage and cargo with a sheet of canvas tied down to keep the load from shifting and to keep out as much dust as possible. Bessie had advised everyone to wear old clothes for the trip and pack something respectable for the Friday and Saturday. There had been a slight rain two days previously but not enough to lay the dust. Though morning dew now held the dust somewhat in check, Bessie passed Mary a light scarf to protect her hair. She had a larger scarf that fit over her own hat, and she was pleased to see that Amelia had remembered her instructions and was likewise equipped.

"Morrie dear," Bessie called to the driver, "if the wagon and the team kick up too much dust, I think we should drive in front."

"Sure, just let me know when. Father told me the way and I'll wait at crossroads if I'm not sure."

Before they reached Lower Jemseg, Roger's day was made perfect when Morrie asked him to help drive, and then again giving him the reins on a straight road toward the Narrows. Morrie took them back on the hills. Hills needed a special driving technique, putting on more speed to produce momentum before the climb started, and then controlling the descent so the whiffle tree would not hit the horse's hind legs.

Their five o'clock breakfast was a faded memory by the time Mod signaled they should stop at some cleared land by a burnt out farm house with trees close behind for "exploring." It was customary for women and girls to "explore" first to relieve the urgency, but on this occasion there was enough woodland close by that everyone could seek privacy in different directions at the same time.

But for Jock, it was work duty first. He tied the horses loosely to a part of the house still standing where they could reach plentiful grass on which they immediately began grazing. Before extracting dinner from under the canvas, Bessie ordered everyone to shake like Trixie to remove road dust from clothes and hair. She wanted no grit to mingle with the carefully planned picnic. Because of Morrie's clever driving, the occupants of the carriage put up with no more dust than those in the wagon. He hung behind far enough for the worst of the dust raised to settle ahead of them. Amelia set out the picnic on a white tablecloth while Bessie presided. Amelia and Jock sat a little off to one side of the family, as was proper. Mary and Roger were parched, drinking their ration of raspberry cordial as though it were their last but hoping for more.

"We might not stop again for ages, so best not to drink too much," Bessie warned the two. Mary was nearly bursting before this stop and the opportunity to "explore," so she heeded her aunt's words and chose an apple instead. As they travelled on, Roger continued to sit with Morrie and, from time to time, take the reins on flat stretches of road. Mary was happy for Roger but felt a pang of envy as her spirit of adventure was aroused. She could learn to do this, she was sure. She'd seen a woman in Gagetown driving a carriage by herself so she wouldn't be the first in the world. Horses seemed to belong to the world of men and boys. She made a plan to get Morrie by himself and ask him to let her sit up with him for a while and practice taking the reins.

*　*　*　*　*

If asked, the whole Meadowland contingent would have agreed that the adventure of going to Sussex for the Kings County Fair was beyond expectation. Mod sold his colts for even more than he hoped. The Percherons took three first prizes in their class, one for the stone boat haul, one for the best turned-out team, and one for synchronized manoeuvering. Bessie and blushingly surprised Amelia won first prize for their gingerbread, second for pickled beets. A Sussex woman took all the prizes for mixed pickles. Though Mary reveled in the exciting confusion of the fair, and spending time with her eleven year old cousin, Emmy, her most precious memory was Morrie's handing her Horsey's reins on the way home. She loved the excitement of being the "driver." She decided to wangle her way into doing this more often. Now, she knew there were at least two "women" in the world that could take the reins.

Bessie was relieved to see that cousin Henry's wife, May, had advanced into middle age, returning to her sweet nature and leaving behind the sourness of her change of life, which had all but ruined their last meeting with mutual cousins in Saint John. The only disappointment for Bessie was the quality of the boarding house in Sussex. It was none too clean, the supposedly "hot food" was not, and generally the whole place was below hoped-for standards. She knew it was her fault. By the time she started

224

inquiring for accommodation it was far too late; her first two choices were already fully booked. Next year would be different. Next year! Yes, she was already thinking about her submissions for 1907.

A mood of tired triumph surrounded the returning procession on Sunday. All were reviewing the past days, crammed with the stimulation of unaccustomed activity, sights, sounds, and people. Lulled by the rhythmic movement of the horses, and spiked with the inevitable sharp smell of fresh manure—a familiar smell that increased the sense relaxation—some heads lolled on chests, briefly catching a little sleep. Jock was more than happy with the outcome, both for himself and his employer. Roger, like Mary, found taking Horsey's reins a highlight, though the games they played going and coming with Aunt Bessie and Amelia were the sort of fun he'd remember well into his adult years. Morrie, for his part, now had proof that dedication and hard work bore results. The experience made him even happier that he would be in the first class of students at the Nova Scotia Agricultural College in Truro next week. He felt ready to stretch himself.

As the journey home began to cover familiar territory, Bessie thought of the coming few days. She had been looking forward to seeing Morrie launched into the greater world, but now it was so near an unwanted sadness, like a cool breeze on an already cold day, crept over her; every day Morrie seemed to become more responsible, more willing to discuss subjects beyond childhood, more of a companion than a responsibility. She knew she would miss him, probably more than she had missed the girls when they left for school.

Elizabeth and Gertrude, just thirteen months apart, naturally turned to one another for companionship or solace. Mary and Roger, with nineteen months between them did the same. Morrie, being the eldest, gravitated towards the grownups even more when the girls were gone, though he also found being the big brother was satisfying, if not required for too long at a stretch. As they approached their Meadowlands' home, Bessie was unable to squelch a shiver of pride as she watched Morrie's straight back supporting a head of summer bleached light brown hair, which refused to lie flat for long. Her pride ran into confidence that he would do well at Truro. The experience would surely wipe out the ignominy of being expelled from the Grammar—though quite unfairly—and help prepare him for life's vicissitudes.

31

Morrie Goes to Truro

Bessie took a bittersweet pleasure in packing Morrie's trunk, showing him the best way to do it, filling every little crevice, keeping the layers level. He checked off the list as she lowered each article, mostly practical, hard wearing gear suitable for field work but also less rugged apparel for sitting in a classroom. After some discussion one evening over the usual tea and cake, Bessie and Mod agreed he should accompany his son to the college, taking the riverboat to Saint John and the train from there to Moncton where they would change to the Halifax train that ran through Truro. Morrie feebly protested that he could go on his own but was half glad that he didn't have to. Mod explained that he wanted to see the college, the grounds, the farm it had been built around, and a get a feel for what his son would experience for the next two years. He would stay in Truro overnight, retracing his journey the following day, spending two nights with cousins Lucy and Will in Saint John, and have time to shop for a much needed pair of good leather boots.

After they had hugged their brother goodbye, Mary and Roger stood close to their Aunt Bessie while Morrie transferred the trunk from the wheelbarrow to the wharf and then to the larger of the rowboats, along with two valises. As Morrie took the oars and Mod gave a little wave to the stay-at-home three, Bessie slipped a handkerchief out of her skirt pocket, lifted her glasses and dabbed her eyes before her sight was completely fogged by the unexpected tears. Morrie saw the gesture, and was suddenly waylaid by the same emotion Bessie was inadvertently showing. He swallowed hard, fighting back his own tears as he paused rowing and waved an extended arm toward the three, now standing close, looking forlorn and in need of consolation. They stood there until the travellers were scarcely visible, dots in a toy boat, toothpick oars dipping rhythmically into the water on the wide expanse of the St. John River.

* * * * *

It was not until Sunday that Jock rowed to the Gagetown wharf to meet the late afternoon riverboat from Saint John. Mod handed over his valise and his well wrapped new boots and then carefully stepped into the boat. He held his throbbing head in his hands, disinclined to make much conversation, except to tell Jock that their young farmer seemed to like the new college. Mod had been well entertained by cousin Will and his repeated generous offerings from his extensive wine cellar, which Mod had no trouble accepting. His hosts knew that Bessie did not look favourably on imbibing and assumed, correctly, that alcohol was kept for medical emergencies or very special occasions. So why not give Mod a little treat? On the first afternoon of Mod's visit, when their bridge game was nearing the end and Mrs. Morrisey, a pretty widow who lived nearby, occupied the fourth chair, the maid served glasses of sherry.

They all found the last two hands were even more enjoyable than the previous ones. When Mrs. Morrisey left, much to Mod's disappointment, thinking she might have been asked for dinner, the glasses were filled again. By now, the aroma of roasting sirloin slipped under the swinging kitchen door, perfuming the hall and the drawing room with its delicious aroma. By the time the maid announced that dinner was ready, Mod realized he had consumed three generous glasses of sherry, which must have been the reason for his less than straight route to the dining table. With the first course of sole came a white wine of indescribable delicacy followed by a mellow claret with the succulent beef and then a refill to accompany an irresistible encore of roast.

"I hope you like this Apple Charlotte, Mod, Dear," Lucy said as the maid offered the dessert to Mod's left. "It's Cook's specialty."

He helped himself to the whipped cream covered concoction. Taking rather more than he intended, he lost a sizeable blob without noticing. The blob landed on his still pristine napkin and then wobbled off and dropped to the red Turkish carpet. The maid, needing no prompting, placed the dessert platter on the sideboard, bent quickly in the direction of the blob and discretely removed it with a cloth, forestalling the danger of the guest's shoe mashing it into the carpet, compounding the eventual clean up. She then finished her serving, after which the three sipped on their dessert wine in silence. Lucy hoped Mod's face would return to its former hue before it was time for the nightcap.

After the nightcap and before Mod unsteadily ascended the stairs, Lucy announced, "Breakfast is a moveable feast. It will be available when we want it—sometime between ten and eleven would be suitable, but earlier if we feel like it." Mod was relieved. At this stage he could not envisage bounding out of bed for a repast at a normal hour. He made a little speech of gratitude for the delightful evening, which he had trouble bringing to an end. His bed had been turned down and an electric lamp on his bedside table had been turned on. With minimal preparations required, Mod soon had the joy of assuming a horizontal position, his floating head on a soft pillow, and with no sensible conversation expected of him for hours.

A persistent thirst announced the day. A glass of water had been thoughtfully placed on Mod's bedside table. He took a grateful drink, turned over and continued his slumber. Lucy was accurate in her estimation of the time her cousin would want his breakfast. All three met in the dining room at 10:45. Will had plans for Mod. They would visit his favourite boot and shoe emporium, then his club for a late lunch and some afternoon bridge. When they eventually returned home smelling of cigar and pipe smoke, Lucy and Mrs. Morrisey were smiling over their pre-dinner sherry. The evening was not unlike the previous one, with the addition of the female guest's charming wit.

When Mod arrived back at Meadowlands in the late afternoon of the following day and was about to slake his thirst with a cup of tea Amelia had made for him, Bessie descended from her nook to join him in the parlour. She pummeled him with questions. Mod attempted to do three things at once—quiet his pounding head, quench his thirst, and answer his sister's questions. How was the trip? Did Morrie seem to settle in? Did he have a room to himself or was he in a dormitory? Was there a proper campus? Were the trains on time? What did he do at Will and Lucy's? Did they play bridge? Did Lucy look well?

Mod answered two questions as well as he could under the circumstances, drained his teacup, and said he would dearly like another. When his sister left the room to fetch the teapot, Mod put his aching head in his hands trying to will it back to normal, which is how Bessie found him when she returned. She poured another cup of tea and placed it on the little round table next his armchair.

"Oh, oh... oh, thank you Bess."

"It looks as though Lucy and Will entertained you more than necessary," Bessie said with a slight smile.

"They were certainly very generous hosts," said Mod as he tried to raise his head to a normal position, but only half succeeded.

"Relax, dear, before the children come back. I've sent them to Jock's with some soup for his mother. She hasn't been well. They'll want to hear about your trip, too, perhaps over supper. I'll go up and finish a letter I started to Jack and Addie."

32

Morrie Visits Edgehill

Morrie was pleased to find a minimum of rules at the new agricultural college: no smoking in bedrooms because of the danger of fire and no intoxicating beverages in bedrooms. But the director was a realist. He initiated a smoking room and a glass of beer was an option with dinner on Saturday nights. Best of all there were no silly restrictions on letters, coming or going. Morrie took advantage of that before the end of his first week. In his letter home he asked whether his father or Aunt Bessie would ask the headmistress at Edgehill to let him write to his sisters and they to him. They were almost within shouting distance—well, less than an hour by train.

Miss Smith was aware of the new Nova Scotia Agriculture College opening its doors this autumn and thought it admirable the Scovil girls' brother would learn how to manage their family farm. Unfortunately, he had not honed his academic abilities at King's College School—the nearby equivalent to Edgehill for boys, or almost the equivalent, smiled Miss Smith to herself. But he must be an able young man or he would not have been accepted. Elizabeth and Gertrude were now quite senior and had given no trouble; in fact, they excelled in many areas. She accepted Mr. Scovil's request that his children be allowed to exchange weekly letters. Though this was an irregular request, she saw no reason to deny it. The girls letters, it went without saying, would be viewed by a mistress in the usual way for grammar and spelling mistakes and especially for unnecessary references to negative aspects of their lives. Elizabeth and Gertrude's brother would undoubtedly be corresponding with his father and Aunt. Parents must maintain confidence in their children's education and not be worried by minor problems.

The Scovil girls displayed excellent writing skills and were not given to rule breaking so the reviewing mistress' workload would not be measurably increased. Their brother's letters were not expected to be a problem, either. He was older and would not want his younger sisters to be inconvenienced by unsuitable content. After three weeks of letter writing, Morrie suggested he visit Windsor on a Saturday afternoon when there were no compulsory activities at the college, just informal sport. An efficient rail connection, running for the last six years between Truro and Windsor, made the trip less than an hour and the cost of a day return ticket was reasonable. The girls asked Miss Smith if Morrie could visit as proposed. Somewhat to their surprise, she readily agreed, providing that he escorted them back to the school. A mistress would accompany them to the Windsor station in time for his arrival. They could spend the afternoon at The Armitage Tea Room after showing their brother the prettier parts of Windsor. There would be three and a half hours between trains, which should be enough time for a satisfactory outing. The first Saturday in November was scheduled for the visit. Wowsie and Trudy were amazed at Miss Smith's positive approach. Wowsie joked that she must be wearing less restrictive corsets, but that was unlikely, as the whalebones still showed their unbending form through her dresses.

When Morrie's train puffed into Windsor station, Trudy found the bottoms of her feet itching with excitement. Wowsie waved enthusiastically even though the train had not completely stopped and no one looking like Morrie peered out of the windows. Surely he hadn't missed the train. Then, when a cloud of steam cleared, there he was, smiling, with his arms outstretched.

After hugging them both, he slipped his arms through theirs, and, with a sister on each side, said, "Show me your town!"

Their first stop was "The Arm," as the tearoom was commonly called. The girls had saved enough of their allowance money to treat their brother. He objected, saying he expected to treat them. But, they reasoned, he had already spent on his ticket so it should be their treat. They had an unfair advantage, two against one. Morrie graciously gave in.

The owner of the tearoom, Mrs. Armitage, recognized the girls as coming from the school, dressed, as they were, in navy serge uniforms. And that must be a brother, she surmised, judging by their similar facial features. Town gossip knew there was a preponderance of porridge and rice pudding at Edgehill, which inclined Mrs. Armitage to make sure that when students came to her tearoom they were served a special treat. Remembering the appetites of her twin girls before they left to look after children in Boston, she told the waitress to serve an extra piece of cake to each of the three young customers.

Perched on her stool behind her mostly supervisory desk, Mrs. Armitage looked out over the heads of the laughing young folks into the cool November day and wondered whether the sun was shining in Boston. Were Annie and Alice, her ambitious girls, meeting in the nearby park with their little charges? Annie had two and Alice only one, but her demanding employers had another child on the way. The girls both wanted to become office workers. They were saving money from their wages and were taking typing courses at night school. Six months away from home and their mother still missed them every day. Her reverie was interrupted by the entry of a small group of well-dressed, middle aged women, seeking unneeded nourishment and convivial conversation.

*   *   *   *   *

The following Tuesday, the Meadowlands' family was treated to three slightly different versions of that Saturday afternoon. Wowsie's and Trudy's letters were without grammatical or punctuation errors, of course. Bessie noticed that Morrie used dashes to excess and ignored the need for new paragraphs, but all that faded with the joy of hearing about the siblings' happy afternoon in Windsor.

"Jammy humbugs," said Roger, copying one of Morrie's expressions. "Getting an extra piece of cake—free!"

"I wish I could have been with them for the afternoon and then just sprouted wings and flown home afterward," Mary said wistfully.

"Perhaps one day you can try it again, dear."

"Could I have another piece of apple cobbler, please Aunt Bessie?"

Mary really did want seconds, but even more she wanted to change the subject. So much talk of Windsor—Morrie meeting the well-corseted Miss Smith and all—brought many unhappy memories to the surface again, almost to the point of bringing up tears.

Bessie sensed Mary's discomfort and switched to reading a letter from Addie that had come in the same mail. As well, there was a rare letter from Barclay, his handwriting a work of art. Bessie passed the letter around the table for the other three to admire before reading each neatly written page.

Barclay reported that he continued to be happy with his decision to leave his accountant's desk on Broadway for a life so utterly different. Paying treaty money to Indians gave him a life in the fresh air and contact with nature again. He had completely lost his persistent cough. Riding horseback to remote reservations allowed him to renew his almost faded interest in horses and produced a contentment he failed to find in the noisy confusion of New York. Barclay answered the question that surfaced in Bessie's thoughts whenever she thought of her youngest brother. He wrote he had only two regrets leaving New York for the West. One was the absence of family and the other was the absence of the New York Public Library, or anything approaching it. He missed its convenience for delving into family history and history in general. In the West he had the feeling he was making history instead of reading about it. But bird song and spectacular sun rises, as he and his guide set out on horseback for days of riding were a satisfying compensation. He wrote that the train journeys, which often preceded these rides, produced startling views of mountain peaks and black-green lakes. He liked to sit on the back platform of the caboose with the off-duty crew and enjoy the open vista of the landscape.

Bessie paused, when she finished reading, swept back to her own experiences of crossing the country by train on her way to British Columbia to speak on behalf of Lady Aberdeen's Victorian Order of Nurses.

"It is just like that — startlingly beautiful," she mused out loud. "I could scarcely believe what I was seeing when I made that cross-country trip. Around each bend there's a view more remarkable than the one before. Barc needed to do something adventurous like that."

Mary's confused thoughts about Edgehill vanished, along with her second serving of cobbler. She imagined sitting with her interesting Uncle Barc at the back of the train, her eyes resting on mountain peaks and mysterious lakes.

*   *   *   *   *

Encouraged by the headmistress, the Edgehill Board of Governors decided that last year's Christmas closure of the school for renovations was such a success that it should be repeated, but with no need of renovations this time. The Treasurer, in particular, was most encouraged by the prospect of a reduction in running expenses. In late November all parents received notices, signed by the Chairman of the Board and Miss Smith, that the school would close for a month for Christmas holidays as the move was so appreciated by parents and students the previous year. The dates would be from December twelfth to January tenth. The same large house in Windsor as last year, owned by a governor of the school, along with a supervising mistress, would be available to accommodate the students who could not travel home.

When Morrie heard about this, he quickly wrote to his Aunt Bessie suggesting that since he was now experienced in such matters, including making connections, the three girls travel with him by train to Saint John, His college holidays began on December thirteenth and ended the same date as Edgehill's. As Morrie explained, this was no accident; the daughter of the college's director was in her first term at Edgehill.

Morrie did not want to miss the last day of classes before the holiday began so he wondered whether his sisters and Ayleene could leave on the

8:30 a.m. train from Windsor on the morning of the thirteenth. He would meet them at the station in Truro where they would make the connection with the Halifax to Moncton train, and then change again for Saint John. Letters whizzed back and forth among all concerned until everything was settled. Mod assured Bessie there was plenty of time between trains for easy transfer. He thought it was time for the young to spread their wings a little toward independence, especially with Frank right there at the other end to unravel any problems, such as lost luggage.

The odd job man with his donkey cart for luggage, along with a mistress, accompanied the three girls to the Windsor railway station in good time for the 8:30 train. So the adventure began, amid puffs of excitement and great gushes of steam and smoke. Morrie, early by a half hour, paced up and down on the wooden platform at the Truro station, wondering what he would do if the three girls were not on the train coming from Windsor. He thought of reasons his sisters might not appear but realized speculation was a waste of time; it was better to think of a plan. There wasn't another train from Windsor that would make the connection to Saint John until tomorrow. If things went awry, he would send a telegram. To whom, he was not sure. He would decide later, if necessary. He knew Wowsie, in particular, was careful with details. This thought reassured him. He checked again that the train was expected on time. It was.

Just as he began to wish he had not suggested this complicated way of travelling home, the 9:36 appeared as a dot far in the distance with a cloud of smoke like a top hat hovering above the engine. Once the train stopped and a door opened, the three girls were the first to descend the metal steps and the firm stool a porter placed on the station platform. They were greeted with hugs of relief by their grinning organizer. Each carried only a small valise, easily managed by the owner, so no porter had to be hailed. Like others waiting for the Halifax to Moncton train, they crowded into the steamy waiting room, a pot bellied stove at one end, well stoked with coal. Freed from the restrictions of their institutions of learning, the four were almost giddy with conversational possibilities. If there was a moment of silence from then until they caught sight of cousin Frank on the Saint John station platform, it was not measurable.

With several hours of this freedom behind her, Ayleene abandoned all ladylike reticence and flew into her father's arms with a force that nearly dislodged his balance, but which he regained in time to welcome hugs from Wowsie and Trudy and a firm handshake from Morrie. To make adequate room, Frank, instead of his chauffeur, had driven the motor to the station. After the valises were stored in the trunk, he motioned for Morrie to take the front seat beside him, and for the girls to make themselves comfortable in the spacious rear seat.

Several dustings of snow had fallen since the beginning of the month, but none had stayed, so Frank surmised his irreplaceable cargo would be safe in the motor today. His thoughts were often on transportation this time of year. He had to decide on the best time to switch from wheels to runners. The wrong decision could be costly. It was best to keep to the wheels of the coal hauling wagons on the road as long as possible before switching to runners. There had to be a firm bed of well-packed snow before making the change. A good team straining to pull a heavy load of coal over an insufficient foundation of snow, with the metal runners grating over the cobbles, and with "Frank Starr and Son" written across his wagons was not good advertising.

Once the girls were settled with a buffalo robe tucked around their ankles and he and Morrie had protective leather aprons over their chests, Frank Starr's thoughts returned to the present. He could now enjoy the exhilarating task of wheeling his motor through the city and, almost like magic, delivering his eldest daughter and her cousins to the door of his house. Answering many questions about the workings of his motor made him realize what an intelligent lad Morrie was and kept half of Frank's brain well occupied. The other half concentrated on safe manoeuvering through the still mostly horse-drawn traffic of the bustling city on this late afternoon in mid-December.

33

Unsurpassable Skating:
Reachers At Last

The two families had arranged that the Scovil children would spend two days with the Starrs before being collected by Mod, probably in a carriage. Before Frank's motorcar had glided into his driveway, Morrie told him he felt capable of escorting his sisters back to Meadowlands on the riverboat. The water was still open and the boats were still running.

"I don't see why not," Frank replied. "You've proven yourself a good traveller today. Write to your father as soon as we get to the house. I'll add a few lines if you want, and we can send it off tonight. If it freezes up by the sixteenth, I'll take you to Meadowlands. It would be a good change—getting away from coal dust."

"That's most kind," Morrie replied, looking at Frank with admiration and gratitude for his endless generosity. "Father says you should always have a plan B."

Frank could see that even one term at Truro had matured the boy into a young man who was going somewhere. Dear Hattie would have been so proud of her first born. There followed two full days of dizzying activity including a morning of shopping with cousin Madge who insisted they all pick out warm woolen jerseys as a Christmas present. Wowsie chose a blue one to match her eyes, Trudy a deep turquoise, Ayleen a green, and Morrie a cinnamon brown. Mary and Roger were not forgotten. They all agreed Mary would like a red one and Morrie thought Rog would be happy with one the same colour as his.

Though the sixteenth brought a temperature low enough to produce a thin skim of ice on the river, the big boat could handle it. Cousin Frank did not have an excuse to get away from coal dust and the three young Scovils felt quite grown-up making the familiar trip to Gagetown without an adult. In two days, major river traffic ceased, though the larger of the Scovil's two rowboats could still make a crossing to Gagetown for supplies before their biannual island status returned. That night the mercury in the thermometer just outside the kitchen window sank to well below freezing

237

and stayed there the next night and day. There was no wind, no snow. The cold season was settling in.

The young scarcely noticed the isolation. Together again, the five siblings went out to admire the colts; they hiked up the bare, rock-hard Jemseg road and tested the thickness of the rapidly forming ice. Trixie, the border collie, clearly happy to have them all back at Meadowlands, accompanied them in a frenzy of excitement wherever they went.

Once this initial activity was over, Morrie announced he needed to do some "work" alone. He had a special ability to draw, so choosing from the art supplies Bessie always had on hand, he shut himself away to make Christmas presents. The other four all decided to do the same, though Mary and Roger wanted to work together, agreeing not to peek. Water paints, coloured pencils, pen and ink, and paper were distributed accordingly. Bessie was pleased with this creative enthusiasm and with her own foresight in collecting the supplies needed.

With only five days left before Christmas, Bessie and Amelia consulted Meadowlands cookery books and the collection of handwritten, often food stained, favourite recipes that were kept on the same shelf above the kitchen table. As Amelia's magic came together, spicy reminders of past Christmases tickled the noses of everyone whether they were stretched in front of the Franklin stove in the parlour or finding privacy in an out-of-the-way corner near a register where the hot air from the wood burning furnace rolled up into the house. The creativity at work during these days produced bookmarks, calendars, little paintings of winter scenes, woven mats of painted paper strips, and other ingenious novelties that seemed to delight the maker as much as the eventual receiver.

Just after dinner on the twenty-fourth, Mod looked out of the sitting room window at the ice covered river before he settled in for his cup of tea and likely a small doze. He could scarcely believe his eyes. A brave or very foolish man was testing a homemade ice sail. He had apparently made two frameworks from thin strips of wood, which were covered with light cloth and attached to his arms. Mod called to the family still lingering at the dining room table to come see a "miracle." As one, they stood up and rushed to the front windows to see what Mod was referring to.

"It's a bird man," quipped Morrie.

"I think it's Barry Hector," said Mod.

"Let's go down and watch him," Mary exclaimed, reaching for her dark spectacles. "Hurry up, before he leaves."

Buttoning coats and pulling woolly hats over their ears, the entire family plus Amelia who, surprisingly, left the dirty dishes in the sink, rushed to the river's edge. The "bird man" was well out toward the middle of the river, but when he spied the spectators at Scovil's wharf made a graceful turn in their direction; he manoeuvered his wings to catch the breeze at an angle that brought him closer to shore.

It was Barry Hector all right. He greeted his appreciative audience with a big grin. He raised and lowered his wings and changed their angle to increase or retard his speed and alter his direction. Everyone waved and clapped their mittens in admiration and to keep their hands warm. No one had taken the time to put on a second pair as would be usual on such a cold day. When Barry had finished his repertoire of tricks, he waved a wing and set out across the astoundingly smooth ice for mid-river where the wind was brisker.

Mary was the first to express what everyone was thinking; "Now we can all skate! Can't we, Father?"

"Certainly looks safe. What do you think, Bess?"

"If they're careful and listen for cracking."

"Let's go," shouted Morrie as he started for the house. "We need to dress more warmly." Wowsie and Trudy each put an arm through one of Aunt Bessie's as they followed.

"It's such a treat to be home with you and Father for Christmas, Aunt Bessie," Wowsie said with an emotion that surprised her.

"And with the whole family," added Trudy.

"It's lovely to have you both here. I expect the long Christmas break will be the rule from now on."

"I hope so," added Trudy. "They must save a lot of money, not having to feed us for a month."

Mod headed for the carpenter's shed where he collected the skates he had asked Jock to sharpen on the grinding stone earlier in the month, knowing this day would come. He dropped them on the kitchen floor and asked Amelia for a hot cup of tea, which he took to the sitting room and the Franklin, getting back to his routine that had been pleasantly interrupted by the appearance of the "bird man."

In spite of their excitement, the need for warm feet and hands was the priority as the young placed their boots around the kitchen stove and went off to collect extra socks, mittens, scarves, and sweaters. As soon as she was bundled up, Mary grabbed her dark glasses and announced she would get one of those old kitchen chairs in the carpenter's shed.

"Me too," Roger offered always eager to follow Mary's lead.

Once they all reached the riverside, Morrie supervised the strapping on of skates, making sure they were tightly snugged up with no loose ends.

They all wore reachers, except Mary and Rog whose blades ended at their boot toe. Children learned on these short blades and only progressed to reachers, with much longer blades, when they could skate well enough to avoid tripping. Reachers encouraged lengthy strides, which made distance skating less tiring and more pleasurable.

As Morrie was tightening Mary's straps she said, "I wish I could wear reachers. I think I'm ready."

"See how much your feet remember from last year. Maybe try tomorrow, if the ice's still good."

Mary didn't argue with her usually wiser brother. With this wide expanse of perfectly smooth ice calling, she wanted to get started skating immediately. Mod joined the party, followed by Bessie who said she hadn't skated for a long time and wanted to try again. Morrie and Wowsie came to her assistance. Mod lit a much appreciated bonfire.

That first skate of the 1906-1907 season became etched in everyone's memory — perfect conditions for days on end, never surpassed nor even approached ever again. Decades later, when the siblings were together and reminiscences began, the superb ice at Meadowlands on that Christmas Eve afternoon, was a prime topic of conversation. They would all look into the distance of memory, imagining the limitless stretch of blue-black ice, no lines of snowflakes indicating cracks, no ruffles stuck to the surface impeding speed. They remembered no biting wind, just a warming winter sun glistening off tiny silver bubbles caught under the surface of the ice, and then how, when they stopped and kneeled, discovering those endless sparkles far down, down, down, seemingly to the centre of the earth. They remembered the crisp, white ribbon clinging to the shore — the result of the water's persistent lapping in the freezing air — just asking to be shattered with the merest touch of a boot's toe, which then revealed the frozen earth underneath. Most of all they remembered their Aunt Bessie and Father coming down to watch and their aunt sitting on one of the old kitchen chairs while Father kneeled down and strapped skates to her boots. They remembered Morrie and Wowsie rushing to her side, each taking an arm until the grey-haired woman's legs suddenly recalled their youthful expertise and began gliding forward while the other children stared in disbelief. They remembered Father collecting driftwood and some dry branches fallen from a nearby tree, and, with proud side glances at his still upright sister, starting a fire that grew into a large blaze where they came to warm themselves.

"Where did you learn to skate?" Morrie asked his beaming Aunt when they returned to the warmth of Mod's fire.

"In Saint John," she told them, "when I was young. It was very popular, even with adults."

"You're wonderful," piped up the usually quiet Trudy.

"I'll have something special to tell Helen in my Christmas letter, besides the "bird man," Mary thought to herself. "She'll be surprised."

Morrie and Bessie struck out again and headed toward mid-river. The others clapped their mittened hands in admiration and followed while Mod built up his fire. The contrast between cold air and the substantial fire, helped by the exertion of skating, brought out red cheeks in everyone, even in Bessie, who normally had a sallow, almost olive, complexion. Even the threat of a lowering sun did not break up the skating party, though it did send them back to Mod's fire with increasing frequency. On any other day, Amelia would have brought down a jug of hot chocolate, but this was Christmas Eve and was far too busy a time in the kitchen. The growing darkness, cold, and hunger failed to drive the family back to the house, but no one argued with Amelia's bell; not a crumb, or a slice, or a dollop of her Christmas Eve supper survived the skaters' appetites.

Christmas Day took on the usual routine with morning church in Jemseg, but by carriage this year instead of by sleigh. Jock made sure the sleigh bells were attached to the harness, all the same. The unlikely combination of sleigh bells without a sleigh was odd and disconcerting, but they managed to make the adjustment with the help of their usual carols. Everyone's nostrils were primed for the proof of a perfectly roasted turkey. They all remembered Uncle Jack's odourless turkey disaster of the past, which made them especially thankful for Amelia's well-done offering.

The artistic presents—drawings, paintings, bookmarks, mats, and sewing cases were distributed and appreciated. As usual Bessie had squirreled away, weeks ago, books ordered through *The Ladies' Home Journal* for everyone except Mary who was handed a parcel shaped not at all like a book, but long and thin. The gleaming steel of her very own reachers dazzled her eyes. After a stunned silence, she rushed to her Aunt Bessie and to her father to give them full-blown hugs. Wowsie, Trudy, and Morrie, who had taken part in cousin Madge's shopping expedition, had passed all the new woolen jerseys to Aunt Bessie for safe keeping so the young ones would be surprised on Christmas Day. When they were brought out and unwrapped, Mary and Roger were delighted to have the same kind of jerseys as their older sisters and brother.

Bessie and Mod were genuinely pleased with the books Madge had bought for the children to give their elders. Mod's was a well-illustrated book on fishing and Bessie's was Susanna Moodie's, *Roughing It In The Bush*. Bessie was intrigued with the choice but somewhat amused by the title. Though written fifty years earlier, and well known as a classic of pioneer life in Canada, she had not read it. Bessie had several volumes by the author's more famous sister, Agnes Strickland, who had remained in England and concentrated on the lives of British royalty.

The siblings all tried on their colourful jerseys. Mary was beside herself with happiness—a red jersey, her favourite colour, and reachers. She could not stop smiling. Roger was very pleased his jersey was the same colour as Morrie's and not a "girl colour."

By this time it was three o'clock and Bessie suggested they all play some games.

Mary quickly interjected, "I want to try my new skates."

"Let's play games this evening," Trudy added, hoping to please everyone. "This weather won't last. Shouldn't we skate first?"

Aunt Bessie could not disagree with this logic and nodded her agreement with a smile. Morrie put all the boots around the stove and then his new jersey back over his head.

"These jerseys are quite special," he said remembering cousin Madge's generosity. "Just perfect for skating on Christmas Day."

His four siblings followed his example, admiring the bright colours, like so many flowers come to life. They reluctantly covered themselves with the necessary coats, and gathered up their scarves, hats, and mittens. As Mary picked up her skates and held them in front of her as though they were a silver platter heaped with delicacies, she turned to the grown-ups, "Are you two coming?"

"Not today, dear. The muscles in my legs are telling me I shouldn't."

"And I need to let my excellent dinner digest," said Mod, looking forward to a rare cup of coffee and an even rarer brandy, both part of the annual indulgence. He then added, "But we'll watch you through the front windows to see how you get on with those reachers."

The feeling of disappointment that ran through Mary was quickly replaced by common sense. Of course, someone as old as Aunt Bessie would be stiff after yesterday. Anyway, she could still show off on her new skates and they would still see her, though from a distance. Roger walked close to Mary reveling in her shining acquisition, but not without a trace of envy. He knew it would be a few years before he was ready for reachers, but he wondered if he could maybe try them out, just a short borrowing.

Though the afternoon was well advanced, nearly two hours of skating was still possible. The siblings took turns forming up in all combinations — singly, in twos and threes and fours and all five together in a "whip," which they liked best and took turns leading and tailing. Mary was a little disappointed with her performance. She wished she hadn't fallen so many times at first. She knew it was a matter of getting used to her reachers, and she more or less mastered them after practicing with a kitchen chair for a while. Her sisters also helped by each taking one arm and all three striding and gliding, keeping toes well up, which they said was the secret. All this produced a family troop of happy, exhausted, and pink cheeked Scovil children marching from the river to the house in answer to Amelia's supper bell after the sun was quite set.

Bessie encouraged Amelia to produce a simple evening meal after their elaborate, traditional Christmas dinner. She prepared a supper of baked potatoes, cold ham, bottled tomatoes made into a scallop, and apple sauce over pound cake, which everyone, especially the skaters, much appreciated. They were careful not to spill anything on their new jerseys, which they kept on through the meal and for the evening of family game playing.

34

Skating to Gagetown

Boxing Day was still snowless. Morrie suggested they all skate over to Gagetown to visit the Peters and the Caswell cousins. He offered to pull a sled in case anyone got tired. Mod said he hadn't yet seen horses and sleighs on the ice so skating would be the best way over. Though Morrie did want to see family friends and cousins, he really wanted to see Maizie. Mary told him she had not seen her more than a few times during the fall term since she was looking after her mother. Bessie insisted each should have a sandwich tucked into a pocket, just in case there was sickness and no one asked them for dinner. This would, at least, give them enough energy to skate home.

"Take care, son, you're in charge," Mod instructed. "Make sure the ice is safe as you approach the wharf. You know how deep it is there. Watch to see if anyone else is on the ice."

"Yes, OK; we'll be careful, and we'll let you know if we see any sleighs."

Both Bessie and Mod followed the precious cluster starting out—all skating and Morrie pulling a sled. While they were still in sight they stopped so Roger could take a rest riding on the sled.

"I like the way Morrie looks ahead," Bessie mused. "Wouldn't Hattie be proud of her babies if she could see them now."

"Perhaps she can," replied Mod as he quickly looked away and summoned a cough that gave an excuse to bring out his handkerchief. After a pause, he reloaded the Franklin stove.

There was no need for the sandwiches. Aunt Mira Caswell welcomed them all with hugs and an invitation to dinner. Marion, Edith and Frances, each about two years older than Wowsie, Trudy, and Mary, were more than pleased with an opportunity to catch up with their cousins. Roger, though only eight, was not left out, nor little Jimmy, only four. Marion, well past her eighteenth birthday, told some funny stories about her experiences at the Montreal General Hospital where she was in nurses' training, and now back for a week's Christmas holiday. Edith was planning on doing the same, after a year at Edgehill that she would start next autumn. Frances, not yet thirteen, declared she wanted to be a nurse, as well. At that, the usually gruff Uncle Albert managed a smile and joined the conversation.

"With my three girls as nurses," Dr. Caswell bragged jokingly, "there won't be a sick person East of Montreal. And what about you Scovils? Are you going to cure the halt and the lame?"

"We haven't decided, but probably not," Wowsie spoke for the three. "Aunt Bessie's hard training has put us off."

"Times have changed, m'girl. But it's still tough."

"I'm thinking I'd like to be a physical training teacher," added Wowsie.

"You're on the right track, m'girl. Anything that will improve health."

Platters of cold turkey and fixings were passed a second time along with dishes of hot potatoes, a gravy boat, and mashed turnips with some special seasoning in it.

The girl who looked after Jimmy had left that morning for a few days with her family in Jemseg and so had the housekeeper. The Caswell family always let their help go home at this time of year, but not before the big day was over. Marion, in particular, was a great help. Jimmy could feed himself, but was a little messy, so Marion corralled his food into more manageable mounds and cut up his turkey. Edith and Frances removed the plates and first course serving dishes before bringing in two golden, hot mincemeat pies from the accomplished hand of the absent housekeeper. While conversation buzzed, they drank tea. Mary and Roger preferred cambric tea, as they didn't really like the taste of regular tea. Jimmy drank a little too.

"You girls look like a flower garden in your colourful jerseys, and you boys look like red squirrels," Aunt Mira observed after thoughtfully taking a sip of the hot tea.

As Trudy ventured an explanation about the new jerseys, the doctor turned to Morrie, sitting next to him, and asked; "How d'like Truro, boy?"

"I'm learning a lot. There're only four of us from New Brunswick, one from Sussex. The rest are from Nova Scotia."

"You'll get on," the doctor said encouragingly.

Morrie took another sip of tea and, with everyone else busy talking, quietly asked Dr. Caswell the question burning in his head.

"How's Mrs. Biddiscombe?"

"Not doing too well."

"What about Maizie?"

"She's in the early stages."

Morrie blinked. Had he hear correctly?

"TB?"

"Yes, boy. Don't go near her. Don't go into the house."

"Could she get better?"

"She doesn't have the right sort of care. The young sister has stopped school to support them."

Morrie's fingers froze around the handle of his teacup. He did not want to imagine beautiful, clever Maizie coughing up blood; her bouncy curls sunken into her pillow.

"She got the scholarship from the Normal School," the doctor continued. "Everything paid, she a smart girl."

"Will they were hold it for a year?"

Dr. Caswell lowered his voice; "She probably won't last a year. Look boy, as hard as it is, you owe it to your family not to go into that house, write her a letter, make it optimistic. I shouldn't have been so frank, but you can't risk getting infected. Keep the seriousness to yourself."

Morrie felt he had aged ten years in two minutes. He wanted to ask for pen and paper, but knew he needed a quiet time to compose a letter. He wanted to leave the table, run out doors for fresh air, run and run away from the facts. He wanted to doubt his uncle's medical judgment but no one ever did. He had a reputation for being right. Instead, he ate an imaginary crumb on his plate and drank the last drop of tea, distractedly swallowing a leaf and stared at the remaining leaves in the cup.

Aunt Mira suggested they all spend the afternoon playing games after they put the dishes in the sink. The doctor announced he had a call to make.

"Do you want some fresh air, boy? Come with me, just a mile or so out of town."

Morrie could not have been more grateful if the doctor had placed a one hundred dollar bill in his palm. He had to get away from the jollity of the others. The two men excused themselves and the party continued.

The usual favourite games were played, taking into consideration the span in ages. Even Jimmy almost managed "Hold Fast All I Give You." Pencil and paper games were beyond him, but he sat on his mother's lap and enjoyed the fun. Marion suggested they try the new game they received from a relative in Boston that had just come out this year called "The Landlord's Game." Each player had a little figure of a man who advanced, according to the number on two thrown dice, around a board marked off with properties named for streets in New York. The player had the option of buying the property with pretend paper money and could then build houses and hotels on it and charge rent when other players landed on it. The goal of the game was to become the richest landlord and put all the other players out of business.

Aunt Mira busied herself elsewhere while the seven players became quite engrossed in the game. After a while it got so complicated that Roger became bored and sold his land to the others. He joined Jimmy who was playing with wooden building blocks. Soon Roger was building high towers for Jimmy to knock down, which produced peels of laughter every time. The last tower used every block on the floor. Jimmy clapped his hands in anticipation and then swiped the whole structure, laughing and laughing. Suddenly, Roger saw the little boy's eyes roll back in his head. He started to shake and then fell over and thrash about on the floor, turning from side to side and groaning. Roger was terrified.

"Aunt Mira, come quick!" he yelled,

The commotion brought all six girls as well. The Caswells, who were all used to this situation, automatically moved furniture out of way of the thrashing boy while his mother put a pencil between his teeth, which, she explained, would keep him from swallowing his tongue. The Scovils stood in frightened astonishment, which abated a little when they saw how relaxed the family was. They had heard that Jimmy had "fits" but had no idea what they were. After several minutes the little boy's thrashing ceased and he lay quiet with his eyes closed. His mother carried him to a couch and covered him with a blanket.

"He'll sleep for a while now," Mira explained, "and then he won't remember what happened. It's epilepsy. He won't have another episode for days or maybe weeks. It's why we've kept the nursemaid on. Ruby's good with him. The doctor's uncle had it. It's not on our side of the family so don't you worry about getting it."

Mira smiled reassuringly at the Scovil children as their expressions relaxed from alarmed to attentive.

"Father's giving him medicine for it," Marion added from her medical knowledge. "Bromide; a very low dose as he's so small, but it means they're not so often."

The girls returned to the "Landlord's Game" and started picking up the pieces that had been scattered to the floor when Mary upset the board in her rush to see Jimmy.

"It's getting late; we should be going as soon as Morrie gets back," Wowsie announced, feeling responsible without her brother there. "It's hard to see cracks when the sun starts to go down."

Wowsie invited the three cousins to spend a day at Meadowlands and proposed the day after tomorrow.

"If the ice is still clear, we can skate over," Frances replied enthusiastically. Marion and Edith were equally fond of the sport.

Before long they heard foot stomping on the back porch, which was automatic on entering in winter, even without snow. The doctor and Morrie took off their boots and moved to the kitchen stove to warm up, rubbing their hands vigorously over its warm surface. In spite of Morrie's cheerful red cheeks, his face looked pinched and worried.

"We should go as soon as you're warmed," Wowsie said, suggesting they all take advantage of the Caswells' luxurious bathroom as well.

"OK, give me a minute," Morrie replied.

Aunt Mira hugged her sister's children with special feeling. They all responded with many thanks. Once they were again layered against the cold, they picked up their skates and, with their uneaten sandwiches still sitting in pockets, started for the river.

"See you well before dinner on the twenty-eighth," Wowsie called out as they started down the hill toward the river, half turning and waving. As they strapped on their skates, they spied three horses and sleighs out for cautious trots on the frozen river, which meant the ice was more than thick enough to be safe even where the water was less deep than by the wharf.

The five were nicely launched into good strides with Roger doing his best to keep up, when Trudy suggested they should eat their sandwiches. All agreed, in spite of their more than adequate dinner and took turns resting on the sled while eating. When they finished, Roger was quietly grateful when Morrie offered to pull him on the sled. Roger felt sure his legs wouldn't get so tired if he were wearing reachers.

"I'll wait a few days," he thought, "before asking Mary for a try. Her feet are about my size, so the straps won't need much changing."

Morrie's long strides, so close to his brother's face, and showing a gleaming blade with every rhythmical stroke, mesmerized Roger. In his weary state, he hoped he could stay put for the rest of the trip home.

Morrie was not concentrating on his long glides. He was thinking only of Maizie. He was thinking about the time Maizie hugged him, the way her hair bounced when she walked, the way her freckles bunched in some places and faded out in others. His thoughts turned darker as they approached Meadowlands.

"How could there be a god that allowed this to happen. Why should clever, pretty Maizie suffer in this horrible way just because her family is poor? There's something in the Bible about children being punished for the sins of their fathers. That doesn't make sense. Maizie's father died. There's no sin in that."

Wowsie put more effort into her skating than necessary, moving her arms vigorously as well as her legs, hoping to increase her muscle power for the tennis season, though that was months away.

"Perhaps I should think again about nursing. Marion seems to like it. She didn't mention mopping brick floors, like Aunt Bessie had to do. I suppose things have changed in thirty years. Maybe the dried up sandwiches on night duty have too, but maybe not. I'll ask Marion more about it."

Trudy copied Wowsie's arm movements, hoping to increase her speed and keep up with her sister.

"Marion might like it, but I'm not going to be a nurse," thought Trudy. "I'd like to help make people well but without touching their smelly bodies and hearing their screams, and no rest for twelve hours. Makes me tired to think of it. I think I'd like to make people well by giving them the right sort of food. Aunt Bessie says that's almost as important as nursing. Maybe I could go to that place in New York with the funny sounding name that Miss Smith talks about; 'Pratt,' I think she called it. They won't take me until I'm seventeen so I have two more years to decide."

Mary tried to remember not to look down at her new blades. "If I keep my head up my toes stay up better. I've only tripped once since leaving the Gagetown wharf. Must try longer glides. I wonder if Helen is skating, if she has reachers. I expect so. What a lot to tell her. I bet she's never seen anyone having a fit. My legs are getting tired. I'll see if I can catch up with Trudy and Wowsie."

With a burst of speed, Mary called out; "Can I skate in between you two? My legs are too short and getting tired."

The big sisters left off their thoughts of the future, returned to the present, and linked arms with Mary. It was the boost she needed to avoid the humiliation of asking for a ride on the sled. Roger, wanting to redeem himself a bit from that same feeling, called out to his "horse."

"Hey, stop a minute. I want to stretch my legs."

Meadowlands was now in sight and Roger skated the rest of the way home. The sun was gone by the time the skaters slowly walked up the frozen slope to their house, all youthful energy thoroughly spent.

35

And Then Comes the Snow

The next day was again bright and snowless. By afternoon, young muscles had somewhat recovered and none could resist another skating session. But on the twenty-eighth they awoke to a soft, bright quietness. Snow had begun early enough in the night to have already produced a four-inch covering. Keeping a big patch of ice clear of snow became the most pressing morning chore. When the Caswell girls arrived by sleigh, driven by their father's hired man in late morning, they joined the shovelling and sweeping, all hoping for an afternoon skate.

Dinner and the games that followed took a good two hours. Amelia had produced her usual superb spread—two turkey and vegetable pies, with the last of the bird and a fluffy mound of creamed potatoes plus a giant Queen-a-pudding with more strawberry jam than usual lurking in the corners. Amelia was a good judge of appetites. Even with eight hungry young, no one wanted for seconds. Bessie said that skating was not unlike swimming—a good while should be allowed for digestion.

The snow had continued to fall, so when the games were over, several more inches had to be removed from the ice. But no one minded as the jokes and teasing that passed among the cousins while shovelling and sweeping were almost as much fun as the skating that followed. The snowfall slacked off and the skating was good. There was little light left when the Caswell horse and sleigh arrived at Meadowlands, having spent much of the day making sure the doctor reached his most needy patients. Turn around time was brief, allowing only a short pause for the girls to thank their aunt and uncle, warm their mittens over the stove, and provide a cup of hot tea for the driver while Morrie held his horse. The snow had resumed falling, and though the moon was almost full it shed no light on the darkening scene. But the general whiteness of the snow covered river and the kerosene lamps on each side of the sleigh would provide the visibility needed for making the trip back to Gagetown. The Scovils watched from the front windows as the yellow glow from the sleigh's kerosene lamps faded into the snowy night. Mod knew that Doctor Caswell had great confidence in his driver and, of course, the horse knew the way home.

Snow fell for two more days and nights. Keeping a clear skating patch became an obsession. Horsey and the cutter established the river road to Gagetown. Morrie cut small spruce trees and "planted" them along the way so even with falling snow and failing light the route could be safely travelled.

As soon as Morrie had composed and then several times rewritten his letter to Maizie, he delivered it to her house. He was still not satisfied with it, but he knew he would never be since he couldn't say what he was really feeling. He hoped, perhaps, to have a glimpse of her through a window but he knew that was not likely. The house was quiet. He slipped the letter into the crack at the edge of the door and left feeling low and mean that he had not knocked on the door to make his presence known. But his uncle's words of warning kept his knuckles in his pockets.

There were more trips to Gagetown, during the holiday time, visiting the Peters, the DeVebers and the Caswells again. Sometimes Bessie and Mod joined the young in the larger cutter. The days vanished too quickly. January tenth had a double significance this year. Mary would be eleven and both Edgehill's and Truro's new terms would begin. In order that both would occur without disappointment, Bessie suggested that Mary's birthday should be celebrated on the fifth and the students should leave for Saint John on the seventh, after confirmation with cousin Madge that she still wanted them to stay three nights before Alyeene joined them for the train trip back to Nova Scotia.

Mary spent all year looking forward to Christmas and to her birthday, though a pity, she always thought, that they were so close together. To have her whole family home for her eleventh was a treat. Well, not her whole family exactly. She liked to imagine that her mother could pay a short visit each January tenth — her pretty mother with her soft lap, whose face was fading and needed to be revived by a look at photographs. They helped, but she was never smiling in the photographs as she often was in real life.

Amelia took a lot of care over Mary's cake. It had three layers, stuck together with coconut frosting and a liberal covering of the same on top, sprinkled with more sweetened coconut recently purchased from McKinney's store. Coconut layer cake was one of Mary's favourites. When the eleven candles were lit, she let them burn while she thought of her wish until they almost singed the coconut. And then, as she suddenly blew them all out at once, she knew there would soon be a letter from Helen. Morrie's present was a little sketch of her on the new reachers, wearing her new red jersey. He had accomplished this with coloured pencils in his room after bedtime. He made it into a birthday card, which Mary kept for many years. She was also given homemade cards from everyone else. The best fun of the day was making molasses candy. Making it was almost more fun than eating it. With buttered hands, it had to be pulled out in long ropes again and again until it was getting firm and just right to twist and leave for a while before cutting into small pieces. The pieces were then allowed to harden like stone before wrapping in little pieces of waxed paper.

There was no shortage of snow for firm sleighing to Saint John and back on Sunday the seventh. They took the large cutter with comfortable double seating. Bessie considered going but thought better of it as she was much behind in her correspondence. Everyone else went, well bundled up with heated bricks under straw at their feet, warmed cushions, and every buffalo robe that could be found. Morrie did most of the driving. They stopped at the Evandale Hotel to rest Horsey and for hot drinks. They took their cushions inside to keep them warm.

The Evandale Hotel had indoor plumbing of which they all made good use. The girls always looked forward to visiting the Starrs and the luxury of their seven indoor bathrooms. The lack of indoor plumbing and the use of the outhouse and commodes in the bedrooms were the only depressing part of returning to Meadowlands. Swimming and sponge baths were fine in the summer, but bathing otherwise meant that the big tin tub had to be filled with hot water and then emptied as each member of the family took their weekly bath. During the Christmas holiday, Wowsie had a serious talk with Aunt Bessie about the possibility of having a proper bathroom installed. She explained that it was embarrassing to still have such primitive arrangements when entertaining guests and visitors. Bessie, quite aware of this situation, had responded positively and told her niece she would talk to Mod about making the improvement.

The streets of Saint John were covered with just enough snow to prevent the runners from scraping, even as they ascended the hill to the Starr's big house. Hugs and greetings and a hot meal awaited the travellers. As always, Mary's emotions were conflicted when she said good-bye to her sisters headed for Edgehill. But when she and Roger and their father set out for Meadowlands she was more relieved to be going back to her known and comforting world than she was disappointed not to be returning to the rigid and frightening world of Edgehill.

*   *   *   *   *

Though Mary was more than satisfied with her early birthday celebration, she had no problem being the centre of attention again on the real day, January tenth. Her teacher always wished each birthday child a "Happy

Birthday," and if it fell on the weekend or upcoming holiday would do so in advance. Mary put up with eleven spankings from her classmates. One classmate, Dorothea, greased Mary's nose with a finger-smear of butter from her lunch sandwich. She had picked up the custom in Nova Scotia where she spent summers with her grandmother. It was meant to be humiliating, but Mary preferred it to the spankings, which she found a little too fierce. Everyone endured them on their birthday and no one ever complained.

January proceeded as usual. Mary and Roger tried to have a skate most days after school, though clearing the snow often took more time than was left for skating. They missed their siblings' muscle power, especially Morrie's. After one especially heavy snowfall on the night of the twentieth, Jock asked Mod it he could help clear the skating area. Mod readily agreed, pleased with his groom's thoughtfulness. Jock missed his own son and enjoyed helping Mary and Roger. Since the groom's mother died, seven-year old Willie had gone to live with a family in Jemseg. Though this was hard for Jock, it was a better arrangement for Willie, now that he was school age. Jock tried to see him at least every week or two.

Near the end of Jock's snow clearing efforts, Amelia appeared with a well-wrapped jug of hot cocoa and three enamel mugs. When Mary and Roger found the cocoa cooled just enough not to scald their tongues, they drank it down and returned to their task. Jock's drink seemed to take longer to cool. As he stood talking with Amelia, he said something that made her smile, then laugh. Mary looked up from her sweeping, and thought how pretty Amelia was, though now getting quite old, well into her twenties.

The final days of January produced the usual thaw. Skating became impossible, staying that way until well after Groundhog Day. But then, one cold morning, the sun shone on a hard, smooth surface again. The school day dragged by until at last, back at Meadowlands, the children rushed from the house to their renewed playground on the river ice. Mary was always kind hearted toward Roger but now, with her reachers, a lonely feeling came along with a sense of being different. Though it was hard, it prompted her into letting Roger use her new skates. With the help of an old kitchen chair and a large dose of determination, he tried to keep his toes up so as not to trip and fall. But his difficulty with the reachers let them both knew his performance did not rate a pair of his own.

Having shared the use of her skates relieved Mary of some of the burden of being different. She had seen this in Roger's eyes as she had mastered those long, silver blades and he had not. But he was used to being in Mary's shadow. After all, Mary was a year and a half older and no matter how hard he tried that would never change. There was a photograph on the mantle piece over the Franklin. It showed him with curly hair, wearing a dress with lace around the neck, just a baby at that time. It had been taken at a studio in Saint John on August fourteenth to mark his first birthday. He was looking out at the camera with pretty Mary leaning her head toward him with her blond bangs and curls and half smiling. She knew what was written on the back; "Roger, aged one year, Mary aged two and a half, 1898."

36

Improvements at Meadowlands
1907

The year of 1907 brought several surprises along with the expected routine. The river ice broke up in late April pushing Meadowlands into its island mode once again. During this time, Bessie and Mod decided to make two major improvements — divide one of the larger upstairs bedrooms for the installation of a modern bathroom and make the leveled and seeded tennis court Mod had earlier proposed. The bathroom would be the most costly, but it was Bessie's idea, prompted by Wowsie's recent plea, and the bill would not be unbearable. She wanted the girls to be unashamed of their home, especially when Ayleene or others visited.

As soon as the river boats were running, Bessie and Mod made a rare trip together to Saint John, staying overnight with cousins Lucy and Will, where Mod was constrained by his sister's presence not to repeat the indulgence of his previous visit. They had lunch with Madge and Frank, partly to glean advice on the choice of bathroom fixtures and the name of a reliable dealer in the city.

Frank, in his usual way, did more than give advice. He insisted on taking Bessie and Mod in his motorcar to the recommended store. With seven bathrooms in his house, they had no doubt about Frank's views being well founded. Madge was not without input, recommending basins with large rims for sundries and emphasizing the need for their proper height. Decisions were reached, orders were given, and an agreement for installation concluded. The installer would make two trips. One, in a week's time to advise on what was required for preparation, and another, with an assistant to accompany the well-wrapped porcelain fixtures. Frank offered to lend one of his wagons, drawn by two black Percherons, for that journey, which was graciously accepted. Remembering her own youthful enjoyment of surprises, Bessie suggested to Mod and the children that they write nothing of the indoor bathroom to Edgehill or Truro, not even a hint that a surprise would be waiting for them.

They regarded the construction of the tennis court differently. Bessie and Mod thought it was important to involve the children in a Meadowland's project that was chiefly for their use and enjoyment. They were all told about the firm decision to construct a proper grass tennis court that spring. Ideas flew back and forth. The project was the main topic in Meadowlands' letters during the late winter and spring, partly to steer away from the bathroom secret and partly so everyone would have some say in the plans. A proper tennis court would not only benefit them now but for years it could be a focal point of summer activities, along with swimming. There would not be much extra expense. Mod would arrange with the hired man and Jock to plow, level, plant and roll the area where the makeshift court had been. Mod found a special grass seed well suited for this use in Burpee's catalogue, which he added to his annual order.

Work began as soon as the ground was dry enough for plowing. After careful grading and leveling, the grass seed was evenly broadcast over the smooth soil and a roller applied to the whole area. Daily inspection by everyone insured not a seed would sprout without notice. By June seventh, the new tennis court was covered with a light green blanket, waiting to be hand mowed, rolled, mowed, and rolled again. Soon, when the house was full once more with family and guests, lively games of tennis on a near perfect court would be enjoyed.

By the time the grass on the tennis court was showing healthy growth, the glistening bathroom was in use. The installation was complete by the end of the third week in May. Each day, as renovations and installation were in progress, Mary and Roger flew to the site of the new bathroom as soon as they landed at Meadowland's wharf. The smell of paint was almost intoxicating; it was the forerunner of change, of luxury, dignity, and progress, of a city way of life! No more outhouse, no more sprinkling lime down the hole after each use; no more flies; no more outhouse odour; no more need for Amelia to regularly empty the bedroom washing basins and chamber pots!

*　*　*　*　*

Morrie graduated from his two years at Truro, in mid-June. The entire Meadowlands' family attended, with an overnight stop each way at the Starrs in Saint John and a train trip to and from Truro. The Edgehill term finished the previous day, so Wowsie and Trudy, now seventeen and sixteen, were able to attend their brother's graduation ceremony as well. Ayleene joined them. They travelled unescorted on the train from Windsor to Truro, after having been accompanied to the station by a junior Edgehill

258

mistress. Mod was more than a little proud of his manly looking son walking with confidence to receive his diploma. Bessie, seeing her "dear boy" on the edge of adulthood, was so moved it was all she could do to restrain her emotion and hold back the tears. The girls and Roger clapped longer than anybody else as Morrie received his diploma and shook the college director's hand.

They all spent a night in Truro, then took the trains to Moncton and Saint John where Frank, now with a larger new motorcar, waited to carry them back to the Starr's mansion for an overnight stay. The next day saw the seven Scovils on the riverboat, well laden with large trunks and small valises. In order to keep from bursting out with the secret of the bathroom, Mary and Roger talked enthusiastically about the tennis court and how beautiful it was. With this great improvement uppermost in the minds of the returning three, the tennis court was the first place they went once safely ashore. They touched it and gingerly walked on it. They admired the smooth surface of the ground and the deep green colour of the close cut grass. Mod explained a little of the work involved. They all thanked him and made plans for painting the lines at the first opportunity. Trudy suggested he might like to learn to play, but he said his exercise would be in watching them.

Finally, finally, or so it seemed to Mary and Roger, the returning students greeted Amelia in the kitchen and began to walk up the stairs to their usual rooms. Mary and Roger, bursting with the secret, pushed them into the glistening bathroom. Amid the surprised laughter and hand clapping, Wowsie turned to her aunt to give her a big hug for listening to her pleadings during the Christmas holidays. Bessie was almost crushed with all the hugs.

"Won't Ayleene be surprised when she comes in July!" was the first thing Wowsie exclaimed after releasing her grateful hug.

"We'll all miss those jokes pinned up on the outhouse walls, won't we?" Morrie asked innocently.

"We can do without those," Bessie replied with a little smile.

37

The Groom Takes a Bride

Jock had become increasingly fond of Amelia's hot chocolate. In addition, he was now frequently coming to the kitchen to ask Mr. Scovil's opinion about some matter having to do with the horses or a farm project when previously such consultation was not needed. Of course, this afforded opportunity for conversation with Amelia as well. Mod understood the reason for this change in Jock's behaviour and was sympathetic. He could see the attraction was becoming mutual.

Though fifteen years his junior, Amelia saw that Jock, in many ways, would be a perfect husband. She could continue to work for the Scovils some of the time, and would become the mistress of her own neat little house right here at Meadowlands. There were no young men in Jemseg she enjoyed walking with and talking to. There had been one boy who seemed to like her when they were sixteen, but he married a girl from Young's Cove.

Jock knew so much. He made her laugh and she enjoyed hearing him talk with that lovely Scottish burr. He was not a tall man, just a little taller than she was, but, as she found out one evening when no was around, he knew how to kiss, which made her toes tingle. He had not been forward; she let him know in a modest way that his attentions were welcome. After that, her days had a happy new feeling of quiet excitement and she looked forward to Jock appearing at the kitchen door.

One evening a few days later, after the chores were done, Jock suggested they go for a walk on the road to Jemseg. Jock was a good talker and it didn't take him long to propose marriage. Her acceptance was confirmed with another toe-tingling kiss.

The ceremony was scheduled to take place on Saturday, July third, in the Jemseg St. James Anglican Church. The rector would read "the bans" on three previous Sundays, which was required for a marriage to be legally recognized by the Church. Jock considered himself a Presbyterian when he left Scotland, but he settled for Amelia's Anglicism, which was her family's church. The only other church in Jemseg was Baptist.

The occasion would be grander than usual when a servant married. Jock was a professional of sorts, a qualified groom, and regarded by all with high esteem. Amelia had made a good catch. But it would be the attendance of Mr. Scovil, Miss Scovil, and the five Scovil young occupying their usual front pew just under the pulpit that would make the marriage of Amelia and Jock a special event. Jock had no Canadian relatives except his son, Willie, who was too young to act as best man. Morrie offered to fill in and Jock happily accepted. The two had worked together and were like friends with each other.

Amelia's parents and surviving siblings still at home lived in a tidy but small house, too small for a reception after the wedding. So Bessie suggested the reception be held in the church hall and persuaded the fledgling Women's Auxiliary to provide sandwiches and tea. She knew Amelia was likely to be the best cook in her family so suggested she make the cake with Scovil ingredients at Meadowlands.

Bessie found pictures in *The New York Times* and *The Ladies' Home Journal* showing modern wedding cakes with two and three tiers. Why not try one with two tiers, Bessie asked Amelia, who blushed with pleasure at the thought of being such a special celebrity. But there was a small problem; the little pillars needed to hold up the second layer could be found only in Saint John and there was not enough time to make such a trip before the cake needed to be baked. Morrie, who was working at home for the summer, got wind of the dilemma and came up with a solution.

"What about cutting bits off an old broom handle and covering them with frosting?"

At first, Bessie and Amelia just laughed at Morrie's suggestion. But then, on further consideration, Bessie said, "Why not?"

"It's worth a try," Amelia chimed in.

Morrie produced eight "pillars," four inches high. He smoothed the rough edges with a small file. Amelia scrubbed them clean. She then made a small batch of "Royal Icing," which the cookery books said was the right sort for wedding cakes. She tried rolling the pillars in the frosting, but then found it stuck better if applied with a knife. Bessie showed Amelia how to make a paper cone with a small opening at the narrow end, which, when filled with frosting, enabled her to squeeze small blobs on the top and bottom of each pillar. This gave them the appearance of real pillars with a base on the bottom and a capital on the top. She stood them on end and carefully placed them in the pantry to harden.

Some of the pictures in *The Ladies' Home Journal* showed three tiered wedding cakes, but two seemed quite enough to Amelia. Bessie recommended making pound cake, which is firmer than the traditional fluffy wedding cake and the pillars won't poke holes in it. Each cake called for ten eggs but that was not a problem as the hens were laying well. But to lessen the chance of a disaster, small pieces of butter paper were placed at either end of the pillars and then covered with a smoothed layer of Royal Icing when the cakes were being assembled.

On the evening of July second, Jock drove Amelia back to her family home in Jemseg in the small carriage with the wedding cake in a basket on her lap, which minimized the effect of bumps. Her wedding dress, which Miss Straight produced on Bessie's instructions, was a simple design made of fine white cotton that Amelia could wear for years as the basis for her best summer outfit. It was carefully folded, riding in a dust proof box at the back of the carriage. Amelia's grandparents had first settled in Jemseg when they were young, so just about everyone knew the family and dozens turned up to see her married to an upright and settled man who could provide a good life. Almost as many comments were made about the innovative cake as about the lovely bride.

Bessie insisted that Amelia take a week off to become used to her new life as a married woman in her own little house. The girls were becoming more capable and Trudy was now showing a real interest in making nourishing food. The week passed with only two burned pots. Amelia had left them well supplied with seven loaves of bread. By the end of the week all agreed the last one required toasting with more than the usual amount of butter applied.

A sensible solution to Amelia's dual role as maid and wife was decided upon. She arrived in time in the morning to prepare breakfast and was joined for dinner by Jock and again for the evening meal, unless he had a sick animal to attend to, in which case Amelia would take food to him. Jock, not wanting to be deprived of his bride's company more than necessary, became adept at drying dishes, which lightened her kitchen work. The new bathroom cut nearly an hour of work from her daily routine. She now had her own little house to organize and care for on her own time but that was entirely a labour of love.

Willie wanted to stay on living with the McLeod family in Jemseg. Jimmy McLeod, about the same age as Willie, was like a brother. Having lost his mother to an early death and then his granny two years ago, Willie was not keen to give up his playmate and his place in the McLeod family. This was a good arrangement all around. It gave Amelia a chance to know Willie gradually on his Sunday visits, often with Jimmy. Jock continued to pay Mrs. McLeod one dollar a month, which, she said, was more than enough. She enjoyed having Willie as part of the family especially since he was willing to be helpful when asked.

38

The Last Family Summer at Meadowlands

The day after the wedding, July fourth, was Morrie's eighteenth birthday. There had been no time for birthday preparations since the wedding preparations came first. But Bessie could not bear the thought of a cake-less anniversary for her dear boy's eighteenth, especially as he had been so helpful with the wedding cake. She had, as usual, squirreled away a book for him as a gift, and she knew the others, led by Wowsie, were planning something by way of celebration.

Bessie awoke a little earlier than usual on the fourth. In spite of yesterday's excitement the significance of today banished the weariness in her limbs and pushed her from her bed into the strangely empty kitchen. As she fed the stove with paper, kindling, and some stouter pieces of firewood and then lit it, Bessie decided on a layer cake for Morrie; two Victoria sponges which would take less time and need a less hot oven than more complicated recipes. Mashed fresh strawberries and a little whipped cream would be right for the filling plus the usual butter frosting and as many candles as could be found, though she wasn't sure there would be eighteen. And of course they must have strawberry ice cream. That would require two trips to the ice house by Bert, the new hired man — the first to carry in enough ice to chill the mixture of cream, sugar and berries, and the second to fill the ice cream maker's outer shell, along with coarse salt to promote melting.

Bert had been hired a short time earlier to help Jock with the horses and generally lend a hand with farm and household tasks. He was a strong young man and a willing worker who thought nothing of walking back and forth from his family home in Jemseg. Fetching the slabs of ice and breaking then into small chunks to chill the ice cream mixture and then to fill the ice cream maker would be pleasant task on a warm day. Bessie would make sure he had a generous serving of the final product. Bert was pleased to be working at Meadowlands and the Scovil's were pleased to have him.

Mod, knowing there would be a morning rush for the new facilities, was up and about before his children. As he descended the stairs, he wondered, with Amelia away, whether his usual oatmeal porridge would be waiting for him. It pleased him every morning, year round, like putting on his Stanfield's "unshrinkables" long underwear—thick ribbed wool in the winter and a lighter version during the warmer months. He was not disappointed. A pot of oatmeal was sitting at the edge of the stove, cooked and keeping warm in a double boiler. By the time the young were up and took turns using the still novel bathroom, the smell of baking cake was rising to their nostrils. They all noisily wished Morrie a "Happy Birthday."

The children fell in with their Aunt's partially prepared breakfast, finding what they needed if it was not on the table. Trudy put on an apron and offered her services as a kitchen helper. She had definitely made up her mind to become a dietitian when she left Edgehill in two years and decided she should learn as much as she could about kitchen food preparation even before then. Bessie suggested she start by dishing up her father's porridge, putting the cream in a jug and then helping with some lunch preparations. There was easily enough porridge for two servings so Morrie, having clearly reached the age of manhood, joined his father, copying him by adding a sprinkling of salt to the porridge before the yellow cream.

Trudy was pleased that Aunt Bessie asked her to work on lunch, but felt conflicted when Morrie announced that this was the day to paint the tennis court lines and put up the net. Wowsie unearthed her measurement notes from last summer. Morrie and Roger mixed up a pail of whitewash, found the brushes, borrowed the kitchen ball of string, and a yardstick. The team of four got to work laying out the string according to the right measurements and staking it down.

After an hour of chopping vegetables for what her aunt called a "hearty soup," Trudy's help was no longer needed. She quickly joined her siblings and took her turn painting lines and then helped erect the new net that Mod had asked Frank to ship from Saint John along with proper holding posts that would keep the net tight. Mary walked back and forth over the whole area determined to find any little rock or twig that might have found its way on to the nearly perfect blanket of green. By eleven o'clock the work was done. They were all hot and sticky.

"The whitewash needs a few hours to dry," Morrie announced "There's time for a swim before dinner."

They all agreed and ran to change into their swimming costumes.

Bessie and Mod came from the house to view the court, agreeing, even before any tennis was played, that it was a splendid and civilized addition to life on the farm, a good investment indeed. Mod was thinking a cup of tea on the verandah, where he could enjoy watching the swimmers would be perfect, but Bessie had another idea.

"Mod, dear, I don't have enough strawberries for the ice cream. Would you help me pick some?"

"Of course, Bess."

Ordinarily, one or more of the children would have been happy to help if asked, but on this special day, Bessie wanted tennis, swimming, and celebration to dominate. Sister and brother both found straw hats and berry pails, which they filled in twenty minutes, which was long enough for both under the noonday sun.

Lunch began with Bessie and Trudy's hearty soup accompanied by Amelia's still fresh bread and butter. Bessie carried in the layer cake, oozing with cream and strawberries and placed it in front of Morrie. They all sang out "Happy Birthday To You" with Mary's perfect pitch voice leading the way. When not a smudge of strawberry stained whipped cream or cake was left, Morrie carried the ice cream maker to the now partially shaded verandah. Bert had filled the circular space between the outside wall and the canister with chopped ice and salt. Trudy brought out the chilled berry, cream and sugar mixture, which also had a touch of salt and vanilla, and poured into the central canister. Bessie inserted the paddle, fastened the lid, and clamped on the crank and gearing mechanism. The young folks all took turns cranking. At first, it was easy, then became harder and harder as the mixture began to freeze and it took more and more strength to keep the paddle turning inside the canister. Roger lost patience when the cranking became more and more difficult, but stopped complaining when he was reminded that everyone was sharing the work so they could share the reward.

Eventually, when the self-appointed expert, the birthday boy himself, could barely turn the crank, he pronounced, "Enough!" He opened the lid, withdrew the paddle and passed the canister of ice cream to his aunt for dishing up. No one objected when Morrie turned his back and began licking the paddle on which a good deal of ice cream remained. This was a privilege of his birthday. (Years later, as a prisoner of war in Germany, down hearted by the length of his incarceration, Morrie would recall the creamy taste of that fresh strawberry ice cream. He would savour the memory of standing on the edge of the verandah at Meadowlands, the sun warm on the back of his neck while licking the cool ice cream from the paddle on his eighteenth birthday.)

Normally, after such a satisfactory and celebratory meal no energetic activity would be undertaken. But, this time, no more than ten minutes passed, with conversation still centered on the making of ice cream, before Mary burst out with the question that was in the back of everyone's mind.

"Do you think the lines will be dry by now?"

"Let's find out," Wowsie shot back.

Mary took off like a streak. She was a fast runner and reached the tennis court first.

"The lines are perfectly dry," she announced as she swiped her hand across the whitewashed grass. "We can start playing."

They took their ice cream dishes to the kitchen sink before collecting tennis racquets and balls. All five practiced for a while, Roger mostly with two hands. Then, they began games of four with the fifth as "ball boy," at which they all took turns. Wowsie and Trudy supervised the scoring since they were the experts. Bess and Mod nodded to one another from their comfortable wicker chairs on the verandah, taking great satisfaction in the way their good idea had worked out. They were especially heartened to see the balls bouncing most satisfactorily off the almost shaved turf.

"Just about as good as Westfield," called Trudy to the onlookers as she returned a near perfect ball to Morrie.

"We can't expect higher praise than that," Bess remarked to her brother.

39

Morrie Joins the Militia

By the time Ayleene came the following week, tennis had become a daily activity, often followed by swimming. She confided to the girls that she thought Meadowlands was the most perfect place in the world now that there was a real bathroom and a good tennis court.

Mr. and Mrs. Jock McTavish returned to work after their honeymoon vacation week. Amelia made good use of the time in putting her mark on the little house, which went with the groom's position and was now her home. Jock was skilled at doing almost any kind of work and responded with pleasure to his wife's suggestions for home improvements.

Morrie gravitated more and more to the barn, helping Jock with the horses and working on the tack. At Truro he definitely realized he had an affinity with animals, especially with horses, rather than an interest in developing improved potato or apple varieties. One afternoon, after thinking all this through again and finishing up in the barn, he joined his aunt and father who were relaxing on the verandah with their cups of tea. Morrie was ready to spill out his decision.

"I need to talk to you two," he started in. "I'm really a horseman, at least for now. I met a fellow at Truro who thinks as I do. He's going to join the militia in Saint John, working with horses. We'd have basic army training, then be attached to a cavalry regiment. It would only be on the weekends and some evenings."

"What would you do in the day?" asked his disappointed father, who hoped his son would stay at home to improve Meadowlands.

"George has that all worked out. His uncle owns a business in Saint John—Rideout's Insurance, on lower King St. He's expanding and needs more workers. We could stay at his home, at least at the beginning. They have two daughters but they've married and left home so there's plenty of room."

"You certainly have very good handwriting, dear, good for office work," Bessie responded with a tone of encouragement.

"I could always come back to the farm if you really needed me, and I'd visit of course." Morrie was beginning to feel guilty he would not be repaying his elders properly for all they had done for him by leaving Meadowlands so soon.

Mod stroked his moustache, dealing with a certain sadness. Bessie sipped on her tea, digesting the implications.

"You must decide what you'll do with your life, son. I know Jock says you understand horses and I've noticed it, too. This seems like a good way to hedge your bets. Training in an office would help in the future if you went in for farm management. And you have some distinguished military ancestors, you know. Col. Beverley Robinson, the elder, fought at the side of General Wolfe on the Plains of Abraham and survived. And his son, the younger Col. Beverley brought his regiment from New York to the Fredericton area of the Saint John River to remain loyal to George III."

"I don't want to be a Colonel, Father, I just want to see that horses are treated well."

"Have you decided when you might move to Saint John?" Mod asked.

"Now that I've told you, I'll write to George. We thought we might start at the end of August or early September. That would suit his uncle and allow lots more holiday time yet this summer. When I hear back from George, we'll spend a day or two in Saint John. Mr. Rideout wants to meet me, of course, and I'd like to see where I'd be working. We will visit the militia headquarters, as well and see how we sign on and all that. We'll get paid for it, too, George says. So you don't have any big objection?"

Morrie looked from his aunt to his father.

"You seem to have thought it out well, son. It's an exciting time of life for you. Try it for a couple of years, and see how you like it. There's always the farm, if you don't," Mod replied, half-hoping two years would be more than enough.

Relieved to have spilled his decision and found it more or less accepted, Morrie announced he would celebrate by joining the others for a swim. In between swims, when all were sitting on the wharf, he told them of his plans. They were full of questions. Alyeene's asked, "Does that mean we'll see more of you in Saint John?"

"Probably, but it looks as though I won't have much time for myself. I don't know how many hours I will have to give the militia once I sign on."

"Now that you've talked over careers with Father and Aunt B, it's a good time for me to do the same," Wowsie interjected. "Come on Trudy, you need to do this too. They should know what we're planning."

Morrie, Mary and Roger slipped back into the water like basking seals, while the eldest sisters went to the house to change from their bathing clothes and matching mob caps which did nothing to keep out the water.

After shaking out and drying their hair, they changed into flower spotted summer dresses, which seemed to weigh twenty pounds less. The girls replenished their elders' teacups, returned to the kitchen for glasses of strawberry cordial, and rejoined their father and aunt on the verandah. They were both eager to spell out their vocational plans.

Wowsie, seventeen on August sixteenth, had her mind set on studying Physical Training at Randolph-Macon Women's College in Lynchburg, Virginia. They would accept her at eighteen, next autumn. The two-year course would prepare her for teaching. Miss Smith and the physical training mistresses at Edgehill had encouraged her and recommended Randolph-Macon. Cousin Frank and cousin Madge were enthusiastic about this plan and would pay all the bills. Wowsie's plan of becoming a Physical Training teacher was generally known to the family, but she felt the need for her father and aunt to approve the details. Trudy was in the same position.

Before Aunt Bessie or Mod had time to respond to Wowsie, Trudy followed her sister's lead and set out her plans. Though she could not enter the Pratt Institute in New York to become trained as a dietician until she was eighteen, which was two years away, Trudy wanted the general approval of her father and aunt. Miss Smith was encouraging, especially as two other Edgehill girls had studied dietetics at Pratt in recent years and both have responsible positions with large hospitals. In her enthusiasm to change the world, Trudy added, it was a pity they hadn't returned to Edgehill to improve the food there! The Starrs would also cover Trudy's expenses.

The girls sipped the last of their cordial, leaned forward in their wicker chairs to fluff out their long hair, still drying in the late afternoon sun, and waited for questions or comments.

"Well," Bessie responded at last, "we are overloaded with information! It's very gratifying that your headmistress is encouraging both of you. She obviously believes you will be successful and I'm sure you will. Determination and a sort of 'calling,' a passion, you might say, has a lot to do with it. It takes you over the rough spots; at least it did for me in nursing. It's so good of Frank and Madge to offer their continued support. Dear Hattie is still looking after you both."

"Yes," Mod added. "Your mother would be so proud of you, as am I. What accomplished young ladies you will be! You both certainly have my blessing."

Nothing the girls said was completely new to Bessie or Mod. Frank and Madge had previously confided they would continue to finance Elizabeth and Gertrude through any further education that interested them. A letter from Miss Smith accompanied their last report cards that mentioned her endorsement of their plans for future education. But today seemed to be made for these dramatic disclosures that needed specific approval. The girls both stood with satisfied smiles, kissed their elders and headed for the tennis court, now cooled with late afternoon shadows.

* * * * *

Ayleene finished her "perfect" Meadowland's visit as planned, and returned to the Starr summerhouse in Westfield by riverboat. As in former years, Wowsie and Trudy were invited for two weeks of tennis and parties at the Westfield country club with an impeccable court and impeccably turned out boys and girls from well-heeled families, now summer friends. Suitably chaperoned dances, picnics on the beach and playing Whist—a forerunner to Bridge—in the evenings when cousin Frank was out from the city more than filled their time. Madge was training a new girl to care for the three younger children. She needed to supervise evening and bedtime activities and sometimes did not join the others. Exuberant Frank had no difficulty keeping the girls on their toes and well on the way to playing Bridge.

Wowsie and Trudy arrived back at Meadowland's in time for Roger's birthday on August 14th and Wowsie's on the 16th. Bessie suggested a combined party on the 15th, for which the Caswell's were invited. Even the doctor spared a couple of hours.

"What this place needs is a telephone system," the doctor said to Mod as they settled down for a pipe on the verandah after a more than sufficient birthday lunch, now about to be extended to include blueberry ice cream. The nine young people were all putting their muscle power into making this new, late summer flavour of the Meadowlands specialty. They now considered themselves experts after at least one ice cream feast every week since Morrie's birthday. Today there were fourteen present, including Amelia. That meant initial small portions for everyone and then, without washing up, filling the canister a second time with the chilled mixture of cream, sugar, vanilla, and berries, packing in more chopped ice, and cranking rapidly until the new batch was ready for serving. The large birthday cake vanished without difficulty, having done its job of focusing "Happy Birthday" on the two celebrants. No one was in need of further nourishment, but no one refused the second helping of ice cream.

While lunch was settling, the young assembled on the new tennis court, mowed and rolled yesterday so it would be in prime condition. Marion and Edith had both played tennis before; Frances had not, nor, of course, little

272

Jimmy. All the rest took turns except Roger, who still found the racquet too heavy for his wrists. He was happy to amuse Jimmy but was careful to avoid anything too exciting, for fear of triggering another fit, though he half wanted to see Jimmy have one again, now that he knew he wouldn't die from it. Mary, nearly two years younger than Frances, showed her how to hold a racquet and shared advice on playing the game. Wowsie and Edith partnered against Trudy and Marion with Morrie volunteering to be ball boy.

During the last week of August, Morrie was launched into independence with his departure for Saint John. Wowsie and Trudy set about restocking their trunks under their aunt's guidance. Bessie continued with her writing and answering her many correspondents. Mary and Roger savoured the last days before school. Mod surveyed this year's squash crop and consulted with Amelia about what variety's seeds to save for next year's planting.

One weekend, when the leaves were turning colour and flying off the trees, Morrie returned for a visit with tales of his new life. Roger so envied his big brother that he took to asking for second and sometimes third helpings, hoping they would hasten his growth to adulthood. Letters to and from Edgehill continued and now, occasionally, Morrie's handwriting could be spotted on an incoming envelope.

40

"Mr. Evinrude" Comes to Meadowlands
1910

One cool evening in mid-March, 1910, after Mary and Rog said "goodnight" and had gone upstairs, Bessie settled into her chair near the Franklin while Mod added three sticks of hardwood to the still glowing embers. Amelia brought in the tray with a padded tea cozy, covered with a field of tiny embroidered violets. This tea cozy was last year's Christmas present from Addie in appreciation for her sister-in-law's generosity. Mod never lost that little boy love of cake, or his anticipation of what each evening might bring. Of course, it was often the same as the previous night, though rarely three nights in a row. Amelia had the knack of turning yesterday's cake into today's pudding, enhanced and disguised with palate pleasing additions. Mod's mouth became moist just looking at tonight's offering. He could not guess exactly what it was and was happy to wait until Bess had passed him his cup of tea. Then her knife sliced a serving and he was rewarded with the sight of black currants embedded in a golden pound cake. Mod smiled at his sister and she at him. It was one her favourites, too.

"Have you finished your seed order for spring planting, dear?"

"Not quite. I thought I'd try some new, dry, buttercup squash, but neither of these catalogues has them. I'll wait for Burpee's. They're often best, anyway. I'm way behind reading *The Times*. Do you want a section?"

Bessie accepted the part of the New York paper Mod handed over and they both settled into their evening reading ritual.

Bessie suddenly interrupted the silence; "Oh, Mod, I must read you this advertisement; just listen to what it says: 'Throw away the oars, buy an Evinrude detachable motor.' There's a company in Milwaukee making motors that can be attached to rowboats. Isn't that just what we need? The children have taken over much of the rowing, but a motor would be an enormous help. Let's write them for details. My shares are doing well and it would be a good investment, don't you think?"

"Let's have a look at that," Mod replied as he reached for the page Bessie was holding. "I wonder if we'll need new row boats?"

Mod studied the sparse but intriguing advertisement. He knew that small boats with on-board motors were now being built, but this was something different. He imagined taking his ease in his heavy boat while it skimmed over the water like a large dragonfly. "I've been rowing to Gagetown and back since 1880 — thirty years," he thought. "It's time I slowed down a little. With Morrie in Saint John, and Elizabeth and Gertrude home only for some of their holidays, Mary and Roger are mostly the rowers, but with a motor my summer trips would be much easier and without the sweat. Little Mary is plucky, the way she stands in the boat in the middle of the river and catches the mailbag thrown to her by Jimmy Gilchrist, the boat captain. It would be much safer if she could then speed away instead of being rocked by the wake of the big riverboat."

"What's your opinion, dear?" Bessie asked, rousing Mod from his reverie.

"Capital idea. I was just thinking what an advantage it would be. I'll write for more information in the morning. In the mean time, how about another slice of that currant cake?"

School morning breakfasts were always a rush. Mod decided he would wait until the three of them were bundled into the sleigh before he mentioned the topic uppermost in his thoughts since last evening. As they started across the still passable ice road to Gagetown, he told them about the Evinrude outboard motor. He hadn't imagined Mary and Roger would think of so many questions to ask.

Mod's letter of inquiry brought a prompt reply from the Evinrude Company along with additional information to which they gave careful consideration. It seemed a bit like "buying a pig in a poke" since no one they knew had seen this new invention in action or even heard about it. They had only the pictures and the glowing description in the publicity brochure to go by. Nonetheless, Bessie's keen interest in modern improvements and her usual optimism prompted her, with Mod's approval, to place an order accompanied by a cheque. There was a possibility it would be a poor investment; but, if the company brochure was to be trusted, the advantages were so great it seemed worth the risk.

A week later, the ice broke up and Meadowlands reverted to its semi-island mode. Bessie kept an eye on Mary and Roger's homework, trying to maintain the weekday mornings for their studies. When their concentration deteriorated, she would announce a half hour recess. The day had to be really miserable for Mary and Roger not to dash for the door, buttoning coats on the way and slipping their feet into Wellingtons — much quicker than lacing boots and more suitable for the season of mud and puddles. On a break of thirty minutes they were outdoors for twenty-eight!

Though having outgrown childhood, Mary and Roger's enthusiasm for milk and cookies had not diminished, which they knew would be waiting for them when they heard Aunt Bessie ring the old school bell. Whether they were in the barn or down by the river trying to spot something interesting on the ice floes—like that hen perched on a branch they remembered from years ago—the bell calling them back to their studies could easily be heard.

As she finished her cup of tea and the "students'" moist fingers blotted up the last cookie crumbs, Bessie opened the family copy of *The Last of the Mohicans*, by James Fenimore Cooper. She had chosen this book because she thought the story would appeal to Roger, whose reading skills needed improvement. It was well written and exciting enough to hold the children's interest. It had been a favourite of her father who had read it aloud to his family. Bessie well remembered how the words came to life with his expressive voice and well articulated vowels. No doubt, listening to his own father—Bessie's grandfather—preach from the Trinity Church pulpit in Kingston all those years of his childhood and youth impressed him with the benefits of enunciating and pronouncing clearly.

Twice a year, since she had returned to Meadowlands and when the river was closed to traffic, Bessie had employed reading aloud as a multi-faceted learning tool. It seemed to be an appropriate settling down activity after an outdoor recess. She started the reading and after five minutes passed the book to Mary, who read rather too quickly her aunt thought but said nothing, as she made no mistakes. It was then Roger's turn. His reading had much improved in the last four months, though he did have to spell out some difficult-to-pronounce words, like "unprecedented." Reading for five minutes especially suited Mary as it gave her eyes a rest for two-thirds of the time, cutting down on that pulled feeling resulting from her extreme astigmatism. She was forever grateful for her glasses, which were a huge help but could not remove the problem entirely. Bessie's love of words and the joy of reading absorbed her so completely she often exceeded her turn of five minutes, sometimes doubling it before she noticed Roger and Mary smiling at each other in amusement and realized she had gone on much too long.

The two students spent the last hour before noon on essay writing. Bessie, at first tried going up to her nook to resume her own writing during this time but found that Roger and Mary's concentration and quality of work fell short when she was absent. She now brought her own writing to the dining table for the hour, which improved her student's concentration and their essays. Bessie reminded them that their teacher had asked to see three of their best essays from their enforced absence, which also sobered the two into making an improved effort.

Gradually, the Meadowlands' noon meal had become "lunch" though the evening meal was still referred to as "supper." Sometimes, however, supper became "dinner", partly because Wowsie and Trudy had become accustomed to this usage at school and when they stayed with the Starr's in Saint John. With Mary and Roger expending so much energy rowing back and forth to school each day and having only sandwiches at noon, Bessie saw the need for a full dinner at the end of the day. Her reasoning also took into account that Mary and Roger now had nearly adult digestive systems and went to bed much later than previously. They could well handle a sizeable "dinner" in the evening.

*　*　*　*　*

One day the "Royal Sandwich" was on the menu for lunch, which reminded Bessie of how this creation came to be. Shortly after she had returned to Meadowlands from the United States in 1903, the women of the Fredericton Cathedral were putting together the *Fredericton Cathedral Cookbook*. They asked her to contribute recipes. She sent in two: "Royal Sandwich" and "Cheese Potatoes," both good ways to use leftovers. Building leftovers into household and institutional menus was one of the basics of being a skilled cook who consistently produced nourishing food that all found agreeable, and, at the same time, operated her kitchen in an efficient and frugal way. Bessie was a firm believer in making good use of leftovers, a skill that saves time, effort and expense. She had often mentioned the importance of this practice in her articles and books.

When the *Fredericton Cathedral Cook Book* was published and she acquired a copy, Bessie was struck by the contribution she had made in addition to her two recipes. She had sent the editor a long list of possible contributors, relatives and friends she respected for the quality of their table. The editor had followed up on her recommendations, and there they were, generously sharing their treasured recipes: Mrs. Dibblee, Mrs. J. R. Howie, Mrs. Lee Street, Mrs. George J. Bliss, Mrs. Caswell, Mrs. W. V. B. Bridges, Mrs. R. F. Randolph, Lady Ashburnham, Mrs. J. Delancy Robinson, Mrs. W. W. Hubbard, and Miss DeVeber were prominently featured along with many others Bessie had suggested. The *Cathedral Cookbook* was a great success, the sale of which added to the Cathedral's restoration coffers.

Though she knew her recipes by heart, Bessie enjoyed taking the well-made little book off the shelf and opening its stout cover. It had a tendency to open to the page where both Bessie's recipes appeared. Her eyes first lit on "Royal Sandwich."

278

Mix 1 cup of flour, a pinch of salt and two teaspoons of baking powder to a batter with 1 cup of milk; pour into two buttered Washington pie plates and bake. Have ready a mince made of any cold meat, seasoned with pepper, salt, celery salt, or poultry dressing as preferred; heat it with a little gravy or melted butter and boiling water, and spread between the cakes. Gravy can be served with it if desired.

"I've certainly made good use of semi-colons," Bessie observed.

"Cheese Potatoes" was shorter and simpler, and depending on the quality of the cheese, she really preferred it to "Royal Sandwich." She remembered the day she devised it, wondering what to do with some bland, old, cooked potatoes.

Cut enough cold potatoes into small pieces to fill a pint measure, cover with a pint of white sauce, spread a layer of grated cheese over the top and cover with bread crumbs moistened with water, bake half an hour.

Every now and then, especially when the necessary left overs were waiting for inspiration, Bessie would suggest to Amelia, that one or other be on the day's menu. Mary and Roger were not displeased when either appeared, but Mod had never warmed to them, especially to "Royal Sandwich." However, complaining about anything that had Bess's stamp on it was outside his thoughts, or at least his expression of them. After all, she had given up her successful nursing career for him and his children. She had made a search for a second wife and a mother for his children unnecessary. Their sibling bond allowed them to understand one another's decisions and thoughts with little explanation. Her independent income was a huge help in providing for the family's wellbeing. Without her largess, he could have maintained the farm, but life would have been very different; Morrie might not have attended college at Truro; they would not have a tennis court, or an indoor bathroom, or many other extra comforts. Her presence in the household had lifted the intellectual and social level of the children's development. He could never thank her enough.

Mod had been so upset for so long after dear Hattie's death that his possibilities of attracting a suitable wife would have been slim at best, especially with five children under fifteen to care for. He also knew it would have been a poor start to pretend he wished to marry a woman because of her charms or the usual reasons. Hattie was such a perfect wife. He would always be making comparisons and anyone else would come off badly. Bess was an efficient manager and organizer and not afraid of hard work herself. She was a good influence on his children, a cheerful companion and clearly enjoyed life on the farm.

Mod considered that with Mary and Roger nearly grown he could encourage Bess to get away more. She was still very active in her many organizations but she usually said "no" to their requests to address conferences and to head committees to do with the nursing world. He would now encourage her to say, "yes."

Mod knew now he would not remarry. Mrs. Morrisey, whom the Saint John cousins, Will and Lucy, always invited for Bridge when he was there, charmed him, reminded him of his past desires and fulfillments, but he could not imagine her sitting across from him at the Meadowland's dining table. Whatever their talents, the Mrs. Morriseys of the world he might chance to meet were unlikely to endure the isolation of living at Meadowlands. Bess was unique. She nourished an inner life, a dedication to the values, principles, and connections of her chosen career *and* to her family that no other women of his acquaintance possessed. And even if a perfect woman fell from the skies to take over Meadowlands, what would happen to Bess? No, if he had been going to remarry he should have done so before Bess gave up her career. He would remain a widower.

As for the physical side of marriage, he had found a generous hearted, attractive widow woman on the outskirts of Gagetown. Her impecunious situation had compelled her to earn her living making needy men's lives happier. He did not discuss this with Bess. Perhaps she was aware. She was generally very observant, and a realist. With all these thoughts and feelings settled in his mind, Mod still reserved a sense of guilt with regard to Bess. "She gave up her career for Hattie, for me, for our children. She left that school a couple of months early for her summer holidays, to help Hattie, and then stayed. That was seven years ago! Dear Bess never mentions regret at not returning to her nursing career. But, of course, she wouldn't."

*　*　*　*　*

Once all the ice floes had passed and the river was running normally again, Meadowlands was no longer an isolated island. Mary and Roger rowed back and forth to school and visits were made to friends and relatives. When the riverboat resumed its schedule, heaps of mail, accumulated over three weeks, slid out of the mail sack. Among the envelopes of different sizes was one from the Evinrude Company. The letter stated that payment had been received, the receipt was enclosed, and the ordered boat motor had been dispatched. Then, under the latest copy of *The American Journal of Nursing*, Bessie found a notice from the Saint John Post Office that a heavy box addressed to Morris Scovil would be shipped as soon as the riverboats were running again. Another message stated the crate would be unloaded at the Gagetown wharf on April eighteenth.

They all realized with a start that was in just two days! From then until everyone was in bed that night, all conversations and thoughts centered on the coming of the Evinrude motor. This new invention had taken on near magical properties in their imaginations. The anticipation of what was coming accompanied them to their beds and into their dreams. Mod was confident there would be instructions on how to operate the motor. He had asked Bess to stipulate the need for instructions when she sent the cheque. He had never dealt with the mechanics of an gasoline engine before.

At breakfast the next morning, Mary asked, "Father, who will be the first to dart over the water?"

"Well, I thought I'd ask Jock and Bert. Bert's young and strong and seems willing to try anything. He's named after your Uncle Albert, you know—he delivered him. When mothers run out of names around here, the new baby boys are sometimes called 'Albert,' not in honour of the good Queen's husband, but after the good Gagetown doctor."

On the eighteenth, Jock and Bert set off in the large rowboat in good time to meet the riverboat at the Gagetown wharf. As usual Mary and Roger had rowed to school in the small boat that took less muscle power. Mod found difficulty in settling to anything until he finally saw the two men carrying a crate up from the wharf. He met them at the workshop door, joined by Bessie and Amelia. By the time Bert had extracted the nails from the crate and those holding slats in place to keep the motor steady, in panted Mary and Roger, having run all the way up from the wharf in time to see the marvel being lifted from its nest.

"What a gleaming miracle!" thought Mary; "It's almost delicate, the way that thin arm supports a windmill sort-of-thing." At first, she thought the "windmill" was meant to work the air and push the boat along, but then quickly realized it went in the water to do the same thing. All were impatient to see the miracle in action. They had imagined its possible performance so many times. With hope that its equivalent of muscle power would equal that of the strongest man, Mary christened the new acquisition, "Mr. Evinrude."

"It will be fun to say 'rude' in front of grown-ups," she whispered to Rog, who grinned conspiratorially.

"Gasoline and oil must be kept on hand at all times," Mod announced, quoting the original brochure. He had stocked up on six one-gallon cans of gasoline and three quarts of oil, having no idea how greedy the machine was.

At the bottom of the crate lay a substantial booklet of instructions, which Mod now picked up and began to examine. The diagrams made preparation, installation, and operation all seem quite simple. Even so, Mod went on to say that the instructions, extra gasoline and a pair of oars should be kept in the boat at all times.

Bessie looked on with approval and a little trepidation, conscious that in the excitement her cheeks were becoming flushed. As the men went over final preparations for trying out the new acquisition, she felt curiously on the sidelines — a position she was not accustomed to when important things were afoot. She smiled to no one in particular, except perhaps to Mr. Evinrude, now freed from his packing case and waiting, shining in the mid-afternoon sun coming through the grubby shed window. Everyone trooped down to the wharf, looking forward to the launching but a little anxious. Would a piece be missing? Could it be attached easily to the rowboat? Most importantly, would it go? Mary and Roger knelt on the wharf so as not to miss any proceedings. Mary, in particular, followed every detail of how to operate this mechanism and tucked it all into her memory. With gratifying speed, the motor was attached to the rowboat, gasoline mixed with the right proportion of oil, poured into its gas tank, and the cover screwed on.

When all was ready, Jock turned and addressed Mod; "Bert and I'd better take it for a little run first, just to make sure."

"Yes, that's what I had in mind," Mod replied with confidence in Jock.

Jock grasped the handle on the flywheel and gently gave it a spin. After two more false starts, Jock, who was used to the gentle touch with horses, gave the flywheel a mighty spin. The motor started with a bang and the boat immediately shot out into the river, surprising everyone. Jock pulled back on the throttle, grabbed the steering stick, and cut two wide circles partly to get a feel for how to handle the steering and then partly to show off a little. Everyone on the wharf clapped. Mary jumped up and down, her long black stockings adding to their wrinkles around her ankles.

Considering that Mr. Evinrude had been acquired because of Bess's suggestion and money, Mod encouraged her to be first for a little trip into the middle of the river.

"Can I go, too?" Mary asked, still jumping around in excitement and trying to control her bladder.

"Me too?" chimed in Roger.

Before Mod could object, Bessie beckoned to the children, "Come, sit by me, both of you."

"Best if Miss Mary sits at the prow for better balance." Jock suggested.

As Mary stepped adroitly into the boat, Jock extended his hand, which she took only briefly out of politeness rather than necessity.

*　*　*　*　*

The spring and summer of 1910 — the spring and summer Mr. Evinrude entered their lives — brought lasting changes to the Scovil household, and to others both directly and indirectly in the Gagetown vicinity. Initially, Bert took the children back and forth to school. Then one day, after about a week, when Mod was standing on his wharf to admire the miracle gliding home, there was Mary with her hand on the tiller, her dark glasses perched on her sizeable Roman nose, wearing the smile of a conqueror.

"I hope you don't mind, Sir; she's very good at it," Bert called out as the boat approached the wharf.

"No, no, that's alright," Mod replied. "But show them both how it works and what to do if it goes wrong. And you should all have a good look at the instructions. I've just hung them up in the shed."

Mary and Roger were elated at their father's confidence in them. Roger felt he might soon follow his sister in taming the beast. Up to now, his job had been looking for eelgrass and rocks near the shore, which they had to keep the motor away from. He longed to get his hands on the tiller. Mary and Roger followed Bert as he carried Mr. Evinrude up to the shed. They were both determined to study the instructions and to increase their knowledge of how to operate the miracle motor.

As the days passed, Mod spent more and more time studying the instructions, absorbing the fine points of operation. Then, after asking Bert to mount the motor, he began taking practice trips up and down the river in front of the house. One day, to Bert's disappointment, Mod announced he would take the children to school, though Bert could collect them. More often than not on the homeward trip, Mary had her hand on the tiller and occasionally Roger.

The thought of a breakdown in mid-river was not far from Mod's concerns so he was careful to obey his own rules of extra gasoline and oars. He insisted Bert follow these rules as well. Eventually, as Mod gained confidence in the reliability of the engine and learned from experience how much gasoline it consumed crossing the river, he relaxed the rules. The oars were always in the way so he substituted two old blades with broken off handles that could more easily be stowed in the boat just in case. One calm morning in May, Bessie accepted an invitation from Mod to try the new arrangement and was impressed with the increase of space and comfort without the regular oars. She laughed like a schoolgirl as Mod increased the speed, and the rush of warm air, like a wind, loosened her bun so that stray hairs danced past her ears.

News of the Scovil's acquisition spread from the very first day the rowboat was seen skimming over the water like a sailboat without a sail. Unlike a sailboat, however, it put a strange clattering noise and the pungent smell of burned gasoline in nearby ears and nostrils. Men and children gathered at the Gagetown wharf, pummeling Bert with questions. Mary and Roger stepped up to answer some of them, glowing with the feeling of importance. Doctor Caswell soon heard about the new contraption and was there to meet it one morning. He asked Bert, whom he knew from birth, to take him for a little spin. In two minutes he was convinced one of these motors would make his practice much easier. He told Bert he wanted the details for ordering from Mr. Scovil.

Within a month there were two Evinrude motors, turning stolid rowboats into prancing stallions. By mid-July, the Peters and the DeVebers added to the Evinrude Company profits. But no one benefitted quite as much as the Scovils, now able to shorten the distance between Meadowlands and Gagetown to just a few minutes. Doctor Caswell also benefitted greatly from having an Evinrude motor. He could now get to Jemseg to see patients or respond to an emergency in a fraction of the time it had previously taken.

*　*　*　*　*

Once Roger finished school, he tried to become knowledgeable about horses and farming and growing a garden by doing the work instead of mostly watching. In their spare time, he and Mary planned activities together just as they did when they were children. On Sunday afternoons or sometimes on long summer evenings during the week, they would take a rowboat with or without Mr. Evinrude and go exploring. They would sometimes go downriver toward Foxtown or more often upriver to a creek above the Gagetown wharf, making their way upstream until they could see "The Mount."

According to local lore, the formidable stone structure was built by the French to protect their women and children from Indian raids when the men were off fighting the English. Another version was that an original Loyalist, a Mr. Peters, built it for his family. It was an imposing structure with grand fireplaces on each of three floors. Swifts nested in the chimneys and barn swallows now colonized the interior, coming and going through the open windows. Mary and Roger had a mutual feeling about its air of mystery and the stories that must be hidden in this ruin.

284

They beached their boat and walked up to the house, treading carefully over the broken stone steps, not wanting to disturb the birds or any leftover memories of previous occupants, imagining how frightened and isolated they must have felt. After a little exploration they sat on a log near their boat with their feet in the water, talking in whispers, hoping to see muskrats or beaver at work on the other side of the creek. A family of mallards kept well away, the tiny ducklings paddling furiously, not to be left behind, timid looking but determined to follow, to learn, to avoid being grabbed and sucked under by enemies unknown.

"I can't believe the ancestors of the gentle Pauls would have killed French children," Mary whispered to Roger. "They all speak so softly and have such kind brown eyes. I thought the French and the Indians were mostly friends."

"Maybe some of them were and some of them weren't," Roger offered.

Mary knew more about the Indians than Roger. Though Father and Aunt Bessie said she shouldn't, she had visited the Indian encampment at the far end of Gagetown several times and had gotten to know the Paul family. It was a secret she shared with her brother.

Mary remembered she had six cookies in her pocket and handed three to Roger. They ate them slowly in small bites, extending their special time together. The last of the crumbs were thrown to the mallard family, which quickly paddled over to consume them, then scooted away looking for more food.

"Will you try to shoot them this fall, Rog?"

"Maybe not these very ones. They look too smart."

*   *   *   *   *

While Mary and Roger were enjoying the simple pleasures of Meadowlands, their older sisters were making their way in the somewhat rare world of well-educated, professional women. On September 4, 1908, less than a month after she turned eighteen, Wowsie arrived by train in Lynchburg, Virginia to present herself at Randolph Macon Women's College, where she had been accepted as a student. At first, the imposing buildings seemed a little intimidating, but she soon made friends with girls in her dormitory, though none ever became as close as Raynsley Hensley at Edgehill. Wowsie embraced her studies in Physical Training with enthusiasm, taking on the option of learning massage therapy in her second year. No one was surprised that upon her graduation in the spring of 1910, her first application for employment was accepted. She wanted to return to Canada so a teaching position at Rupert's Land Girls' School in Winnipeg suited her perfectly—almost like being back at Edgehill, but now with power and responsibility.

At the beginning of her last year at Edgehill, Trudy found life without her older sister like being in a boat without an oar. She relied on Ayleene's friendship even more and discovered untapped abilities. Miss Smith told Trudy she had "blossomed" in the final year at Edgehill and was ready for professional training at Pratt Institute in New York. She applied and was accepted. With newfound confidence, Trudy took up the study of dietetics and excelled in her courses. After graduation in 1911, she became employed as an assistant dietitian in a New York hospital, occasionally visiting her cousin Bess and her Aunt Addie in the city.

*　*　*　*　*

After a visit to Meadowlands in the summer in 1911, Uncle Jack just stayed on, returning to New York only for brief visits. Jack had lost his job as an accountant when President Theodore Roosevelt closed the credit unions. Jack had been unable to find another position. He became a disappointment to everyone, including to himself. When no further employment could be found, he was unable to control his need for alcohol.

Bessie embraced and welcomed her "sister" into the family from the time Jack and Addie were engaged. She kept up a regular correspondence and often visited when she was living near New York. She sent cheques for special purchases, to tide them over when funds were low, to help with the children's summer camps, and to pay for an operation.

When it became clear Jack was not likely to work again and his health difficulties would probably get steadily worse, remaining at Meadowlands seemed the best solution. Addie now lived in an apartment with daughter Bess, who was working as a librarian after withdrawing from Columbia University before her graduation due to a shortage of funds. She was now the family breadwinner.

41

Mary and Carl
1914

Near the end of June 1914, Mary was on the verandah trying to teach Trixie to sit on her hind legs and beg for food when she noticed a rowboat with a lone occupant approaching the wharf. As a tall blond man climbed out of the boat and tied up, Mary and Trixie started down the path to meet him, one with a quizzical smile and one jumping and yapping, still looking for treats.

"Hello," said the visitor. "I'm Carl Brown, a distant Scovil cousin. I've sailed up from Saint John with a friend. Which one are you?"

"I'm Mary, the next to the youngest. My younger brother and I are the only ones still at home, and this is Trixie," Mary added to hide her sudden delight over this unexpected encounter with the most handsome man she had ever seen.

"I'm glad to meet you both. My mother said I should call here if I came to Gagetown."

As Carl bent down to pat Trixie, Mary had a good look at his head of tousled hair, slightly curling behind his ears, which were tanned the same shade as the back of his neck.

"Is your mother our cousin Dora Brown? I've heard Aunt Bessie speak about her."

"Yes, you're right. Mother has a very high opinion of your aunt."

"Come up and meet her. She's writing, I expect but she'll be pleased to meet you. So will my father."

Bessie had caught the movement of an arrival out of the corner of her eye from her nook. She screwed the cover on her Waterman inkbottle and went down to meet the unexpected visitor.

"Aunt Bessie, this is cousin Dora's son, Carl Brown. He's sailed up from Saint John."

"You are most welcome. I hope you will stay for lunch." Bessie smiled as she looked into his mother's delphinium blue eyes.

"Mary, do tell Amelia we have a visitor for lunch and to bring some raspberry cordial to the verandah. It's quite warm enough and perhaps the mosquitoes are not too hungry."

As they walked toward the verandah, Bessie asked Carl about his family in Centreville and was he living there? Another part of her brain was thinking about the lunch menu, which was expandable—ham and potato salad with berries afterward.

"My parents are both well," Carl replied. "As a doctor's wife, Mother is always busy and I have a sister and two brothers still at home. Father's life was made simpler a few years ago when he bought a motorcar, a Hupmobile. It's bright yellow and caused quite a stir at first. Centreville is about the size of Gagetown but he has patients all around the countryside so the auto has changed his life."

Mary reappeared carefully carrying a tray with glasses, a pitcher of cordial, and a plate of cookies. "Amelia has her head in the oven so I'm in charge of serving," she explained.

After a few more pleasantries were exchanged, Bessie drank a small glass of cordial and returned to her writing. Mary and Carl drank seconds, ate uncounted cookies, and began exchanging details of their lives. Carl explained he had come upriver with his friend Jim, who owned a sailboat and had relatives in Gagetown. They wouldn't be returning to Saint John until tomorrow afternoon.

Mary was pleased to hear that but didn't trust herself to comment. "I can show you around the farm, if you want," she offered.

"I'd like that," Carl said, hoping the tour would include a bathroom or an outhouse.

Mary, having the same need, started with a tour of the house, giving them both an opportunity to be more comfortable without making it a topic of conversation. She then showed Carl the professional looking tennis court, which was a real surprise. They next went to the strawberry field where Roger's assigned work for the morning was a major picking for the first boiling of jam and, of course, for immediate meal planning. Mary had intended to join him but the appearance of their visitor now required her attention. Roger was glad to meet Carl. They were both above average in height and could talk eye-to eye, a rarity for both. Roger was in no rush to again curl his long back toward the strawberries, but when Carl offered to help and Mary joined in, the task became less daunting for him. They continued their conversation, which included the state of the crop and showing Carl where to find the best berries.

After a half hour of steady picking, they had filled several containers much to Roger's delight. Mary was keen to continue with her tour, in case Carl had to leave right after lunch. They patted this year's foals and fed the chickens handfuls of corn much to their surprise. They greeted this midday treat with enthusiastic clucking. They threw tiny green apples to the pigs and admired the Herefords and Jerseys in the far pasture. There were no awkward silences. When Mary paused, Carl took over with comments and questions. He was impressed by the assurance and knowledge with which Mary responded to his comments and answered his questions. They were at the far end of a big hay field when Mary realized it was nearly lunchtime. Carl confirmed with his pocket watch and they began the walk back through knee high timothy and wild flowers. As they ambled along, Mary picked wild daisies, buttercups, Queen Ann's lace, and purple vetch to make a mixed bouquet for their lunch table.

"Let's see if you like butter," Carl said as Mary straightened up. He held a buttercup under her chin and sure enough, there was a reflection of yellow. They both laughed at the old childhood game.

"Fair is fair," Mary responded. "Maybe you do too."

She stretched up her free hand, repeating the test by holding a perfect flower to Carl's chin. They both laughed again. Mary could see that Carl had perfect teeth, straight all around, with no pitting in the front from scarlet fever, like hers.

Conversation over lunch was fulsome. Mod's questions about agriculture and farming methods in Centerville prevailed. Mary was impressed by the way Carl dealt with the conversation, admitting ignorance when he was out of his depth. Not only that, she noticed he made it a point to draw out the usually shy Roger, asked her opinion, was respectful to Aunt Bessie and her father, and expressed appreciation for the meal—especially for the dessert of fresh strawberries and thick, yellow cream.

After lunch, they all went immediately to the verandah except Bessie, who first had a word with Amelia who soon brought out a tray with the large, blue and white china teapot and matching cups and saucers. Bessie poured and lively conversation continued. The old elms on the riverbank produced dappled shade that was comfortable for all, though Mary, as always, popped her sun hat on her head. She sat with her back to the sun and, with the help of the elms, managed to keep her dark glasses in her pocket.

"Do you play tennis?" Mary asked Carl at a lull in the conversation.

"Yes, but I'm not an expert. Would you like to play?"

"After our lunch settles," Mary replied. "Aunt Bessie says it's a bit like swimming. We should wait an hour."

"I hadn't heard that, but it makes sense."

"I'm glad you think so," Bessie said as she stood, excused herself and, with a second cup of tea in hand, returned to her writing nook to finish an article that was on deadline for publication. Mod retired to his easy chair with the latest *New York Times*, now filled with unsettling news from Europe. Roger returned to picking strawberries.

"There's somewhere I haven't shown you," Mary said, "one of my favourite places — Nelson's Mound. It's a little way along the road to Jemseg. The walk will help settle our lunch."

At this invitation, Carl stood up and asked, "Who was Nelson?"

"Come, I'll show you."

As they started along the road, Mary elaborated on the character of Nelson. "He was an old workhorse who was allowed to live even when he was past working. He would tolerate any number of children on his back, walking at a dignified pace, never skittish, eating gently from little hands, baring his yellowed teeth but only to make his soft lips available for a carrot or an apple."

"What happened in the end?" Carl wondered, catching the spirit of the story.

"He had to be put down," Mary replied softly. "He limped so much and was in terrible pain. Aunt Bessie said he had arthritis. We couldn't bear to see him suffering but we didn't want to lose him either. Finally, the groom couldn't watch him suffer any more and put a bullet through his head. We all cried. He was buried at a place up the road we came to call 'Nelson's Mound.' But his mound became a happy place. We often came here for picnics, especially when we were little."

As they stopped in front of Nelson's Mound, Carl looked at Mary and then back at the rounded form of earth, which marked so many memories for her and her family.

"I can understand why it's so special. Thanks for bringing me here and telling me about it. That big aspen helps make it a beautiful place. I've always liked the way a breeze shows the underside of aspen leaves."

After a long pause, Mary said, "You seem to like the country."

"Yes, I've spent most of my life with the countryside close by. And I love the river. Meadowlands seems strangely familiar, though I have never been here before."

Carl realized they weren't just making conversation. He felt so happy and relaxed with this quick witted little Mary and so moved by what she had shared with him. Without speaking, they both sat down with their backs against the aspen and watched a butterfly make its way over Nelson's Mound.

His thoughts moved to the fact that he and Mary were related and wished it were not so. Surely he wasn't falling in love, was he? But would that be so bad? He suddenly had a sense of where meeting Mary might lead. His mother had told him of the family relationship. The Meadowland children were the great, great grandchildren of Samuel James Scovil. Samuel Scovil's brother, the Rev. William Elias Scovil, was the father of William Elias II, who was Carl's grandfather. Not exactly first cousins, and it's not unheard of for even first cousins to… Carl pulled back from where this thought was going and refocused his attention.

"Butterflies are so delicate; I'm surprised the wind doesn't tear their wings," Carl heard himself saying as he broke the silence with something impersonal, not wanting to reveal his thoughts.

"Do you think our lunch will be settled enough for a tennis match?"

Mary smiled in reply without speaking, which was unusual for her, but was all she could manage as she too pulled her attention back from an unexpected and exciting reverie.

Carl reached for Mary's hand and pulled her up as he stood, hanging on a little longer than he intended. They stood smiling at each other, neither wanting to move but knowing they should.

Carl's height and strength were huge advantages on the tennis court, but Mary's determination to impress this Adonis and the excitement of the day gave her extra energy. Her occasional, well-placed backhand shots surprised them both. They each won a set; then Mary deliberately missed an easy ball. She had succeeded in showing her skill and knew boys felt crushed if they didn't win, especially against a girl; and after all, he was a guest. They both laughed with exhaustion and triumph, sinking to the ground.

"I'm parched." Mary said, after her breathing nearly returned to normal. "Let's have some cordial on the verandah."

"I'm with you on that."

"You don't have to go back until after dinner, do you?"

"No, that's right. Jim isn't planning on sailing back until tomorrow afternoon. We sleep on the boat."

"Good, you'll stay for dinner, then. I'll tell Amelia."

Amelia responded to the news with her usual resourcefulness. "It's jam day, so nothing special, just a stew in the oven. But I can make tonight's cake into a dessert with strawberry jam and cream."

"That sounds good. I'll tell Aunt Bessie."

Mary would normally linger in the kitchen on jam day, smelling that sweet berry steam, that special aroma of summer like nothing else, but not today. She stayed just long enough to organize a tray of cordial and cookies. She then made a detour to Aunt Bessie's nook to fill her in on plans, and then to the bathroom which included tidying her hair. She left her comb near the basin, in case Carl wanted to do the same.

"All's settled; you won't starve," Mary reported on return to the verandah. "Here's some cordial. Do you want to wash your hands first?"

Carl said he did and returned with well-combed hair.

"If there's nothing you'd sooner do after we rest a bit, I thought we might help Rog with the strawberries again," Mary suggested. " His long back isn't meant for it, but he's trying to learn about running a farm. My older brother went to agricultural college for that, but he seems to like being in the militia in Saint John better."

Bessie had trouble concentrating on her writing. She could look down on the part of the verandah where Mary and Carl were sitting, talking earnestly, laughing frequently, and clearly enjoying one another's company. "Oh dear," the thought crossed her mind, "I hope nothing serious comes of this. Mary's future happiness is important but it cannot involve marrying a cousin. They absolutely mustn't. I won't worry Mod, yet."

After a half hour of animated conversation with Carl, Mary filled a blue trimmed, white enameled mug with cordial, grabbed her larger sunhat, and they both set off to cheer up Roger. When he saw them coming, Roger straightened up, resting his hands on his lower back. He picked up a basket filled with berries and walked it over to the shade at the edge of the field where his visitors also headed. The cordial and the presence of two volunteers gave the future farm manager a much need physical and mental boost. Over the next hour of steady picking, the three workers filled containers with a harvest that would satisfy Amelia's jam pot and the dinner table.

Cups of tea on the verandah after dinner allowed conversation to continue on many topics. Carl asked his cousin Bessie if she would talk about meeting Florence Nightingale and having tea with Queen Victoria, both occasions having been mentioned by his mother. Bessie, though a little startled that he would know about these events, was happy to elaborate, not least because it broadened the topics of conversation.

Roger eventually stood up, stretched, put his two hands on his lower back, and excused himself; "Farming isn't meant for bean poles like me! I'm going to turn in early. I'm glad you stopped by, Carl, and thanks for the help picking berries."

"I am too," Carl replied, as he and Roger shook hands. "I hope your back recovers. I should be going soon. It's a bit of a row back to Gagetown."

Carl thanked Bessie and Mod for their hospitality, both of which replied by saying how much they enjoyed having visits from cousins.

"Mr. Evinrude and I can take you back to Gagetown," Mary suddenly offered, rising from her seat. "It will be much easier. We can tow your boat."

Bessie's back stiffened a little, but she made no objection and neither did Mod.

Let's go," Mary said. I'll introduce you to Mr. Evinrude."

With a small wave to their elders, the two set off for the carpenter's shed behind the house where the motor was kept. Carl carried it to the wharf and Mary took an extra can of gasoline, just in case. With Mary looking approvingly over his shoulder, Carl took his time attaching the motor and tying on his small rowboat with a length of rope. He checked and rechecked to make sure both were securely fastened. When all was ready, Carl sat back and left Mary in charge. He wanted to watch her in action and was not disappointed. When they got underway, the motor made too much noise for conversation and they had to be content to exchange smiles from time to time. As they approached the Gagetown shore, Mary slowed the motor and, with the minimum of words, pointed out where her DuVernet cousins lived and a little cove where ducks nested every year. Before long, they saw the sailboat docked at the Gagetown landing. Mary slowed the motor to an idle and then shut it off as they drew up to the wharf.

Carl turned to Mary and asked; "What were you thinking during the crossing?"

"I was thinking about what you might be doing tomorrow morning," Mary responded without hesitation. "I think you said you won't be going back until afternoon."

"That's right. I've nothing planned. Just hang around on the boat waiting for Jim, I expect."

"I could come and pick you up for some more tennis, if you like."

Mary busied herself with the boat, not wanting Carl to see how much she hoped he would agree.

"I'd really like that. But you mustn't let me win next time! You're too polite."

Mary blushed, thinking her ploy had not been noticed.

"I hope your father and aunt won't mind."

"Oh, no. They like visitors. You can stay for lunch. Mr. Evinrude will collect you and take you back when you need to be here to set sail for Saint John."

Carl was just as pleased as Mary with their arrangement and didn't hide it. "That would be perfect. I'm looking forward to it already," he replied as he tied up the tender.

"What time in the morning should I be ready?"

"How about nine? Is that too early?"

"I'll be waiting for you. Would you like to come aboard and have a look?"

"Yes, but I'd better get back now. Perhaps tomorrow; oh wait don't forget your boat."

Mary untied the small rowboat and handed the rope to Carl.

"Thanks for such a great day," he said as he unhitched Mary and Mr. Evinrude. "I can't remember when I've enjoyed one more."

"Me too," Mary replied, after unsuccessfully looking for words that reflected her feelings.

They smiled and waved as Mary pulled the throttle and steered the boat toward open water. She turned repeatedly looking back at Carl standing on the deck of the sailboat. They continued to exchange waves until both were barely visible in the distance.

42

"… a sweetness in the still air …"

Mary was wide-awake by six the next morning. Normally, she enjoyed awakening to the bird song coming from the elm tree near her window. But today, her first thought was of the fading view of Carl, waving from the sailboat, as Mr. Evinrude took her away from him. She imagined the reverse scene in three hours, coming nearer and nearer. She went over the events of yesterday, smiling at their perfection.

Carl's eyes were more than the usual Scovil blue; they were several shades deeper. He had escaped the Scovil beak of a nose, like hers. His nose was perfectly straight. In fact she could think of no fault, either in appearance or behaviour. She suddenly realized she didn't know what Carl was doing in Saint John. She did know he was twenty-two, so must have decided on a profession, though obviously not medicine, like his father or he would be studying at a university. Oh, it's holiday time, so perhaps he's just visiting his friend.

On arriving back at Meadowlands last evening, she had immediately mentioned to Aunt Bessie that Carl and his friend, Jim, were not leaving until Sunday afternoon, and that she had asked him to play tennis in the morning and would it be all right for him to stay for lunch?

"Of course, dear, that's the reason we have the tennis court, so young guests can play, and lunch is fine. But do remember he is a cousin so don't let your heart become involved. We shouldn't desert a visitor, so I think we can skip matins at Jemseg and go to evensong at Gagetown."

Mary turned away and bent over to retie her shoe, concealing the strength of her heart's involvement that had already blossomed.

"All right," Mary said, though it was a reply to only the last part of her aunt's comments.

Mary ate her breakfast as slowly as possible, chewing each mouthful of her boiled egg, toast and marmalade for longer than necessary. At eight-thirty, though still a little too early she sauntered to the shed to pick up the motor. She then used up ten minutes putting it in place. "There," she thought, "that's about right for a two-minute past nine arrival, though I might have to put brakes on Mr. Evinrude."

295

Carl was waiting on the deck and able to spot Mary's arrival from a long way off, waving enthusiastically, which Mary returned. Jim's hosts had not yet picked him up, so introductions were made and Mary accepted the owner's invitation to "come aboard." She was amazed at how cleverly the tiny interior had been arranged, with two long, narrow bunks, storage room underneath, a "kitchen" of sorts and a rudimentary bathroom.

"When do you need your crew back?" Mary smiled at Jim as she climbed back into her boat.

"After you properly trounce him at tennis," Jim teased, and then added, "Two should be good."

"Right, we'll be here if Mr. Evinrude behaves."

"Mr. Brown should behave, too," quipped Jim as he pushed them off from the wharf.

Mary tried to hide her blushing. Clearly, Jim had received an earful about Mary. She pulled the throttle open, and expertly brought the boat around in a graceful curve before straightening out for the shortest path to Meadowlands. They waved to Jim and he waved back.

Above the motor's roar, Mary managed to ask, "Did you sleep well in your narrow bunk?" Carl shook his head. "No, I kept thinking of today."

"And how you will kill me at tennis?" Mary teased.

"Not exactly," Carl replied without elaborating.

Then, emboldened by the perfect June morning, a sweetness in the still air, the soft sun not yet fully awake, Carl blew little Mary a kiss instead of more words. The astonished girl blew a kiss right back, partly because she knew of no other honest way to respond. The rest of the trip was punctuated with smiles and thoughts about the next four hours. Carl dangled his hand in the water, which was still cold from its distant sources in northern New Brunswick and Maine. The coldness shocked him in contrast to the warmth of heart he felt about this relationship. Like Mary's, his heart was already entangled. As they secured the boat, both fore and aft, to the wharf, Mary announced there would be no need to take off the motor, as they would be using it again in four hours.

"Unfortunately," added Carl. He put his hand on Mary's left shoulder as they started walking toward the house. Mary briefly touched his hand with her right one and looked into his crinkling eyes. Then they both dropped their hands as they came in sight of the house. Bessie was tidying up on the verandah.

"Lovely to see you again, Carl. I hope you will stay for lunch."

"Thanks, cousin Bessie. I'd like to. We're sailing back at about two, so I won't have to leave before one thirty."

"We'll have lunch a little after twelve, so there will be lots of time to eat."

"That's kind of you."

As they collected racquets and tennis balls, Roger appeared and volunteered to be ball boy. After a warm-up they played in earnest, each, for their own reasons, determined to win. They each won two sets and were evenly matched until Carl lost his concentration, missed a ball, and then a second.

"You're too good for me," laughed Carl as flopped on the grass to catch his breath.

"You just need more practice," smiled Mary, fairly confident Carl had really tried to win. "Thanks, ball boy! Do you want a game?" Carl offered.

"No, thanks I'll keep my back for the strawberries. I'll see you at lunch. Father wants me to do something in the barn."

"Let's have some cordial on the verandah," suggested Mary

"OK, and then let's walk up to Nelson's Mound. I'd like to see it again."

Carl and Mary quickly drank their cordials and set off. Bessie was at her writing desk, finishing up a review of two medical reports for the September issue of *The Canadian Nurse*. She paused and looked out the window. A shadow of concern again crossed her mind as she saw the pair walking briskly down the Jemseg road.

When they were well out of sight of the house, Carl again put his hand on Mary's shoulder and she put her hand on his.

"This has been the happiest weekend I can remember."

"You mean you've never tasted such delicious strawberries?" Mary teased.

"What I've tasted is the joy of being with you; you're like no other girl I've ever met."

"Oh, I think I'm rather dull."

"You have lots of good ideas but that's not one of them." Carl tweaked Mary's shoulder playfully.

They reached their destination and sat down under the aspen with their backs to the trunk. Carl looked up through the branches at the gently fluttering leaves.

"I wonder how many leaves there are in this tree?"

"Thousands I imagine. We'll never know, unless we make it our life's work," Mary replied, her gaze floating upwards.

"We could have a rough number, if we counted the leaves on a typical branch, counted the branches and multiplied. That would do it. You choose the branch."

"How about the one that's fourth from the bottom with the little bump on it."

"That looks about right."

Mary started counting out loud from the base of the branch outward, pointing at each leaf as she went. As she got to twelve, Carl gently took her hand.

"Your arm will get tired if you don't have some help. You have a long way to go."

Mary laughed in surprise, but did not resist. They counted one hundred and fifty leaves, then, still holding Mary's hand, Carl counted the branches pointing to each one. The total was sixty.

Mental arithmetic was never Mary's strong point, so she was relieved when Carl said, "Now we know. This aspen tree has nine thousand leaves—at least. We must be the only people in the world who know that; it can be our secret."

Mary smiled, giving Carl's hand a little squeeze of agreement. What a fascinating thought, she silently mused; we've only just met but it feels like we've known each other forever.

After a pause, Mary said, "It's nearly lunch time; we should go back."

"I suppose we should, but I hate to leave this almost magical place."

Carl stood and extended his hand to pull Mary upright.

"You have such tiny hands compared to my great paws," he observed. "Wouldn't it look strange if I had yours, and you had mine?"

"Yes," Mary replied, "we are the way we're meant to be."

Hand in hand, they started out. As they rounded the bend and came in sight of the house, Carl placed Mary's hand by her side.

"It's time I gave this back to you. Thanks for lending it to me."

Mary smiled, feeling her hand had been given special properties.

Lunch was as convivial as yesterday. Bessie kept her eye on the interaction between the two cousins, though nothing in particular alarmed her. By one-thirty Carl said his good-byes and he and Mary set off for the wharf. The trip across the river was much the same as the others, the minimum of conversation and the maximum of happy expressions and smiles, but now tinged with regret that the weekend, and their time together, was coming to an end.

Jim waved from the deck of the sailboat as they approached. He was already putting up the sails. Mary cut the motor and manoeuvered along side. As he was getting out, Carl covered one of Mary's hands with his, looked into her eyes, and said, "I'm sure we'll soon meet again."

"I hope so," Mary said, holding steady to their parting gaze.

As Mary opened the throttle and pulled away, the two sailors waved to her, which she vigorously returned. Jim went back to work on the sails but

Carl continued watching and waving, as did Mary, until they were again barely visible to each other. She slowed the motor for the remainder of the trip home, savouring the day, wondering whether Carl was playing some kind of boy game, toying with a girl's heart. It was new to her, but probably not to him. She knew she would enjoy spending time with him every day. He made her feel entirely special.

Evensong at St. John's in Gagetown was even less appealing than usual. The rector went on and on, seemingly unable to finish his sermon, losing more than Mary in his vagaries.

The drone of his voice, like bees in clover, was overlain by her thoughts of the Adonis who had lifted her weekend out of the ordinary, in fact, had transformed her whole experience of life. Did he mean what he said about meeting again? And what would that mean. When the organ interrupted her thoughts, Mary automatically stood and started singing the hymn she had sung a hundred times before, "There Is a Green Hill Far Away." She needed no hymnbook. No "Green Hill" would ever again be appealing to her unless Carl was standing on it, waving a welcome to her.

43

"… on the edge of complete happiness …"

On Thursday, Mary received a letter with a Saint John postmark. She dared to hope and was not disappointed. Carl's letter recounted how much he had enjoyed the weekend and hoped Mary would allow him to try to defeat her at tennis the weekend after next. Jim was planning another sail to Gagetown and wanted him as his crew. The next weekend was not possible because he had a preliminary examination on Monday in his efforts to become a chartered accountant and needed Sunday to prepare. He also had to work Saturday afternoon to make up for taking the morning off the previous Saturday.

There was a letter from Helen in Ottawa in the same mailbag. A letter from Elizabeth about enjoying her position in Winnipeg, and one from Gertrude, full of her duties, as a dietitian in New York, had also arrived. Bessie read both of them aloud while they were all still at the lunch table.

Mary took advantage of the conversation over all this correspondence to mention that Carl had enjoyed last weekend so much he would like to come back the weekend after next to try to beat her at tennis.

"Jim is sailing up to Gagetown again," Mary explained. "Would that be OK?" she added, looking up at Bessie and Mod.

"I hope he does," put in Roger, "he's mighty quick at picking strawberries. I suppose they'll be nearly over then. But the raspberries should be ready."

With Roger's approval of the visiting cousin and with Mary's obvious enthusiasm, Bessie replied with only a slight hesitation; "That would be fine, don't you think, Mod?"

"By all means." Mod concurred. "He's a personable young man. Dora has done a good job raising him. I like to see more young life around here, especially family."

Mary bridled her enthusiasm and simply said, "All right, I'll say we all look forward to his visit."

She climbed the stairs to her room and with a feeling of elation wrote a carefully worded letter to Carl. She then replied to Helen, telling her about Adonis. With her correspondence completed, she offered to take the mail to Gagetown in the afternoon. Her aunt had two well-filled envelopes.

* * * * *

The following nine days seemed like nine years to Mary. She spent many hours with Roger finishing the strawberry crop, often walked up to Nelson's Mound, once trying to count the flickering leaves, one by one, but the breeze was too active and confused those which had been counted with those that hadn't. She picked wildflowers again, looking hard at the buttercups, adding more to her bunch, though knowing the petals would soon fall. She decided to try swimming and found it cool but bearable after a few minutes of vigorous sidestrokes.

Mary's preoccupation with filling time was disturbed by her father's summary of the unsettling news from Europe. But there was nothing especially new about that. Europe always seemed to be unsettled. Mod thought it his duty to inform his family about what was happening in other parts of the world. Though they lived in a backwater that was no reason to be ill informed.

With no one remaining in New York to send their copy of *The New York Times* to Meadowlands, Bessie had ordered a subscription for her own information and to enhance Mod's basis for his opinions. Sometimes, several copies arrived on the same day. Though Mary was disinclined to read books because it tired her eyes, she found the short columns in the paper of interest and manageable. She often read the full article of which her father had given a summary over the previous meal. And Roger, too, would sometimes pick up the paper to read for himself what the others were talking about.

But now, though her intention was to read the papers, Mary's ability to concentrate on world news eluded her. Her thoughts of Carl caused all others to pale. On the Thursday before his return, another letter arrived from Saint John, to say how much he was looking forward to Saturday. He and Jim planned to leave after work on Friday, spend the night in a cove along the way, and arrive at Gagetown by eleven Saturday morning at the latest. If she and Mr. Evinrude were not there, he would row over. The examination on Monday was not as difficult as he had imagined it might be.

Being early or late at the Gagetown wharf would not do, so Mary aimed to be on time. As it turned out, she first spied the sailboat when the anchor splashed into the water. In another minute, she saw a wide wave of welcome to which she responded by increasing Mr. Evinrude's speed.

Much of this second weekend in July at Meadowlands unfolded along expected lines, though everything else was quite unlike any previous weekend for Mary. Yes, they played tennis on the recently cut, rolled, and

302

painted court. Mary realized there was no point in deliberately losing, so she played her best and consistently won. Yes, the family conversation flowed naturally over lunch and dinner and over cups of tea afterward on the verandah. Yes, they helped Roger pick a good crop of raspberries, and, yes, they spent time under the aspen tree. But what was different from two weeks ago, or at least intensified, was the degree of "togetherness" they both felt—that hard to describe feeling of rapport between two people, which they hope will continue forever, the feeling of being on the edge of complete happiness.

With the afternoon tennis match over and the two sitting under the aspen, Carl lifted one of Mary's hands, squeezed it a little and asked, "May I kiss you?" Mary smiled her consent. Being kissed by Adonis was like nothing else she had ever experienced in all of her eighteen and a half years, as she later wrote to Helen.

"Would you consider marrying me, Mary? You know I love you."

Mary was silent for only a moment, digesting Carl's question and statement.

"Yes, yes, the answer is yes!"

They kissed again and sat quietly with their hands entwined, savouring the moment.

Mary was the first to speak. "The grown-ups might object. I know Aunt Bessie is not keen on cousins marrying. What about your parents?"

"The subject has never been discussed, as far as I know. We're not first cousins, after all. Do you think I should speak to your father after dinner this evening?"

"Please. I would like to have it settled, but I expect Father will say he needs to talk it over with Aunt Bessie," Mary replied, and then added with emphasis; "I can think of nothing better than being married to you!"

44

The Calamity of Being Cousins

Little Mary and her tall Adonis mutually relinquished hands as they rounded the bend and came in sight of the house. The suitor was disappointed but impressed by Mary's accurate assessment of the hurdle they might face. Over the last few days he had rehearsed what he might say if Mary accepted him, including acknowledging the shortness of acquaintance and being distant cousins. He believed these hesitations could be overridden by their love for one another and the fact he would soon be a chartered accountant and in a good position to support a wife and family.

Mod was not surprised when Carl asked to speak with him after dinner. They retired to the parlour. Carl found explaining the situation, and the depth of his feeling for Mary, easier than he had imagined it would be. Mod was impressed with his sincerity and maturity.

"Well," said Mod, after a pause, "I can see you two enjoy one another's company, but because of your being cousins, I'll need to talk it over with Bess. She's a nurse and understands these things better than I do. And what about your parents? Your father's a doctor. You probably haven't told them."

"I wrote to them after my first visit and said how much I enjoyed meeting you all, especially Mary."

"I'll talk it over with Bess later this evening. I suggest you bring your parents up to date as soon as you can. I must say, confidentially, that Mary is my favourite child, so sharp, so inquisitive, and quick to learn; her eyes let her down, but she manages. I want her to have a happy life."

"I understand, sir."

"Will we see you tomorrow?"

"I hope so. Mary has invited me for tennis and lunch. I'm sailing back early in the afternoon, like last time."

"Come and see me after lunch tomorrow."

"Yes sir, thank you."

The two men shook hands.

Carl's expression was neither radiant nor dejected, mirroring his feelings—in limbo—when he and Mod joined the others on the verandah. He smiled at Mary and raised one eyebrow to show not all was settled.

Mod and Carl both accepted second cups of tea, still warm with the help of a cozy and now considerably stronger. Carl had trouble remaining composed and sitting still. He desperately wanted to share the results of the conversation with Mary. He chose an appropriate moment, thanked his hosts, and mentioned he should be getting back to the sailboat for the night. As he and Mary walked toward the shed to collect Mr. Evinrude, Carl picked up Mary's hand and told her she was right.

"Your father and aunt will talk it over this evening and I have to tell my parents."

Before Carl picked up the motor he bent and kissed Mary.

"I love you so much," he said and kissed her again.

Mary floated down to the wharf beside Adonis. Both his hands were busy carrying the motor so she grabbed the edge of his shirt to keep up with his long strides.

The almost engaged-to-be-married couple spent Sunday morning being optimistic, though neither had slept well the night before. They played tennis, wandered about the farm, checked on the aspen's leaves, discussed where they might live in Saint John, and who they knew that already lived there. Mary was sure Carl and Morrie would be good friends, though her brother was older.

Lunch was a little stilted. Roger dominated the conversation, which was a surprising change. Amelia exceeded her usual expertise with a raspberry dessert to surpass all others; seconds went without saying. Carl and Mary smiled gently at one another from time to time in keeping with their guarded optimism. Bessie organized the meal, as usual, but both she and Mod were clearly preoccupied.

At last, lunch was over and tea served on the verandah. After a few sips, Mod nodded to Carl and both men stood and walked to the parlour.

"Your cousin Bessie and I had a thorough talk last evening. Though you are an admirable young man and would make Mary a steady husband, we can't give our permission to marry. Bess knows of too many cousins who married, with dire results, some if not all children having mental and sometimes physical abnormalities. Bess will write to your mother. If your father thinks the risks are minimal then we will re-consider."

Carl moved his gaze from Mod's face to his own hands, so recently enfolding Mary's.

"Perhaps we could arrange not to have children," Carl offered as his already flushed cheeks became more so.

"You can ask your father about that, but nothing is fool proof, by my understanding."

Mary could see the outcome on Carl's face as he returned to the verandah—bleak. He shook his head slightly in Mary's direction, thanked his cousin for the hospitality, said good-bye to Roger and turned to Mary,

"I must go."

Mary willed her tears not to flow until she was walking by Carl's side toward the wharf, her little hand in his. When he told her the details of the conversation, she could no longer dam the flow. She took off her glasses, mopped her eyes but continued to cry.

"There's a tiny bit of hope. If my father thinks there's not much risk, your folks will reconsider. But if a nurse knows of lots of sad outcomes, then a doctor certainly will as well."

Carl gave Mary another kiss, perhaps their last one, each thought. Before he climbed on to the rocking sailboat, greeted by Jim, Carl squeezed Mary's hand.

"We should know in a week or so. Let's hope."

They blew one another kisses, as Mary slowly separated from the sailboat and Adonis. As usual, they waved until they were tiny dots to each other.

Mary put Mr. Evinrude in the shed but did not go directly into the house. She wandered to the horse pasture and patted the horses that came close to the fence. They had such hard facial bones, such sleek coats, such uncomplicated lives.

From her nook, Bessie saw Mary arrive at the wharf just as she blotted a letter to Dora, hoping for a prompt reply. She had ended the letter by writing; "The young are in a state of anticipation which should either be removed or encouraged."

When Mary eventually came into the house, Bessie could easily see her niece was a very red-eyed, downhearted, and miserable eighteen-year old. Bessie had felt such responsibility for the welfare and happiness of all Mod's children since their mother's death, but especially for Mary, and now this.

"I'm so unlucky. Everything nice turns to dust," Mary said with a vacancy in her voice that her aunt had never before heard.

Bessie suddenly had the sense of a person torn from their moorings and was almost at a loss for words. Finally, with caution, she replied.

"He seems to be an admirable young man, dear, and his one fault is not his doing. You need to guard your heart against a negative reply from his parents."

Mary turned from her aunt, tears again flowing. "I won't be going to evensong. I'd be an embarrassment."

"Whatever you think best. You might hear some helpful words."

"Not unless there's been a change of rector. This one puts me to sleep."

"He's not the most inspired, but he has a good heart."

"I hadn't noticed. He's very hard on sinners."

"It's part of his job to be critical of sinners, to discourage them."

"Ever since, I came back from New York where I saw all those Santas on the street corners, and you told me there is no Santa Claus, I've had a problem believing in God. To me, they're both make-believe."

"I hope one day when you're older, dear, you will think differently."

"That's unlikely. I'm going for a walk. I can't sit still. Where's Roger?"

"He's meeting John Young in Jemseg for the afternoon."

"I might meet him on the road on his way back."

With that, Mary turned, opened the kitchen door and walked out, leaving Bessie with an unsettled feeling that was new to her.

When Mary reached Nelson's Mound and the aspen tree, she sat down and idiotically again began counting every leaf, trying, all the while, to quell her feelings and collect her thoughts. "Is there any hope? A doctor must know more than a nurse. Perhaps there are other reasons for idiot babies, like the mother falling. Will I be doomed to being an aunt to Rog's children? Surely he won't marry John Young's sister, but who else is there? All the interesting possibilities are related to us. If I can't marry Carl, I'll be an old maid but without the kind of careers Aunt Bessie and Wowsie and Trudy have. They don't write about admirers so maybe we'll be 'those unfortunate Scovil girls, all old maids.' I'll try to hope. Carl would want me to hope."

In spite of her resolve, Mary's eyes again filled with tears. Eventually, she got up and started walking rapidly toward Jemseg. She had covered nearly half the distance when she saw Roger loping along toward her in his relaxed way. He had left right after lunch so had not heard the news. Mary told him what had happened so far, and that there was a tiny bit of hope, but not much.

"That's too bad," Roger replied. "He'd make a good brother-in-law, I'd say."

The letter Bessie received from Carl's mother confirmed her views. Dora had consulted her husband after a very happy letter from Carl, which told them of his love for Mary and desire to make her his wife. They both objected strongly for the same reason, to the point of forbidding their son to marry his cousin. Dora said she had told Carl it would be best if he did not see Mary again, but that he should write to her promptly, bringing the relationship to a close.

"It is a great pity," Dora concluded. "Carl's letter was so optimistic, saying he had found the 'perfect girl' to be his wife."

Bessie showed the letter to Mod.

"Poor girl," he murmured. "I guess it's the only possible decision. She'll be very down."

45

Mary's Collapse and a Brother's Care

Mod's forecast was an understatement. Mary took to her bed, complaining she couldn't see properly and her eyes hurt, even when she closed them. The next morning, Mod lost no time in motoring over to Gagetown for Bert Caswell's opinion. The doctor said he would be over the following day; he had a birth expected today.

When the next day dawned and breakfast was over, Bessie kept watch from her writing nook, frequently looking up from her work. She alerted Mod as soon as she spied the doctor in the distance. Mod met him at the wharf. As they walked up to the house, he gave Bert a quick summary of events leading up to Mary's problem and that she hadn't complained about her eyes hurting recently. After a full half hour with Mary, the doctor told her he would have a word with his colleague, Dr. Addy, in Saint John, and be back in a few days. In the mean time Mary should wear her dark glasses, get up if she wanted to and eat regular meals. Away from Mary's hearing, the doctor told Bessie and Mod that Dr. Addy had studied nervous diseases and should have some suggestions regarding treatment. "If she isn't interested in food," he added, "make sure she has enough liquids. But of course you would do that, anyway, Bess."

Within four days the doctor was back. Dr. Addy wrote that the patient appeared to be having a "nervous breakdown" brought on by her great disappointment. Since her eyes were probably her weakest organ, the symptoms have settled there. He advised bandaging her eyes for four months, removing them briefly once a day for bathing them, but she should keep her eyes closed then.

Doctor Caswell told Mary what Dr. Addy has prescribed for treatment.

"I don't care what you do to me. My life is over."

"Life hands out some cruel disappointments m'dear. Just sit up a bit so I can wrap this bandage around better."

Mary smelt a mixture of the doctor's office, tobacco and sweat stained tweed, as she gave in to the repeated wrapping of the cloth bandage around her head and over her eyes.

311

"Try to eat something at every meal and get up when you feel like it, I'll be back in a few days."

Aunt Bessie went into Mary's room as Mod walked down to the wharf with Dr. Caswell.

Mary smelled lavender. When her father came back and entered her room, Mary smelled tobacco and sweaty tweed. That's odd, she thought, I've had little awareness of people's smells before.

"I've brought you some cambric tea, dear, not too full. It's in the spout cup. I'll put it on your bedside table. Can you manage?"

"It doesn't matter."

Mod was disturbed to find his cheerful little Mary so defeated, so empty. Then it hit him; "She must have really loved this fellow." The love Hattie and he had shared suddenly welled up and the heartbreak of his daughter, mixed with his own, overwhelmed him.

With great effort, he regained his composure, squeezed the limp and unresponsive hand of his daughter, and said, "There'll be better days ahead, Mary." It was all he could think of to say and it felt so inadequate.

A bit later, Roger came in and sat on the bottom of her bed. Mary immediately noticed he smelled of horses, which was strangely comforting.

"I bet Carl feels as bad as you do," Roger offered in his plainspoken way. "Do you want me to write to him for you?"

"No point now."

"How do your eyes feel?"

"Awful."

At the end of the week, Roger announced he would like to take his lunch up to Mary's room and eat it there, to encourage her. She had refused most food all week except tea and bread and butter, even from Bessie's patient hands

"She isn't very big. She'll disappear if she doesn't eat."

Roger carried two plates of food to Mary's room. He set one on a small table near the end of the bed and the other on a bed tray, which had been made for Hattie more than a decade ago and was now being used by her daughter. He asked Mary to sit up so he could put the tray in front of her. She lifted her bandaged head off the pillow and wiggled into a more or less sitting position.

"I'm not hungry. What is it? I can smell onions."

"It's potato scallop, ham and chow-chow. Amelia's cut the ham into small pieces. I'll put the tea on your bedside table. It's the cup with the spout, so you should be able to manage it."

Roger sat on the end of Mary's bed and started eating his lunch.

"Amelia makes a pretty good potato scallop, just the right amount of pepper."

The pungent smell of onions, and the matter of fact presence of her beloved "little" brother suddenly did something to Mary's previously dormant appetite. She picked up her fork, stabbed at something and directed it toward her mouth, then another, and another, and another, until the plate was nearly empty.

"Help me with the tea, Rog."

When she had finished the tea, he said, "There's apple sauce and cookies, want some?"

"I'll try."

In order not to destroy the momentum by going down to the kitchen for another serving of dessert, Roger passed his to his sister. Amelia was so used to Mary's tray being returned, untouched, she thought it wasn't worthwhile adding dessert today. Roger tucked the napkin under Mary's chin to keep runaway applesauce off the bedding. As she began chewing on a cookie, her eyes began to smart and tears began to flow. Roger noticed her bandages becoming dark and damp under her eyes.

"What's the matter?"

"He said he loved Amelia's cookies almost as much as he loved me," Mary replied in a softly sobbing voice. "He'll never taste them again. It's not fair."

Mary turned and slipped down into her pillow. Roger removed the tray. He hated seeing his energetic sister reduced to being an unhappy invalid, but he had achieved his objective. After that, Roger began eating his meals at the bottom of Mary's bed. Her appetite improved and the bond between sister and brother was a comfort to both of them.

After breakfast one day, Roger said, "I'll be back in a minute." Mary could soon hear and smell Trixie. She put out her hand for Trixie to lick as the dog tried to climb onto her bed. Roger was ready with an old sheet to spread over the counterpane. He had wiped the dog's feet, but Trixie was, after all, an outside dog, a border collie who liked nothing better than herding cows through the barnyard. The animal settled in the curve made by Mary's bended knees, nuzzling her hand while the invalid rubbed her pet's ear with the other one.

"OK for a while, Sis?"

"Thanks for Trixie."

After a few days of this routine, Bessie could see that Mary spent more time sitting up, playing with Trixie and was generally more responsive.

"How about a nice warm bath, dear, and then maybe getting dressed? You can have one of your father's walking sticks. Are your eyes a little better?"

"They hurt a lot, but not as much."

*   *   *   *   *

On the afternoon on July 29, 1914 Mod was in Gagetown with Gabe DeVeber who could talk of nothing else but the assassination of Archduke Ferdinand of Austria, heir to the throne of Austria-Hungary. It had happened the day before and the papers were full of it. Mod couldn't wait for the issue of *The New York Times* to come that would tell him more about it, so bought a Saint John paper. Because a Serbian had pulled the trigger, Austria-Hungary declared war on Serbia and Europe held its breath to see if other countries would become involved, which, of course they soon were. On August 1st, because of complicated loyalties, and after hearing of Russia's mobilization, Germany declared war on Russia and then invaded Russia's ally, France, through Belgium, violating Belgium's neutrality, and causing Great Britain to declare war on Germany. Because Canada was tightly tied to Great Britain, it was automatically involved.

On August fifth the Governor General declared war between Canada and Germany. The newspapers reported Sir Wilfred Laurier as saying: "It is our duty to let Great Britain know and to let the friends and foes of Great Britain know that there is in Canada but one mind and one heart and that all Canadians are behind the Mother Country." Quickly following Laurier's pronouncement came Prime Minister Robert Borden's offer of assistance to Great Britain, which was gratefully accepted. Though most Canadians thought the militias would be the first to be readied for fighting, instead the government raised an independent Canadian Expeditionary Force.

Mod and Jack spent much of one evening wondering how Laurier's words would go down with French Canadians. Though Laurier was one of them, Mod felt certain he did not speak for them all. *The Saint John Globe*, like many other newspapers, thought the war would be over by Christmas. How long it might really last was discussed at every family meal, along with the chance of sons or young fathers being called up or enlisting for the adventure or for a chance to be heroic for King and country. Mod and Bessie and Jack, when he felt up to it, regularly talked over the incoming war news during their evening conversations over tea and cake. Everyone hoped the conflict would be short lived. Morrie, with his long experience with the militia, would almost certainly enlist. They hoped there would be no need for Roger to go. With his height, he would not last five minutes on the battlefield.

46

The Five-Month Cure: "I will always love him"

Gradually, Mary adapted to her sightless life. Although her arms and legs were covered in bruises from bumps and stumbles, she was reasonably mobile by the time her sisters arrived for a coordinated ten-day holiday. Gertrude came from New York and Elizabeth from Winnipeg in time for her birthday on August 16th. After lunch and sometimes after dinner, Mod and Mary often went to the verandah where he would read aloud to her from *The New York Times*. Roger was always there for Mary when she wanted to take a walk, pat the horses, or go for a blow with Mr. Evinrude. Morrie, unable to return to Meadowlands for his birthday in July, made a point of being there the weekend nearest the sixteenth. Bessie organized the birthday meal for the seventeenth and made sure everything was at hand for the ritual of making ice cream. They all took a turn "churning" the ice cream maker, even Mary. At one point, Mary spontaneously laughed at one of Morrie's jokes, which was as much of a surprise to her as it was to everybody else. It was the first time anyone had heard Mary laugh since she had taken to her bed. They caught one another's eyes and silently rejoiced. Weekly letters had been continuous, so the siblings all knew of Mary's great disappointment and how it had affected her. Bessie had advised them all not to bring up the subject of Carl Brown, but if Mary did, to encourage her to talk.

Morrie was now a full-time captain in the militia with the 28th New Brunswick Dragoons. He had given up his office job when offered full responsibility for the horses and overseeing new recruits who worked with them. He admitted he did not dislike being in the insurance business but much preferred training horses and training others to work with them.

On the subject of careers, Gertrude confessed she was still not used to the noise of New York, which scarcely had a quiet corner. She was thinking of returning to Canada and had been in touch with cousin Edward DuVernet. He had recently moved to Vancouver as a doctor, having trained at McGill, like his father, Uncle Ned. He told her the Shaughnessy Hospital there was looking for a dietitian. She had applied and was waiting to hear. Elizabeth enjoyed teaching Physical Training at Rupert's Land Girls' School not unlike Edgehill, but larger, and with the great convenience of being in the middle of Winnipeg. She was also on call for occasional work at the hospital for therapeutic massage. She had nearly passed up this option of the training but was now happy she had acquired this additional skill.

Mary quietly listened to details of the exciting lives of her siblings, realizing once more that she would be left on the farm, gradually fading away, probably looking after Roger's numerous offspring, her occupation destined to be stated in official records as "at home." What a lot of heartache sat behind those two little words. She would be more aware the next time she read them—if she ever read again—so simple, and yet so complicated, laden with disappointment.

* * * * *

Once her two career sisters returned to their working lives, Mary settled back into her less than exciting life. She made a point of not going to Gagetown to be a spectacle to be stared at and not going to church at Jemseg for the same reason. She told family members that if anyone asked where she was to simply say, "She's having trouble with her eyes," which was a truth that even Aunt Bessie could not argue with. Mary felt the summer leaving and the crisper autumn air, a little more each day. She heard the dry leaves rustling under her feet when she and Roger walked along the road toward Jemseg.

One afternoon in early November, Bessie looked up from her writing desk and spied Doctor Caswell motoring across the river. By the time he had tied up at the wharf and walked to the house, Amelia had a fresh pot of tea ready at Miss Scovil's request and had carried it on a tray into the sitting room where Mod and Bessie were waiting to greet the doctor with a lazy fire in the Franklin. Roger steered Mary into the room and to a chair by the doctor.

"Well, m'dear, how are those eyes of yours?" the doctor began. "Behaving themselves? No more hurting?"

"Yes, behaving themselves and no more hurting, not even a migraine," Mary replied.

"Good girl. I've been in touch with Dr. Addy. He's made an appointment for you on November 15th. If you're still pain free, I expect he'll take off those bandages for good."

"At last," Mary said with a genuine feeling of anticipation.

While the others caught up on family and community news—who had enlisted, who was still at home—and talked over the progress of the war, Mary's thoughts moved to expectations of normality. She would be

316

able to take Mr. Evinrude out by herself before the ice came, see the first snowstorm, write directly to Helen instead of a sending a few sentences in Roger's hand, and read her sisters' and Morrie's letters.

Bessie made arrangements to stay with cousin Lucy and Will Robinson for three nights, the fifteenth, sixteenth and seventeenth. The Starrs asked them for lunch on the seventeenth and Bessie thought a little shopping expedition was in order by way of celebration, if the bandages were in fact removed. Mary's appointment was for four o'clock in afternoon on the fifteenth. Bessie and Mary caught the morning riverboat, which was still running in spite of a sheen of silvery ice hovering on patches of water near the shore in the early mornings.

They arrived at Dr. Addy's waiting room on time and were promptly shown into his office. After a few minutes of conversation with both Bessie and Mary, Dr. Addy asked to see the patient by herself. He told the nurse to pull down the blinds to cut out the late afternoon sun. Mary had brought her dark glasses, as instructed, and of course her regular owl's eyes, in case of good news.

"When did your eyes last hurt?"

"I can't remember, exactly. Before my sister's birthday, I think, and that was August 16th."

"Come and sit on my lap, Mary. It will be easier to take off your bandages."

The slim, five-foot-one-and-a-half-inch eighteen-year-old slipped from her chair and, with the smell of tobacco and sweat on wool in her well-tuned nostrils, found her way to the doctor's ample lap. While Bessie's clean bandage was gradually unwrapped by the doctor, he chatted encouragingly to Mary, saying how brave and courageous she was, how she would have a happy life, and how lucky she was to have such a famous and supportive family.

"You've turned a page in your life m'dear. Keep your eyes closed when I take off the last round, put on your sunglasses and then open your eyes."

Mary did as instructed. She put on the glasses opened her eyes and looked up. The round, pink face of a stranger with bushy eyebrows and a receding hairline was smiling at her.

"No pain, no pain!" she exclaimed and laughed in relief. Dr. Addy gave his patient a little hug and placed her back on her own chair. She closed her eyes again, put on her regular spectacles, then the sunglasses on top.

"It's so bright!"

"Nothing hurts?"

"Nothing."

"Good, the cure worked."

*　*　*　*　*

All through the second day in Saint John, Mary marveled at the smiles she observed on people's faces as much as the sharpness of colours and light. She enjoyed just looking around as much as shopping for a new outfit. Mary chose a navy blue serge skirt, matching jacket, and shiny winter boots. She managed to persuade Aunt Bessie that it would be much easier walking if the skirt came only to her ankles. Bessie thought a new topcoat was in order, but Mary selected a wool jersey and a cozy scarf instead. On the seventeenth, Morrie joined them for lunch at the Starr's, just a seven-minute brisk walk from his work on King Street. Mary hugged him hungrily, happily, so different, they both realized, from their August meeting. Morrie looked into his sister's eyes and gave her a second hug.

At Bessie's urging, the Starrs reported on their children: Ayleene was well into her second year of nurses training at Montreal General; Ruth was trying to decide what she wanted to do; Constance was a promising pianist; Penniston, the youngest, was at Rothesay Collegiate School. Though Bessie assumed her nieces were keeping their benefactors informed, she reciprocated with news of Elizabeth enjoying her work in Winnipeg and Gertrude planning to take a position at the Shaunessay Hospital in Vancouver.

After Bessie and Mary returned to Meadowlands, several days passed before Mary collected her courage sufficiently to walk up to Nelson's Mound. The experience was made easier because all had changed so much since those sunny, summer days. The six thousand leaves were gone; the grass was rust coloured, cold and soggy. Almost everything was different. It was not hard to imagining five idiot children sitting there with Carl on one side and she on the other, all crying. She gave the children varying degrees of idiocy. The pictures in her mind made her think of the photograph of her own parents and their five children taken in 1903, the year her mother died. No one was crying in that one. Tears came just a few weeks after that picture was taken. "I suppose I'm lucky. Like Dr. Addy said, I've turned a page in my life, but I will always love him."

On the following Sunday, Mary put on her new outfit and joined the family attending matins at St. James Anglican in Jemseg. With the familiar warmth of the buffalo robe around her as they travelled up the Jemseg road, she felt a kind of pride and a sort of newfound happiness. With her sight restored, a sense of freedom made it comfortable for Mary to again take her place in the Scovil family's front row pew at St. James.

47

Under the Cloud of War

As usual, there was a whirlwind of activity before the river froze, which included more than the usual number of trips to Gagetown for visits to the Peters, the Caswells, the DeVebers, to McKinney's store and to St. John's Anglican for Sunday evensong. The exchange of family and village news was dominated by conversation about the war and how it was proceeding. Those with hazy knowledge of what countries made up the Austro-Hungarian Empire and the Ottoman Empire became experts after studying newspaper maps. Adults hoped it would be over soon, that their boys would not have to go. Sixteen-year-old boys hoped it would last long enough so they could go.

The length of time it took the river to freeze over was more of a deprivation than usual for the Scovil family—no war news. Thanks to very cold temperatures for two weeks in early December, the river ice became safe for travelling and life at Meadowlands settled into its winter rhythm. With no appreciable snow for weeks after freeze up, the skating conditions were ideal.

Mary and Roger dusted off their reachers, sharpened them, and made good use of miles of uninterrupted gliding. They would often swing into Gagetown in the afternoon to pick up a Fredericton paper. A new rail line from Fredericton had opened the previous year and a train now stopped at Gagetown every day. The Saint John newspapers carried more news, but they were available only in the summer off the riverboats. Some of the rail line from Gagetown to Westfield, which would connect with the line from Saint John, had been laid, but was then pulled up and shipped to Europe to help the war effort. Residents of the Gagetown area had mixed feelings about this. A rail line through to Saint John would be such a convenience and very much appreciated, but if the sacrifice would shorten the war everyone agreed it was a good move.

Christmas was soon in the air. Morrie managed four days off during Christmas week, including the twenty-fifth, which was more than enough reason for celebration. The Caswells were invited and all came for lunch and an early dinner. Morrie, Mary, and Roger were glad to see their cousins.

The three Caswell girls were home for a week's holiday. Aunt Mira told Roger that Jimmy's epilepsy was now better controlled. Doctor Caswell was eager for a little time out from his medical practice and hoped no emergencies would interrupt the holiday.

But the ongoing war was the topic hovering just under all the pleasantries. It tended to dominate the conversation, though Bessie did her best to eliminate it at mealtimes. She managed to entice all the cousins into playing afternoon games, which she had prepared. Morrie, who really wanted to take out his pipe and talk with the men, joined in the games, though he scarcely considered himself to be young anymore. He knew his participation would please his aunt. In the back of his mind he also knew this might be the last time he would join in such games.

Tea was served before the games began. Morrie mentioned he had recently met Alan Otty, a classmate from his schooldays. He was working in Saint John, had joined the militia, and they renewed their friendship.

"If the war is still in full swing when spring comes, we may enlist if the militia can find replacements for us." Morrie reported. "It's been nearly five months since the war began and nothing's been settled. I read there's been a raid on Scarborough and Hartlepool about a week ago. The Germans must have been aiming at shipping. And there was heavy fighting in a couple of places in France — Givenchy and Champagne after that."

"I hope some of them had a good drink," quipped Roger.

"Probably not too much time for that," Morrie replied.

"Let's play some games," interrupted Bessie. The thought of so much needless loss of life, and without enough nursing, created a gloomy atmosphere she wanted to disperse. As pencils and papers were being collected, Roger turned to Morrie.

"What are the girls in Saint John like?"

"Like girls everywhere, I guess," Morrie replied in an off-hand way. "Some pretty and some ugly, some smart and some stupid." He paused, and then added, "But I'm not too interested in Saint John girls. I've met one from Amherst who's pretty and smart; she came top of her leaving class at Edgehill, *cum laude*, it's called. She overlapped with Elizabeth and Gertrude some. Her name's Madeline Bliss. Her father's a doctor. I'd like to marry her one day, after the war."

"You old devil. How did you meet her?"

"At a birthday party of a friend. His parents in Amherst were having a party for him. They suggested he bring a friend. They were short of men. We drove over in his Tin Lizzy. Now you know why you don't see much of me!"

"I think her brother, Denison, was at Kings when I was at Edgehill."
Mary interjected. "His ears stick out. He didn't last long, like me. I heard
he ran away. I expect he was bullied, too."

"I've met him," replied Morrie. "He's a bit of a headache for the family.
He's Madeline's half brother. His mother died when he was born. His older
brother is studying to be a doctor in Halifax."

What a legacy, thought Mary. Sounds familiar.

48

Morrie Enlists
1915

The winter of 1914-1915 passed with the war and its consequences on everyone's mind at Meadowlands. The "killed and missing in action" column was the first to be read in each new edition of the newspaper. Familiar names appeared, prompting Bessie to go quickly to her nook to compose a letter to the bereaved parents. When the ice broke up and the riverboats had resumed their schedule, Mary asked her aunt if they could get out of the Meadowland's rut by spending two or three days in Saint John. She wanted to visit Dorrie Lee, a distant cousin she had been corresponding with and had occasionally met. She wanted to invite her to come to Meadowlands for a visit. They had a lot in common as well as being cousins. Dorrie was a year older, but also unmarried and "at home," They had the same sense of humour. Dorrie, in a way, was a replacement for Helen, who was now married with one baby and expecting another. They still exchanged letters at birthdays and Christmas, but Helen's interests had changed.

Bessie, agreed. She too felt the need for a diversion after the long winter. She wrote to cousins Lucy and Will, always so hospitable. Would three nights be too many?

"Stay as long as you like. We are looking forward to having you both with us," came the reply.

Bessie also wrote to Morrie, hoping he would have the opportunity to drop in to see his Robinson cousins while she and Mary were with them. He wrote back that he would be in Amherst that weekend visiting Madeline and planned to enlist in the 6th Canadian Mounted Rifles in the Canadian Expeditionary Force. His rank as captain would be maintained.

Morrie was twenty-eight on that sunny spring day he enlisted, April 6, 1915. He had been with the 28th New Brunswick Dragoons for five years. According to the captain who signed his enlistment papers, the five foot eight inch recruit, in good health, still considered himself to be a "farmer." With his knowledge of horses and men, Captain Morris Allaire Scovil hoped to contribute to defeating the enemy of the Mother Country and

Canada. The family at Meadowlands was a little shaken by the news, but not really surprised. They were all proud of Morrie. He had warned them last August that he would probably enlist in the spring, if the war was not over.

Shortly after enlisting, Captain Scovil was appointed to command of the New Brunswick 28th Dragoons. With so many new recruits to train, he remained on Canadian soil throughout most of that summer but was told in early August he would be posted overseas before the end of the month and to arrange a pre-posting leave immediately. He did so to coincide with Elizabeth's birthday on the sixteenth. As he hoped, Gertrude was able to take her holidays then, as well as Elizabeth. The Scovil family was reunited at dear old Meadowlands for that week, perhaps for the last time, a somber and depressing thought they all shared but none expressed.

Morrie suggested they should ask Alan Otty and his sister, Molly, over from Gagetown for ice cream and birthday cake on Sunday afternoon. Alan, a school chum of Morrie's, was being posted, too, and Molly, was back from the University of Chicago where she was studying journalism. After the ice cream maker had been cranked until its contents was too stiff to turn and the last of the ice packed around the canister to promote further freezing, they all gathered on the verandah for a photograph with a large Union Jack firmly pinned to the back wall. Elizabeth still had her prized Box Brownie camera. As Mary joined the lineup, an entirely unrelated thought popped into her mind; all the women here are unmarried, five "spinsters." Perhaps it's a new trend, not to be despised.

As usual, Bessie had organized the preparation of enough ice cream mix and enough ice to be brought from the icehouse for two churnings, one strawberry and one raspberry. A new variety of strawberry now produced fruit all summer and the raspberries were at their peak. Morrie claimed the right to lick the paddle, more to make Mary laugh than for any other reason, though he knew he was storing up memories as important as anything he would ever put in his rucksack. Meadowlands' ice cream, made from the farm's own fresh cream and berries, was incomparable.

Morrie was prohibited from telling anyone when his troop ship was sailing. They begged him to write, even just a few lines, as soon as he could after he arrived in England. Within three weeks, proof that he had done so tumbled out of the mailbag. He could not be specific about anything, even the weather, so although the short letter was mostly generalities, they all cherished it as though it were a full-length book. Their replies were rewarded about every two weeks with another cheerful letter with nothing the censor could disapprove. Morrie remained in England training recruits until mid-March 1916.

Through clever inspiration, he was able to sidestep the censor and inform his family of his movements.

> *Cousin Clara has invited me to visit her around the middle of March. I am looking forward to it.*

When Mod read that over the dinner table, he was a little confused until Bessie explained that cousin Clara was a distant cousin who married a Frenchman and was living in France. No one spoke for a few minutes, all thinking of what might lay before Morrie. Roger broke the silence.

"Clever of old Morrie to think of a way to tell us."

There was something in them all that did not want to think about what he might have to endure with this move, but they were also grateful they could accompany him in their thoughts.

*   *   *   *   *

Attending matins in Jemseg and evensong at Gagetown, until the ice was unsafe, took on an increasingly important role for the Meadowlands' family. Even Mary was keen to pray for Morrie's safety just in case God was more substantial than Santa Claus. One evening, on their return drive from Jemseg, Mary asked Bessie a question that had been uppermost in her mind during the hour-long sermon.

"There must be millions of German Christians who are also praying to God to protect their sons. If He answers all these prayers and doesn't allow any soldiers to be killed, no side will win or lose and the war will go on forever."

Bessie was taken aback by Mary's logic, but realized she, too, had sometimes wondered about this. In order to avoid serious doubt, she replied, "I feel certain, dear, that God is on the side of right and He will help us, ultimately, to win, though it's a pity anyone has to die."

Mary digested her aunt's answer for the rest of the way home but found herself still confused. Surely the Germans believe they are on the side of right as well. If a god does exist he must have a perpetual headache.

Every mailbag was scrutinized for Morrie's familiar writing. After a gap, there would sometimes be two letters thanking everyone for theirs and painting a vague picture of reasonable comfort. He again cleverly cleared the censor.

> *When I eat cousin Clara's food, I think of all those splendid meals we had at Meadowlands and can almost taste last August's ice cream! I am looking forward to seeing something of cousin Charters before long.*

"So he's been in France for a while," observed Mod. "Doesn't Charters live in London?"

"Yes," replied Bessie. "Morrie must be expecting some leave time in England. I visited cousin Charters Symonds in London when I was there in the nineties. He is a well-educated and much honoured doctor. He was born in Saint John, but went to London to study medicine and stayed. I had a letter from Fanny, his wife, not long ago to say he is now a Colonel and in charge of medical services. She didn't say exactly where but wrote, 'He will be glad to revisit the place we both like so much.' I knew that meant he would be stationed in Malta, a place they often visited. But Morrie wouldn't know that. We can be sure he will be on leave in England."

There was general relief that for a time he would not be risking his life. Mod did not dampen their optimism by saying leave is often granted just before a big push. He swallowed the thought along with more mashed potato and gravy. In fact, Capt. Scovil was granted leave on March 28, 1916. One letter arrived from the leave with "cousin Charters", then a gap of several weeks, then another short letter, then nothing.

49

The Dreaded Report
1916

In early June 1916, Brigadier-General McLean contacted Mod to say he had heard from his brother that young Morris and others had been unofficially reported missing. A news story then appeared in *The Daily Gleaner* in Fredericton with the heading,

Capt. Scovil and Lieut. Morrisey reported missing.

Though this news did not convey the dreaded certainty they all feared, it was, nevertheless, a blow to everyone at Meadowlands, even though each member of the household had tried to prepare for it. The assumption that hovered behind the tentative report was that these two local men, and probably others, had not survived the latest battle, and that their superior officers would do everything in their power to return personal possessions to their next of kin, should that be necessary.

Bessie hid behind her sorrow by saying newspapers liked to dramatize their stories. No one slept well. Mary could hear her father walking in the night, his long heavy stride, up and down the hallway. Bessie would sometimes join him. The footsteps would descend the stairs and brother and sister would share their worries over cups of tea.

On June fifth Mod received a telegram from Ottawa to say that Capt. Morris A. Scovil was officially reported missing in action. He sent the information on to *The Saint John Globe*, which printed a lengthy article on June sixth, including a photograph of the officer taken while he was still serving in Saint John. To have Morrie officially missing increased the level of gloom at Meadowlands and in Gagetown. On the seventh, Mod went over to talk with Gabe DeVeber about Morrie's chances. He took a copy of *The Globe's* article so Gabe could read it himself. It began:

IS OFFICIALLY REPORTED MISSING
Capt. Morris Scovil, of Gagetown

Captain Morris Scovil, Mounted Rifles, has been officially reported from Ottawa as missing. This information has just been received by his father, Mr. Morris Scovil, farmer, Gagetown, but no other details are given by the Adjutant General. The news will be received with regret in the southern part of the province, and in St. John particularly, for he had become well known in the city. He left St. John as captain in B Squadron, 6th Mounted Rifles, under Major C.H. McLean. He had during the months that the 28th Dragoons were acting for the Imperial remount depot been in command of the St. John detachment and was a first class officer of cavalry, a good horseman and a steady disciplinarian whose influence in the corps was everywhere acknowledged. When the Mounted Rifles were sent into training as infantry, he volunteered to take the course and retained his rank.

Nothing much came from the conversation with Gabe, except it helped Mod to be able to talk with him.

Dozens of letters descended on the Scovil family from both close and distant relatives and friends and acquaintances, all very much regretting the news, but offering comfort that there was still hope. Even Carl Brown wrote to Mod and asked that his concern for Morrie's welfare be conveyed to all members of the family. Cousins Frank and Madge Starr wrote saying that Morrie had grown to be a fine and responsible young man, that they always enjoyed his occasional visits, and if there was anything they could do, just ask. Further letters arrived after more articles were printed around the middle of June.

Then, suddenly, a letter arrived from Morrie that had been written on June 10th. Everyone at Meadowlands breathed a huge sigh of relief. Mod sent copies of the letter to *The Daily Gleaner* and *Saint John Globe*.

The Gleaner reported as follows:

CAPT. MORRIS A. SCOVIL WAS BURIED IN A MINE SHAFT AND CAPTURED WHEN HE CAME OUT
Writes from Officers' Prison Camp at Gütersloh in Germany
GRAPHIC STORY OF THE THIRD BATTLE OF YPRES
Was Partly Buried Several Times and Was Saved by Steel Helmet

Capt. Morris A. Scovil, of the 4th Canadian Mounted Rifles, is now a prisoner of war at Gütersloh, Germany, where he is at the prison camp for officers. Today his father, Mr. Morris Scovil of Gagetown, received a letter from him written under date of June

10th from Gütersloh, in which Capt. Scovil gives the first story of his miraculous escapes from death in the Third Battle of Ypres and tells how he happened to be captured by the Germans. The letter, which also contains the information that Generals Mercer and Williams had just arrived at the Canadians front line trenches on an inspection at 8 o'clock on the morning of June 2nd when the Germans opened their bombardment which continued until 1 o'clock in the afternoon and marked the opening of the Third Battle of Ypres, follows:

"We are only allowed to write four post cards and two letters of six pages and eighteen lines to the pages each month, so I must try to get as much as I can in the allotted space. I want to tell you how I came to be taken prisoner. I was not scratched except some bruises on my cheek, which I got when buried in the trench. Generals Mercer and Williams had come up to look over our lines, and I was eating my breakfast when I went out to meet them, pulling on my rubber boots. As I went out the first shell came over at 8 o'clock on June 2nd, a lovely fine day. I went up to the other end of the trench as I knew no other officers were there. Shells and trench mortars were bursting all around. Of course at that time we did not realize that it was to be anything but an ordinary bombardment; but they kept it up until 1 o'clock.

Only Two Left

"I never lived through such a Hell, and of the men saved only two were in the front line. I am the only one who has been heard of as yet. At 12 o'clock the sergeant and I were the only living men I could see--and he was killed soon afterward. I was partly buried several times, and my steel helmet undoubtedly saved my life on several occasions."

Capt. Scovil made his way to the opening of a trench where others were taking refuge.

The article and quotation continues:

"I crawled in but before doing so seized a shovel, which I saw lying outside. It certainly saved all our lives as a shell lit on top of the opening and the roof caved in, imprisoning us, and we had no air. However, we dug with the shovel, and just as we were giving up all hopes, struck light. We enlarged the hole and crawled out,

intending to go back to our support lines; but we saw Germans on every side and told to go across to their trenches. None of us had rifles or revolvers; what had been our trench was nothing but shell craters.

Other Officers Prisoners

"We were well treated by the Germans, who were kindness itself. Naturally I was pretty well shaken and could hardly hear. They gave me wine and after a wash I was able to continue marching about fifteen miles where we met some other officers of another regiment, and spent the night there. I thought I was the only survivor of the officers of the 4th Mounted Rifles but next morning Col. Ussher, Dr. Park, and Capt. Lightburn and two of my lieutenants, Smith and Wood, came. The only reason they escaped was because they took refuge in a tunnel, and the men who escaped death were there also. I will never forget the experience as long as I live; even yet it seems like a bad dream. The camp we are in is the best one in Germany, and I am very comfortable. I have a fine warm bed and the food is well cooked, although plain. I have made arrangements through a London firm to forward a parcel of food each week, the same as the other officers here do. A lot of English officers are here and they are kindness itself, and have fitted me out with a change of clothes so that I am all right until mine arrive, which will not be for six weeks."

On June nineteenth, *Saint John Globe* printed a long article and a photograph with slightly different information as follows:

CAPT. MORRIS A. SCOVIL SAYS GERMANS TREAT OFFICERS WELL

Writes Interesting Letter to Father from German Prison Camp

GAGETOWN OFFICER SENDS PICTURE TAKEN IN CAMP

Officers Allowed Out Twice a Week Without Guards, He States.

Captain Morris A. Scovil, who was taken prisoner during the fighting early in June last, has written to his father, Mr. Morris Scovil, of Gagetown, stating that he is being well treated by the Germans in the camp where he is a prisoner.

The Scovil family had absorbed Morrie's letters thoroughly before they were in newsprint. After the news story about Morrie's situation was printed, Mary at first came to feel the situation was more hopeful now that anyone could read of his plight and share in his experiences. But then she wondered if thousands knew what had happened to him, did this in someway make the situation worse, enlarge it and make it more difficult to bear? Mary shared her quandary with Roger who knew what she meant but thought the news reports would mean others would talk about it and that would be a good thing, sort of like spreading the sadness thinner.

"Look at the good news," Roger offered. "Morrie is a prisoner in as comfortable a place as possible and off the battlefield, so we can be more hopeful."

After rereading the story in the paper when they were all having tea on the verandah at the end of the day, Bessie brought up the subject again, unable to let it rest.

"Surely there is enough factual drama without writing that the dear boy was 'quite badly wounded'. According to what Morrie wrote in his first account, that's not true."

"Perhaps the journalist thought being practically deaf from shellshock was enough to qualify," Mod said as he passed his cup for a refill.

"Poor old Morrie, having to walk fifteen miles after an experience like that, with just some wine and not even finishing his breakfast," added Roger.

"At least he writes he's being treated well. Do you think he just said that so the rest of it would get through?" asked Mary of no one in particular.

"We won't really know until he returns, but I think it is probably true. I like to think well brought up German officers are every bit as civilized as ours," Bessie replied, putting things in a positive light. She was thinking of the courteous Germans she had met during her working career, a time when England and Germany were bound together by numerous ties including intermarriage between royal families. Even "Brunswick" was a German name.

50

A Prisoner of War

Mod wanted to know where Gütersloh is located in Germany and asked Roger to bring the world atlas from the bookcase with glass doors in the parlour.

"I wouldn't want to carry this very far," Roger said as he placed the large leather covered volume on the dinner table in front of his father. "It weighs a ton."

Mod found the page devoted to Central Europe, then scanning Germany eventually found Gütersloh.

"Looks as though it's at least fifty miles east of the border with the Netherlands, so probably too far to risk escaping and even then he wouldn't be safe. The Germans have taken over that whole area of Europe."

They all crowded around Mod looking closely at the place on the green map to which he pointed. There, amidst other unpronounceable names was Gütersloh, the place their dear Morrie sat in prison.

"Lets send him a parcel," Mary suggested. "Let's think of what we can send that will cheer him up. He might be getting one from London, but I'm sure he'd like one from home."

"Draw up a list, dear," Bessie quickly replied. "We can all add suggestions. If there's too much for the first parcel, we can send subsequent ones."

"Since he said the food is plain, we should put in some spices," Mary offered. "Oh, and peanuts; he always liked peanuts. Let's make molasses candy and add that. It will remind him of home. How about a sewing kit and a first aid box and socks?"

"Write it all down. Lets keep a list on the dining room table and we can add ideas as we think of them," Bessie directed.

"Was he really smoking a pipe in the photograph?" Roger asked. "I mean does he have tobacco? Even if he has, we could send his favourite."

Within two days a sizeable list was drawn up; they all had opinions on what was most important. Bessie suggested she and Mary take the list to Gagetown to see what they can find and then a day in Saint John for the rest.

"I'm sure I have some strong white cotton in the house. We'll need to wrap the parcel securely and then sew it closed. We must ask at the Post

Office about the maximum measurements," she added, always looking ahead in order to avoid problems or disappointment.

Mod and Mr. Evinrude escorted Bessie and Mary to Gagetown where they acquired most of the items on their list. Morrie's favourite tobacco, however, and several other items, could not be found.

"Looks as though we'll have to go to Saint John or Fredericton," Mary said as she screwed her face into an expression of mock displeasure. Bessie responded in kind, knowing both of them would very much enjoy two days in the city.

"Yes, I'm afraid we'll just have to go. I'll write cousin Lucy and see whether we can stay with them. They're so much closer to shopping than the Douglas cousins. Saint John is more convenient than Fredericton."

The reply soon came. "Will and I are so looking forward to your visit. Do plan to stay two nights."

Bessie wrote back with thanks and to confirm the dates. Mary was delighted with the thought of a little more liveliness than Meadowlands could provide, and she did want Morrie to be really pleased with his parcel. Now that it was late June, the strawberry harvest was in full swing. The morning his aunt and sister set off for Saint John, Roger had a basket of freshly picked berries still covered with morning dew ready for cousin Lucy. Mary picked up their two small valises while Aunt Bessie took charge of the basket of berries, which she carried snuggly arranged in a sturdy cotton bag. Mod and Mr. Evinrude delivered them to the Gagetown wharf and the two women set off for a calm, sunny riverboat trip to the city.

Bessie and Mary returned from Saint John refreshed from the change of scene, delicious food, lively conversation, challenging bridge, and an entirely successful shopping expedition. However, next day, when they laid out everything for the parcel, they realized something was missing; they had forgotten to make molasses candy. Mary wanted to get right at it, but Bessie demurred.

"It's going to be the hottest day of the year so far," her aunt observed. "How about if we wait until evening when it will be a bit cooler, or until we prepare another parcel?"

But Mary was all for having it in the first parcel and even volunteered to do most of the work.

"It's the thing that will remind Morrie the most of Meadowlands!" she said emphatically.

No one could argue with that.

"But I agree to wait until evening."

Once the dinner dishes were put away, Amelia placed all the necessary ingredients on the kitchen table, and then announced she needed to rest her feet; she had been on them all day processing strawberries. Mary set to work. When she decreed the candy ready for pulling, they all pitched in. Though it was hot work, they all wanted to be involved as a way of showing, if only to themselves, their desire to sweeten the confined life of their "dear boy" and give him a taste and memory of home.

Once the long twisted ropes had cooled and were chopped into bite-sized pieces, it was obvious the pile of candy was too large to all go off to Morrie. After everyone had one or two samples, Mary found two tins, a square one just the right size for the parcel and a round one for storing the surplus. By now, they all displayed beet red faces. No one disagreed with Bessie's suggestion that a spell on the verandah with glasses of strawberry cordial would be cooling, especially since an evening breeze off the river had come up and would discourage mosquitoes.

The next day the parcel took shape, wrapped with stout white cotton and sewed together with strong thread. Mary thought Aunt Bessie should print the name and address as she had such neat penmanship, though her father's was not far behind. Even after the parcel was on its way, the contents were discussed. Roger mentioned the tobacco was in a well-sealed tin that would keep its smell from affecting everything else, especially the socks and underwear, though maybe Morrie wouldn't mind. Mod suggested any smell that didn't remind him of a trench would suit the captain.

Preparing and sending monthly parcels to Morrie became part of life at Meadowlands. They varied the contents according to comments of appreciation in his letters, which arrived somewhat irregularly. They knew his letter writing was rationed and he would certainly be writing to Madeline as well. Bessie established a regular correspondence with her future niece-in-law, letting her know when they received a letter and the general contents. Madeline did the same, so between them the two families heard from Morrie about once a month, except when letters seemed to have been lost, probably when a ship was attacked and sunk. There was always a chance Meadowland's parcels would meet the same fate, but that was never mentioned. They imagined only Morrie's pleasure at receiving them.

During his time as a prisoner of war, Morrie was moved from camp to camp. Each time he was moved, Mod received official notification from Ottawa. On May 5, 1917 he was moved to Krefeld, on July twenty-fifth to Schwarmsteadt, on August eleventh to Fursternberg, and on October seventeenth to Holzminden. Morrie received the treasured parcels from Meadowlands until November 1917. After that, only parcels from the Red

Cross were allowed, chiefly food. The Scovil family felt the cut off as a deprivation, especially Mary, who had taken on the preparation of parcels as her special project. They compensated by trying to make their letters more descriptive, more detailed, more full of life, more "nourishing."

5**1**

Conscription Looms
1917–1918

During this time, Uncle Jack's health became an increasing concern. His general health had never been strong and was now clearly failing. He still smoked a pipe and enjoyed the limited amount of alcohol Bessie was willing to provide, a ration that was surreptitiously augmented by Mod who purchased an additional supply when he knew his brother's had run out. Jack had chronic chest troubles and sometimes broke out in boils. No name was given to his failing health, not even by Dr. Caswell. Jack could not have found a more agreeable environment than Meadowlands in which to spend his declining years. It was his brother's and sister's home and had been his parents; besides, there was no alternative.

In early September 1917, Bessie wrote to Addie in New York with an update on Jack's health:

> *Dearest Addie,*
>
> *Jack has been writing you so regularly that I know you are fully informed about him. The tenderness is very much better; his neck is not nearly as painful, so I hope the gland will not suppurate. We are using ichthol ointment and keep it bound up. He coughs very little and does not expectorate at all. His appetite is good and he sleeps a good deal, though not always at night. He has nourishment six times a day. When it is damp, or the wind is very high, he stays in bed. He wears very thick flannels at night and has a down comforter, though he seldom uses it. He is able to read a good deal and has plenty of magazines and books. The Times would be a great pleasure to him, I am sure...*
>
> *We have not heard from Morrie for a little time and are constantly anxious about him.*
>
> *I hope Bess is feeling better and able to begin work. My love to her and Charlie.*
>
> *Ever,*
> *Your loving sister, Bessie*

Jack survived a little more than a month after Bessie had written this letter to Addie. He died on October eleventh. On December nineteenth, Bessie wrote to her niece, Bess.

Dearest Bess,

This will be a sad Christmas for us all. It is many years since we have had a break in our immediate family and even I, who had not had him at Christmas for a great while, miss your dear father now. We cannot but be thankful he did not linger and suffer through this cold winter …

We have been deep in politics and feel that we have little left to do now the election is over. General McLean, the Union candidate for this riding asked me to organize the women voters of the parish of Gagetown as this is the first time women have had the vote. It was given to the wives, sisters, mothers and daughters of soldiers. We had 45 in Gagetown and got 31 to the polls. The majority everywhere was overwhelmingly in favour of conscription. We have a majority of 40 seats in the Dominion Parliament. Quebec, being French Canadian, voted almost solidly against it.

I hope the change to Philadelphia did both you and your mother good. She must have many lonely hours. I am so glad you are able to be with her instead of at the Library.

I am enclosing a very small gift. Please get some little things for her, yourself and Charlie.

We have had cheerful letters from Morrie from Fustenberg in Micklenberg, where he now is. He says it is a great relief to be treated as an officer after their miserable summer.

Uncle Mod joins me in love and many good Christmas wishes to you all. My love especially to your Mother.

Your loving,
Aunt Bessie.

That evening, over tea and cake with Mod, Bessie shared her concern about Addie and the fact that young Bess now had the sole responsibility for the support and care of her mother. Cousin Nell Burpee in Philadelphia had offered them hospitality when Bess was on a leave of absence from her employment at the General Seminary Library, due to it being enlarged and modernized.

The difficult circumstance of their lives was a cause of sadness for Bessie. She was grateful that her financial resources would allow her to continue assisting as needed.

*　*　*　*　*

With the national election of 1918, women at last won the right to vote. General McLean recruited Bessie to help organize the newly enfranchised women of the area to reach the polls. Bessie was well known as a leader for the advancement of women so this request was not surprising. As a result, the subject of all women being granted the vote was frequently on Bessie's lips. Mod was pleased to see his sister give voice to her enthusiasm for the cause, but was not shy of offering an opposing view.

One evening after the election, Mod ventured a rhetorical question; "Did all those thirty-one women voters know who they were voting for and what they stood for, or were they told where to place their X?"

"Do you think all the men who voted understood what the candidates represented?" Bessie promptly replied. "There has to be a beginning. Once a person votes they will take more interest in politics. I'm sure it won't be long before all adults will have the vote, except those who are in insane asylums, of course."

Mod did not further challenge his sister's view on the subject but rather turned the conversation to a complication of the war that now concerned him.

"Conscription seems the only possible route at this stage in the war, and no patriot of the Mother Country can really be against it," Mod observed. "But it does mean that Roger will eventually have to go. Morrie told him not to enlist. His height would be against survival."

"Let's hope it will all be over soon and Roger won't be called up." Bessie replied.

"It can be argued Roger's needed on the farm, but he wouldn't like that excuse."

"Perhaps he could serve in a noncombative role, say as a medic?" Bessie mused. "But then his back would never stand up to being a stretcher bearer and his height would still put him at risk."

Sister and brother paused their conversation when they heard Mary and Roger banging their snowy boots on the back porch. Together they had put away Horsey and the sleigh after a musical evening in Gagetown the Peters had organized on a Christmas theme.

"Come join us by the Franklin," Bessie called out. "Would you like some cake and tea?"

"I couldn't eat a crumb, but some hot tea would help me thaw," Mary said, standing in the doorway still in her heavy clothes, face bright red and glasses completely steamed.

"Same here," Roger chimed in. "There's a fierce wind getting up, blowing snow everywhere. Good thing those trees were in place to show Horsey the way."

Roger moved a chair close to the Franklin for Mary.

"Pearl insisted on putting our bricks in the oven for a reheat so at least we had warm feet," he added as he wrapped his large hands around a warm china cup.

52

The War Ends and Morrie Returns
1918–1920

Early in May 1918, Mod received notification from Ottawa that Capt. Morris A. Scovil had been moved to Holland. There was unease mixed with happiness at Meadowlands over this news. No one knew what it meant until a reassuring letter from Morrie was received. Holland was clearly a great improvement over his experience in Germany. The prisoners worked as farm labourers to help feed badly nourished German troops and the population generally. This was the happiest period of Morrie's internment. The extreme boredom of the previous camps was over. He wrote:

> *I pretend I am planting and weeding at Meadowlands, which greatly adds to my contentment, but the air has a different smell, so few trees, only two or three as far as the eye can see.*

Though the family's worries over Morrie's welfare lessened, they began to be concentrated on Roger's. At nineteen, lanky Roger had less than perfect eyesight, though with his spectacles he was deemed fit to become cannon fodder, or, more politely, "to serve the Mother Country in her Dominion's efforts to remove evil and encourage right to prevail." In spite of Morrie's caution that his unusually tall brother should avoid combat, the situation in the late summer of 1918 was such that he had no alternative. For sometime he had been aware that mothers of soldiers were beginning to give him critical glances. At least no one had passed him a white feather. Everyone in Gagetown knew he was doing essential farm work. Even so, when he was conscripted it was, in a way, a relief,

In the days after his twentieth birthday, and just before he was required to report in Saint John for induction, Roger contemplated his chances of survival. He did not like killing, not even ducks when he and Mary went out in her birchbark canoe on Foshay Lake every autumn. It was a manly ritual, but he was glad there was never a single bird in the bag. Blaming Mary for not holding the canoe steady or laughing too much was always a good, if feeble, excuse. He presumed he would be taught the fine points

341

of shooting to kill another man, perhaps younger than himself. Morrie had not enlarged on this detail of basic training.

Roger had never lived entirely in a man's world, always having his Aunt Bessie and at least one sister in his life. He asked his father what he might expect. Mod had no first hand experience of military life, though conversations with Jack when he was training with the militia and with military cousins and ex-military acquaintances gave him some idea. He passed on to his son what good advice he could summon, mostly comments on surviving in an exclusively man's world, though he was no expert. When Roger thought over their conversation, he realized Father passed on fewer than a half dozen recommendations.

"If you drink alcohol, drink slowly, with food if possible, and not past the point of beginning to feel unsteady. Do not be pushed into consorting with women you do not know.

Always refer to your superiors as "Sir". Never answer back even when you know they are wrong.

Always be punctual."

Roger's letters home during his basic training in Saint John were guarded. He did not mention his sore feet, his aching back, and his exhaustion at the end of the day. He knew his family could do nothing to change his sufferings and they must be mild compared with what Morrie had gone through. His father had given him the chance to avoid all this by applying for special status as a farm worker. Mostly, he was still glad he had not taken that route, though he knew that would probably change once bullets were whizzing past his ears. His target practice scores were improving. Each day his body found the ordeal a little easier. Marching for miles, setting up camp under canvas according to barked orders, taking part in manoeuvers was somewhat satisfying, especially in retrospect.

It was all so alien to the relaxed life he was used to. He made a friend, Jake, a farm boy like himself who was impressed when he said his brother was a prisoner of war. Roger wished he could talk to Morrie about life in the trenches. He tried to banish the knot that appeared in his stomach whenever he thought of being in combat.

The Canadian Expeditionary Force was desperate for more men whether fully trained or not. They needed to fill the gaps created by the killed, wounded, and taken prisoner. By October 30, 1918, Cpl. Roger Peniston Scovil was given a week's pre-embarkation leave. When he returned to Meadowlands he reported that he had been told by his commanding officer that he would have been put in for officer training had there been more time before going overseas. Roger was glad not to be in a position of authority. After only one night back in the Saint John barracks, Roger and his regiment were sent to Halifax. On November tenth he boarded the troopship, half elated to soon be in the fray and half in dread of seasickness or inadequate performance in battle. Then came November eleventh! The Armistice went into effect. Roger's ship did not leave port.

The war was over! Bessie and Mary allowed themselves tears of joy that both Morrie and Roger would be coming back to them. Mod hugged the two women. Hooters, honkers, church bells, gongs and drums in Gagetown and throughout the British Empire and its allied countries provided noteworthy noise at eleven o'clock on the eleventh day of the eleventh month, the official time of the armistice.

Little time was lost in clearing troops from ships in Halifax harbour to make space for those returning from England. Roger was back in Saint John, demobilized and home within two weeks. Canadian forces in Europe were not so lucky. As the weeks passed and soldiers were still in British barracks, riots broke out in protest. Mod eventually heard that Morrie was to be moved from Holland, to North East England, on November twenty-second.

A few days before Christmas, Morrie walked through the Meadowland's door, now promoted to the rank of Major, which he was entitled to use, as a civilian, for the rest of his life. The joy in the Meadowlands' farmhouse over Christmas 1918 needs no description to be imagined! There were, however, occasional unusual noises from Morrie's room in the middle of the night—shouts and muffled moans—as he relived his trench experiences. On the twenty-seventh he took the train from Gagetown to Fredericton and then on to Amherst to visit Madeline. They laid plans for their future together, deciding to put off marriage until they knew what kind of land grant would be given to the Major as a reward for his services. The Canadian government wanted to expand the cultivation of the Prairie Provinces to increase its tax base. Land grants for large-scale grain farming were in prospect.

Mod was disappointed Morrie and Madeline did not choose to remain at Meadowlands, construct a modern, well-insulated house for their anticipated family and take over the farm. Bessie felt likewise but knew from her experience that the attraction of wider horizons and greater prosperity were not lost on the energetic couple. Despite Mary's negative social status of being "at home," she had a deep attachment to Meadowlands and hoped Morrie would feel the same. Roger had long known he was not a good candidate to take over the farm and would be happy to have Morrie do so. But he also knew that with Morrie's education and with the experience and rank he had acquired during the war, he would likely be attracted to other opportunities.

With the appearance of motorized transport and farm equipment, it was clear the demand for hay and horses was beginning to decline. The rise of large-scale grain farming was based on the never-ending need for wheat, a farm product for which the market was now increasing. Morrie's training at the Truro agricultural college, his experience at Meadowlands, his work with the cavalry, and his military service gave him significant status and a real advantage in applying for a land grant property.

Morrie and Madeline eventually chose a property near Selkirk, Manitoba, about fifteen miles from Winnipeg, not far from the Red River. It took some months for the paper work to be completed and arrangements to be made. While waiting, Morrie divided his time between Amherst and Meadowlands where he worked with the horses. The reality of their intelligence, their smooth necks, soft snorts, and head tossings, along with their general responsiveness to his care, helped diminish most of the war's horrors still lurking in his head.

Mary Madeline Bliss and Major Morris Allaire Scovil were married on March 17, 1920 in the Anglican Christ Church at Amherst. The Rector, Reverend Horace Dibblee, who also had family connections to the groom, conducted the ceremony. Both the bride and groom wanted the occasion to be low-key, but the essential guest list swelled to the point the church could scarcely contain them all. The rambling Bliss house had no difficulty providing space for a reception. Three days later the couple with all their "worldly goods" set off on the long train trip to Selkirk, Manitoba and their new life as prairie grain farmers.

53

A Disaster Averted

Seeing Morrie and Madeline so happy together made Mary restless. After a long winter and the excitement of the wedding, she felt the need for a little city life, which appealed to Bessie as well. By the end of April the riverboats were running again, which gave the two women the means of independent travelling. They could choose between Fredericton and Saint John. Mary pushed for Saint John, not least because she could visit her friend, Dorrie Lee. Bessie's letter to cousin Lucy asking for a few nights hospitality was answered in two days.

> *Stay as long as you like. Plan on at least four nights. We want to hear all about the wedding. Will and I are so looking forward to having you both with us.*

Thinking Bessie might be tired after the river journey, Lucy invited no one else for dinner that first evening. The four just played a little bridge after the usual sumptuous meal and a touch of wine. Lucy knew Bessie did not approve of generous libations. Mary had arranged to have lunch and spend the next afternoon with Dorrie. Bessie and Mary both wanted to make some purchases at Manchester's. Lucy accompanied them and the three ladies enjoyed a morning shopping expedition. Mary then went to Dorrie's for lunch and a pleasant afternoon of conversation. Bessie and Lucy remained downtown enjoying a prolonged lunch in an attractive restaurant, recently opened. Will, as was his frequent routine, visited his club. The Robinsons and Bessie were back at the house by three-thirty for a bit of rest and a change of clothes before dinner to which guests had been invited. Mary returned at five, feeling the happy afternoon with Dorrie had vanished too quickly.

Lucy's great friend and close neighbor, Mrs. Morrisey, was frequently asked for dinner, especially when there were visitors. She possessed all attributes desired in a dinner guest, as Mod discovered some time ago. On this occasion, Mrs. Morrisey's house guest had also been invited which made it unnecessary for Lucy to think of someone else closer to Mary's age to balance the evening's conversation.

At six o'clock Mrs. Morrisey and a Captain Geoffrey Beaumont arrived, introductions were made, and places taken at the table for glasses of sherry before the meal. Lucy arranged for the captain to sit next to Mary. Captain Beaumont turned out to be a sea captain, the son of an English colleague of Mrs. Morrisey's late husband. He often stayed with Mrs. M. for a few days while his ship was being unloaded at the Saint John docks and then reloaded for the return trip to Liverpool. He was happy to talk to Mary. She asked questions that revealed he had served in the navy during the war and was lucky to have survived. Mary judged the reasonably good-looking captain to be about thirty-five or maybe forty. She decided to find out the answer to the obvious question.

"It must be hard on your wife and children, having you away so much."

"Oh, my sort of work doesn't encourage a family life," Captain Beaumont replied, noting Mary's carefully phrased question, and then added; "My mother is used to me being away ever since the war."

"Yes, I suppose she would be," Mary managed, weakly, hiding her amazement that this mature and confident man was not married.

The sherry loosened everyone's tongue a little, though Lucy was careful to produce some canapés — "blotting paper," Will called them. Dinner was perfection with a tender Crown of Lamb providing visible drama and the most superb gravy exercising the taste buds. Bessie made a mental note to ask Lucy what her cook's secret ingredient was, if she would divulge it. By the time four courses with various wines came and went, Miss Scovil became Mary and Captain Beaumont, Geoffrey.

A game of bridge followed. Lucy said she needed to get on with her needlework and Mrs. Morrisey joined her, so Will partnered with Bessie and Geoffrey with Mary. The captain was not a little surprised that the girlish-looking, owl-eyed Mary was such a skillful card player. Will, the ultimate host, organized the games so all felt comfortable with their wins and losses.

"I hope we will meet again," the captain said as he and Mrs. Morrisey took leave of Mary, her aunt, and then of their hosts.

"Yes," Mary replied with a small smile.

When they reached Mrs. Morrisey's house, Geoffrey asked whether she had Mary's address. He wanted to write to her.

"I don't, but I can easily obtain it from Lucy Robinson," Mrs. Morrisey replied. "I'll have it for you in the morning."

Dorrie had happily accepted Mary's invitation to return with them for a visit to Meadowlands. She met Mary and Bessie at the riverboat wharf on the day of their departure. The girls walked around the deck, speculating on the captain, but coming to no particular conclusions except, as Dorrie suggested, he may be looking for a wife. Mary was not surprised and somewhat pleased to receive a letter from him three days after they returned to Meadowlands. Captain Beaumont wrote that he had enjoyed her company and he hoped to see her again when he was back in Saint John. Could he call on her while he was waiting for his ship to be loaded? Could she recommend a hotel in Gagetown? Mary passed the letter to Bessie after she had read it, along with a cryptic comment.

"A letter from an old man; he must be thirty-five or forty," she said with a bemused look at her aunt.

"Maybe not," Bessie replied encouragingly. "Spending time at sea gives men a weathered look that makes them appear older than they are."

Bessie quickly absorbed the one page letter.

"Would you like to see him again? He seems personable with an educated voice and refined manners. We could ask him to stay here overnight, if you like."

With Mary launched into her twenty-fifth year, Bessie felt encouraging a possible romance was the least she could do for her spinster niece after the debacle over Carl Brown.

"What do you think, Dorrie?" Mary said, handing the letter to her.

After reading the message, Dorrie answered her friend, "He seems keen."

"All right; nothing to loose," Mary concluded. "Father will enjoy having a new bridge player to demolish."

The "girls" thoroughly enjoyed one another's company. Early May was still too chilly for summer activities, but they went for long walks, quietly watching ospreys building nests with surprisingly large sticks, and observing tiny turtles swimming in the still flooded ditches along the Jemseg road. Mary taught Dorrie the intricacies of paddling and steering her birch bark canoe without taking the paddle out of the water and how to avoid Mr. Evinrude's fits of temper. When the week was half used up, Amelia told Miss Scovil she would not have time to make a cake to go with the evening tea because she wanted to make a start of spring cleaning. Mod and Bessie, along with Mary and Dorrie had nearly finished the cake on hand the previous evening.

"That's OK, Amelia, I'll ask the girls if they would like to make a cake," Bessie replied.

The day was cloudy with a hard wind so being inside was no sacrifice. Mary proposed a coconut layer cake — one of her favourites. She took down the *Boston Cooking-School Cook Book*, which, after a few flips of the pages, fell open at 699 — "Butter Cakes" and then on to the page of "variations." Though published in 1896, it was still the most used cookbook in the house, the proof of which could be seen by its ingredient discoloured pages.

Mary and Dorrie, well swathed in aprons, took over the kitchen for the morning, laughing their way through the making of a two layer cake. While the layers were cooling, and before preparing the frosting, they mixed up a batch of molasses drop cookies and popped them in the oven. They were optimistic about the results, since even licking the raw batter off the wooden spoon was irresistible.

Very little preparation was needed for lunch. Amelia reappeared shortly before noon to heat up a hearty soup waiting overnight in the larder and to bring out a loaf of bread from yesterday's baking. By this time the layer cake had been assembled and placed in the cool larder ready for the evening ritual. The filling between the layers consisted of sweetened, shredded coconut pressed into white icing well flavoured with vanilla. The cake was topped with a generous application of this same frosting. The molasses drop cookies turned out perfectly and waited to be served with their after-lunch cups of tea.

"You're really good at baking, Mary," Dorrie said, as they gave Amelia a hand with setting the table.

"It's the only thing I can do properly, beside handling a canoe and operating Mr. Evinrude. I can't read books so I can't study anything. Even with my glasses, reading for any length of time is just too much of a strain on my eyes. Aunt Bessie said she would send me to the Miss Farmer Cooking School in Boston, if I want to go."

"Do you?"

"I'm thinking about it. I could always earn a living, then, if I had to. Aunt Bessie is keen on that. Her father's bankruptcy still hangs like a cloud over the family; she was only nineteen."

*   *   *   *   *

After Dorrie returned to Saint John, life at Meadowlands became predictable again, but then, suddenly, she had something different to look forward to. When Captain Beaumont returned to Saint John he found Mary's letter of invitation waiting for him at Mrs. Morrisey's. He immediately wrote back thanking her for their invitation to stay at Meadowlands. He expected his ship would remain in Saint John to be loaded for at least a week and he would plan to arrive at Gagetown on the afternoon boat on the twenty-eighth of May. Could he be met?

That was in five days. Mary wrote a quick note in the affirmative, saying she would be at the Gagetown wharf with the family motorboat. Her interest in this "old man" was curiously sharpened.

As usual, Mary arrived on time. She was surprised by his lively wave and her quickened heartbeat as she saw him walking down the gangplank. Geoffrey Beaumont's visit was more fun than Mary expected. He was not thirty-five or forty, but thirty-three, very agile at climbing over fences on walks around the farm, and, indeed, he and Mary provided quite a challenge for Mod and Roger over bridge. Bessie spent much of her time during the visit at her desk as she was in the middle of writing an article.

Though a spinster, Bessie was no fool in the elements of courtship, pronouncing on such matters with, "The watchers see most of the game." She knew the captain was not here for the fresh air and she was aware that Mary knew it, too.

As their guest prepared to leave on the afternoon boat on the thirtieth, Bessie bade him a gracious farewell with obvious warmth.

"Do come and visit us again, when your ship docks."

"Thank you. I should like to very much," Geoffrey replied with feeling, knowing that whatever happened at Meadowland's was under the benevolent eye of Aunt Bessie.

More visits followed. In June the tennis court was prepared. Geoffrey had previously been introduced to the game but was not proficient. He was willing to be instructed. Roger offered to be ball boy partly to make sure he behaved himself and partly to see how he would behave if Mary showed her superiority. He reacted graciously. Mary decided Geoffrey had the makings of a passable tennis player.

The summer advanced and so did Geoffrey's attentions. On a visit in early fall he proposed marriage, which Mary accepted. She was sure Geoffrey would be her last chance. She did not love him the way she loved Carl, but she had grown fond of him and decided that was enough. She and Bessie set to work on a "bottom drawer" after a visit to Manchester, Robertson and Allison's to purchase sheets, pillow cases, huckaback towels, and other linens to embroider with S/B suitably entwined.

Mod looked forward to Geoffrey's enlivening visits, but he was curious that he said nothing much about family or his life in England. Questions on the subject were answered briefly with no details. Mod mentioned this to Bessie one evening when they were alone; she agreed it seemed a little odd.

"I think I'll have him investigated. I know a man in Saint John, a private detective, who will do this discretely. I'll write to him."

"Whatever you think best, dear."

The result was unfortunate, but prevented a disaster. A letter arrived three week's later from the detective.

> *I regret to inform you that Captain Geoffrey Beaumont is already married. He lives with his wife of ten years, in Liverpool, England. There are no children. They separated for a time and there was talk of a divorce but they reconciled. Captain Beaumont's mother also lives, independently, in Liverpool. Is this sufficient information, or do you require more?*

Mod passed the letter to Bessie without comment.

"Oh, the scoundrel!"

"Who's a scoundrel?" Mary asked as she walked into the room.

"Sit down, Mary, before you read this."

Mary's face flushed as she read the letter, but she did not burst into tears as expected. She just said, "That explains a few things; like why he wanted us to have a house in Saint John, near my friends and family, he said, because he'd be away so much. Well, good riddance. If he could lie about that he could lie about anything. Imagine! I nearly married a bigamist! I'll write to him and send a quotation from the detective's letter."

"Do it immediately if you can, dear," Bessie advised, and then added, "Surely Mrs. Morrisey didn't know and certainly not Lucy and Will."

"At least invitations haven't been printed or sent out," added the ex-bride-to-be before she climbed the stairs to her room to write a letter to Dorrie, who was to have been her bride's maid. As Mary wrote, "Dear Dorrie," the twenty five year old spinster removed her spectacles and the tears flowed.

Three days before Captain Beaumont had been due to visit again, two letters arrived, one for Mod and one for Mary. In the one to Mod the captain apologized for his behaviour but excused it because he and his wife were only technically married; they shared the same address but he usually stayed with his mother when he was in Liverpool. An attempt had been made at divorce but failed because of her religious beliefs. The letter to Mary also apologized for misleading her. He said he genuinely loved her and no one else and wished her a happy life. He added he explained his behaviour more completely in the letter to her father. Mary wrote back, mostly to help dissipate some of her venomous feelings toward the would-be-bigamist.

> *Captain Beaumont,*
>
> *I hope you are suitably grateful to my father for saving you from prison, to which you would surely have been sent when your*

deception was eventually discovered. Your name will be blackened in Saint John, so I would not waste your charm on more young women there.

Mary Scovil

Mary showed the letter to her father, who just said, "capital." As the days passed, so did Mary's anger and disappointment. Attacking the contents of her "bottom drawer" with scissors, snipping away all the entwined initials, helped to further dissipate her anger. She should have left them but she was not clairvoyant. She hung up her trousseau and began to wear pieces to church and to gatherings in Gagetown. Aunt Bessie said the greater family and close friends who had been told of the expected wedding should be informed of the change. Mary told Bessie she could do that if she liked.

Her siblings were all astonished and said it was good to be rid of him. Others sent sympathy notes as though someone had died. In a sense the potential bride in her had died. She gave up ever being one. At least, her apparently happy and considerably older sisters were still single, so it wasn't a state to be despised, necessarily. She would like to have one or two children if they could just be dropped in her lap, and not go through a long nine months of sickness, backache, and great dark circles under her eyes, like she noticed with some of her school friends in Gagetown who now had children. She once read in *The Ladies' Home Journal* how kangaroos in Australia produce tiny offspring that grow up in outside pouches; a much better arrangement, she thought. Mary knew it was odd to have thoughts like this but sometimes life was really odd so maybe her thoughts were just part of this oddness.

As before, when love was shot down, Roger came to the rescue. He hadn't found a girl he wanted to spend the rest of his life with, nor did he want to spend it at Meadowlands where, as everyone was saying, machines would eventually take over from horses. He and Mary were in the same boat, literally sometimes. Before the days became too cold and while the colour of trees along the riverside was still a treat for the eye, brother and sister enjoyed each other's company by taking long day trips on the river with Mr. Evinrude.

54

A Manitoba Land Grant Farm
1921

During the winter of 1920-21, Bessie hatched a plan. She first mentioned it to Mod, then to Roger. She then wrote to Morrie and Madeline. Letters from Selkirk had indicated they were short of manpower. The farmers helped one another on major projects, like barn building, but there were never enough hands. Would it be a good idea for Roger to join them next spring to help with the work? Everyone thought it was a good plan. Roger was excited at the prospect, especially since Morrie had purchased a tractor with the last of his army demobilization gratuity. Roger knew nothing about tractors but looked forward to learning.

Roger was set to take the train to Selkirk, Manitoba in early April. Mary was pleased for him but sorry to lose his company. She now looked forward to visiting Selkirk, perhaps once Morrie and Madeline could afford to increase the size of their little house. Mod and Bessie agreed it was time Roger had some experience of another part of the world even though they would miss his quiet good humour.

Roger spent much of that winter imagining life in Manitoba based on Morrie's letters and some sketches he had sent. Once the ice had gone out, Bessie helped Roger make a list of what he would need to take with him. Train travel was so quick and easy from Gagetown to Fredericton. Bessie, Roger, and Mary made a day trip, finding much of what was needed at Edgecombe's department store, including a trunk. They went to a store on York Street specializing in work clothes, where they found the heavy-duty leather boots needed for winter. Roger already had summer work boots and a good pair of rubber boots.

As the three of them, laden with Roger's parcels, climbed into the train to return home, Mary wished they would move to Fredericton, especially with Roger leaving, but she knew there was no hope of that. The very air of the city had a different smell, suggesting excitement of which lazy little Gagetown could never boast. She felt she had outgrown Meadowlands and Gagetown, but part of her still loved them both.

When Roger boarded the train at the Gagetown station on April 12, 1921, with his trunk stowed in the luggage car, Bessie thought he looked more like an overgrown school boy, full of anticipation yet edged with regret at leaving the only home he knew. Mod had mixed feelings.

Perhaps he should have done more to launch his youngest son into some sort of career in Saint John or Fredericton. His unsophisticated ways and trusting nature seemed to naturally place him in a rural setting and certainly he had picked up a lot about farming. Mod hoped Roger would find the West to his liking.

Mary was surprised at the size of the crater Roger's absence caused. The day after he left, she took a long walk on the Jemseg road splashing through the spring puddles in her rubber boots. When she returned to the house, she first wrote a letter to Dorrie and then announced to her aunt that she felt like doing some baking.

"By all means, dear. How about an apple pie? Amelia has some dried apple slices soaking which you can probably use. Check with her."

"You're welcome to them," Amelia responded to the request. "I don't have time for more than apple sauce today, but a pie would be better."

The complications of pastry making — chilling, rolling, filling, decorating the top with pastry leaves, glazing with beaten egg — filled most of the remaining afternoon. As evening came, Mary again thought about Roger, still on the train, making his way all alone to Manitoba. She then remembered something he had been doing during the week before he left — feeding carrots to each of the stabled horses in the barn. It was the time of year when the remaining supply of carrots in the root cellar were beginning to shrivel but were still regarded as delicacies by the horses. Mary picked up the basket Roger had been using for this task, made her way to the root cellar and then to the barn where the horses responded with soft nickerings to what they knew was coming. Mary's acute sense of loss seemed to fill the hollow of the great barn and tears filled her eyes as she fed the basket of carrots to the patiently waiting horses.

When Mary picked up the mailbag the following day, it brought a letter from Elizabeth that contained surprising news.

> *… I met a charming Englishman last year here, when he was investigating a possible business enterprise. We have been corresponding. He has recently returned and has proposed marriage. I have accepted. We plan a simple wedding here on October 21st. We don't expect anyone from the East to come, but hope Morrie and Madeline will, to represent the family, as they are near and perhaps Trudy, though Vancouver is not exactly on my door step. His name is*

"I hope he's not a cousin or already married," Mary cynically commented.

"We must be pleased for her, dear, though I'm sure an Englishman in the family is painful for you. By the time they are married Elizabeth will be thirty-one, old enough to know what she wants in life. I was nearly that age when I began my nurses' training and knew that was what I wanted."

Eventually, the mailbag brought a letter from Roger. It was full of surprise at the size of Canada as he had seen it from his train window and at the strangeness of the prairie landscape — so many trees for so long and then none.

*   *   *   *   *

When Roger arrived in Manitoba, the nights were still cold and the ground too wet for plowing and planting. Morrie took the time of waiting to show his younger brother what prairie farming was all about. Like most of the farmers in the area, they went into town by horse and wagon. Roger was impressed by the size of Selkirk. Main Street was lined with businesses housed in big buildings with large plate glass windows. A huge hotel, several stories high, dominated the centre of town. Motorcars were numerous, though most horses still shied away from them, which indicated they were a recent change the horses did not like. Morrie said he planned to buy a motorcar if this year produced a decent crop of wheat. Their first year had been a disaster, not a drop of rain when it was needed, a complete crop failure.

"Most farmers have loans from the bank," Morrie explained. "Aunt Bessie is our bank, but that can't go on for ever. If we get rain at the right time this year, we'll have a bumper crop and really cash in."

Last year, when the wheat was not worth harvesting, Morrie's neighbours had time to help him build a proper barn with room for his horse and cow, hay for the winter, and to house his new tractor. They had already put up a separate chicken house and were making plans for a pigpen. Madeline looked after a kitchen garden, which she hand watered during the drought along with the flowers she had planted around the house. A well had been sunk on the property before they arrived, which provided a good supply of water for household and farm use. The house, for now, was rudimentary, a small wood frame structure with basic conveniences. Madeline's creative ingenuity along with Morrie's assistance helped to turn it into a comfortable home. They had the makings of a prosperous modern farm of the kind Morrie had been educated to manage. What they needed now was the cooperation of the weather.

One morning in early May, Morrie and Roger went to Selkirk to buy wheat seed before the best was gone. Mad, who planned the day for bread baking, gave Morrie a list of essentials she needed for the next two weeks. The seed store was close to McFayden's, a grocery and general supplies store where old men with leathery faces sat around on nail kegs, shootin' the breeze, chewing tobacco, and aiming for the spittoon, which they usually hit.

When they returned home, Morrie wanted Roger to have a first lesson in learning to drive the tractor. Morrie's tractor was the kind of new steel-wheeled machine that was taking the place of multi-horse teams for prairie farming. He started it up and backed out of the barn where it was easier to see the operating levers and pedals. Morrie gave Roger a demonstration of how to operate the formidable machine—starting, putting it in gear, stopping, turning, increasing and decreasing speed and so on. As Morrie headed for the outhouse he said, "Have a go. Do a little practice driving around the yard. You'll get the hang of it."

Roger climbed into the metal seat, put it in gear and started driving forward. He suddenly realized he had failed to turn away from the barn in time and now had to stop the tractor—but how? How to stop had flown from his mind. He grabbed a lever and pulled, but it was the one to increase speed, which the tractor obeyed perfectly, as it smashed through one end of the small barn and out the other. The impact dislodged a main beam and part of the roof collapsed behind him. Morrie was in mid-flow when he heard the noise. He bolted from the outhouse, hitching up his trousers on the run only to discover a partly collapsed barn and Roger, still in the tractor seat, steering in a wide circle around the yard, wondering how to stop it. Morrie ran after him shouting,

"Take it out of gear and step on the brake peddle."

Roger did as he was told and it worked. The tractor came to a stop. Madeline appeared in the kitchen door and then rushed to Morrie's side. Roger sat, stunned, in the operator's seat. Morrie started laughing. There was nothing else for it but to laugh. Roger was horrified by what had happened but then, with great relief, joined in when he saw Morrie laughing. Madeline looked at the two men and managed only a slight smile.

"Could have been worse," Morrie came up with after he stopped laughing. "You could have flattened the house!"

"I guess I thought it would be as simple as the Evinrude," Roger offered. "I panicked and couldn't remember how to stop it."

"Once the Evinrude starts, you've got the whole river in front of you, not a barn in sight," Morrie said, putting his arm around his brother's shoulder, the two of them suddenly remembering their Meadowlands' home.

"It's not quite the end of the world," Morrie added. "The neighbours will help rebuild it after planting. I help them with their plowing."

Morrie and Roger set to work shoring up the roof over the cow's stable and to protect the hay that remained in the barn. The weather was likely to be dry through spring planting in any event. The nights were now warm enough for the horse to stay in the pasture with a blanket strapped to his back. The sturdy tractor was undamaged.

The following day, well away from the house and anything vaguely upright, Roger received more tractor driving lessons. Morrie sat on the fender beside the driver providing step-by-step instructions until Roger had mastered all the details of operating the machine. Morrie realized he should have done this in the first place; it would have prevented the barn disaster.

Several weeks later, the fields were dry enough for plowing. The two men hooked up the three-row plow to the back of the tractor and drove to the nearby field. Morrie plowed two lengths of the field while Roger watched. Roger took over and plowed the next two. They stopped and talked over the details of handling tractor and plow, especially how to make turns in order to keep the furrows straight. After the turned over furrows dried out a bit, a harrow was hitched to the tractor and pulled across the field until the soil was worked enough for seeding. Next, the drill seeder was hooked up to the tractor, filled with the precious wheat seed, and pulled across the field in perfectly straight lines. The Fordson tractor accomplished all this in a fraction of the time it would have taken using horses. Morrie and Madeline had the financial resources to begin farming with this modern equipment. Many of their neighbours were still using horses and welcomed the use of Morrie's tractor when it came time to put in the crop.

Roger eventually became a real asset. His help allowed Morrie get his planting done even faster and made it possible to offer more assistance to his neighbours. Madeline came to appreciate Roger's presence, especially because he was helpful around the house and was always cheerful and easygoing.

A week after the fields were seeded a delicate green covered them as far as the eye could see. Mad congratulated the two farmers on their productive work. That evening, Morrie said they should do an inspection tour around the fields in the morning to see how evenly the wheat seed had germinated. Mad was also keen to get a close look at their future prosperity, but when morning came she felt unwell. Her stomach was upset and she didn't feel like eating breakfast. Morrie was concerned but Mad told them to go ahead with their tour. She said she must have eaten something that disagreed with her and just needed to rest. Morrie thought that was odd. They had all eaten the same meals and neither he nor Roger had any symptoms.

Mad rested for a half hour and gradually began to feel better. The nausea had gone. As well as resting, she had been thinking. She knew morning nausea could mean she was pregnant. Morrie and Roger returned from the first part of their tour shortly before noon. Mad greeted them and asked Morrie to come into the bedroom.

"Are you feeling any better?" Mod asked with a worried voice.

"Yes and no," Mad said with a smile. "It may take nine months before I feel normal again. I think we're going to be parents. We should make an appointment with a doctor."

"What great news!" Morrie replied giving his wife a hug and a kiss. "I hope we'll do a better job raising babies than we have of wheat! I'll take you to see a doctor, or, if you'd rather, I'll arrange for him to come see you."

*   *   *   *   *

The doctor confirmed that Mrs. Scovil was indeed pregnant. She should expect the birth to be near the end of December or early January. The weather can be pretty fierce around then, he said so they should make plans accordingly.

"I like to attend first timers myself, if at all possible," the doctor said reassuringly, "but I'll give you the name of a good midwife who will provide helpful instruction and be here for the birth if I can't get there. I'll give you my home telephone number in case you start over the Christmas holidays, but that would be a little early. In the mean time, let me know if you have any problems. Best to check every two or three months, anyway. You might feel nauseated in the mornings for up to three months."

Mad and Elizabeth had developed the habit of telephoning one another every two weeks or so. Winnipeg was only twenty-two miles from Selkirk. Elizabeth had recently released the exciting news of her engagement. Now it was Mad's turn for congratulations. The sisters-in-law discussed the possibility of Mad attending the wedding in late October, seven months pregnant.

"I'll be as big as a house," Mad said, "but let's see how I feel at the time. I'll be a great advertisement for marriage! Come and visit us as soon as school holidays begin in June."

Elizabeth agreed. She said she was considering not returning to Meadowlands in August, but saving the money for her trousseau. A visit with them would be more than welcome. Roger began treating his sister-in-law as though she were made of glass, forever offering her a chair, carrying anything weighing more than a pound, opening doors, until Mad had to ask him to stop.

"I'm not an invalid," Mad explained, "but I really appreciate the way you have taken over the kitchen garden work."

"I did a lot of gardening at Meadowlands," Roger replied, feeling some pride in the knowledge that experience gave him.

Neighbours helped rebuild the barn in that slow period when farmers looked at the greening fields with pleasure and the sky with anticipation, hoping to see rain clouds forming up on the horizon. But as the days passed, fewer and fewer clouds came into view, and then none, like last year. The wheat stunted and then went into maturity much too early. The grain heads formed irregularly, failed to fill out properly, and then withered. It was shaping up to be another year of total crop loss. Nothing could be saved. Special prayers were said in all churches, beseeching the Almighty to have mercy. In a bitter moment, Morrie suggested the "Almighty" could do with an ear trumpet.

55

A Crop Killing Drought

When the news of the crop failure came to Meadowlands, Bessie had a serious talk with Mod. She had been thinking about the sad plight of the "Selkirk children." She was happy to send Morrie and Madeline enough money to tide them over into another year, especially with a baby on the way, but, if there were a third drought, would it not be better for them to return to Meadowlands and run the farm?

"You and I and Mary, and Roger, if he wants to, could move to Fredericton and leave the farm in Morrie's hands. That's what he was educated to do, after all. Madeline seems very adaptable and capable."

Mod smoothed his moustache and nodded. The thought was not a new one for him.

"That's a capital idea, Bess. Morrie understands mechanized farming, which is the way of the future. I'm too old to start that. Mary could do with more young friends and Roger, too, for that matter. Write to Morrie, outlining the plan and tell him I approve. It's an alternative he can think about over the winter."

Morrie's reply was prompt in coming. He and Mad embraced the generous offer. He explained how disheartening it has been to work so hard and have nothing to show for it. Weather in the East might be difficult but at least you know roughly what's coming and when. He praised Roger's willingness to work hard but observed he is not really cut out to be a farmer. Some kind of work in town would probably suit him better. Even if the crops are reasonably good next year, Morrie said he might still consider taking up the offer of Meadowlands. Even if you have a good crop one year, drought may very well bring a crop failure the following year. You can never be sure.

"Morrie was always sensible," Mod said as he handed the letter back to Bessie.

Later that day, with her brother's approval, she wrote to the Douglas cousins to tell them that come next summer or fall she and Mod might be looking for a 4-bedroom house, with accommodations for help, in central Fredericton so they would not need a horse and carriage. Cousin Sophia wrote back to say they would keep their ears and eyes open and report any good prospects. They would certainly look forward to seeing more of their cousins should they make the move.

*　*　*　*　*

Bessie wrote to Elizabeth in early September, enclosing a generous cheque as a wedding present. Part of it was just that and part of it was the money she and her father would have spent on attending the wedding. She told them that though they would dearly like to be there, it seemed more sensible for them to use the money as a nest egg to take to England. They would be with her in spirit on October twenty-first with their fondest love. Bessie was glad Morrie and Roger, and perhaps Madeline, would represent the family, and possibly Gertrude if she could get away, which was not settled yet.

Morrie and Roger packed their best clothes and were glad to leave the dead, dry fields behind for two days away in Winnipeg. The doctor recommended against Mad making the trip over the bumpy, unreliable roads. She knew she was beginning to look like a pumpkin and was not comfortable sitting in one position for a long time. Remaining at home seemed best. If she needed assistance, the nearest neighbours, a Ukrainian couple with a two-year old boy and another baby on the way, were two miles away and on the same telephone line. Ulla, the mother, was rapidly picking up English with Mad's help. They had become good friends and Mad knew she could rely on Ulla and her husband if need be.

Morrie "gave away" his eldest sister at the ceremony in St. Michael and All Angels Anglican Church. The cornerstone had been laid the previous year so the church building still had that pristine look and smell. The congregation had outgrown the original, small wooden church building. When winter came it was to be pulled across the road to serve as a church hall.

Morrie and Roger could not help but notice that women's fashions were changing at an alarming rate. Ever since the end of the Great War, a great change was taking place and Winnipeg seemed to be in the forefront. Dresses and skirts had gone from ankle length to mid calf, and now, in some places, nearly up to the knees. Elizabeth wore a handkerchief hem oyster dress, with beige lace trimmings that came somewhat below her knees. She hoped it would do as a best dress in England, so it would not, like many wedding dresses be worn only once. If Gertrude had been able to get away, she would have been her sister's bride's maid. As it was, Isobel Hotchkiss, an English mistress filled in, wearing her best pale blue dress,

362

with the hem taken up to match the bride's length, though a handkerchief hem was too much of a challenge.

Morrie and Roger took to their new brother-in-law, Hayden, immediately. He was about an inch taller than Morrie, a firm though clipped voice, steady eyes, and a full smile showing straight teeth. They were careful to make a note of his appearance. Aunt Bessie and all at Meadowlands would want an accurate report.

Elizabeth found saying "good-bye" to her brothers very hard, representing as they did in her mind, all of her family, all of Meadowlands, all of Canada, for that matter. She had no idea whether she would ever see them again, but tried to put that out of her mind. She was looking forward to her new life in England and to renewing her Edgehill friendship with Rainsley Hensley, who had married well and was living in London. They had been best friends and corresponded since school days.

Roger's neck nearly twisted off his shoulders during their short Winnipeg visit but Morrie's thoughts were not on the height of the buildings, the shortness of skirts, or the wide, smooth streets. He insisted on an early start for home the day after the wedding, and was relieved to find Mad happily baking bread and eager to hear all about the wedding.

There was no harvest, of course, except from the garden, which Roger and Morrie enlarged and faithfully watered to ensure good production. With adequate watering, the fertile prairie soil produced an abundance of basic vegetables for eating fresh and for canning, pickling, drying, and stowing away in the root cellar for winter use. The brothers also occupied themselves by pulling up the dead wheat plants, self tying them in bundles big enough to use as kindling through the coming winter, and storing them in the barn along with the hay. The native grassland hay crop, though sparse, had done better than the wheat. It matured earlier while there was still moisture in the ground from the spring snow melt. A large loose pile of wheat straw was kept as bedding for the horse and cow. In the hardship of the drought, they could afford to waste nothing.

Madeline had grown up as an active, outdoor girl as well being top notch at academics. Her resourceful mind and practical skills went a long way to sustaining their effort at prairie grain farming, which, unfortunately coincided with a multi-year period of drought. She had often accompanied her father on autumn hunting trips. He owned property on the Tyndal Road five miles outside of Amherst, Nova Scotia where he had a rustic but substantial hunting camp, which they used on these trips. He had taught her how to shoot deer in a way that avoided maiming and made sure of a clean quick kill. She became skilled at bringing down wild ducks and geese as well, all of which provisioned the Bliss household table. She now realized her time roughing it with her father partly prepared her for life on this isolated western farm. She wrote to her father expressing her appreciation and thanking him for all he had taught her. Her father had been twice married. Madeline had three older stepbrothers from the first marriage and two older sisters and younger brother from the second. But her mother also died and her father had not remarried. He wrote that her little brother, Donald, needed more care than he could provide and would soon be sent to Rothesay School for Boys, near Saint John. Her three older stepbrothers were busy with their own lives, so she now heard family news through her father and her two sisters. They had both graduated from nurses' training and, now that Mad was pregnant, were writing more often offering little snippets of advice from their medical knowledge, but not from personal experience.

Daily walks, which had been encouraged by her sisters, were part of Mad's routine. Morrie and sometimes Roger accompanied her. The brothers' days were no longer filled with essentials of farming as they had been. Spending effort, time, and tight money on farm improvements for the future seemed inappropriate, considering it was likely they would be leaving in a year.

The men, instead, turned their attention to household work and projects related to the immediate future. On Mondays they took over the scrubbing and washing, lifting and wringing of towels and heavy linen sheets, hanging them on the outdoor line where they eventually became mostly dry, even if they froze stiff. They made a cradle and a changing table for the coming baby, which were really Christmas presents for Mad but could not be kept secret since they did their woodworking in the house. Mad was never idle. She was constantly knitting. Morrie teased her she was knitting enough for quadruplets. In between producing little garments, Mad worked on a Christmas present for Morrie—a new sweater, which he dearly needed. She hoped to have time to make one for Roger, but it looked as though he would need to be content with a wooly hat and mittens.

Mad pushed her increased bulk around the kitchen sufficiently to produce a Christmas dinner, which more than satisfied them all. Presents were given, tried on, and appreciated. Mad rocked her imaginary baby in the new cradle. The Ukrainian neighbours visited by sleigh on Boxing Day bringing special little cakes tasting of almond and dusted with sugar. Mad reciprocated with date squares that were equally new to the Ukrainian palates. Morrie insisted on making the tea for their visitors, so Mad could sit with Ulla. His eyes returned to her every few minutes for signs of discomfort. The doctor said, "any day now."

As Mad stood up after supper on December thrity-first to serve the last of a Christmas cake she felt a strong twinge. She set the cake back on table and turned to her husband, "Better telephone the midwife, dear."

Morrie flew to the telephone, cranked the handle for the operator who immediately asked, "Do you need the midwife yet?"

"Yes, please call Mrs. Siskin, thanks," Morrie replied without asking how she knew. He had often thought that telephone operators knew more than God himself and this more or less proved it. He would never say anything on his party line phone that he didn't want the whole community to know.

Mrs. Siskin was there within the hour. The prospective father had organized the delivery room according to previous instructions — a rubber sheet on the bed, a layer of old newspapers, a sheet and a draw sheet. Roger looked after filling kettles with water to heat slowly on the stove to be ready for the baby's first bath, but that was hours away. Mad changed into an old but clean nightdress, added a dressing gown. She gently walked about the room as Mrs. Siskin instructed, waiting for the next contraction.

At five o'clock on New Year's morning, 1922, red haired Elizabeth Courtenay Scovil made her appearance, and none too soon for the four present in the house, all of whom had had a sleepless night. The number could have been extended to five if the newborn had been able to express her opinion. Efficient Mrs. Siskin stayed until nearly midday, making sure all was well. She returned the next morning to find mother putting baby back in her cradle after her second feeding of the day. Father and uncle had nearly recovered from the experience and were out burning up their excitement by shovelling wider paths to the barn and chicken house.

During the rest of the winter, when the two men took the horse and sleigh into town, they found the talk among the farmers at the provisioning stores was of little else but the coming growing season. Some churches were beginning early with prayers for abundance, hoping to increase attendance and boost the amount put in the collection plates since no one person could give much. Pennies were more common than silver.

As days grew longer and snow retreated, banks were busy writing up loans for farmers so they could buy seed. Like the previous two years, spring and early summer were promising with that eventual green blanket covering the fields. Farmers cricked their necks looking at the sky, watching the weather signs. But, like the previous two years, rains ceased just when they were essential. Crops withered; another season of failure.

Mad and Morrie and Roger, too, were grateful to have Meadowlands waiting for them and their little redhead, who they now called "Courtenay Elizabeth," after one of her maternal grandfather's names, which is used for both girls and boys. "Elizabeth" was, of course, after her great Aunt Bessie, but the parents decided there were already enough Elizabeths to keep track of in the Scovil family.

56

A Return to Meadowlands and a Move to Fredericton
1922

The Douglas cousins were faithful to their promise. They reported a doctor in Fredericton was retiring and moving from his quite modern house in the six hundred block of King Street, within walking distance of the Cathedral, the City Club, shops and stores, and most amenities. It appeared to be just what Bessie had in mind. She wrote to the owner and made an appointment to see the house. The Meadowlands trio took the train from Gagetown for a day trip to Fredericton, viewed the house, and all were pleased. The Robinson lawyer was contacted. He suggested various checks on the house and, if they proved satisfactory, an offer would be made. He recommended the Scovils offer $200 less than the asking price. The doctor said he would meet them half way and accept $100 less. The deal was signed at the end of August.

Morrie had written earlier to tell Mod and Bessie that again the rains had failed to come at the crucial time of the season and the crop would again be lost. He had given up walking in the fields to inspect growth. The exercise was too depressing. Like the last two years, the grain heads partially developing too early, drooping, and turning brown on the dying plants. They had kept the kitchen garden going by hand watering. It was ironic to have such an abundance of living green in the garden while the landscape around them was brown and dead. Yes, please, they would like to return to Meadowlands and start over. It would probably take a while to sell the farm and its equipment. It will be easier to sell the horse, cow, and chickens. When would be a convenient time to move?

When the Fredericton house was firmly in Scovil hands, Mod wrote they could make the move any time that suited them. The house they had found in Fredericton had room for Roger if he wanted it. Amelia and Jock will stay on at Meadowlands, at least for a while and so will Bert who now knows a lot about horses and general farm work. They would make the move to Fredericton around the middle of September, so anytime after that Morrie and family could plan their return.

Mary was delighted, but, in a way, also disappointed. She couldn't wait to move to the city and have Roger back and old Morrie and his family nearby. But the opportunity to visit the West had now vanished. Maybe she would travel to Vancouver one day to stay with Gertrude.

The doctor from whom Mod and Bessie purchased the Fredericton house was moving into a smaller residence and was happy to leave the excess furnishings in place and sell them to the Scovils. This meant that the furniture and household equipment in the Meadowlands house would remain there. This, in turn, enabled Morrie and Mad to sell their household goods, along with the farm, and ship only a few small items they especially treasured, including the cradle.

A completely furnished house was an added incentive for the young farmer and his family who decided to buy the Manitoba farm. No one could remember more than three years of drought, including bank managers, so there was optimism that the seasonal rains would return. By including the tractor, all the farm equipment, the horse, cow, and chickens, Morrie had enough cash to pay back a small loan, buy rail tickets to New Brunswick, and have enough left over to get through the coming winter. The temporary "westerners" arrived home the end of September.

Roger had the choice of Meadowlands or Fredericton. He chose the city, partly because Mary would be there, partly because he was interested in city life of which he knew little, but mostly because he had lost interest in farming — so little to show for so much work. Morrie was delighted to be back at predictable old Meadowlands, and was soon thinking about making it into something more than a hay and thoroughbred horse farm. He knew they could make a living from this kind of operation for now, but with more and more mechanization there would be less demand for hay and for horses. He would talk over the possibilities with Mad during the winter. Morrie was thankful she was good at making practical plans and making them work. Mad was especially happy to be in a house with a full bathroom, to have household help, and to be nearer her family in Amherst. She knew she would have to get used to being cut off from Gagetown for a while in both autumn and spring but that was just a fact of life at Meadowlands. The isolation did not overly concern her; it was much less than she had endured on the Manitoba farm.

Mary and Roger investigated nearly every corner of Fredericton that fall while the brilliantly coloured leaves and sunny days lingered. Both close and distant relatives and friends asked the Scovil household to dinner parties, tea parties, "at-home" afternoons, and bridge parties Most of the hostesses were middle aged or older. Sometimes there was a sprinkling of under-thirties. Mary and Roger were often considered a "couple" especially for bridge or to balance the seating at dinner parties. When Bessie secured live-in help, invitations were sent to reciprocate hospitality. Ethel, a widowed woman with a daughter working as a maid in Boston, was no Amelia, but she was a skilled cook and knew how to fit in without overstepping boundaries.

Church attendance at the Cathedral for Sunday matins needed no four-mile journey or a boat trip, rather just a five or six-minute walk though much more time was taken up in conversations afterward. Invitations for Christmas socializing began to accumulate, propped up on the mantle piece over the fireplace. Mary thought she should have at least two new dresses for her new life and a new hat. Her aunt thought one dress would sufficiently augment those from her trousseau, if the lengths were adapted a little, but she did agree to a new hat and new trim for the old one. Cloches were what all the young were wearing, Bessie knew. To her they looked like upside down stewpots and not at all flattering, especially to Mary with her Roman nose, which really needed a sizeable brim for balance.

The smart new cloche and dress with a dropped waistline and loose pleats in the skirt were soon "christened" at Bishop Richardson's where Mary had been asked to pass sandwiches at an afternoon tea so that a visiting dignitary could meet selected parishioners. Whether she was emboldened by her modern hat or a little bored with encouraging bodies to consume more than they needed, she seized the opportunity of saying to a boney woman, about to sit down next to a white haired man wearing a too-tight clerical collar, "Miss Horsey, have you met Canon Cowie?" Mary could not completely contain her mirth at this fortuitous coincidence but managed to channel it into a broad grin as the two began to converse while helping themselves to tiny swirled sandwiches from Mary's plate. Imagining Roger's laugh when she related the scene, kept Mary going for the remainder of the tedious afternoon.

Mod joined the City Club on Carleton Street, barely a two-block walk, where he met Lord Ashburnham, a compatible bridge partner with whom he quickly struck up a lasting friendship. Now he knew why cousin Will Robinson spent so much time at his club.

Bessie continued her family correspondence with special attention to her niece, Bess, in New York, Jack and Addie's daughter. She continued to write articles for various publications and answered letters from readers of *The Canadian Nurse*. She composed occasional speeches to nursing groups. She had kept her little walnut desk with the twisted legs and brass tassels for drawer pulls. There was no nook in the new house, but her bedroom was much larger and afforded a bright corner with a view of King Street life instead of Scovil's wharf.

At seventy-three, she felt she could decline inconvenient requests and accept only those that appealed to her. She was sometimes introduced as the oldest living, nursing graduate in North America, along with other accolades. She knew her words need not be wiser because of them, but she hoped they were. Bessie joined the Cathedral's Women's Auxiliary and encouraged Mary to sign up for the junior WA, which she did, only to be trapped into passing more sandwiches.

Roger could not decide what he wanted to do with his life. Mod and Bessie discussed it between them, then with Roger and Mary. He had no burning wish to join any profession. He had been persuaded to teach a Sunday School class at St. Margaret's Anglican Church at Salamanca, just before Morrison's Mill at the far end of Waterloo Row, a twenty-minute walk from the King Street house. The rector thought there was a little too much laughter coming from Roger's class of nine-year old boys, but at least the new, tall, young man seemed to have their attention. But that was only a once-a-week activity. What did he want to do during the week — work in a bank, an insurance office, or as a sales clerk? Nothing especially appealed.

Then, an opportunity for Roger appeared from an unanticipated source. Two of his maternal uncles, Hattie's brothers, Robert and William DuVernet, left Gagetown when young to establish an orange grove in Florida. Unfortunately Will died of a fever. Within five years Rob had built a fine orange grove, then a house, then acquired an English wife, Ella Pratt, and before long two children. In1895 their orange grove was hit by freezing temperatures that wiped out the crop. After the ruinous weather, Rob had the bright idea of digging long trenches and throwing in the oranges ruined by freezing. In the spring, hundreds of orange tree seedlings appeared, which he transplanted and sold. Encouraged by a friend who lived in Greenville, South Carolina, Rob and his family moved there. When he arrived in Greenville, he secured land on the outskirts and started The Piedmont Plant Company, inspired by his Florida experience. Remembering the late planting season in his native New Brunswick, Rob started with cabbage plants, advertising in northern newspapers. He then expanded to producing and shipping seedlings for other crops.

Rob and Ella DuVernet were among the many extended family members to whom Bessie wrote letters in early December. She explained why they had a new address, that they were still getting used to living in the city, and that Roger had not yet settled on a position and was rather at loose ends, but they were hopeful something would turn up that would appeal to him.

A few days before Christmas, a letter with an invitation surprised them all. Roger's Uncle Rob and Aunt Ella asked him to visit them, to stay with them and their numerous children, to help in the business while he was looking for something he'd like to do with the rest of his life. Roger brightened at the prospect and was grateful for the opportunity. He talked it over with Bessie, Mod, and Mary. He reasoned that he hadn't travelled except to Selkirk, he hadn't found anything to do in Fredericton, he had never met this uncle and aunt and all those DuVernet first cousins; it seemed interesting, like an adventure. He'd give it a try, especially as it wouldn't be just planting and hoeing; there would be advertising, packaging, organizing.

Bessie and Mod were relieved something had appeared that grabbed Roger's interest. Mary was pleased for her younger brother but, yet again, sad for herself. Perhaps she could visit. Roger's trunk was again filled for the long journey and, perhaps, a new way of life. A large can of maple syrup was included to remind Uncle Rob of his Canadian roots.

57

City Life
1923

On an early spring morning in 1923, Bessie sat at her walnut desk in the Fredericton house, preparing to open her mail. She picked up her silver letter opener with the mother-of-pearl handle from where it lay in one of the desk's cubbyholes. She was then ready for the ritual of stacking the envelopes in order of priority. The envelope that ended up on top was from the Victorian Order of Nurses post marked, Saint John, the twenty-second of March. The VON was dear to her heart, not surprisingly as she helped launch it twenty-five years ago. Her curiosity was piqued. She held the business sized envelope and slit open the end. They had not forgotten her. At the request of Lady Aberdeen, she was being invited to speak at their Annual General Meeting on May fifteenth about her early involvement with the VON and her connection with the organization since that time. The VON had grown to be an organization so perfectly suited to the sprawling Dominion, sparsely covered by doctors, that Bessie would forever use any power her nursing qualifications might bring to further the growth and service of such an admirable movement. She would accept the invitation without further thought, as soon as she dealt with the remainder of her letters.

A fat envelope with Roger's unmistakable hand was next on the pile, no doubt full of his news about life in South Carolina where he was helping his Uncle Rob DuVernet with his seedling company. She set it aside for reading aloud this evening when they would all be together. Mod and Mary would hang on every word. She flicked through several envelopes dealing with business, including one from the Curtis Publishing Company, which was still the mainstay of her accumulating wealth. She placed those likely asking for donations in a separate pile.

As the sun streamed in through the east window of her bedroom, Bessie sat musing about her unexpected trip before accepting and asking for details. She thought she would make a little holiday of it, perhaps arrive two days before the speech and stay two days afterwards. With two days of travel on the riverboat from Fredericton to Saint John and back, her time of absence would total a week. She had always been fond of Saint John, her birthplace, and enjoyed catching up on her relatives' lives face to face instead of through letters.

Always the organizer, Bessie had an urge to plan possible activities for Mod and Mary for the week of her absence. She knew they were perfectly capable of spending the week as usual, playing two-handed bridge when they were at loose ends. Morris had a reputation at the City Club for being a first rate bridge player where he and Lord Ashburnham were usually partners. Mary had become quite a respectable player, as well. Mod and Mary might rather like being on their own for a week, spending their time in the usual ways. Even so, Bessie decided she would make a list of possible activities for father and daughter, either together or separately. She had to admit, this was more for her satisfaction than theirs. May was two months away, so there was no rush to accumulate suggestions; she would note them as they were advertised or mentioned by friends or relatives.

As the winds of March abated and the slushiness of April's rapidly melting snow arrived, Bessie's calendar for the week she was to be absent had accumulated several entries. Mary had been asked to pass sandwiches at the Bishop's post Easter tea, the Montgomery-Campbells had invited both Mary and Mod for dinner one evening, there was to be a lantern show in the Cathedral Hall about the treatment of lepers, and a talk at the Opera House titled, "The Family," obviously well suited for a father and his adult daughter to attend. On her morning of departure, Bessie checked her valise for her speech notes and other essentials, and then left the list of definite and possible activities on the mantle, telling both Mary and Mod it was there.

On the five days of the week when Ethel came in to clean and cook, Mary and Mod settled down after breakfast to a couple of hours of two-handed bridge. They were able to tick off all of Bessie's suggestions until the Friday and then wondered what a talk on "The Family" would tell them that they didn't already know. Bessie would no doubt ask about the lecture and would be disappointed if they had not attended. The evening was mild and the walk through to Queen Street and the three blocks to the Opera House—in the same building as the City Hall—would take not more than ten minutes.

On the way Mary asked her father, "What do you suppose this is going to be about?"

"I'll tell you better on the way home," Mod quipped.

"It's probably not religious or it would be in a church hall," Mary said, keen to eliminate that possibility.

"I've heard it's a woman from Scotland, so perhaps it's how to make better porridge," Mod chuckled.

They had dallied too long over Ethel's treacle tart so were only just on time. The hall was quite full, but they spied two empty seats three rows from the front where they just had time to settle, before the speaker for the evening was introduced. Two people sat on the stage, a well-bearded and moustached gentleman and an attractive woman with curly dark hair. They spoke quietly to each other and then the gentleman stepped to the lectern.

"Good evening, Ladies and Gentlemen. I have the honour of introducing to you this evening a world famous biologist. This is not Dr. Stopes' first visit to New Brunswick. She was here in 1910 at the invitation of the Canadian Government to work on plant fossils on the shores of the Bay of Fundy, which settled a dispute about the age of those rocks. Tonight Dr. Marie Stopes, a highly regarded doctor of science, and an author will talk about her most recent book, *Married Love*.

Mod shifted his feet uneasily and crossed his legs. Mary blinked several times as she adjusted her owl eyes glasses. The speaker, fashionably dressed in a beige cloche hat, slim brown skirt and pale green jacket approached the lectern and smiled confidently at her audience. Dr. Marie Stopes read passages from her book and elaborated on their meaning. She described the science behind birth control and the precaution of abstinence at certain times of the month. She informed her stunned audience that enhanced foreplay helped satisfy both women's and men's sexual needs.

"Many men imagine that the turgid condition of an erection is due to the local accumulation of sperm and that these can only be naturally got rid of by an ejaculation. This is entirely wrong."

Scarcely anyone could concentrate on the rest of her presentation. She did not mention porridge.

Mary found herself getting warm around her neck, so she unbuttoned the top three buttons on her navy blue serge jacket. She assumed her face was red, though she hoped not matching her father's, which looked like a well boiled beet. Her friend, Margaret Hall, in front and three seats to the right was positively aflame, her curly orange hair setting off her bright red cheeks in an alarming fashion, nearly ready for the fire engine, thought Mary. At least Margaret was here with her aunt, which would be slightly less embarrassing than being here with one's father.

When Dr. Stopes finished, there was polite, thin, hand clapping. An invitation for questions brought one cowardly query about the rocks of the Bay of Fundy, which the expert cleverly answered using biological terms, attempting to bring back the topic to the avoided subject.

After all was over, no one made eye contact with friends, strangers or neighbours. A silent bolt for the door took place in as seemly an exit as was possible for an audience all wanting to appear broad minded. Outside, an unexpected drizzle had come up and provided a bland topic of conversation between Mary and her father on their walk home. The only reference to "The Family" from Mod was, "Women like that should be reined in a little."

Mary followed with, "I wonder if Aunt Bessie knew …"

*　*　*　*　*

Later that year, Bessie received a letter from an old friend from her Boston days, a Mrs. Violet Agnew. She was a childless widow living in Arizona. They had corresponded, with long letters, at Christmas over the years. This year's letter was a little late, she explained because she was having some health difficulties that would require an operation and nursing at home afterward. The letter continued; "Is there any chance, dear Bessie that you could leave your present responsibilities for a short few weeks and come to my aid? Besides, Bessie dear, it would be lovely to see you again."

Bessie showed the letter to Mod and Mary. Would they mind? Could they manage?

"You must do what you think is best," Mod replied.

"Of course," Mary added. "We'll manage just fine."

Bessie took the train to Arizona and was gone for three weeks. She then wrote to say she was bringing Mrs. Agnew back to Fredericton to continue looking after her. She did not need nursing, as such, anymore but did require care, which would be easier in Fredericton. She could have Roger's room.

It turned out that Mrs. Agnew's enormous bulk and personality filled every room she occupied and unsettled the routines of the house. Bessie explained to Mod and Mary that she and Mrs. Agnew had been very good friends in their younger days. She had endured a difficult life in various ways and would soon settle down. Mary noticed Mrs. Agnew was indeed settling down — settling down to eat! She had an enormous appetite. Edith adjusted her recipes to allow for Mrs. Agnew's second helpings of everything. Mary also noticed that whatever Mrs. Agnew wanted, Mrs. Agnew was given. Aunt Bessie produced a new lap rug when Mrs. Agnew complained of feeing chilly, a new walking cane when she said hers was too short, and she asked Edith to make Mrs. Agnew's favourite dishes more often.

Mod spent more time at his Club, quoting Lord Asburnham's witticisms on his return. Mary wished she had a club where she could escape.

376

She had met Margaret Hall at a party. They were about the same age and she, too, had lost her mother. Margaret helped out most days in her father's bookstore on Queen Street. Mary now often visited the store to chat with her when she wasn't serving a customer.

Mary also began to regularly call on the Col. Montgomery-Campbells household, which included three unmarried daughters close to her age. One daughter, however, was the subject of the exclusive attentions of a handsome bachelor at parties, so might leave that category before long. The Montgomery-Campbells lived in a spacious house on the corner of Regent and Aberdeen Streets, and seemed to have some connection with the Scovil family or perhaps the Robinsons; Mary wasn't quite sure but it made her relationship with them special. Her wit and spontaneity were appreciated and she always felt welcome; something she now felt less and less in her own home. The Montgomery-Campbell house was on extensive grounds with many large hardwoods and smaller evergreens, which help cut the noise from the railway tracks not far away. Mary surmised the house was older than the tracks.

Mrs. Agnew did not play bridge, nor was she interested in learning. The conversation at meal times usually centered around Mrs. Agnew, her previous life and her views on everything. Mary occupied a good deal of time writing to Roger every week. She kept up a steady correspondence with Dorrie, and with her sisters, Gertrude, and Elizabeth. Gertrude was busy with her job in Vancouver and Elizabeth was happy in England, having most recently written they were expecting a baby next January.

58

Mary Takes a Bold Step with Denison Bliss

One day in midsummer when Bessie was in her room at her desk, Mary knocked lightly on the door.

"Come in, dear," her aunt responded.

Mary closed the door and asked, "Would you still be willing to send me to the Boston Cooking School?"

"Of course, dear, if that's what you would like to do. I think it's a good choice I'll give you the address and you can write for an application form. A term will be starting in September, I expect."

After various mailings of forms and references, Mary was accepted for a one-year diploma course beginning on September third, which could be extended for a second year if she wished to specialize. She and Bessie began planning for this big step.

Every now and then Morrie and sometimes Mad with baby Courtenay would take the day train to Fredericton, usually on errands relating to the farm. The baby, now an enthusiastic walker, with only occasional falls, was the object of everyone's devotion as she tottered from room to room. Mary found sitting on the floor was the best position to amuse and keep track of her niece.

During one visit, Mad explained that Courtenay was not yet christened and they were planning on having this done at the Amherst Parish Church in early August where Mad had been welcomed into the Anglican faith.

Aunt Bessie," Mad asked, "Would you be Courtenay's godmother?"

"That's very thoughtful of you, dear. I should love to but I can't leave Mrs. Agnew. Perhaps Mary would stand for me."

"Oh! Yes, that would be nice," Mad replied, disappointed, but gracious.

"I would be honoured," Mary responded, pleased to have something to look forward to while waiting for Boston.

The christening was set for Saturday August second. Mary would stay for two nights in the rambling Bliss house on Church Street in Amherst, which had stained glass windows on either side of the front door, a spacious entrance hall with embossed wallpaper covered with green and purple peacocks that went all the way up the curving staircase to its eight bedrooms.

Mary was familiar with it from being at Morrie and Mad's wedding where she met Mad's two sisters, Fuddy and Gwen, one little brother Donald, and three older half-brothers, Gerald, Botsford, and Denison.

Elizabeth Courtenay howled, as expected, at having cold water splashed on her forehead on an otherwise warm day, but the sight of Mary's familiar owl eyes glasses and smile calmed her. Botsford, in charge of the kitchen, served a well prepared lunch at the Church Street house. Gerald, the eldest of the three brothers, now with a medical practice in Altoona, Pennsylvania was absent, but Denison, the youngest, the one Mary had noticed at the Edgehill chapel so long ago, because of his big ears, was there. She counted nine sitting around the dining table, plus the reason for the gathering on her mother's lap. After lunch, Dr. Bliss, very much in control, organized everyone for family photographs along one side of the house where ornamental bushes showed to good effect. The arrangement for the photographs had Mary standing next to Denison. When the session ended, she mentioned remembering him from Edgehill so long ago, and then added, "There's nothing planned until teatime; let's go for a walk."

Denison was a little startled by the remembrance and the invitation but smiled and quickly said, "OK."

They made predictable conversation about the day's events as they walked down the street and into a small neighbourhood park where they sat on a bench and began to talk more personally.

"Your brother seems to have got over the war pretty well," Denison commented.

"Yes. You know he was a prisoner for two years," Mary replied. "He told us the worst part of that was boredom, until they were allowed to work on farms in Holland. But he had nightmares about being in the trenches and under attack for a while after he came home. What about you?"

"Not good. I still have nightmares. Thunderstorms drive me crazy. Dad thinks I should get a job but I don't like being around a lot of people. He's lined up one that might work—timekeeper at the railway station in Fort Fairfield, Maine. There's a little house near the tracks that goes with the job. I'm going next week."

"Must be hard to go through all that. Lightning scares me, too. When I was little I saw a barn go up in flames after being hit by lightning."

They sat there, side by side, each silently remembering their terrors. Denison had confided in her. Mary felt comfortable doing the same.

"I'm fed up with being at home. Aunt Bessie has sort of adopted a fat slob to look after, an old friend who has taken over the house. I'm going to escape though, I'm going to a cooking school in Boston in September."

"Do you like to cook?"

"Sort of. Individual dishes, like cakes and pies. I wouldn't be able to do what Botsford does, a big meal for a crowd, doing everything at once."

"Gerald has the brains in our family. Bots and I were no good in school. He cooked in lumber camps a few winters. That's where he learned to do it. I haven't found anything I'm good at doing. At least, I now have a job that might work out."

The two unsettled souls, each with their own thoughts, sat looking at the faint clouds barely moving over the treetops.

Mary turned slightly toward Denison and decided to take a bold step; "I've been thinking. We both seem to be equally unhappy. We could try to make one another happier if we were together. When I'm due to leave Fredericton for Boston in late August, I could change at McAdam, take the train north and cross over to Fort Fairfield. We could elope. There must be a minister in Fort Fairfield who could marry us."

Denison, who had been staring at his hands, sat up and looked directly into Mary's eyes. She noticed how blue his eyes were and that he seemed to have grown into his ears. They seemed almost normal.

"Are you serious?" he asked with both unbelief and elation in his voice.

"Yes, but it must be our secret. I don't think our folks would approve. Aunt Bessie wants me to have some qualifications, but I'm fed up with my life."

Denison's hand shot over and grasped one of Mary's as though he were grabbing a lifeline in a rough sea.

"Dad has warned me not to get tied up with a girl until I have a good job, but the one in Fort Fairfield might lead to something better. If you're serious, I'm all for it."

"I'm serious. Let's make a pact. Agreed?"

"Agreed!"

Denison looked around, saw no one, bent toward Mary, and planted a quick kiss on her cheek to seal the agreement. He suddenly saw this sister of his brother-in-law quite differently. She seemed to believe in him when everyone else had more or less given up, he'd messed up so often. Perhaps she would help chase away those nightmares. He wanted to kiss her again, give her a big hug and a real kiss, but that wouldn't do in public, so he squeezed her hand. She squeezed back and considered herself engaged-to-be-married. She smiled broadly at her future husband.

"Write to me with your address when you get to Fort Fairfield. I'll give you my address. I'll write back and let you know when I'll arrive," Mary said, organizing her thoughts and then added. "We should be getting back.

We need to be there for afternoon tea. Oh yes, and find a minister to marry us shortly after I arrive."

Mary stood up and glanced back at this now memorable park bench, never to be forgotten as the place where desperation had pushed her to propose to a man. But her life now had a strange new feeling about it, which she liked. It wasn't exactly romantic excitement, but it was the next best thing. Denison, too, was suddenly feeling different about his life. His sense of drifting had been replaced by the anticipation of being a married man. He wanted to grasp and hold Mary's hand as they walked back to the house, but instead they were content to exchange secret smiles, somehow knowing what the other was feeling and that they should give no sign to the others of what had happened between them. Just before they entered the house, Mary quietly reminded Denison about the letters they needed to exchange and added that he should also write back to confirm he had received hers about the date and time of arrival. She was taking no chances. Later, she found a piece of paper, wrote her address on it, and passed it to her intended.

*   *   *   *   *

Mary and Bessie gradually filled two medium sized trunks over the rest of the summer. Mary made no objection when her aunt recommended mostly practical clothes. She was not expecting a demanding social life in Fort Fairfield. As Bessie talked of what she might expect in Boston, Mary could not look her in the eye. Over all those years since Bessie came to Meadowlands after their mother died, giving up her career to care for the family, she had never before knowingly deceived her aunt on important matters. She could only hope Bessie and her father would understand.

During the second week in August, Mod, Bessie and Mary spent a day at Meadowlands. Mary encouraged Mad to talk about her family. She said that Fuddy, was not really her sister, but her cousin. Fuddy's mother was her mother's sister who died when Fuddy was two and her stricken father could not cope, so the solution was adoption. Fuddy and Denny were about the same age so it worked out well, especially since Denny's mother died when he was born. Her real name is Frances, but Denny couldn't say that and called her "Fuddy." The name stuck. At that point Courtenay announced she had finished napping so questions about other family members, including Denny, remained unasked. Mary realized that knowing your mother died when you were born must be a terrible thing. She would soon learn more about her husband first hand.

59

Farm and Family with Denny
1924

When Mary got off the train in Fort Fairfield, Maine, she was glad to see Denny but shocked by the primitive house that came with his job. It was a mere shack, but Denny had at least prepared a rabbit stew to welcome her. They carted Mary's luggage the short distance from the station to the house, and then, before eating, walked to the nearby home of the minister Denny had contacted about performing a marriage ceremony. It happened the minister was also the Justice of the Peace and could, therefore, issue the marriage license as well as marry them. For $2.00 and the assurance they were Christians, he performed the ceremony. He was not concerned they were Canadians. They were both over twenty-one years of age and could be married in Maine if that's what they wanted to do.

The living conditions were rough. Denny's pay was very low, and the requirements of the job with the railroad were proving difficult for him to handle. Winter was coming and the shack needed to be improved and insulated to be livable. Before the week was out, Mary had the distinct feeling she had made a mistake, but she was now a married woman and determined to make the best of the situation.

She was, however, buoyed up by the sense of freedom and autonomy she now enjoyed in many small ways, right down to making fudge without asking Aunt Bessie for permission. The immediate bleakness of her situation was modified by the sense that her life was now her own. Denny appreciated Mary's strengths, her determined spirit, skills, and initiative, and he treated her with consideration and kindness. She quickly realized Denny had certain weaknesses that bordered on incompetence but was grateful that he in no way tried to dominate her.

At the end of the first week in Fort Fairfield, Mary summoned the courage to write Bessie, knowing she would be expecting a letter with a Boston postmark. She forthrightly apologized for her deception and explained why she chose marriage over education. Bessie and Mod both wrote back saying how surprised they were at her boldness but understood her decision and wished her happiness in her new life. Bessie included the gift of a generous cheque.

After a few reminders from Mary, Denny finally wrote his father about his new status. Dr. Bliss was equally surprised and said he hoped being married would help "straighten him out." He was more than a little pleased Denny had chosen a respectable girl from a good family, in fact, Madeline's sister in law, rather than the sister of one of his drinking friends. The letter to his father had omitted the detail about who had done the choosing.

Denny's performance as a timekeeper for the railroad did not go well. He tried hard to fulfill requirements of the job, but the demand for close attention and precision recording were simply beyond him. Just as Mary began to think she was pregnant, Denny was fired. She urged him to write his father and ask if they could live temporarily in the Bliss hunting camp on the Tyndall Road near Amherst. Dr. Bliss agreed and urged them to come at once to get settled in before the fall rains or early snow made the dirt road difficult to navigate. Denny and Mary travelled by train directly to Amherst, not stopping in Fredericton, partly to save time but also because she did not want to face her family considering the rocky start of her marriage to Denny.

The hunting camp was a substantial two story building but on a road where electrical lines had not yet been strung. They would use kerosene lamps, an outhouse, and carry water from a nearby brook. Mary, thinking of "Meadowlands," christened their embryo farm "Beaverbrook" in honour of the other nearby residents. Mary wrote to Bessie and Mod explaining the need for their move and describing their present circumstances.

The first task was to bring in supplies for the winter because when snow came they would be somewhat isolated, though travel by horse and sleigh would still be possible. Mary carefully compiled a list of necessities, picturing the Meadowlands pantry and checking with Denny on the tools he might need. He added two more buckets for water, a better axe, and a few other hand tools. Dr. Bliss agreed to bring them out in his Ford.

When Bessie heard of the move she put together a box of linens, including heavy linen sheets, perhaps forgetting there would be no laundry maid. Mary was grateful for anything and everything that came their way. It was especially good news when Dr. Bliss told them his efforts to get a small war service disability pension for Denny had proved successful. At least they wouldn't be destitute or completely dependent on their families.

During visits to Amherst, Mary learned more about Denny's past from conversations with Fuddy. His mother died from "childbed fever" within two weeks of his birth. His father married again and sired four more children. At twelve, Denny was sent to Kings College School in Windsor, Nova Scotia. He hated the experience, ran away, and was brought back home to become a reluctant student in Amherst. At seventeen, he went to work in a lumber camp and discovered the power of alcohol. Later, he and his best friend enlisted in the army to fight in the Great War. Denny saw his best friend killed in front of him and returned home with terrible nightmares. It was called "shell shock" and Denny had come to rely on his "medicine" as a way to deal with it.

Dr. Bliss hoped that with a wife, a child on the way and a farm to develop, Denny would pull himself together and become more stable and responsible. However, Denny became friends with the Trenholm brothers who lived further along the Tyndall Road. They operated a still in their barn, which made Denny's "medicine" readily available.

Mary's first child died after four days of labour and only a breath or two. It was a close thing for her as well, but determination to survive prevented her from joining the baby. After recovery, she worked hard to make Beaverbrook into a successful small farm. They acquired a barn, chickens, a cow, a horse, wagon, and sleigh, mostly through Bessie's generosity. They had only moderate success with basic vegetables until Denny learned how to deal with Colorado potato beetles and other garden pests. After that, and with manure from their animals, garden production improved.

Mary had to wait longer than she expected for some of her hopes to be realized. For her second pregnancy, she abandoned her father-in-law's free medical attention, a decision related to the trauma and loss of the first pregnancy. Dr. Purdy saw her through two pregnancies and deliveries with no complications. Diana Elizabeth was born in 1925. Denny seemed to genuinely enjoy being a father. One evening, while Mary was clearing the kitchen and Diana was fretting before her next feeding, she picked up the baby and placed her in Denny's arms. She instantly stopped complaining and smiled up at her Daddy, who smiled back.

Mary observed all this from the kitchen doorway and then spontaneously asked, "Are you happy?"

"Yeah," Denny replied, "as happy as I'll ever be. Are you?"

"Yes," Mary said, and more or less meant it. "We're a real family now."

One day while Diana was still an infant, she was resting in her cream coloured, wicker perambulator on the front porch of the camp when a large hawk swooped in and upended the carriage, baby, and all. Neither baby nor perambulator were damaged, but Diana's screaming terrified her parents who came running to the rescue.

When Bessie received Mary's letter describing the incident, she insisted her niece and family should have a decent house with an enclosed porch. She wrote that Sears, Roebuck and Company in Chicago has complete house packages that can be delivered to any railway station in North America. The package includes everything needed to assemble a modern two-story house: precut lumber, doors, windows, siding, walls, flooring, stairways, interior trim, roofing, nails, paint, chimney bricks, cement block foundation, plumbing, wiring, all fixtures, and detailed construction plans. Bessie offered to finance the purchase and construction of a new Sears, Roebuck house at Beaverbrook. A few weeks later the house package arrived at the Amherst station. A local carpenter and his crew were engaged to transport the materials and build the house.

Mary was grateful that once again Aunt Bessie had taken command and made this happen. Not only would she no longer have to guard her baby when she was on the porch, but Mary would be able to live with her family in a new modern house of her own instead of a borrowed hunting camp.

Construction went well until the discovery that some essential materials were missing. Repeated telegrams and letters to the company by Bessie brought no results, so she arranged for the missing materials to be delivered from a local supplier. Mary and baby Diana "supervised" this miracle of construction from a safe distance during the summer of 1927. The result was a bright yellow house with varnished Douglas fir interior trim. It had running water that for now needed to be pumped up from a nearby spring, a full bathroom, and a wood-burning furnace in the basement with hot air registers in every room.

The house was set behind a spacious lawn and the next summer a colourful flower garden, planned, planted and tended by Mary, bordered the front and one side. Three shades of blue delphiniums sat near the house, clumps of English buttercups, mauve asters, velvety wine red double Shirley poppies took over the next row and little orange California poppies interspersed with blue forget-me-nots grew next to the lawn. The few houses along the Tyndall Road were either white or weathered board, with perhaps a lilac bush or tiger lilies in the yard. The new Bliss house, with its colourful departure and lovely blooming flower beds caused the drivers of cars and wagons to slow down and admire the plantings as they passed.

The camp was not abandoned. It became a rather grand hen house. The upper floor was put to another "creative" use. A sizeable blot on Mary's happiness was Denny's need to visit the Trenholm brothers at least once a week. Rather than fading with the passing of time, Denny's need to calm his demons with alcohol increased. He was often not back in time to milk Daisy.

Hearing the distressed cow bellowing from the barn tore at Mary's memory of her own burning, bound breasts after her first baby did not survive to suckle.

She repeatedly reminded Denny that leaving a cow past milking time was against the law. The nagging added to Denny's pressures until he found a solution. At his urging, the Trenholm brothers agreed to help set up a still in the upper floor of the old camp providing Denny kept his mouth shut about it when he was in town. No one wanted the Mounties sniffing around. Denny then made a point of milking Daisy every evening before he "inspected" the hen house and collected the eggs. Mary grew to associate her husband's flushed face with a small basket of fresh eggs placed on the white enamel pastry table with the dark blue line around the edge, which stood just inside the back door.

Bessie believed there was a chance that Denison's behaviour could be improved if she helped to establish a proper income for the family. She first provided capital for a muskrat farm. A nearby marsh provided an ideal site and there was a good market for the fur. It involved enclosing an area of the marsh with wire fencing and sinking it deep into the bottom. Alas, the fence was not deep enough and all the muskrats escaped. Then a silver fox farm was created, starting with four spacious pens. Before the new lumber could weather, disaster struck; Denny failed to separate the new kits from the adult males, and the fathers killed them all. Next, a soft fruit farm was attempted, but Denny did not prune the currant, gooseberry and raspberry bushes properly and made no plan for marketing the fruit.

Beaverbrook produced just about enough basic vegetables to see them through the winter. Their cultivated strawberries were enough for summer eating and a good shelf of jam. Wild blueberries in the old field on the edge of the woods produced an abundance of fruit, easily harvested. Cranberries from the marsh were plentiful in the fall. Milk, cream, kitchen churned butter, buttermilk, chickens and eggs were all part of the menu. Occasionally, Denny supplied speckled trout or wild rabbit.

When there was not enough money from the monthly pension left for essentials because Denny had "entertained" his old army buddies in town, an SOS from Mary to Bessie brought quick results. Eventually, to save Mary the embarrassment of a begging letter, Bessie arranged for a regular money order to appear near the end of every month.

In the spring of 1929, a second daughter, Virginia Scovil, joined the Beaverbrook family.

Mary's siblings all sent their congratulations. Bessie wrote that she and Mod were especially pleased, and now that Diana had a playmate there was no need to try for more children.

60

Meadowlands Sold & Transatlantic Sojourning
1926–1934

In 1924, Morrie announced an unexpected change of occupation. He and Mad and little Courtenay left Meadowlands and moved to England. With investment assistance from Aunt Bessie, Morrie went into the automobile garage business in London with his brother-in-law, Hayden Villiers, Elizabeth's husband.

Meadowlands was put up for sale and quickly purchased as a summer home, by Herbert Parlee, a wealthy man from Saint John. Five hundred acres of rich interval land and four hundred acres of woodland that had been granted to Samuel Scovil (1773-1856) over a century earlier now passed out of Scovil hands for the first time. A news story about the transaction ran in *The Gleaner* under the headline, "Meadowlands Sold for $20,000."

In 1926 Bessie and Mod made another momentous decision. They sold the Fredericton house and entirely changed their way of life. Twice a year they began crossing the Atlantic by steamer, spending sunny winters in Greenville, South Carolina and spring and summer in Bishop's Stortford, northeast of London. Roger now had a good paying position as a sales representative for a barbershop equipment company. He was married to Rose and they already had two young children, Roger Jr. and Rosemary. They had a big house and welcomed Mod and Bessie for six month sojourns each year. Grandfather and Great Aunt were helpful around the house and grounds and especially with the children.

When spring came, they packed their steamer trunks, entrained to New York for the comforts of an ocean liner that took them to Southampton. From there they travelled to Bishop's Stortford, to stay with Morrie and Mad and their three children: Courtenay, Ann and Richard. Elizabeth and Hayden, along with sons, George and John, also opened their house at Little Missenden in Buckinghamshire, spreading the responsibility of providing a seasonal residence for their aging relatives. Wherever they were, Bessie more than made sure she and Mod were not a financial burden.

Bessie especially loved arriving in England in the spring where they were greeted on every hand by the profuse blossoming of longstanding and well-kept flower gardens both public and private. There was something about this tradition of tending and care that made her feel "this is the way the world should be."

*   *   *   *   *

In 1929, when Mary's daughter, Virginia, was not quite three months old, a financial disaster shook the world. The American Stock Market crashed and what came to be known as The Great Depression changed the lives of millions. Bessie's income came mostly from investments, especially in the Curtis Publishing Company in Philadelphia. Her compensation for sixteen years as a contributing Associate Editor of *The Ladies' Home Journal* was paid partly in Curtis stocks. *The Ladies' Home Journal* was highly profitable and grew to have the largest circulation of any magazine in the world. Bessie often took the option of buying more Curtis stock. Other well-advised stock purchases contributed to her being a millionaire on paper when Black Tuesday dawned on October 29, 1929.

Mary heard about the "Crash" on the large Atwater Kent radio that had come to her after the sale of the Fredericton house. She wrote to her aunt on October 30th, wondering whether her investments had been badly affected. Bessie replied from England:

> *It is all so upsetting, a complete disaster for so many. As I have investments in a number of places, I am hoping some will still pay a little or at least eventually recover. I do not plan to sell anything now. Morrie thinks his livelihood will not be affected very much and I daresay Roger's will not be either, to any extent. We have our tickets to sail from Southampton in mid-November …*

Mary and Denison and their little family fared better than many others during The Great Depression. She heard stories on the radio about men, unable to face financial ruin, jumping from the windows of tall buildings in New York, and of others who were "riding the rails" back and forth across Canada looking for non-existent jobs. Beaverbrook's standard of living remained about the same based on Denny's small pension, varying success with crops and cheques from Bessie, which she was able to manage for the rest of her life.

Mary's ability to weather constant disappointment was supported by the frequent arrival of letters from her siblings, her father, and especially from Aunt Bessie. Walking out to the tin mailbox by the side of the dusty or snowy or muddy road was often happily rewarded with family correspondence. Bessie's letters from England or South Carolina were easily spotted. The envelopes were always a lovely shade of blue. This continual exchange of letters provided contact with others besides her unreliable husband and her two much loved but needy girls. Aside from infrequent buggy or sleigh rides into Amherst, letters were her only reminder of how the rest of the world normally lives. Essential shopping or medical or dental appointments and a few hours of female company with Fuddy continued to be highlights of her life.

Mary's summers were made miserable by hay fever triggered by a field of flowering timothy hay growing between their house and the Tyndall Road. Migraine headaches, unaffected by the latest "cures" continued to flatten Mary, driving her to her darkened bedroom which gave some relief from the coloured lights but not from the pain. Dr. Purdy once told her they could be brought on by worry, but he knew better than to suggest she stop worrying. There was not much the residents of the little town of Amherst did not know about Dr. Bliss's wayward son.

Concern for her girls' futures was always at the back of Mary's thoughts, unexpressed but increasingly urgent. The East Amherst one-room schoolhouse did a moderately good job, but only until grade nine. How could they afford to move into Amherst? Town life would not suit Denny. Perhaps Diana could stay with Fuddy and Joe during the week when the time came. Would they want a country girl in their childless, neat-as-a-pin, beautifully decorated home? Diana was becoming very strong willed. Would she agree to the change? Would Virginia be too lonely without her? Were there other solutions?

Mary had always been gregarious and longed to have women friends. A few letters a year from Dorrie Lee in Saint John were not enough. Activities in Fredericton as depicted in the Daily Gleaner—a gift subscription from Bessie—became less and less relevant to her life at isolated Beaverbrook. Denny's answers to her questions about the greater world when he returned from cashing his pension cheque in Amherst were disappointingly vague, always tinged with his friends' entertainment.

With each letter from her relatives, Mary imagined their changing experiences as best she could. Her knowledge of life outside the Maritimes was limited to her childhood experience of New York and Atlantic City, and a visit with her Edgehill friend, Helen Heaney, near Ottawa years ago. Listening to the radio gave her a sense of what was happening in the larger world, but it was all second hand and often depressing news.

Bessie's letters were a lifeline for her quick mind and vivid imagination. They were so full of description and detail that Mary sometimes felt like a fly on the wall, looking out of her aunt's window toward St. Michael's spire, through an English mist. When Morrie and Mad drove them to visit rhododendron and azalea gardens, heavy with blossoms, Bessie wrote they were like peonies on bushes, only with a greater variety of reds plus yellows and oranges, knowing that Mary would never have seen these exotic plants but would enjoy imaging their beauty. These imagination stretching letters with their splashes of colour, excitement, and vivid descriptions landing in her roadside mailbox kept Mary going through those lonely years.

61

"You have two roles, Miss Scovil,
the nurse in charge and the patient."
England 1934

A heavy fog had not completely dispersed, though the little blue enamel clock on her bedside table announced to Bessie that midday was approaching. She must have been napping. From one of her two windows she saw the remaining wisps lift off St. Michael's steeple, an inspiring view in any weather. It was nearly the same view depicted in Morrie's watercolour that now hung on the wall to the right of the window. He must have done the painting from the window of this bedroom she had been using for the last six months. Bessie suddenly remembered the drawings and paintings Morrie made as Christmas gifts for family members in the years after she came to Meadowlands. That was long ago but seemed almost like yesterday. She was glad to see Morrie was still painting.

Madeline had long since cleared away the breakfast tray, though Bessie had not been aware of it. It had held a four-minute egg, two pieces of toast standing in a little silver rack, a pretty little dish with a daisy design of Seville orange marmalade, a pot of Darjeeling tea and a small jug of milk all laid out on a tray cloth embroidered with forget-me-nots that Courtenay had done in her school needlework class.

This had been the routine for the past week—ever since Madeline called the doctor following Bessie's wave of weakness when she was hurrying to go shopping in the High Street with Mod, a routine she initiated to help them both get daily exercise. Her brother had become more and more sedentary since recovering from an operation last year and was putting on unhealthy weight. Her medical knowledge reminded her it was easier to prevent weight gain than to reduce it once it was a fact. Mod was eleven years her junior and usually tried to act on her good advice. With Bessie's sudden weakness, there was no walk that day, nor since. Dr. Prentice ordered bed rest for the once vigorous, eighty-five year-old Canadian aunt of Mr. Scovil. She complied, of course, having spent

393

her working life paying attention to sensible doctors and finding ways to incorporate her occasionally differing views. She knew he was right. She knew her strength was diminishing.

Her mother would have said she was "breaking up" but she could not believe she was there yet. There were so many more things she planned to do. She wanted to complete and publish a series of one page children's stories that she had started to amuse Ann and Richard when they were only seven and four at the beginning of her annual six-month visit. She needed to do something about bringing her will up to date, now that her stocks were worth so little, though Morrie and his lawyer had looked after that on the basis of percentages rather than on fixed amounts. She knew hand written wills were legal so she would write a page or two, distributing her few personal possessions to her family.

Bessie leaned back and closed her eyes. "Will Mod and I ever cross the Atlantic again for those sunny winters with Roger and Rose and their two little ones in Greenville? It had been the perfect solution for eight years — six months on each side of the Atlantic. I was sensible to sell the house in Fredericton once Mary and Roger left. I don't think we are much of a burden, at least not financially. I see to that. And we visit Elizabeth and Hayden and the boys once a month nearer London to give Madeline and Morrie a little time without us. It's lovely to see Elizabeth happy with her two dear boys. Hayden is a little stiff, but I think he is just shy; so many Englishmen are."

As Bessie reflected further, her innate optimism was tinged with realism. "My dear mother lived to be well over ninety I could do the same, but I'm beginning to think that's unlikely. Is it even desirable? I have written so much about looking forward to life after death … now is the time to think more about matters of faith. Mod is so much younger, but I don't think he'll make very old bones; he has that washed-out look, not a healthy colour. He would not be penniless or at least could afford to help whichever son he would end up staying with. If I had consulted a clairvoyant in the spring of 1929, as Elizabeth and I did two years ago about her boys' weak chests, there might have been a different outcome. She just might have forecast the crash that autumn. I would have sold my shares for a good sum and not lost a fortune, as I did. Oh, well, Mother coped with Father's bankruptcy and didn't become bitter."

Madeline knocked and opened the door. "Aunt Bessie, are you ready to move to the window? Lunch will be ready in a little over a half hour."

"Yes, Mad, dear, just give me your hand. I should empty my bladder while I'm up."

Medical terms had stayed with Bessie. Mad's two sisters were nurses and her father a doctor so they did not seem inappropriate. Once Bessie was comfortable in the armchair near St. Michael's window, Mod called out through the half open door, whether the patient would like a visitor.

"Of course, dear. Come in, I'm all settled."

Mod arranged a chair so Bessie would not have to twist her head to look at him. They talked about possible readiness for travel. It was now mid-October. They usually left before the November dampness was too advanced.

"Let's see how I am in a week or two. Dr. Prentice said he would call tomorrow afternoon. I hope he says I can walk around a little. What about you? We should both be fit enough to enjoy the voyage."

"Anytime Bess. My scar area doesn't hurt any more."

"We better not reserve tickets until the doctor gives permission. I don't want to be under the care of a ship's doctor. They always seem to be escaping from something on land—a poor diagnosis or an unpopular decision."

Ann and Richard, home from their dame school for lunch, peeked in through the open door.

"Come in, dears; did you have a good morning?"

"Yes." laughed Ann as she tossed her head, swinging a swath of straight, blond hair across her shoulder. "Miss Nicholson had a streak of chalk on her big nose and couldn't understand why we were all laughing. She was very cross when she couldn't find out why but the head called her outside for something and when she came back there was no chalk mark, so we went back to boring sums"

"They made an awful din. We could hear it in my Form," Richard piped up as he climbed up on to the plaid rug covering his great Aunt Bessie's lap.

"You remind me so much of your Daddy," Bessie said to the cuddling five year old, as she thought of her "dear boy," Morrie, in the Meadowland days so long ago.

"How was your morning?"

"We learned the six times table—like a little verse. It was sort of fun."

"Lunch is ready. Wash your hands and come now," their mother called. She shooed them into the breakfast room where lunch was set, since there would be only four. Madeline brought in Bessie's tray and set it on the small table, making sure she could reach everything. Madeline really missed Courtenay, now thirteen and in her second year at boarding school. She had been a great help with the little ones, making sure they were on time for school and talented in so many ways. Madeline could always count on seeing Court's red hair pop up when summoned by Miss Tucker to receive first prize for English and for her artwork at the end of term.

Mod took Richard's hand to make leaving the comfort of Bessie's lap easier and helped him get promptly to the lunch table. He realized how much he would soon miss this little ritual with his grandson. Once the children were fed and tidied, they returned to their school a short walk up the street.

Madeline had an afternoon committee meeting of the Women's Institute at the home of a neighbour. Before she left she told Bessie and Mod where she would be if they needed her. They did not. Mod dozed in a comfortable armchair in Bess's room most of the afternoon. She did the same after turning over in her mind how well she would need to feel before reserving places on a steamship. What if the doctor did not give her permission to travel? She could ignore his caution or they could travel later than usual. The gales that come with the Equinox were now past, but there could be bad weather almost anytime in the North Atlantic, but that wouldn't deter them. A little smile played across her face as she thought what good sailors they had become over the past eight years. She felt sure Madeline and Morrie would not mind if they waited until late November or even early December. Bessie drifted off, occasionally opening her eyes to focus a bit on St. Michael's spire, which was the highest point in the town and seemed to beckon the red brick and half-timbered houses up the hill from the flat where the commuter railway station stood beside the Stort River.

When her meeting was over Madeline did not linger with the chatty hostess. She knew tea would be appreciated at home. Bessie and Mod heard Mad in the kitchen and were fully awake when she came through the bedroom door with a tray of tea and digestive biscuits. Bessie requested Madeline's arm for a trip to the bathroom, after which they all concentrated on enjoying the tea and biscuits.

"I would like to get up and dress for dinner," Bessie said as they finished the tea. "I'm feeling much stronger."

"If you're sure." Mad replied. "A little exercise shouldn't hurt. I just want to put something in the oven, then I'll come back and help you dress, and perhaps you can have a bath first."

Mod announced he would go for a walk toward Ann and Richard's school, as it is nearly time they were let out. Madeline ran the water, made sure Bessie had clean undergarments to put on, her robe nearby and left her to a relaxing bath. Bessie stretched out in the high, porcelain tub, letting the liquid warmth soothe her old joints, noting how thin her legs had become, almost emaciated. For an instant a vision of Meadowlands shot past her consciousness, the days before their splendid bathroom, the days of bathing in that old tin tub. "I'm like an old cat," Bessie thought, "already on my ninth life! Saint John, Douglas, Boston, Concord, Newport, Meadowlands, Fredericton, South Carolina and Bishop's Stortford plus all those interesting trips to the Italian Lakes, Alaska and a dozen other places. Must make an effort to get back on my feet. Mod needs a winter in South Carolina. I can see such sorrow in Morrie's eyes when he looks at me now. I have no fear of death, but I will be sad to leave my dear boy and all my family."

A little shiver wrinkled through Bessie's body. She bent forward and turned on the hot water tap for a few moments. The gas flame in the water heater jumped to life with a hiss. Slowly, she set about washing herself. Madeline knocked and came in, discretely offering her a large, white bath towel as she finished and then helping her over the high-sided tub.

"That was refreshing, dear, but I think I will have a little rest before I dress."

Madeline hoped she had not been rash in suggesting a bath, especially without the doctor's approval. As soon as Bessie was back on her bed, her eyes had difficulty staying open. Madeline returned to the children who were chattering about the excitements of school while eating their "tea" of sardines on toast, followed by baked apple stuffed with raisins and topped with Bird's custard. By the time they finished, their mother had the dining table set for the grown-ups dinner and the smell of roast leg of lamb was beginning to announce the menu.

"Can we play out a bit, Mummy," asked Ann, already headed for the back door with Richard. "We need to do more training to get Alphonse to jump through a hoop. He's the laziest cat in Bishop Stortford!"

"Alright, if you don't scream. Aunt Bessie is resting and Grandfather is probably dozing over the paper. Oh, and bring me six sprigs from the mint bed."

Madeline had time to clean the Brussels sprouts before she glanced at the clock and realized Morrie's train would be arriving in less than ten minutes. She checked that Mod was awake and told him he was in charge — children playing in the garden, Bessie resting. She grabbed the keys to the old Rover and called to the children, deeply engrossed in enticing the wary cat, that she'd be a few minutes going to the station and not to forget the mint.

Morrie had no wait. He walked out of the station door just as his wife drew up. He kissed her on the cheek after sliding in beside her over the well-worn, brown leather upholstery. They briefly caught up on their day. He told Mad that Anthony Hoists, the company in which he was one of three partners, was expanding.

After Morrie and Hayden sold Hamilton Motors for a good price, they teamed up with Anthony Hoists—an American manufacturer—to run their London branch. Oddly, Morrie had taken to business and the English way of life, though initially he wondered whether he should give up on agriculture completely. Luckily, Madeline easily fell in with what was expected of her in English society, already having had a taste of British ways and manners through her years at Edgehill, which was staffed almost entirely with mistresses from the Mother Country.

As soon as the Rover was garaged, Madeline warned the children they had five minutes before bedtime. Morrie examined the progress Ann and Richard were making toward "Puss-In-Boots" becoming a circus animal. Since Alphonse was a compliant feline, they were able to push him through the hoop, but he hadn't yet made up his mind to do any jumping. On her way to check on the lamb, Madeline opened Bessie's door a crack and found her awake.

"How are you feeling?" she inquired.

"Help me to the WC, please," Bessie responded.

As she offered the assistance needed, Mad noticed Bessie's weakness and unsureness of step seemed greater than earlier in the day. She was glad the doctor would come tomorrow.

"I think I'd better have a tray, Mad," Bessie reported as she settled in the armchair by the window. "Sorry to put you to more trouble, but I don't have the energy to dress."

As she rested, Bessie watched St. Michaels spire being enveloped in early evening wisps of smoke-like fog. She wore her heavy dressing gown plus the warm, Black Watch plaid rug on her lap and tucked around her knees. Mod and Morrie joined her, each with a glass of sherry in their hands, while Mad hustled the children through the last of their day and into their beds.

Morrie could smell the lamb and knew he was expected to make the mint sauce. He had noticed the leaves, not yet wilted, sitting on the chopping board where Ann had put them. Mad flattered him by saying he sprinkled just the right amount of sugar on the leaves before chopping and adding just the right touch of vinegar. He looked forward to this simple ritual; it was at least something he could do to help his competent but overbusy wife. It was also self-interest, being partial, as he was, to a good mint sauce with his lamb.

After preparing the mint sauce, Morrie poured Mad a glass of sherry and left it on the kitchen table where she was on the point of spooning the sprouts and baked potatoes into serving dishes, sliding the leg of lamb on to a platter, and popping four fat Bramley apples back into the oven to reheat. Morrie started up the stairs to say goodnight to the children. Mad said don't be long; she just had to finish the gravy before dinner would be ready.

*　*　*　*　*

Dr. Prentice visited mid-morning the next day. Bessie was still in bed, though she had finished most of her breakfast and Mad had removed the tray. The doctor went through the usual routine: taking the pulse, listening to the heart, looking in the eyes, and at the tongue.

"Mrs. Scovil tells me you were a pioneer nurse and even knew Florence Nightingale," the doctor said with a tone of deference when he finished. "So you will know just why I am doing all of this"

"Indeed. Knowledge has improved since my day, but the approach is about the same. I need your frank opinion, Doctor Prentice. Do you think I will be fit enough to cross the Atlantic, with my brother before the end of November?"

"I can't say yet, one way or the other. After a week of bed rest, a little gentle exercise walking around your bedroom, and sitting up a few hours every day, we will be in a better position to make an assessment. Your heart is a little weak at the moment. I will give you a tonic with a tiny quantity of strychnine that will act as a stimulant, as you know. That may be all that is necessary. We will know after a week. I'll be back the day after tomorrow to see how you are getting on. I can't stay now but I'd like to know a little about the good Miss N. I understand she was a bit of a Tartar!"

"She knew her own mind, shall we say." Bessie responded with flash of memory and carefully worded understatement.

Mad heard the visit coming to a close, met the doctor at the front door out of Bessie's hearing and asked his frank opinion. Mod, whom Dr. Prentice knew from his recent operation, joined the conversation.

"Her heart would not tolerate an Atlantic crossing as it is. There is a slight possibility the strychnine will be enough, but I am afraid an eighty-five year-old heart will not respond sufficiently. I told her we should know at the end of a week. Hope is also a good tonic, but I think my patient is much too experienced and realistic for that "medicine" at this stage. I'll be back in two days. Here's the prescription."

"Let's have some tea," Mad offered.

"That's just what I need, but I mustn't stop. I have several more patients to see this morning. Call me if there's any change."

Mad showed the doctor to the door and returned to the kitchen to make a tray of tea for three, which she took to Bessie's room where

Mod had already settled in for some realistic conversation with his sister. But her comments made anything more unnecessary.

"At least he hasn't said absolutely 'no,'" Bessie began, clearly indicating she was not hopeful. "I'd like to sit up in the chair for lunch, but in the mean time, all this conversation has tired me. I'll rest a little after I finish my cup and take the usual trip to the WC; please, Mad, if you can help me. After lunch, would someone bring me that box under my bed, I want to try to finish some little stories and some other writing."

In order to feel useful, Mod pulled out the covered box he knew was the one wanted and carried it over to the table beside Bessie's window chair. He then walked as briskly as he was able to the chemist's to get her prescription filled.

In spite of taking the tonic as stipulated, Bessie knew there was no change in the way she felt, so presumably no change in her heart function. She cooperated with Dr. Prentice on his next visit. She knew he had to go through the motions of checking. He announced, as though a great triumph, that Miss Scovil's heart was no worse and he thought he might have detected a modicum of improvement.

"So you have no objection to my sitting by the window, taking the occasional bath and doing what I feel capable of doing?"

"You have two roles, Miss Scovil, the nurse in charge and the patient!"

A shared knowledge allowed them both to smile at Dr. Prentice's answer to her question.

"I'll be back at the end of the week."

62

"No regrets, no regrets…
One can't go on forever."

The doctor's visit made Bessie even more determined to work on her short stories, but today she wanted to collect her thoughts and revise the list regarding the allocation of her few personal possessions. She pulled a folder from the box Mod had placed beside her chair.

"Disposition of My Belongings, July 21, 1933." She read over the two pages and decided only a few changes were necessary. She then added this note:

> *Dear children,*
>
> *I have nothing of value to leave but I thought you would like to have these little things as mementos of the aunt who has always tried, however feebly, to take care of you.*

She read the list over again, wondering what the recipients would say when they received her little bequests.

> *Morrie. Little locket with my mother's picture.*
>
> *Elizabeth. Cameo broach.*
>
> *Hayden. Silver back hat brush.*
>
> *Gertrude. Pearl pin and gold thimble.*
>
> *Mary. All clothing of use to her and crystal beads.*
>
> *Roger. My bedside clock and silver letter opener.*
>
> *Madeline. Amethyst broach and beads and Honiton lace collar.*
>
> *Rose. Little grey broach and cameo slide. Fountain pen and white silk scarf.*
>
> *Courtenay. Gold ring I always wear and have worn for more than 50 years. Ivory beads. My watch.*

Bessie leaned back and closed her eyes, now satisfied she had included something for most of those who were close to her by blood or affection or both. She remembered the twins, tiny Pearl and Ruby, not even five feet tall; Pearl sitting at the family piano in their rambling Gagetown house after church, trying to sing, "Oh Hear the Gentle Lark," because of her father's mistaken belief she had a talent for it. And Ruby, with a kind heart eventually funneled into missionary work in China, always encouraging with her quiet attention. And Lou, older than the twins, of normal height, motherly, though none to mother for any of them, all spinsters, like herself. "No regrets, no regrets."

As Bessie opened her eyes, the sun bounced briefly off St. Michael's spire. She focused on the familiar scene as long as it lasted and then, with a feeling of accomplishment, drifted into a restful nap.

Dr. Prentice found no change at the end of the week, in spite of the contents of the bottle of strychnine tonic being suitably lowered. He knew he could not beat around the bush with this patient.

"Miss Scovil, I'm sure you know you are not fit enough for an Atlantic crossing,

Bessie nodded.

"I suggest you take the tonic until it is finished and do just what you feel comfortable doing. Some exercise every day, walking about your room, sitting up for part of the day, and so on. I'll look in next week."

"I understand, Dr. Prentice. One can't go on for ever."

Mod was sorry Bess was not up to travelling but somewhat relieved he would not have to make the effort which steamship life required. He resolved to spend more time talking about the past with Bess, and less about future possibilities.

*　*　*　*　*

As October advanced into November, the children brought in the Bramley windfalls. Morrie picked the apples remaining on the tree and tidied the small vegetable garden for winter, though the sprouts and leeks would continue to be harvested until well after Christmas. Mad cleared the dead leaves from the herbaceous bed, snipping back the browned perennials and planting a few new tulips and narcissi, which she did every year to replace the ones the field mice demolished. Rain now thrashed against St. Michael's spire more often than the sun glinted on it, but everyone expected that in November. Mod and Bessie had never before remained in England so late in the year.

Mod was encouraged to go for a little walk every day, even in the light rain. He knew there was no escape when Mad appeared in her Mackintosh, holding two umbrellas. Mrs. Harding, who came three mornings a week, was usually around when Madeline and Mod went for a walk. She always chose to clean Bessie's room when they were out. She liked to chat. She believed the old lady would benefit from an update of the local gossip. She had the habit of pushing the carpet sweeper back and forth over the same spot a dozen times when she was concentrating on an especially scandalous piece of news. Bessie listened with half an ear, often wondering what Amelia was now doing.

Bessie had written short letters to Roger about the progress of her "weakness" Finally, on November 15th she knew she must tell him they would not be spending the winter with them in sunny South Carolina as they had for the past eight years. She wrote that Dr. Prentice said she was not up to a transatlantic voyage just now, implying she might be later, without actually saying so, which she knew was most unlikely. At the same time she wrote one pagers to Gertrude and to Mary, partly so

403

they would not write to her at Roger's address and partly to prepare them for the inevitable. She knew Hayden would keep Elizabeth up to date but wrote to her as well, saying she and her father often thought about her and her condition and hoped for an easy delivery. Bessie reminded Elizabeth to work on building up her strength, and mentioned it was likely she and Mod would remain in England for a while longer.

On the morning of November twenty-fifth, Madeline knocked gently before pushing the door open and entering Bessie's room with the usual breakfast tray. One look at Bessie, even before the curtains were opened, told Mad breakfast was not needed. She automatically felt for Bessie's pulse and found none. The nurse, educator, author, journalist, woman of the church, loving aunt, generous supporter of family members and worthy causes seemed to have a little smile on her lips as though she had arrived at her desired destination and the sun was shining. Elizabeth Robinson Scovil died just one week before her last great niece, Barbara Elizabeth Villiers, was born.

Afterword

The Enduring Literature of Home

One way to tell if a new literary work is likely to endure is to ask whether it will be read with interest, understanding, and appreciation long after it was written. I first encountered this perspective in an essay by Kenneth Rexroth on the classics of world literature. For example, he points out that poetry of Tu Fu (712-770) is as resonant for us with its portrayal of the natural world and the pathos of human life as it was for his contemporaries. And, in the same way, the essays of Montaigne have been read with pleasure and edification ever since the 16th century. A century and half ago Emily Dickinson composed poetry that when we read it today feels freshly drawn from the spring of universal, recurring, human experience.

This same consideration applies to works of literature that have proven to be of enduring interest for the way they portray the fundamental experiences of home, family, and a sense of place. For example, books by Lucy Maud Montgomery, Louisa May Alcott, Sarah Orne Jewett, Ernest Buckler, and Alistair McLeod have this enduring quality. We return to these authors — and many others — because the characters and narratives they create provide a deeply satisfying engagement with the heritage of human experience, even though the stories, in some cases, may come from times long gone.

Such were my thoughts when I started reading *Meadowlands* by Virginia Bliss Bjerkelund. I was visited by the same feeling that came to me when I first read *The Country of Pointed Firs* by Sarah Orne Jewett — the feeling that I had stepped into a fully realized community of place. In *The Country of Pointed Firs*, the community comes alive bit by bit as the characters and their stories are introduced. With *Meadowlands* you step at once into the environment of a family with its unique characters and into the community in which they lived.

*   *   *   *   *

There is nothing that can be called "exciting" about *The Country of Pointed Firs* or *Meadowlands*. They are both quiet books of ordinary daily life. But, as you start reading, there is something about both books that makes you want to know what comes next. In the case of *Meadowlands*, you want to know what will happen in the lives of its characters and to the life of the Scovil family as a whole. It's a strange experience to have no knowledge whatsoever of a particular family and its members and then, by reading a book, come to know these people and the trajectory of their lives in a way you will never forget.

Since the main characters in *Meadowlands*—Aunt Bessie and "little" Mary—were the great aunt and mother of the author, they are portrayed in such a fully rounded way that the reader is virtually inducted into the Scovil family. When characters in a book stick in your memory like burdocks stick to your jacket after bushwacking through an overgrown hedgerow, you know the author has created a literary work of enduring value.

With the plethora of cosmopolitan novels and works of creative non-fiction that each year jostle for attention in the stream of literary journalism, the story of the Scovil family may seem "provincial." And so it is, but that's precisely what makes it a work of enduring value. I can imagine a graduate student working on Maritime social history some years from now pulling *Meadowlands* from the library shelf and discovering the key to a thesis they have been trying to bring into focus.

The potential of *Meadowlands* in this regard rests in the way the author has included the details of the Scovil family's daily life. For example, a whole study could be made of menu planning, food preparation, meal serving, the communal enjoyment of meals, and the ceremonious attending to tea time and summer refreshments on the verandah. Thanks to Aunt Bessie, the sense of ceremony that comes into play around holidays and birthdays and the visits of guests goes a long way to explain why the Scovil family, despite its great loss of Hattie, was able to recover and flourish.

In a similar way, a substantial paper based on this book could be written on the geography of the Meadowlands/Gagetown area, the social ecology of place, and the role of the St. John River in the life of the Scovil family and Gagetown residents.

In addition, *Meadowlands* is permeated by the technological, economic, and cultural changes taking place over the first three decades of the 20th century—decades that encompass the momentous change from horses to motor vehicles. Under Scovil family management the Meadowlands farm did not make that transition, even though motorized transport was springing up all around them, including their own early adoption of an outboard motor for navigating the St. John River.

Meadowlands is also a compendium of the way the attitudes, values, and mores of the late Victorian Era were changing and how a less hierarchical, more egalitarian, and convivial way of life was emerging. (The popular

BBC television series, *Downton Abbey*, parallels the same three decades and portrays these same changes in England.)

The Scovil family was ahead of the curve in this regard. There is something different in the relationship between adults and children in this family than was typical at that time; something that Aunt Bessie's presence enhances with her progressive views of child development and family life. The children are clearly appreciated for their individual characteristics; they are supported in their interests and accomplishments and flourish as a result.

The sense of family bonding and the fact that the children genuinely care for each other and enjoy each other's company is a large part of what makes the Scovil story so appealing. The siblings eagerly return to Meadowlands for family gatherings even after they begin to disperse. In a time when explosive industrial growth, dire economic conditions, and social fragmentation elsewhere were taking a dreadful toll on many families and society in general, Meadowlands, and its manner of living, served the Scovil family well.

*   *   *   *   *

In the end, however, there is also an undercurrent of loss, displacement, and sadness in this story. Higher education, The Great War, and the economic and cultural changes of the time dispersed the Meadowlands' family as it did so many others. We are fortunate that Virginia Bjerkelund came into the picture when she did and has been able to create this family story in a way that captures the heart and engages the imagination.

I've now read *Meadowlands* several times and, of course, no long wonder what happens next. Nonetheless, I'm always eager to resume reading for the pleasure of being immersed in the story of this unusual and yet quite ordinary family. Thanks to the devotion of the author, the story of the Scovil family at Meadowlands has now become an enduring part of our cultural heritage—a gift from the past to the future.

In his reflections on literature that endures, Kenneth Rexroth writes:

> *The perils of the soul and its achievements are constant.... this is the area where novelty seems to be of no importance whatsoever,... the contemporary novel that embodies paradigms of the great... commonplaces of human life seems precisely "novel," fresh, and convincing.*

> *The fundamental relationships... do not have to be presented as especially grandiose.... There are quiet and idyllic classics, even inconspicuous ones. (The Classics Revisited; 1965, 1986)*

Meadowlands portrays the "perils of the soul" and "the great commonplaces of human life" within the context of a particular family in a specific place and through a period of time now a century past. It does so, however, in a way that family relationships, the natural world, and the sense of community that are embedded in its narrative will continue to resonate with appreciative readers for generations to come.

*   *   *   *   *

Readers interested in geographical exploration can travel to Meadowlands from the Jemseg side of the St. John River or from the Gagetown side by ferry during its seasonal operation. The house and barns are gone but the fields are still maintained. Helen and DC "Chet" Campbell, who hosted the Fredericton Exhibition Horse Show for several decades, eventually acquired the Meadowlands property where they pastured a large herd of Herford cattle and harvested its luxurious hay crop. Through their daughter, Janet and her husband, Bob Stevenson, Meadowlands was passed to the Stevenson family and acquired the name Foshay Farms, after Foshay Lake, which is located on the property.

From 1985 through 2008, the Stevenson family, along with friends of Foshay, regularly hosted equestrian events at the farm. Their son, Dr. Rob Stevenson, became an equestrian athlete, representing Canada at the 1992 Olympic Games. In 2018 Rob and Suzanne Stevenson established Foshay International, a four-day, world class, competitive equestrian event at Foshay Farms. (www.foshayinternational.com)

Morris Scovil, his son Morrie and, indeed, the entire Scovil family would certainly be pleased that their Meadowlands farm is still intact and is being used to keep alive and advance that ancient and uncanny association of humans and horses. For such a historic setting it seems only right that horses still grace the landscape and that its abundant hay crop is still harvested.

Visitors can take the road where it bears right at Lower Jemseg and drive to the shore of the St. John River where the Scovil wharf once stood and where the Gagetown Ferry now lands at Scovil Point. Standing there, gazing out over the river, you can imagine a rowboat powered by "Mr. Evinrude" skimming over the water, and "Mary, with her hand on the tiller, … wearing the smile of a conqueror."

Keith Helmuth
Chapel Street Editions
Woodstock, New Brunswick

408

Acknowledgements

Many thanks to my first cousin, the late (2020) Roger M. Scovil of Atlanta, Ga. (eldest child of Roger P. Scovil, the youngest sibling in "Meadowlands") whose book, *A Scovil Genealogy*, published in 1992, was a great help in keeping track of birthdays and other details. The late Canon Charles Karsten of Gardiner, Maine (grandson of Uncle Jack in *Meadowlands*) made the contents of his mother's trunk (cousin Bess in *Meadowlands*) available to me, which included letters between Addie (Uncle Jack's wife) and Aunt Bessie. I am especially grateful for access to this primary resource material and for his general encouragement. The granddaughter of my uncle Morrie, Anne Purdy of Amherst, NS, was generous in giving me family photographs and articles, some of which I used in *Meadowlands* and some of which will be used in a biography-in-process of Elizabeth Robinson Scovil (Aunt Bessie). As well, I thank members of my two writing groups, "Wolftree" and "Woolastook," whose years of supportive encouragement allowed me to think of myself as a writer. Special gratitude goes to Alison Calvern who nursed my writing ambitions with weekly sessions of herbal tea, expertise, and special care. Finally, and in many ways most importantly, I thank Keith, Ellen, and Brendan Helmuth at Chapel Street Editions for their enthusiasm, attention to detail, and good humour.

ABOUT THE COVER

The cover is a detail and adaptation from the painting by Morris Scovil, *Meadowlands from the Gagetown Side of the St. John River* (Collection of Virginia Bliss Bjerkelund. Oil on board.)

Morris Allaire Scovil, eldest child of Morris and Harriet (DuVernet) Scovil, was born in 1889. In the *Meadowlands* book he is known as "Morrie." After a career in commercial sales and service in England, he returned with his family to Amherest, Nova Scotia where took the position of Managing Director of the Maritime Stockbreeders Association. He took up painting in retirement and studied with Alfred Whitehead, Willard Morse Mitchell, and Fred Nicholson. His regional landscape and St. John River paintings were well received and are now held in both public and private collections. He died in Amherest, NS in 1968.

About the Author

Virginia Bliss Bjerkelund is a Maritimer, born in Amherst, Nova Scotia, educated in Fredericton, New Brunswick, followed by nearly 30 years of living in England where she married and brought up a daughter and son, now both retired. She returned to Fredericton, re-married, travelled widely, practiced Social Work, and is active in the cultural life of the city. *Meadowlands* is her first published book and, although 91, hopes it will not be her last.

Photo by Peter Bjerkelund